Storm Strike

RANDY R. HENKE

RANDY R. HENKE

The characters and events portrayed in this book are fictitious. Any similarity to real persons, living or dead, is coincidental and not intended by the author.

Copyright © 2014 Randy R. Henke

All rights reserved.

No part of this book may be reproduced, or stored in a retrieval system, or transmitted in any form or by any means, electronic, mechanical, photocopying, recording, or otherwise, without express written permission of the publisher.

PROLOGUE

It was an age of monsters. An age of prowling beasts that preyed on any living creature that crossed their path; shattering bones, rending flesh, sometimes swallowing their victims whole. Yet they were not the sort that dwelled under your bed or stirred in the musty depths of your closet. They had no fear of discovery; no innate compulsion to lurk in the shadows.

They were fashioned not of fur, fang nor claw but were no less deadly for it. They were born of a mother's rage at mankind for meddling in her affairs; for desecrating her beauty and timelessness. They were vengeful demons full of fury and raw power, hell-bent on destruction.

Becca Hanson had seen them. She knew what they could do. And she was running from one of them now. She paused in the middle of the dark rain-drenched street to get her bearings, her slippered feet awash in ankle deep water. Sirens wailed incessantly. A sudden blast of wind slammed into her, violently snapping the loose folds of her robe and knocking her back a step. With both hands she tightened her grip on the two precious valuables that meant more to her than her own life.

Six year old Charlotte was on her left, clinging to her stuffed panda bear, eyes clenched tightly shut as if she could will the storm away. On her right, eight year old Graham stood shivering, looking up to his mother for some measure of reassurance that she couldn't offer.

The dull glow from the street lamps penetrated through the rain just enough to tell her that the neighborhood was deserted. The majority of the residents had already sought shelter. She would have been amongst them had she not had to embark on a frantic search for Charlotte and Graham upon finding their bedroom deserted. She had finally found them. They'd been cowering in a linen closet on the lowest level of their house, their arms tightly wound around each other. Being several meters below ground level, she had debated crawling into the closet with them and shielding them as best she could with her own body. But she knew it wouldn't have been enough.

The sky lit up blindingly, white hot tracers arcing between black seething clouds. In the glare of the lightning she noticed a small rectangular shadow gliding across the lawn next to a two-story brick apartment building. She looked higher and spotted a weather drone hovering near the rooftop. She had seen them before but only as tiny, indistinct dots in the sky, dutifully chasing the storms. This one had obviously strayed too close. Its ducted fans were spinning frantically as it struggled against the wind and rain just to stay aloft. As she watched, a sudden gust caught the floating platform, flipping it and sending it crashing into the side of the brick building. Its plastic shell shattered and fell, landing in a heap of debris in the shrubbery.

Another streak of lightning arced down, striking a satellite dish on a nearby house. Sparks skittered across the roof. She glanced down at the flooded street they were standing in. A tremor shot through her as she thought of what would happen if one of those lethal bolts were to strike near enough to electrify the water surging around their feet.

"Let's go, kids!" she said, prodding them onward. She dashed for the sidewalk, dragging her children beside her, their tiny legs a blur of motion as they struggled to keep pace with their mother.

Caulfield Park was still two blocks away but she could already see the flashing green beacon that sat atop the community storm shelter in the middle of the park. It was right next to the playground she took her children to twice a week.

Their bedroom slippers slapped at the wet pavement as they ran. The first block passed quickly. But as her children grew tired, they trailed further and further in her wake. It was like dragging two fifty pound anvils behind her. She slowed as they approached the next street, hoping it would allow them time to catch their breath.

Rain streamed down her forehead and cheeks and cascaded off the tip of her nose. She swung her head back and forth to clear her vision and throw off as much of the water as she could. Then she chanced a look behind her. Her mouth dropped open. Amidst the churning black clouds, illuminated by the near constant flicker of lightning, a rotating vertical column of wind-driven destruction hung down from the sky. It swept back and forth, writhing like a serpent anxious for its next meal. In just the scant few seconds she watched, it grew noticeably larger as it bore down on them.

"Oh my God!" she screamed.

Desperation seized her. She lengthened her stride, praying that her kids could keep up. As she approached the next intersection there was so much standing water that it was hard to tell exactly where the curb dropped to street level. She misjudged the step, her foot dropping to the blacktop before she was ready and throwing her off balance. She went down in a flurry of splashes in the middle of the street, pulling her kids down with her. To her right, Graham hit the water in an indelicate belly flop, arms flailing wildly until he managed to pull himself to his hands and knees. On her left, the momentum of Charlotte's fall plunged her beneath the surface. She came up gasping for air, still clutching the soaked panda to her chest.

Becca climbed to her feet and quickly pulled the children out of the torrent. Another flash of lightning and a glance skyward told her they were rapidly losing their race.

"Move! Now!" she shouted and bolted out of the street and onto the next block, hauling the children along beside her. She lost a waterlogged slipper. The sudden imbalance sent her into a canted lope. Without missing a stride, she hopped on her bare foot and, with a snapkick of her other leg, sent the remaining slipper hurtling off into the darkness. As long as they kept moving there was still a chance, she thought to herself. Just keep moving.

Up ahead, she could make out the shapes of other people. Frenetic moving shapes. All converging on the strobing green light that was beckoning them toward safety. She could hear their frantic shouts as they called out to one another. She could hear something else as well. A low growling rumble that was rising in volume, so deep and resonant she could feel the vibrations in her chest.

Out of the upper periphery of her vision she glimpsed a streamer of fiery blue current lash out like a cobra at the transformer mounted on the pole directly above them. A boom like a cannon set her ears ringing. Charlotte screamed. Suddenly the air around them was alive with burning sparks. Fiery orange pellets of molten metal sizzled as they landed on the wet sidewalk. The street lamps winked out. One of the glowing metal shards settled on her wrist, searing the flesh. She stifled her own scream. The pain told her to release her grip and shake the burning fragment away but it was her motherly instinct, telling her to hang on to her child for dear life, that overrode the first impulse. She tightened her grip, let the ember burn deeper, and pressed on.

Without the glow of the street lamps to illuminate their course, all she could do was aim directly for the strobing green light, relying on the occasional burst of lightning to correct their course and avoid any obstacles in their path.

"Mommy! I'm tired!" Charlotte cried out. Becca didn't slow; didn't dare to. Beneath her bare feet, the harsh slap and scrape of cement suddenly turned to the soft tender prickle of grass. She knew they must be entering the park.

"We're almost there, honey," she yelled. "Just a little bit further!"

The voices of other people were growing louder, more feverish and more urgent. They were all around her now. She saw them with every white blaze of the sky; featureless wraiths in the gloom. They moved with a purpose, although in the strobe-like flashes of lightning they almost appeared to be standing still. They were everywhere. Some ran swiftly. Some hobbled slowly. Some were solitary forms. Some huddled in small groups. Yet all of them were blatantly obsessed with the single-minded goal of reaching the sanctuary offered by that luring green light.

They were close now. She could even make out the arched silhouette of the shelter, perhaps fifty meters away. Suddenly Becca's right foot slammed into something solid. She tumbled, losing her grip on two tiny hands, her arms thrashing in a futile attempt to regain her balance. She landed hard, air exploding from her lungs.

Dazed, she saw a green light coming toward her. Was it the shelter growing still closer? How was that possible when she was lying prostrate on the ground? A strange whirring sound grew louder. Then a sudden fusillade of lightning ripped across the sky, illuminating the object she had tripped over. It was a robotic lawn mower about the size of a child's wagon. Its green status light glowed bright and steady. The plastic cowling that normally covered its blades was missing, no doubt detached from the impact with her foot. That same impact must have also shifted its course. She quickly realized it was heading directly for her face, its rack of knifelike blades spinning furiously.

There was no time to move. No time for anything. She squeezed her eyes shut and prayed the end would be mercifully quick. "Obstruction detected," a tinny voice droned. "Shutting down." She opened her eyes to see the faint outline of the mower as it ground to a halt, the glistening blades only a centimeter away from her cheek. Atop its dome, the green light turned red.

Becca seized the opportunity and leaped to her feet. But as soon as she applied weight to her right leg, it buckled. A knot of searing agony tightened in her knee, forcing her back down into a kneel on her uninjured leg. Placing her hand atop her right thigh she pressed down, testing it. She could feel bones shifting and scraping behind her kneecap. She wasn't going anywhere.

Looking up, she could see Charlotte and Graham hovering over her. Their faces glowed an eerie poison green with each flash of the shelter's strobe light.

"We'll help you, mommy," Charlotte said.

Becca shook her head. "No! Just get to the shelter!"

"We're not leaving without you!" Graham insisted, his tiny hands balled into hard fists.

There was no time to argue. "Okay, come on!" she shouted and lifted up her arms. Her children swept in to either side of her, their mouths set, eyes narrowed as dogged determination pushed aside their fear. She rested her hands on their small shoulders, placing as much weight on them as she dared. Expecting their diminutive bodies to sag under the burden, she was astonished at how sturdy they actually felt.

Pulling herself up on her good leg, she found her balance and began hopping toward the shelter, her children pacing her on each side. The wind was a heaving monster now, threatening to knock them off their feet at any moment, hurling stinging slabs of rain at them. The roar was deafening.

Another jagged blade of lightning tore a hole in the night sky. An ear shattering boom rattled their eardrums. Flames erupted ahead of them. Through the orange haze, she watched as the massive oak tree that towered over the playground split down the centerline of its trunk.

Chunks of bark and splinters of wood filled the air. Several people went down in the maelstrom, crying out in pain as the shrapnel tore into them.

The two halves of the tree parted ways. One section crushed the swing set and snapped a teeter totter in two. The other half came crashing down on the storm shelter's roof. The reinforced steel arches that formed the skeleton of the shelter did their job, resisting the crushing weight. The oak tree rebounded off the roof of the shelter, impacted again and rolled, twisting about its crooked axis. It had nearly come to rest at the very edge of the roofline when the base of the trunk tore away from the jagged stump. Screams rang out as the smoking wooden wreck slipped free of the roof and plunged to the ground, directly in front of the shelter's only door.

"It's blocked!" a man bellowed. Screams of panic erupted from the crowd. People rushed in, tugging at branches, heaving at the unyielding trunk, trying desperately to clear a path to the doorway.

"It's no use," another man yelled in exasperation, followed by more cries of anguish. Then Becca heard an even more blood curdling noise behind her. It was the sound of rampant destruction. Lumber snapping, metal shearing and glass shattering. She saw others turn, their eyes glazed in horror. Then she spun around herself and watched as a cluster of houses were churned into a cloud of whirling debris.

The funnel was huge, easily half a kilometer across at its base, ravenously chewing up and spitting out row after row of buildings. It rocked back and forth, sweeping the ground with its unbridled devastation. It would be on them in seconds. This was the end. Becca went down on one knee and pulled her children close to her, gently covering their eyes with her hands. She could feel them trembling beneath her touch.

"Don't look," she said as calmly as she could. "I love you, Charlotte. I love you, Graham." They didn't answer her. They didn't need to. She lowered her head and listened to the keening howl of the unholy tempest that was about to consume them.

Something shrieked past just over their heads. She felt a momentary wave of intense heat. Looking up, she could make out a flaming ember in the night sky. It took her a moment to realize it was the exhaust of a rocket, spewing out a contrail of gray smoke behind it. It took another moment to realize it was heading directly for the tornado.

Before she could mentally process what this might mean, two more missiles shredded the air above them. They followed on the heels of their predecessor, belching hot gases that turned the rain in their wake to billowing clouds of steam.

Becca held her breath, waiting. She didn't have to wait long. The first missile hurtled toward its target, angling upward for the final few hundred meters. It pierced the swirling wall of wind, penetrating to the very heart of the twister. An explosion bloomed from within, tearing a gaping hole in the flank of the tornado, disrupting the cyclonic forces that fueled it. The funnel shuddered, its tip breaking away from the ground and lashing the air.

As Becca watched in awe, the vortex contracted, becoming denser, almost as if it were rallying its strength, tightening its defenses. But before it could recover, the other two missiles streaked in and detonated, flaring brightly, adding their potent destructive forces to the mix.

Flames gushed outward, tugging the swirling winds with them, diffusing them. Nature's sinister magic spell was broken. The funnel shrank, collapsing in on itself, becoming a ropelike thread. Its base swung free, no longer grazing the ground, thrashing like a wounded eel. Then it came apart in a burst of spiraling eddies that faded into the night sky. The beast was dead.

Before anyone could react, the shockwaves from the three detonations advanced on them. Becca saw them as they neared, rippling the grass in an expanding circle, flinging rain out of their path. They came in quick succession, each one feeling like a solid blow as it swept past.

Then it was over.

A cheer went up behind Becca but she barely heard it as she pulled her two children close to her and broke down in choking sobs of relief. The tornado sirens were still blaring but she thought she could hear a new higher-pitched wail join the din.

She glanced up to see a stormcruiser racing down the street. Its yellow and red warning lights blazed, sending up a shimmering haze as they reflected off the vehicle's glistening armored hull. A fresh triad of red-tipped missiles was already rotating into place atop its roof mounted launcher. She smiled as it passed by and said a silent prayer for the nameless, faceless crew that had just saved their lives.

RANDY R. HENKE

CHAPTER 1

"Kill confirmed. Funnel terminated," Marta heard Kinney announce over the comm system in her helmet. Flipping up her gray-tinted enhanced reality visor to give her eyes a momentary rest, the glowing instrumentation and data displays that had surrounded her instantly evaporated, leaving only stark, smooth consoles of clear glass wrapping around her seat at the right front side of the stormcruiser.

She turned in her seat to glance back at Kinney. His square jaw was set, steel-blue eyes narrowed behind his own enhanced reality visor as he took in the virtual targeting data that she knew would be hovering in front of him. His gloved hands tapped and swiped at controls that were invisible to her unaided eyes. He had about him the calm, focused air of a career soldier.

She heard the familiar mechanized hum of servo motors overhead as three fresh SCH-4 missiles slid into the firing tubes. Then three distinct clunks as they were each latched into place. "Next salvo in position and armed," Kinney added.

"Roger that, Kinney," Marta called back over the intercom and continued to watch him. Then she flipped her visor back down. The transparent console that curved around him came alive with shimmering holographic projections. She felt an electric shiver rush up her spine as his burly hands slid across the surface, deftly manipulating a shifting maze of glowing icons with the steadiness and precision of a surgeon. She caught the subtle shift in his focus as he made eye contact with her. His features softened for a brief moment. He nodded. She returned the stark acknowledgement just as his attention veered back to his workstation.

As she swung back around in her chair, she let her gaze sweep over the man sitting next to her in the driver's seat. She paused long enough to drink in his smooth boyish face and the slight smirk that seemed permanently affixed there. She knew that Chaz was in his element as well. He lived for the thrill of the hunt, the exhilarating rush of speed and the bracing sense of danger that came with taking on one of nature's most destructive and unpredictable forces. At times like these, she found his youthful vigor intoxicating; arousing even, despite the fact that she was nearly old enough to be his mother.

"Coming up on the town of Waurika," Chaz called out in his thick Carolina drawl. His right hand left the steering wheel just long enough to confirm that his crisp tan Stetson was still securely perched on a dark portion of the console beside him where he'd customized the control scheme to leave a void for his hat. Then the squealing whine of the turbine spooled down an octave as they slowed. "Or what's left of it," Chaz added in a low tone.

Marta peered out through the shatterproof nanoglass windshield, three centimeters thick yet flawlessly transparent. It was night but the darkness was being effectively peeled back by piercing beams of white light from the roof-mounted illuminators, shining out in all directions. Despite the fact that she could hear the rain slapping at the hull of the stormcruiser and see the ocean of rivulets sweep up and over their windshield, the view outside the vehicle was eerily devoid of the reflective blur of falling rain.

Such clarity came courtesy of a grid of high intensity LEDS. But the real magic came from the array of infrared cameras that peered out into the deluge, mapping the location of each falling droplet and applying power only to those LEDs where the pencil-thin beam could travel unimpeded. She could detect a subtle flicker as the beams shifted and pulsed in a well orchestrated ballet, effortlessly penetrating the storm's thick veil and revealing a suburban wasteland of twisted trees, flooded streets and wind ravaged houses.

The surreal devastated landscape unfolded before her eyes, further sharpened by her ER visor as thermal data in muted blue, green and yellow hues was overlaid on top of her natural vision. Then a final layer of navigational data was superimposed on top of that. A text cue popped up over a small grassy flat coming up on their left, identifying it as Caulfield Park.

Chaz whistled. "Looks like we done missed the party," he quipped, exaggerating his southern drawl as Marta knew that he sometimes did, often to add a bit of levity to a particularly tense situation; at other times just as an irritant to certain susceptible individuals.

Marta followed Chaz's gaze and saw a group of people gathered around a battered storm shelter. Her ER visor drew crisp green outlines around the huddled forms, highlighting each individual person. As they drove past, one woman in particular caught her attention, kneeling on the ground next to two small children. She was smiling at them as they passed by. Marta allowed herself a brief few seconds to imagine what horrors these people had just witnessed. She smiled back at the woman, knowing it went unseen, and then put herself back in the moment as an urgent tone sounded in her headset.

She tapped a flashing icon on her console and her entire field of vision was suddenly filled by a panoramic radar image comprised of live data from their onboard Doppler array. She instantly spotted three tight clusters of rotating red pixels. A stark white dot gleamed at the center of each swirl indicating where airborne debris was causing the greatest reflection of radar energy. They were the telltale signatures of shredders nestled within the reds, oranges and yellows of the massive spinning mesocyclone that formed the storm itself. A moment later the computer caught up with her instinctive analysis, painting each anomaly with a flashing orange reticle, measuring and displaying relative wind speeds, then finally classifying the funnels and showing her its findings.

A hot burst of adrenaline flooded Marta's bloodstream like molten lava. She savored the primal jolt it provided. Every nerve end tingled in anticipation. She had learned over the years to take a moment at times like these to allow her rampant emotions to moderate and decompress. Such a tactic helped to prevent the making of rash and sometimes regrettable decisions. But it was always more difficult to remember to focus when she was coming down from one of her manic peaks, a time when diametrically opposed emotions were already vying for dominance. She was all too aware that once this mission was over, the adrenaline propping her up would be depleted and she would begin to feel the vitality slowly drain away, replaced by something darker. But for right now, she was right where she wanted to be. This was her moment.

"Okay, people," Marta shouted into her mic. "We've got a pair of F2s ramping up to the south and a lone F3 to the southwest."

The F-, or Fujita, scale was how shredders were incrementally rated according to their wind speed and the damage they were capable of inflicting. The scale was a relic of the twentieth century, modified and expanded several times to enhance its usefulness; the last time to take into account the latest monsters that had only emerged in the past ten years as the climate lapsed further into turmoil.

According to the scale, an F0 was little more than an oversized whirlwind, the strongest of which might lift a couple of shingles from your roof. An F1 could strip that same roof bare. F2s and F3s could effectively remodel your entire house. They also tore wide swaths through crops and threatened the lives of anyone caught out in the open. F4s could relocate your house and were nothing short of devastating.

Until the latest revision of the scale, F5s had been at the top of the food chain. Even though they were every bit as deadly as they were before their demotion, their reduced status along with the fact that their occurrences were becoming far more frequent, imparted a sense of mediocrity to their kind.

F6s through F8s were the new breed of shredders. Thankfully, they were still exceedingly rare. But when they chose to make an appearance, land was scarred and cities fell. The vacuum they generated could steal the very air from your lungs. Their ravenous winds had been known to surpass seven hundred kilometers per hour. Only specially designed above-ground structures had a prayer against their preternatural ferocity.

Momentary radio static in her headset resolved into the deep, deliberate voice of Pete Griffeth, slightly garbled but still intelligible. "Whiskey Romeo One, this is Alpha Alpha Five. We can confirm your Doppler signatures and we also have a visual on those F2s. We are running hot and heavy. Requesting intercept authorization. Over."

Marta grinned, picturing her fellow commander seated in his own stormcruiser's command chair, gnawing on the stub of an unlit Cohiba and calmly awaiting permission to engage. "Sounds like a plan to me, Alpha Alpha Five. Give those F2s a warm Oklahoma welcome, Pete. We'll do the same for that perky little F3. Over."

The radio crackled back with Pete's steady voice. "Will do, Marta. Be sure to save a few party favors for any late arrivals. Over."

Marta glanced down at her console where four rows of missile-shaped outlines glowed red. Only the top row of three was shaded green, visually confirming what she already knew.

Marta shook her head. "That's a negative, Pete. Only one bank of missiles remaining. After this strike, we'll be fresh out and on our way back to base. No worries though. We have two more units, both hot and heavy, on our six moving into position. Over."

There was a short pause. Then, "Roger that, Marta. And you tell that redneck wannabe racecar driver of yours that if that beat up wreck he calls a truck hasn't fallen apart yet, I'm up for a rematch anytime he works up the nerve. That southern luck of his has to run out sometime. "

Chaz glanced over at Marta, like a puppy anxiously awaiting a bone. Marta nodded, giving him tacit permission to answer the challenge. Chaz, one corner of his mouth curling up in a lopsided grin, reached down and stabbed the icon that opened the outside channel on his intercom.

"Mercy, Pete. Sounds like you up and grew yourself a set. I'm proud of you. But not so proud that I won't send you crying home to mama lickin' your wounds just like last time we danced."

A hearty laugh sounded from the intercom. "We'll just see about that, Chaz. Marta, it looks like you've got some ground to cover before you can move in for the kill so I will bid you adieu. Over and out."

Marta studied the F3's projected course and plotted an intercept. As she worked she contemplated Pete's choice of words and how odd it was to refer to what they did as killing. Tornadoes were forces of nature, not living creatures. They could be destroyed, not killed. But she well understood the inherent need to anthropomorphize their enemy, to endow them with human traits and a malevolence that could be hated, a spirit that could be broken. She even found herself thinking that way sometimes.

It was far easier to believe that there were a finite number of them out there and that each time they eradicated one brought them one small step closer to an ultimate victory over their deadly adversaries. But the harsh reality of it was that nature could spawn those monsters any time she chose in endless variety and infinite number. The war would only be won when her rage was appeased and a semblance of climatological balance restored. It was anyone's guess if that was even possible. For now all one could do was fight the battles, reveling in the triumphs and agonizing over the defeats.

Marta's musings ended abruptly. She frowned at the sinuous curves being plotted on the virtual radar screen hovering before her eyes, each mark indicating a potential path the F3 might follow. The paths were based on algorithms that took into account the twister's current course, wind vectors, and the vagaries of the surrounding terrain. Percentages indicating the statistical likelihood of each path hovered over the map. The numbers changed constantly as fresh data was received from the Doppler and incorporated into the calculations.

Most of the paths led to wide open swaths of unpopulated farmland. Crop losses would be significant and that alone was more than enough incentive for intervention, especially considering the fact that Storm Strike was funded by the major farming corporations. But there was one particular track that had Marta worried.

Marta twisted in her chair to address her team. "There's a fifty-six percent chance that one of the Tiburon conglomerate's farms could be hit by that F3 if she continues to follow her current path. Looks like we need to go cross country to get into position. You up for some off-roading, Chaz?"

Chaz's eyes lit up. "Yes, ma'am!"

Marta swept her hand over the course projection and a glowing green orb that represented the raw navigational data shot across the console toward Chaz, where it expanded and morphed into a three dimensional map. Chaz squinted down at it with a juvenile grin.

"Hold onto your personalities," Chaz bellowed. "Things are fixin' to get a might hairy!"

"Aw, shit!" Kinney groaned and gripped the arms of his chair, tight ribbons of muscle in his forearms swelling.

A single violent twist of the steering wheel sent the stormcruiser careening off the road. Marta experienced a thrilling moment of weightlessness as they went airborne, hopping the broad flooded ditch and landing hard at the edge of a corn field. The impact slammed Marta down in her seat. "Woo hoo!" she screamed, jabbing her arms up over her head, letting her still raging energy take her wherever it wanted to go.

The stormcruiser tore deeper into the cornfield, blazing a trail through the towering stalks that folded themselves into the windshield. They exploded on impact. Shredded corn husks, clumps of tassels and pulverized cobs filled the air around them.

Massive tires dug into waterlogged soil. Thick treads gobbled up muddy clods, then spat them back out. A steady barrage of thumps and bangs rang out as the dense clumps of mud slammed into the armored side panels and up against the undercarriage.

Marta was relishing every exhilarating moment. She tightened her grip on the overhead grab bars as they jolted and squirmed over the slick, rugged terrain in a blind, mad dash to put themselves within range for an intercept. The stormcruiser was taking a beating. She knew the mechanics back at base would be sure to let her know about it. But their words of chastisement would mean little as long as they achieved their objectives and kept any innocents out of harm's way.

Marta heard a dull thump behind her as they crested a particularly steep knoll. She turned to see Kinney rubbing the side of his helmet. His face had brightened to a particularly angry shade of red. "Does anyone realize we have thermobaric explosives on board?" Kinney yelled through clenched teeth.

Marta snickered. She knew the warheads they carried were perfectly stable until they left the security of the launcher and their proximity fuses were energized. A half dozen mechanical and electronic safeguards prevented their premature detonation. Still, in a crazy, irrational sort of way, she found herself embracing the thought that at any moment they could be vaporized. It somehow heightened the excitement she was feeling.

Chaz, keeping his eyes fixed on the road, turned his head to the right as if, by doing so, his voice would be heard more clearly over the intercom. "My grandpappy was 95 when he tried blowing up a hickory stump with a stick of dynamite. Ended up sending himself straight to the pearly gates."

Kinney's brow furrowed. "What the hell does that have to do with anything?"

Chaz's face tightened in concentration, his gaze alternating between the windshield and the navigational map on his console. "He'd always told me, he'd say 'Charles'. He called me Charles on account of I didn't go by Chaz back then. He'd say 'Charles, when your time comes, best to go out with a bang.'" He nodded vigorously as if to emphasize the general validity of his point.

Kinney leaned forward in his seat. "In case you hadn't noticed, *Charles*, none of us are quite 95 years old yet."

A mischievous smirk curled the corners of Chaz's mouth. "Well, hell, how old are ya? Gotta be forty-five, if a day. That's pretty damn old in my book. Couple more years and you'll just start wasting away anyhow."

"You want to go out with a bang, just keep it up," Kinney growled to himself.

"What's that, pardner?" Chaz asked, one hand held up to his helmet where his ear would be. At that moment, the stormcruiser bounded over a slope, landing with its wheels askew and skidding sideways. Chaz grabbed the wheel with both hands and fought to regain control. The tires plowed mud and sent up a spray of viscous ooze that sounded like a tidal wave as it slapped the side of the cruiser. Finally he managed to swing the front end back around and correct their errant course.

"My bad, my bad," Chaz offered apologetically. "I reckon I just have to learn to keep both hands on the wheel."

Kinney's eyes flashed. "Or just learn to keep your head out of your..."

"We're in the projected corridor," Marta interrupted. She sat back with a smug look on her face. "That F3 will have to come through us to get to that farm now."

Chaz brought the stormcruiser to a halt in the middle of the cornfield. A gust of wind buffeted them from side to side.

"Winds are picking up fast," Marta said, checking the readout from their anemometer. "Better dig in."

"Roger that," Chaz said and slid his finger over a pair of glowing toggles positioned on either side of a virtual representation of their stormcruiser. Air shocks hissed as the vehicle squatted down close to the ground. Then a quartet of servo motors hummed in unison.

Marta craned her neck to peer out her side window. She watched as a steel arm unfolded from its recessed perch just behind the front fender. An immense rotating corkscrew pivoted out from the arm and descended toward the ground. Like a giant drill bit it dug into the soil, eagerly slipping through the muck and penetrating solid ground. The same process was happening at each corner of the stormcruiser.

The vehicle shuddered as all four anchors quickly found purchase. She heard the grinding as hardened steel displaced compacted soil; the piercing screech as metal encountered rock followed quickly by a loud pop as the offending chunk of ore was pulverized. Finally the sounds of the mechanized symphony died away, followed only by the low moan of powerful hydraulics being charged to tighten their hold on terra firma.

"Anchors secure," Chaz announced.

Marta nodded in acknowledgement. She tried bringing up the radar view in her ER visor but was greeted instead with a flashing red warning telling her no data was available. A moment later her console confirmed what she had suspected. She glanced behind her to see Kinney frowning down at his console. His fingers were frozen in midair as he waited for targeting data to appear.

"Marta, primary tracking appears to be down," Kinney said.

Marta sighed, having known the question was coming and not liking the answer that she had to give. "That's because the Doppler is temporarily offline," she admitted.

Kinney looked up at her quizzically. "Say again?"

Marta let the question hang for a moment. "The radar array lost its directional synchronization due to the rough terrain. It's recalibrating itself now."

Kinney's hands dropped to his lap in exasperation. "So we're essentially blind here."

"Yes, temporarily," Marta said, biting her lip.

Kinney eyed her warily. "How temporarily?"

She glanced down at the glowing red progress bar on her console as it edged toward completion. "Two minutes, give or take."

"Can we at least get a visual?" Kinney asked.

Chaz squirmed around in his chair, trying to get a better angle through the windshield. A soft orange glow was quickly spreading across the sky as morning broke but the towering corn stalks effectively blocked their line of sight. "Ah, that's a negative, pardner. View is a might obstructed at this particular moment."

Kinney unlatched his safety harness, slid his console to the side and climbed to his feet. Keeping his head low, he made his way forward and popped his head into the cockpit between Chaz and Marta. He peered out into the cornfield, trying to focus on the tiny gaps where dark skies were visible. He then fixed his gaze on Chaz. "Why don't you climb up top and take a looksy."

Chaz shook his head sternly just as a particularly vigorous surge of wind shook the cruiser. "No thank you. When I was a young'un I used to like to fly a kite. Don't particularly care to become one though."

Marta stared down at the progress bar. Ninety seconds to go. She was well aware of just how much could happen in ninety seconds. For the moment, they were sitting ducks at the mercy of the storm. She didn't appreciate the feeling of helplessness that thought instilled. Then it occurred to her that it took a little less than ten seconds to deploy a drone. She made her decision instantly and initiated a launch.

"Popping a bot," she announced.

Her visor automatically darkened to block out her immediate surroundings. Live video from the drone's cameras projected onto the opaque inner surface of the lenses. A moment of vertigo tugged at her as she acclimated to her new point of view, hovering just above the stormcruiser. As she turned her head to look around, the drone's cameras panned in perfect unison with her head's movements, deepening the illusion that she was peering out into the storm from the drone's perspective.

Bursts of gale force winds buffeted the flat, rectangular craft; its four ducted fans whining in protest as it fought to compensate and hold position. Marta's right hand hovered over a sensor stud that monitored her gestures. She raised her hand and the drone began to gain altitude. She pitched her hand forward and the drone lurched ahead.

"Got eyes on the drone," Chaz said, peering up and out through the windshield at the flashing navigation lights on the belly of the drone as it drifted into view.

Marta had to consciously prevent herself from flinching as debris whipped past her visual field. Once the drone cleared the tips of the corn stalks, her view of the sky improved dramatically. She squinted hard, trying to make out any telltale funnel shapes in the distance. Oddly, her view to the front seemed obstructed. She twisted her head from side to side and each time her view brightened to the left and to the right but she still saw only darkness ahead.

Then the cause of the darkness became apparent when she saw corn stalks being wrenched from the ground in clumps just ahead of them. She glanced upward and saw only a spinning wall of shredded green stalks. Her eyes widened in horror.

"Fuck me!" she mumbled.

Chaz turned to Kinney. "Buckle up, buttercup!"

Kinney launched himself back toward his seat and just managed to fasten his harness as the twister enveloped them.

Marta's view through the drone's cameras flipped sideways, then spun out of control and plummeted. A sudden wave of dizziness washed over her. She flipped up her visor and shook her head to clear it.

Chaz watched the drone as it hurtled toward the windshield. Instinctively he ducked. A moment later it crashed into the armored glass. The impact sent up a shower of sparks mingled with shattered bits of plastic and left a scorch mark on the windshield.

Savage winds screamed like a banshee. Marta felt the stormcruiser lift up on its shocks and vibrate as the twister tried to dislodge it. She gritted her teeth and listened to the groan of fatigued metal as the frame's structural integrity was put to the test. But the frame held and so did the anchors. A few seconds passed and the winds subsided, followed by a moment of stunned silence as they each realized they were still breathing.

Chaz was the first to break the calm. "Well, Marta. I reckon it just came through us," he said candidly.

Marta shot him an icy glare. "Thank you for that profound revelation, Chaz."

She turned to Kinney. "Major, target that shredder. Let's kick that son of a bitch in the ass."

Kinney nodded and issued an informal salute. "You got it, commander."

He placed his fingers against the surface of the console and tapped out a firing solution. Marta dropped her ER visor back into position. It allowed her to see the same projections hovering in mid-air as Kinney did. She watched as three red lines that represented potential missile trajectories arced away from the tiny virtual representation of their stormcruiser. One tracer held to a straight line toward its target while the other two curved outward and then intercepted the funnel from either side. The location and timing of each detonation was computer directed, carefully orchestrated for delivery of maximum disruption based on thousands of simulations and further refined with data captured from real world interceptions.

"We have a firing solution plotted," Kinney said, his index finger hovering over a strobing red icon.

Marta's eyes narrowed as she coldly uttered a single word. "Fire."

Kinney's finger tapped the icon. A steady tone sounded along with a mechanized hum as the roof-mounted turret rotated to face aft, bringing the missiles to bear on their target. The rumble of fierce combustion shook the cruiser as rocket engines ignited. Through the windshield, the smattering of corn stalks that remained standing withered and smoldered from the hot exhaust gases bathing them.

"Missiles away," Kinney reported.

Marta was out of her chair and swinging the main hatch up before Kinney or Chaz could even react. The rain had lessened to a drizzle as she leaped to the ground. She stood in the scorched, smoking patch of soil that surrounded the cruiser, breathing in the earthy scent of damp loam mixed with the sharp, fresh hint of ozone from the passing storm, and stared up at the rapidly receding missiles. Kinney and Chaz stepped up next to her on either side. They watched as the lead missile shot straight as an arrow for the shredder.

What happened next played out in the wink of an eye. The lead missile swept up behind the twister and spent its thunderous fury, opening up a gaping hole in the dark spiraling wall of clouds. The pair of remaining missiles veered off to either side and swung back in to attack from the flanks. Twin explosions blossomed, staggering the funnel. It wobbled in ever wider undulations until its own weakening forces could no longer hold it together and it tore itself apart. Vaporous whorls expanded out from the fading body of the tornado. Then they, too, simply vanished.

A warm gust of wind swept past, rippling the corn, and bringing with it the stinging smell of burnt explosives that punctuated the end of nearly every mission. Marta recognized this mission as another victory but somehow it still felt hollow and insignificant. She continued to watch as the billowy contrails from the missiles curled and swelled in the hazy sky. The clouds were already dissipating and the delicate hint of a rainbow was visible in the east where the sun was beginning to erupt from the horizon.

"That's one more for the good guys," Chaz said, tilting his Stetson back on his head.

Marta squinted at Chaz trying to hold onto even a tiny shred of the exhilaration that she'd been riding for the past few days. But she knew it was futile. She could already feel her emotional foundation dropping away beneath her, dragging her into a pit that she was all too familiar with. She stared down at the patch he wore on the sleeve of his navy blue coveralls, the same one they all wore, depicting a twister with a red crosshair hovering over it. "Is that what we are?" she mused.

Chaz looked at her and she could see the pity stirring behind his eyes. He knew her too well to not realize what was happening. She forced a smile and threw her arms around both of them, swinging them back around toward the cruiser.

"Come on, boys. I guess it's time to ride off into the sunrise," she said as they clambered back inside.

CHAPTER 2

Dark clouds churned high above Oklahoma City as the stormcruiser sped over the rain slick highway, weaving in and out of the morning commuter traffic. Its imposing hulk dwarfed the cars around it, like a titan amongst mere mortals. Scratches and pits, scars from the recent battle, pockmarked the raised octagonal panels that honeycombed every exterior surface from the hood to the fenders to the side panels. The missile carriage had been retracted; nestled out of sight within the armored black hull. Its siren was silent; its strobes dark. Yet it carried a disquieting sense of grim urgency about it. A latent power that commanded respect.

Inside the cruiser, Marta noted the subtle transition from rolling verdant farmlands to drab, cluttered suburbs with disinterest, knowing their journey back to base was nearly over. Her eyes were heavy but she fought the urge to sleep. The adrenaline high she'd been riding had faded, taking with it her vitality and plunging her toward the inevitable abyss that was waiting for her.

Beside her, Chaz was thrumming his fingers on the steering wheel in synchrony with the music blaring in his headset. Enough of the discordant melody was seeping out from around his helmet to make Marta cringe and consider activating the noise cancellation in her own headset. Youth had its advantages. Taste in music wasn't one of them.

She took another glance at the unsettled sky, then brought up a localized forecast for the sector in her visor. A quick scan of the report and her immediate concerns subsided. She breathed a sigh of relief and felt her body lose some of its tension. Despite the ominous looking clouds, the forecast called only for light drizzle and relatively stable weather patterns. At least for now.

It was all part of the devious game that mother nature was constantly playing. A momentary lull to promote a false sense of security followed by another malicious bout of mayhem. Or so it seemed once one became accustomed to endowing nature with human attributes and actions, not the least of which were malice and cold-blooded murder.

Marta sank back into her chair and gazed ahead absently as they swept past an industrial complex bustling with activity. On her left, steam belched from the cooling tower of the central reactor that powered the surrounding factories. On her right, a sleek maglev train, hovering above a single massive rail, was just pulling away from a storage depot. Up ahead, in the distance, she could see a cluster of towering skyscrapers, their walls a sprawling mosaic of deeply tinted glass panels that caught the sun's rays and used them to power the activities of the inhabitants within.

They were making good time despite the heavy rush hour traffic. The four lanes flowing in each direction afforded drivers in their path the opportunity to quickly move aside, a service that the vast majority of them were eager to provide. Even the vehicles they swept by seemed to edge as far away from them as possible. Some even braked to expedite their passing. And a few pulled to the side of the road and waited for them to leave the vicinity before continuing on. All this despite the absence of flashing strobes or wailing siren.

Marta would have liked to believe that such reactions stemmed from a sense of respect for what Storm Strike stood for. Or that they were a gesture to honor those who had fallen. Or perhaps even a recognition of the innocent lives they had saved. But Marta surmised it was simply their awareness that the cruiser carried a small arsenal of devastating munitions and the quicker they could distance themselves from such potential for destruction, the better. Regardless of the reasoning, it was a convenience that Marta appreciated and that Chaz had no problem taking advantage of. He kept their speed nearly twenty over the posted limit despite the clinging haze that had newly descended, cutting visibility and imparting a monotone hue to the cityscape.

Chaz torqued the steering wheel hard over to the right. The cruiser veered across two lanes, exited the highway and snaked down a steep curving ramp. The ramp spilled onto a private drive lined with an inordinate number of convenient turnarounds and a series of prominently posted signs. The first several warned trespassers in bold red letters of potential fines and imprisonment. For those who ignored the first few warnings, the following ones gave them indisputable notice that lethal force was authorized to be used on any careless souls who chose to journey on.

As they passed by a security checkpoint, Marta waved to the two guards dressed in the mottled blacks, whites and grays of urban camouflage. They saluted in return. Each of them carried a menacing looking rifle; the same kind of rifle that was mounted securely next to Kinney in the back of their cruiser. A gate swung open and they swept past the outer perimeter fence topped with endless loops of glistening razorwire.

Ahead, out of the misty gloom, the stark gray walls of Storm Strike Alpha slowly materialized. The massive structure was cylindrical at its base, vertical slabs rising for the first two stories. Then its shape transitioned into a monstrous truncated cone resembling a stubby inverted funnel, almost as if paying homage to the very force of nature they were sworn to fight.

Constructed of reinforced concrete, Storm Strike Alpha was virtually impervious to any assault that man or nature could mount against it and stood as a testament to mankind's defiance in the face of overwhelming adversity. A symbol of hope, unity and strength. Sometimes Marta saw it that way. But if she had learned anything in her thirty-eight years, it was that there was always more than one way to look at any given situation. And at that moment, with her enthusiasm depleted and her outlook dismally pessimistic, she saw it more as a symbol of rebellion against a natural order that perhaps wasn't meant to be tampered with. A futile gesture of defiance akin to giving a speeding truck the finger just moments before it runs you down.

As they approached, Marta began to hear the familiar droning hum of the phased array radar that was housed within the massive cone towering above them. It was audible even above the steady whine of the cruiser's turbine. Hundreds of megawatts of vibrant energy were being pumped out into the atmosphere. An ocean of electromagnetic waves that collided with any objects in their path; from a single raindrop to a three-kilometer-wide F5 twister. The waves were then reflected back to their point of origin, where they were processed into a high resolution map of airborne activity, updated continuously. Fifteen other smaller dedicated radar installations complimented Storm Strike Alpha's coverage and provided them with contiguous surveillance of the entire swath of the country known infamously as tornado alley.

The road they were following led straight to a single overhead door; one tall and wide enough for a stormcruiser to safely navigate. Marta tapped a code into a glowing keypad that appeared on her console. In response, a bright slit of light appeared at the base of the door. The opening grew in height as the door rolled upward. Chaz slowed to a crawl and guided them in.

The door eased shut behind them. Marta squinted as her eyes adjusted to the sallow glare. They had traded the foggy gloom outside for a cavernous labyrinth of gray, lit by the sterile glow of luma panels overhead. A row of parked stormcruisers drifted past like dormant mechanized ghosts. The floor dipped downward and they descended another level.

There was purposeful activity here. Maintenance bays lined each side of the passage with stormcruisers occupying the majority of them. Technicians hurried about, prodding the vehicles with their instruments, poking their heads in open access panels, rolling around carts piled with tools and diagnostic equipment. Air tools whirred and thudded. Showers of sparks jittered across the cement floor and an occasional blue-violet glow of superheated plasma marked where metal was being wrought.

Marta's eyes were drawn away from the frenzied work to a dimly lit bay on the right where a cruiser sat parked in shadows. A group of technicians huddled by the entrance to the bay in deep discussion with a pair of supervisors. There was a great deal of head shaking and arms being thrown up, either in frustration or as a gesture of futility.

Curious, she wondered what could prompt such solemn deliberations. Then, as their running lights played over the bay, she saw the cruiser. The hull was marred with countless dents and gouges. Its wheels were cambered outward at odd angles. The right front tire hung half a meter off the floor, as if the frame itself had been twisted and deformed. Several body panels were scorched and blistered where the reactive armor had been penetrated, activating explosive packets designed to repel incoming debris. A few curls of black smoke still drifted up from the front end. Then Marta's mouth dropped open as she saw the gaping hole in the right flank, adjacent to the cockpit where the commander would have sat. A dark stain ran from the jagged opening down the side of the cruiser and led to a small puddle of red-tinged fluid on the ground.

One of the supervisors turned to watch their cruiser pass by. He made eye contact with Marta and she quickly averted her gaze. She could feel hot tears welling up for whatever crew endured such a tragedy.

A man in a fluorescent green safety vest and holding a pair of glowing red cylinders motioned them into bay twelve. A crew was already waiting to assess and repair any damage incurred on their recent outing. The moment the cruiser rolled to a stop, they descended on it, tools and probes in hand.

The hatch behind her swung open. Kinney was the first out. Marta took a moment to compose herself as Chaz unstrapped his safety harness and started for the hatch. He hesitated and placed a hand on Marta's shoulder, obviously sensing her distress.

"You okay, girl?" he asked.

Marta forced a smile and nodded. "Yeah. Let's get out of here."

Peeling off the gloves that allowed her to interact with the stormcruiser's systems, she placed them on the center console. Then she slipped off the thin white shell of her helmet, freeing her long auburn hair to spill out behind her. She hooked the helmet over the back of her seat. A faint hum and a flashing blue indicator light on the headrest told her the inductive charging system was working, topping off the helmet's battery that powered the ER visor as well as the active energy absorption system that could sense a violent jolt and transmit acoustic energy through the helmet to cushion the impact.

Marta followed Chaz out into the bay. Kinney was waiting beside a maintenance supervisor who handed Marta a data pad. She took it and signed her name with the stylus, relinquishing her command status over the ended mission and acknowledging the return of the stormcruiser and its military grade ordnance to a secured area.

"Briefing in ten minutes, commander. Room 310," the supervisor said as he took back the data pad, slipped on a pair of reading glasses and glanced down at the display.

"Don't you mean debriefing?" Marta asked.

The supervisor's eyes shifted upward to study her from above his spectacles. "If I'd meant debriefing I would have said debriefing. And its mandatory attendance," he added with conspicuous emphasis on the last two words.

Marta huffed her displeasure, turned and exited the bay. A personnel transport with a bench seat facing rearward was waiting for them. She sat in the middle of the seat out of habit and with the good sense of keeping her feud prone crew separated. Kinney and Chaz dutifully filled the bench on either side of her.

Kinney tapped the rear fender twice, signaling the driver, and the transport departed with a lurch, heading back in the direction they had entered from. Marta was careful to lower her gaze as they passed the bay containing the wrecked cruiser. She took deep breaths and focused on her tightly clasped hands but she could sense Kinney and Chaz taking in the carnage from beside her.

"Damn," Kinney said.

"Someone had a very bad day," Chaz added bleakly with only a touch of his twang evident.

The transport brought them back up the ramp to the ground floor and scooted along a narrow corridor, finally emerging from a short tunnel into the brightly lit administrative section of the building where it rolled to a stop. The majority of Storm Strike's clerical workforce populated cubicles here, their partitions forming a maze of tight passages. The closed doors of offices inhabited by the upper echelon of executives lined the walls. Marta peered east past a ten meter long mahogany reception desk and out through the floor to ceiling glass panels that flanked the main entrance, wishing she were headed in that direction rather than up into the bowels of Storm Strike Alpha.

As they disembarked from the transport, Marta checked her watch and hoped the briefing would be short. Her children would be up by now. But she knew they were used to fending for themselves. Having their mother working a swing shift whenever they stayed with her had prompted an early maturity. They would likely be preparing breakfast at that very moment in anticipation of her return home.

Marta set thoughts of her kids aside and steered for a cluster of lifts along the rear wall of administration. The lifts formed a central hub for the building. On each floor above the first, corridors radiated out from the elevator lobby like spokes on a wheel. They took a lift to the third floor, followed one of the spokes and found room 310. Several crews were already there, seated amidst the rows of long tables set up facing the far wall. Notepads and water pitchers were spaced out evenly on each table. Marta found three empty seats and once more took the middle chair while Kinney and Chaz assumed their usual wingman positions.

There was a great deal of hushed chatter. Marta ignored it, never caring for unsubstantiated gossip. What she needed to know, she'd be told. In her experience, that one simple principle tended to simplify life greatly. Which was good because her life was complicated enough without dwelling on rumors and hearsay.

The room grew still when a small balding man wearing a well-tailored Armani suit shuffled in the door and approached the podium. Marta frowned, a bit puzzled by his presence. Nate Patterson was the chief of operations for Storm Strike and seldom took the time to perform the menial task of briefing or debriefing teams. He gently set a data pad down on the podium, tapped the microphone and cleared his throat.

"Good afternoon," he began in a small, well practiced voice. He leaned forward as he spoke, relying heavily on the amplification of the microphone to distribute his words. His eyes roamed the room continually and he had the peculiar habit of pausing between the phrases within each of his sentences. "Today was a very long and busy day...for most of you...so I'll try to keep this brief...and get you on your way home...as quickly as possible."

He tried for a disarming smile but fell short and ended up issuing a tight sneer before continuing.

"First let me just say that, based on your telemetry feeds and our radar, you all did admirable jobs out there. As usual, commanders, please have your mission reports submitted before your next shift. Now, where to begin…"

He tapped a few keys on his data pad, his face pallid in the reflected glow from its screen.

"Ah, yes. First some good news." He made another attempt at smiling that made his upturned lips quiver with the effort. "I am happy to report that our cloud seeding program is proceeding as planned with very promising results, I might add. Farmers in zones ten through twenty-one have reported a thirty-four percent reduction in hail damage."

He paused to let this sink in and made another slow, deliberate sweep of the room with his head. "Unfortunately, however, our efforts are having minimal effect on the spawning of funnel clouds. And all attempts to use aircraft to engage and terminate them have failed due to the extreme turbulence and electrical interference so prevalent near them. Therefore your stormcruisers with their tightly-focused Doppler radar targeting systems will continue to be our first line of defense for the foreseeable future."

Marta shifted anxiously in her chair and noticed others doing the same as Patterson's painstakingly slow and meticulous style of speaking frayed their already tattered nerves. Patterson, oblivious to the grating effects of his speech, simply continued on.

"It has always been our goal to ensure that your teams have the most advanced and most effective tools at your disposal. Our good friends in the military who have so graciously provided us the means to defend ourselves from nature's wrath have approached us with what we think will be a major upgrade to our defensive capabilities. Here to speak with you about this opportunity is General Coltrane of the United States Army." Patterson stepped back from the podium and gestured toward the door.

The woman who stepped purposefully through the doorway was dressed in a crisp service uniform, hat tucked neatly beneath her arm. Silver hair was tied back in a tight bun. Her features were weathered but she still possessed a residual beauty with prominently high cheekbones and a small, narrow nose. She walked across the room with a sturdy self-assured grace.

General Coltrane stopped and turned to face her rapt audience, still several meters from the podium. Patterson made another invitational motion toward the microphone. The general caught the gesture, walked over to the podium, placed her hat there and calmly walked back to her previous position. Patterson seemed slightly taken aback but, when the general spoke, it became obvious her robust voice needed no amplification to carry to the far corners of the room.

"First allow me to say that you good people out on the front lines of this battle are doing a fine job. I commend you for your efforts." She paused, letting the praise sink in. "As Mr. Patterson just stated, I am here to present a significant refinement to your current modus operandi."

She pulled a small black device from her pocket. Pointing it at the bare white wall behind her, she pressed a button on its face. A beam of intense light spiraled out from the handheld box, projecting a series of slanted and blurred colored bars in a test pattern on the wall. The bars wobbled, then tilted to a perfect vertical orientation and came into sharp focus. The test pattern faded away and a cutaway diagram of a missile appeared on the wall, each part neatly labeled. The image remained remarkably stable and focused despite the subtle movements of the general's hand.

"I'm sure you all recognize this as the SCH series of missiles, or SCORCH as they are commonly referred to. They have proved to be the workhorse behind your endeavors to mitigate the damage to property and the loss of life caused by the new breed of tornadic phenomenon plaguing this area of our country."

She pressed another button on the miniature projector and an animated missile took to the air, reached apex and began to descend toward a thin jagged line representing the horizon.

"The thermobaric warheads these missiles utilize operate on the fuel-air principle whereby a small explosive charge disperses an aerosol fuel into the atmosphere."

Marta watched the animation as it tightened into a close-up of the plummeting missile. A tiny star-shaped explosion bloomed at the core of the warhead and an ocean of tiny spheres, little more than dots, surged out and away in all directions, speckling the white paint on the wall.

"Then a secondary charge ignites it," she continued.

Another tiny star-shaped explosion popped near the cone of the missile. Expanding concentric circles of red and orange engulfed the projection with enough intensity that the entire wall flashed in waves of vibrant destructive color.

"The surrounding air provides the oxidizer," the general said, gesturing toward the flickering wall with her free hand. "In effect, the atmosphere itself becomes an active participant in the chemical reaction. The resulting detonation comes as close to providing a nuclear punch as any chemical explosive ever has. They are, ladies and gentlemen, what make tornado busting possible."

General Coltrane switched off the projector and folded her hands behind her back.

"Stanford Chemistry House, our primary contractor who developed these warheads, has recently completed preliminary testing of an innovative new generation of thermobaric explosive. It utilizes a nanofuel that enhances combustion and exponentially increases the explosive yield. SCH is understandably proud of their new little boy. And it is one angry little boy. It can do everything a tactical nuke can, short of making you glow."

A smug half-smile formed on her taut lips as she paused for effect. "The SCH-4 warhead that you currently use typically requires a triad of missiles in order to be effective against the more powerful shredders. Now…," she said, pausing and taking in the room with her intense gaze. "with SCH-5…," she continued and then held up a single finger. "You'll need only one."

Hushed murmurings filled the room. Marta herself was having a hard time wrapping her head around that level of destructive force. The cyclonic winds that powered a twister usually needed to be disrupted at several different elevations to achieve termination. For one blast to achieve the same effect seemed preposterous. She shuddered involuntarily as she thought of just how treacherous such a weapon could be and how miniscule the margin of error would be when deploying it.

"Technically, these missiles are Uncle Sam's property. They were bought and paid for with taxpayer dollars. But there is a catch. Under the revised Zurich Arms Treaty of 2028, thermobaric explosives are classified as weapons of mass destruction and are therefore banned from military testing or use. However, any non-military organization applying this technology for peaceful, humanitarian purposes is exempt from this limitation. Therefore we feel justified and morally obligated to move forward and begin limited field operation trials," Coltrane said. She raised an open palm to her chest. "Under the military's supportive guidance, of course. Which we are happy to provide in the interest of saving innocent lives."

Muffled chuckles and the guttural sound of throats being cleared made Marta smile. The general narrowed her eyes but let the subtle affront to her sincerity pass without reprisal.

"Initially, only one cruiser will be armed with the SCORCH-5 warhead. Uncle Sam is kind enough to loan you his missiles. But cautious enough to require a commissioned munitions officer to be a member of each of your teams. The most senior and decorated of those officers within your ranks is Major Kinney Keller so his team will be given the honor of testing the new warhead."

The general made eye contact with Kinney, who nodded reverently. Chaz rolled his eyes, leaned forward to peer over at Kinney and made an obscene pumping motion with his fist. Kinney turned to glare back at him. Marta, recognizing an imminent confrontation, planted her elbow into Chaz's ribcage with enough force that she felt the gust of hot wind as the air burst from his lungs. He let out a soft grunt and settled back into his seat, clutching his stomach and trying to catch his breath.

"Your vehicle is already being retrofitted with the new SCORCH-5," she said, speaking directly to Kinney. Then she retrieved her hat from the podium. "More details will be forthcoming at the conclusion of this trial. Good luck and Godspeed."

General Coltrane turned, gave Patterson a quick salute, then strolled from the room. Marta reached for a glass and poured herself some water as Patterson approached the podium once more.

"I don't know if I like this," she whispered to Kinney.

"I don't know that we have any choice but to like it," Kinney replied.

Marta sucked in a deep breath and took a sip of water as Patterson continued.

"I also, unfortunately, have some tragic news," he stated flatly. Marta flinched and swallowed wrong, eliciting a series of gurgling coughs as she tried to extricate the water from her windpipe. She knew what was coming next; had heard it before. Far too many times.

Patterson squinted down at his data pad as he read the report out loud. "Delta Sierra Six, Miller, Taggert, and Dobbs were patrolling just to the southwest of Shawnee when they were caught off guard by a rain-wrapped twister, an F4 so shrouded in precipitation that it proved invisible to the naked eye and evaded detection on their Doppler. They had just started to dig in when the shredder picked up their cruiser and hurled them into a quarry pit. All three perished."

Marta set the water glass down and closed her eyes. Patterson, noticing the increased tension in the room, finished quickly. "Any further details will be relayed to you with all haste. We share in your loss, I assure you."

Snatching up his data pad, he headed for the exit, then paused, almost as an afterthought. "Dismissed," he said and hurriedly departed.

The weary crews filed out into the corridor in silence. In a daze, Marta drifted out of the room, not bothering to wait for Chaz or Kinney. The air had suddenly grown thick, hot and oppressive and she felt an urgency to be alone.

As Marta marched down the corridor she couldn't help but see the faces of the fallen, fresh and vivid in her mind. She had just spoken to Taggert that morning before their shift began. He had asked her if she knew of any intimate but affordable restaurants for his tenth wedding anniversary that was less than a week away.

Taggert had had a wife and two children. Dobbs had been a single parent raising a son. Miller had been engaged to be married. Three lives lost; three families thrown into disarray and despair. It was a steep price to pay but she knew the cost of inaction would undoubtedly be much higher. In the end, they were all pawns in a war that would, at best, end in a stalemate.

Marta turned a corner and found five rookies, not much more than teenagers, standing in the lobby next to the lifts. They were dressed in mission coveralls but she didn't know if they were going on shift or just coming off. She could feel their eyes on her as they briefly checked her out and then returned to their adolescent posturing. She stabbed the down button and did her best to ignore them.

"Have you ever driven straight through one?" she heard one of them say.

"Have you?" another answered.

"Hell, yeah!" the first one replied. Marta could see him out of the corner of her eye. He stood with his chest puffed out and an arrogant sneer permanently affixed to his face. A pompous immature jackass, if ever she had seen one. "An F2, probably close to an F3. I could have sworn our wheels actually left the ground. We came out the other side and launched a salvo behind us. Singed our asses a bit but we took that bitch down."

Marta rolled her eyes and willed the lift to arrive. "It's not a game," she mumbled, half to herself and half with the hope that they might overhear.

"Come again, commander?" the confirmed jackass replied, his sneer now firmly directed at her.

Marta turned and gave him a withering glare. "I said it's not a game."

The rookie chuckled. "Nobody said it was. We're just making things a little more interesting."

Marta shook her head. "You just don't get it, do you? It's life or death out there. And not just for you but for those who are counting on you to protect them."

"You need to chill, lady," he said, eliciting a series of snickers from the others.

Marta felt her blood begin to simmer. She swept the lot of them with one scathing glance. "A team just died, okay? They died!" She fixed her full attention once more on the smart-mouthed jackass. "You think you're better than they were? You think it can't happen to you? Maybe it won't today. Maybe it won't tomorrow. But just keep going out there with that smartass bravado and someday they'll be pulling your lifeless bodies from the mangled wreck of a stormcruiser."

The boy seemed to wither under her chastisement and she wondered if her point was actually getting across. Then another rookie swaggered to the front of the group to confront her. He stood a good foot taller than Marta and she noticed his hand looming dangerously close to his hip and the holstered sidearm that all munitions officers carried.

"He said take it easy, lady. Who are you to tell us how to do our job? You're not our superior. We don't take orders from you." He took another step forward until his face was hovering just above hers.

Marta wrinkled her nose in disgust. "Get out of my face, you insolent little shit."

She gave him an unexpectedly hard shove that knocked him off balance and pushed him back two steps. Enraged, fists clenched and eyes glowing like embers, he started toward her. And met what felt like a brick wall as Kinney stepped into his path. The rookie's head rebounded off Kinney's chest. He lifted his gaze to take stock of his new and unexpectedly formidable adversary. His eyes bulged when he recognized the uniform and his complexion whitened when he saw the face.

Kinney glanced disdainfully at the single gold bar on the rookie's shoulder. "Stand down, lieutenant."

The lieutenant quickly stood at attention, keeping his eyes focused straight ahead. "Yes, sir."

Kinney bent down so he could look the rookie straight in the eye. "You know, you'd do well to take her advice to heart, while yours is still beating."

Getting no response from the lieutenant other than a visible shudder, Kinney turned toward Marta and they entered the waiting lift. Behind them, Chaz stood, thoroughly enjoying the spectacle. "Burn. That was a major burn, y'all." He pointed his finger at the rookies, grinning. When they shifted their attention toward him he quickly followed his crewmates into the lift. "Burn," he uttered once more just before the lift door slid shut.

As they began their descent, Kinney peered down at Marta with a patronizing half-smile. Marta stared at the door, her face still reddening. Just as Kinney opened his mouth to speak, Marta lost her resolve and spun to face him, her finger wagging menacingly just centimeters from his face.

"Before you get all high and mighty on me, I'll have you know I could have dropped that corn-fed cretin like a sack of shit on Sunday so don't you dare give me any of your wiseass remarks or condescending advice or so help me God I will kick you square in your putty makers."

Kinney snapped his mouth shut, swallowed hard, and took a cautious step back toward the far corner of the lift. Marta turned back toward the door. When it opened, she stomped out, heading for the visitor entrance at the front of the building.

The sun was hidden behind a veil of clouds as she stepped through the sliding glass doors. A blast of hot, humid air slapped her in the face and flooded her lungs. Jagged streaks of lightning flared in the distance. With her meteorological senses instantly on edge, she was tempted to pull out her phone and check the latest forecast to see when the next storm front would be rolling through. But what did it matter? She was off shift for twenty-four solid hours. She'd worry about potential storms when the time came that she needed to worry about them. In her current weary and apathetic state, just getting home would be enough for her to contend with.

As her eyes adjusted to the dimness, she noticed a flurry of activity taking place near several news vans that were parked just outside the entranceway. Flashbulbs popped and camera crews jockeyed for position. Then Marta saw General Coltrane giving a briefing to a small crowd of journalists and telepresence reporters.

"So much for discretion," she mumbled derisively to herself and headed for the parking lot at her best possible walking speed.

She had just passed the cluster of news vans when a familiar face broke from the crowd and headed in her direction. She immediately recognized Lydie Wright, a bubbly Storm Strike technician a few years younger than Marta. She was waving excitedly, her blonde ponytail swinging from side to side as she struggled to catch up. Marta forced herself to slow her pace and smiled back.

Lydie was an affable sort and Marta had come to enjoy their conversations whenever their paths crossed. But this was not the time or the place for banal chatter. She wanted nothing more than to get to her car and get the hell out of there.

"Marta! You'll never guess what I just heard!" Lydie said, struggling to catch her breath.

Marta stopped and turned to face her friend. "Let me guess. The army is going to let us play with their new toys."

"Besides that," Lydie said.

Marta noticed that Kinney had nearly caught up to them when a beady-eyed colonel with a thin silvery goatee stepped from the shadows and waylaid him, firmly gripping his arm. "Major Keller, a word?" she faintly heard the colonel say. Kinney glanced down at the hand on his arm and the colonel hastily withdrew it. Kinney nodded and allowed the colonel to guide him off the pavement and out into the grass well out of earshot of any passersby.

"No idea, Lydie," Marta replied, keeping an eye on Kinney who was already deep in conversation with the mysterious colonel. They were speaking in hushed tones and being exceptionally careful to suspend their conversation whenever someone passed close by.

"I'm getting a promotion!" Lydie shouted, bursting with obvious pride.

Marta's attention was drawn back to Lydie. "Promotion?" she asked.

Lydie did her best to stand tall despite her rather diminutive height. "No more working on stormcruisers for me. As soon as a position opens up, I'm going to be in one!"

"You're going to be on field ops?" Marta asked, her attention torn between spying on Kinney and listening to Lydie.

"They're going to make me a commander! Can you believe it?"

"Wow," Marta exclaimed. She had the feeling she should be congratulating her friend but, based on her own experiences in the command seat, she felt more like she should be expressing her condolences.

"I just have to wait for the next command vacancy. And I just finished my managerial classes two days ago! I had no idea things would move so quickly," Lydie gushed.

Marta watched as Kinney pulled a flat palm-sized wafer of translucent glass from his pocket that glowed a serene blue. She recognized it as one of the latest models of G-phones. In response the colonel held out a data pad that gave off a warm red glare of its own. They tapped the devices together and they both began to pulse in synchrony as data was transferred between them.

Lydie rolled her eyes. "I know, I know. You think I'm much better off down in the dungeons twisting wrenches but I want to be out there where I can do some real good. Where I can make a difference."

Kinney tapped his phone a few times and made several swipes across its surface with his finger. Then he held it up to his face. The phone emitted a glaring red beam that Marta surmised was some type of biometric scanner. A grid of red lines danced across his open eye. Then the phone switched back to its tranquil blue glow and he slipped it back into his pocket.

"Saving lives. That's what it's all about," Marta heard her friend say. She blinked and turned back to Lydie, wanting desperately to tell her of the ponderous burdens that came with command and of the horrors she would undoubtedly bear witness to.

Instead, she just said, "I hope you find what you're looking for."

Lydie smiled weakly. "I know I will," she said in a suddenly deflated tone.

Marta silently cursed herself for having inadvertently given her friend the cold shoulder. But it was either that or launch into a desperate tirade, disclosing all of the carnage she had beheld and leaving her friend in abject terror, begging to return to her sterile, mundane existence and her former ignorance of life's arbitrary villainy.

"Goodnight, Marta," Lydie said, already backing away.

"Goodnight, Lydie," Marta replied, trying her best to smile warmly but it was lost on Lydie who had already turned away.

Marta glanced back to where Kinney had been standing but he was nowhere to be seen. Neither was the colonel.

Trying to shake off a sudden bout of paranoia, she eagerly spanned the remaining distance to her car; an opal green, heavily dented, twelve year old Chang'an, one of the last Chinese hybrids to have been imported. Its gasoline engine had been disabled six years ago to comply with the latest emission regulations. But the batteries still gave the ugly little shitbox enough range to get her to and from her apartment twelve miles away in the downtown neighborhood of Deep Deuce.

She placed her fingers in the recessed handle on the door panel. The click of a latch told her that her fingerprint had been recognized by the scanner. She swung open the door, sank down into the seat, and closed her eyes for a moment, trying to collect her scattered wits. The last half hour she had felt her emotions sinking rapidly, expedited by the news of the recent tragedy as well as the realization that another person she cared about would soon be entering the line of fire.

When she finally opened her eyes, she lurched in her seat, high enough that she felt the top of her head skim the roofline. A man was looming over her in the doorway of the car. She relaxed when she realized it was Kinney.

"You startled me," she admitted, trying to slow her rapid pulse.

"Sorry," he said, a sheepish smile crossing his face.

"Where are you off to?" she asked.

"Just calling it a day. Same as you," he said.

Marta glanced around the parking lot where a couple of dozen vehicles were still parked. "Chaz already spin gears out of here? "

Kinney shrugged his broad shoulders. "Don't know. Don't care."

The thought suddenly occurred to Marta that Kinney had probably been aware she was watching his brief impromptu meeting. "Okay. Well, I guess I'll see ya, Kinney."

"You okay, Marta?" he asked, a concerned look in his eyes.

For no apparent reason that she could immediately discern, Marta burst into tears. Her chest heaved with deep sobs and she was powerless to stop it. Kinney bent down and reached for her. Marta held up a hand. "I'm fine. Really."

Kinney hesitated, lowering his arms but still watching her worriedly.

"God, you must be losing all respect for me right now," Marta said between sobs. "I mean...I'm your commander. And look at me."

Kinney smiled. It was a warm, genuine smile that made Marta want to reach up and throw her arms around him. "I still respect you, Marta," he said.

Marta chuckled softly and rolled her eyes. "Now it sounds like we just spent the night together," she joked and then quickly realized how her tone had made the very idea of it sound repulsive. "Not that I wouldn't…" she started to correct herself and, once more, regretted her words. "I'm just going to shut up now," she finally said in defeat.

Kinney was grinning widely, obviously enjoying her string of faux pas. "Probably for the best," he agreed.

Marta watched as Kinney leaned over her, reaching for the center console. He tapped a glowing green icon marked 'Power Up.' The dash came alive with flickering green and blue instrumentation. She watched as the light danced across his chiseled features and glinted in his blue eyes.

"What is it with me sometimes?" Marta asked.

"You're a woman," Kinney stated matter-of-factly.

Marta continued to stare at Kinney, not quite sure how to respond. "Thanks," she finally said.

Kinney was busy tapping icons on the dash, as if completely unaware of the sexist connotation of his last comment. "I just mean that your emotions naturally run closer to the surface. It was a hard day. Followed by some hard news about people that you care about."

"We'll go with that," Marta said. For the second time in the last two minutes she had to fight the urge to wrap her arms around his neck and pull him close.

He tapped one final icon labeled "Home", then extricated himself from the cockpit, bringing himself up to his full height.

"You're sure you're going to be alright?" he asked.

"Yeah," she said, sniffling.

Kinney tapped the roof with his hand. "You have a good night, Marta."

Marta snickered uncomfortably and wiped the tears from her eyes. "I'll try," she said.

Kinney shut the door and backed away. The car's systems were already coming online. There was a subtle thump as the car shifted into gear. A moment later, the rattling Chang'an guided her out of the parking lot and onto the private drive that led away from Storm Strike Alpha. She leaned back in her seat and closed her eyes. She was on her way home.

RANDY R. HENKE

CHAPTER 3

A tranquil chime woke Marta out of a fitful sleep. For a moment, she didn't realize where she was as the shadowy realm of dreams commingled with harsh reality. But her mind quickly sorted things out. She tapped an icon on the car's dash, activating the shutdown sequence and pre-arming the security system.

A hazy warm mist was drifting in the air as she climbed out and ambled toward a shabby five-story brownstone. The elevator creaked and groaned as it hoisted her up to the third floor. Usually she took the staircase but her legs felt too heavy to carry her up that many steep, dark flights of stairs.

At her door, she pulled from her purse a solitary key, its chrome finish flaking. It was the only key she carried. Maintenance had yet to retrofit biometric locks to the doors in her building despite the city ordinance requiring it in all residential apartments. It was a small thing really. As long as they had power, hot water and AC, she would be hard pressed to complain.

She opened the door and winced as the blazingly bright lights from the apartment assailed her. Two blurred forms approached from the small den. She strained against the glare to bring them into focus.

"Hi, mom," came a soft adolescent voice.

Her eyes were adjusting. The two teenagers were dressed nearly identically in bright red jackets and beige pants. The Red Cross badge stood out prominently on their sleeves. Bold white letters emblazoned across their chests spelled out the words Farmer Relief. Normally her heart swelled with pride when she thought of how her children had dedicated their summer vacation to helping the less fortunate. But even that small joy eluded her.

Bonnie was the taller of the two, her long blond hair cascading over her shoulders like a sun-drenched waterfall. Freckle-faced Quinn, his brown hair cropped short and neat, stood beside his sister.

Quinn held out a steaming cup of coffee in both hands. "Thank you,"

Marta said, accepting the offering and taking a small sip.

"What's for breakfast?" Marta asked, trying to sound enthusiastic.

"Oh, we're going to grab something at McDonalds," Bonnie admitted. "We've got a big day ahead of us."

Marta looked down at Quinn. "Where is your troop going to be stationed today?"

Quinn's eyes lit up. "We're going to be helping with immunizations at one of the shantytowns." He squinted as he strained to remember. "Sterling, I think. You'd be surprised how quickly illnesses spread through those places."

Marta nodded. "Not surprised at all, actually," she said, thinking of the endless hours she had spent at the nomadic farming communities that dotted the Great Plains, performing storm shelter inspections as part of Storm Strike's humanitarian efforts. The majority of the semi-mobile towns were nothing more than crudely constructed tin shacks, canvas tents and the occasional wood-framed cabin. They were populated with migrant farmers of every creed and age. The communities shifted around periodically, following the ebb and flow of the planting and harvesting schedules in the region and catering to the whims of the farming consortiums that paid them just enough to eke out a paltry living.

"Do you want us to make you something?" Quinn asked.

"Yeah, sure, mom. We'd be glad to," Bonnie agreed.

Marta shook her head. "No. I'm not really hungry anyway. But thanks for the offer."

"You sure?" Quinn asked.

"Very. My bed is calling my name."

Bonnie motioned toward the den where a reporter's voice could be heard droning on about the latest global environmental summits. "We're just catching up on the news before we head out. Want to join us?"

She shook her head. Even the thought of spending time with her children didn't appeal to her. She shook her head. "Not today," she said, swinging her coffee cup toward the den. "Better get back to it or you might miss something."

Bonnie and Quinn exchanged a pained, knowing look. "If you say so, mom," Bonnie mumbled and placed a hand on Quinn's shoulder to guide him back to the den.

"Have a good day, kids," she called out, knowing that her children could sense that she was near the edge of an emotional precipice and, even worse, not really caring that they knew it.

"'See ya tonight, mom," Quinn said, glancing back over his shoulder.

Marta gave them a wave and a tepid smile, waited for them to disappear around the corner and then quickly headed for the kitchen. With a look of revulsion, she hurled the coffee into the sink, scattering a spray of amber droplets across the countertop. Then she homed in on the cabinet beneath the sink, bending down and rummaging with a fully extended arm. She felt a stab of panic when her initial sweep of the cabinet came up dry. But panic quickly turned to relief and then a fleeting pang of guilt when she finally found what she was looking for. Her hand emerged from the cabinet cradling a half full bottle of scotch.

She poured a finger of the golden liquid into a plastic tumbler and downed it in one gulp, relishing the heat as it bloomed in her belly. Another shot and she could already feel the numbness seeping into her bloodstream, helping to dull the pain and push back the desolation and perhaps even to dilute the nightmares that she knew would be coming.

She left the kitchen, carrying the bottle with her, hiding it behind her thigh. She didn't bother acknowledging her children as she spanned the distance between kitchen and hallway. She just concentrated on each step, taking care not to stumble as she glided across the hall to her bedroom. Let the nightmares come, she thought. She would be ready for them.

CHAPTER 4

Marta lifted the thermos to her lips and guzzled down the last few precious drops of her second cup of coffee that morning. She noticed her hands were still trembling slightly but surmised it was more from the sudden influx of caffeine rather than the lingering effects of the alcohol she'd consumed throughout the past day and well into last night.

With her visor lifted, she gazed out through the windshield of the stormcruiser at cornfields caught in the lustrous fire of a newly risen sun. The skies were a delicate azure with just a hint of fog still clinging to the ground. But more importantly, the skies were clear with not a single cloud, cumulonimbus or otherwise, visible to the far horizon. A storm front had passed during the night and a broad ridge of high-pressure had swept in to replace it, bringing with it the prospect for a pleasant and peaceful day.

Marta's mood seemed to be improving marginally as well. She couldn't tell if it was an artifact of the fair weather or just one of the natural upswings that inevitably followed the precipitous descents. Regardless, she would just try to enjoy the time spent between the extremes. Not surprisingly, it was where she functioned best with little need to resort to attempts at chemically induced moderation.

They were on Route 270 heading east through Oklahoma somewhere between Tecumseh and Seminole. For the moment, at least, they were enjoying a routine patrol. Another front was due to move in toward evening and Storm Strike always preferred to have its assets strategically placed before all hell broke loose. It was late June. During the volatile summer months, the days were few and far between when the weather was stable enough that no stormcruisers prowled the countryside.

"How are those radar diagnostics going?" Marta hollered back to Kinney as he stared straight ahead at his virtual display. His fingers reached out into the empty air before him, nudging sliding controls and tapping icons that only he could see.

"Slow. But I guess you have to expect that," he said wearily.

"Oh? How so?" Marta asked.

Kinney sighed and rubbed his eyes. "The new Doppler signal processor is basically just a tacked-on addition and far from being optimized. You have to remember. This was primarily a military radar system before it was repurposed. Hell, there are still residual operating modes you can select that allow you to track ground targets. We don't need even that capability anymore but the engineers didn't bother to wipe them when they added the weather functionality. More examples of peerless military efficiency."

"Careful. Don't forget who you work for," Marta teased. Then she heard a chime from Chaz's console and recognized it as the low fuel warning.

"I reckon it's time for a leg stretcher," Chaz announced.

Marta reached around behind her seat and tapped the trailing edge of the center console. "Hear that, Kinney? Pit stop."

"Roger that," Kinney replied.

Marta could see out of the corner of her eye that he was already checking his sidearm as he habitually did before any extravehicular excursions. Or EE's as he called them in his strict military vernacular. Chaz, on the other hand, simply called them leg stretchers or walkabouts. The two men were so diametrically opposite it was no wonder they didn't get along. Opposites might sometimes attract between the sexes but when it came to platonic relationships even a rudimentary sense of commonality went a long way.

Chaz steered them into a fueling station brimming with an unusual amount of activity for a weekday morning. Then Marta remembered it was actually Saturday. It wasn't the first time she had lost track of her days. Her crazy work schedule didn't help. But neither did the mood swings. Or the mental fog induced by the occasional bout of self-medication.

They parked next to an open pump. Marta could already see the uneasy looks on the faces of the other motorists. It was always the same. Eyes quickly averted. Children ushered away. Backs turned.

She had grown accustomed to the stigma and the aversive behavior. She certainly hadn't joined Storm Strike for the fanfare. She believed in what she was doing. Crops were being spared, farms protected and innocent lives saved.

Under a different set of circumstances, the public would have considered them heroes. But, in their eyes, Storm Strike was an agency forged to serve the farming consortiums that they loathed, funded by a government they no longer trusted, and supplied and overseen by a military that they feared. No matter how many lives were saved, that image wouldn't change.

"All ashore who's going ashore," Chaz shouted as the hatch popped open.

As security protocol dictated, Kinney was first out the door. His boots clanked loudly on the pair of metal steps. He paused when his feet touched cement and scanned the area for anything suspicious, then he stepped to the side and signaled Marta that it was safe for her to disembark.

Marta slipped a pair of wraparound sunglasses over her eyes, the frames and lenses blending into a seamless strip of chrome. She descended to the ground and pulled in a deep breath of dewy morning air. She was relieved that her head was no longer throbbing but, judging from the still appreciable ache, it was obvious that her brain was not yet done expressing its discontent over the abuse she had inflicted upon it the night before. However, when taking into account the suffering its misfiring synapses caused her on a regular basis, she'd consider it even.

Chaz bypassed the steps completely, grabbing an overhead steel brace and swinging down to the ground. He thumped his chest, stretched and yawned.

Kinney was still surveying their surroundings. "Last time I checked, Storm Strike didn't hire monkeys," Kinney said, delivering the insult without even bothering to make eye contact, then disappearing around the rear of the vehicle.

Chaz took the affront good naturedly. "Someone got out on the wrong side of the stormcruiser."

Marta grinned. She followed Chaz to the pump and leaned against it while he punched an access code into the keypad that would charge their refill to the appropriate Storm Strike account. He was whistling a familiar lively southern ballad that Marta couldn't quite place.

Two lanes away an RV that looked like it could contain two of her apartments pulled up to a station. No sooner had it rolled to a stop than a pair of pre-adolescent boys emerged and began darting between the pumps playing tag.

Kinney was still making his security sweep, just slipping into view at the front of the cruiser. He was walking cautiously, his face contracted into a tight scowl and making the motorists even more nervous than they already were.

"Been meaning to ask ya," Chaz said, grabbing the hose and swinging around to face the cruiser where the fueling port cover was already open. He snapped the nozzle into position and spun the valve. She heard a hiss as the compressed natural gas began to flow.

"Ask me what?" Marta asked, brushing her hair from her face as the warm, gentle breeze tousled it.

Chaz checked the pressure gauge on the pump, then pressed his back into the side of the cruiser and kicked his feet up onto the pump, propping himself between the two. He settled his Stetson further down on his forehead, hung his hands from the dangling lapels of his coveralls and squinted out toward the horizon. In that instant, Marta thought he looked more like a rugged, ranch-hardened cowboy than the wayward, immature, young stormcruiser pilot that he was.

"If maybe you'd be up for a little Sunday cruise out on the lake," Chaz finally said, aiming his squint directly at Marta.

"A cruise? Tomorrow?"

"Yes, ma'am."

Marta furrowed her brow in contemplation. She was flattered that Chaz had asked her but, with their sixteen year age difference and her being on the senior end of that span, she had never really considered the prospect of having any kind of social or intimate relationship with him. That is, until now when the offer had so conveniently and unexpectedly presented itself.

"Let me see. Bonnie and Quinn are going to be spending the day with friends. I could do that," she said, smiling slyly.

Chaz was beaming. He leaped to his feet and slapped his hand on his thigh. "Well, hot damn. I got me a date."

"So where are we going exactly?" she asked.

"Lake Hefner. You'll be on my very own vessel."

"I like the sound of that," she said, raising an eyebrow promiscuously and feeling giddy as a schoolgirl. Her mood instantly ratcheted up a couple more notches. She knew she was still short of a typical manic high but quite possibly high enough to make rash or dangerous decisions. She hoped this wouldn't prove to be one of them.

Just then, Marta noticed an older model fuel-cell powered Hyundai SUV roll to a stop along the curb behind the line of fueling stations. Two stern-faced dark-complected men sat in the front seats. Their attention seemed fixed on the cruiser.

Marta thought it odd they would stop at a fueling station that didn't even offer the antiquated hydrogen refueling service that their car required. But what struck Marta as particularly suspicious was how silently the car had rolled up. There had been no low rumble It was as if the vehicle's pedestrian warning module, a sound emitting system that was required to be functional on all electrics, had been disabled.

They had apparently drawn Kinney's attention as well. He had already circled around behind their vehicle. There he stood; stark still, back arched, hand clutching the grip of his sidearm, senses on high alert. He reminded Marta of a hunting dog on point.

It was obvious the men in the car hadn't noticed Kinney as he slowly crept up alongside their vehicle. They both seemed to be preoccupied manipulating something with their hands. Whatever the objects were, they kept them low and out of sight. Kinney had advanced almost to the operator side window. Marta tensed as the moment of confrontation approached.

In one fluid motion, Kinney spun around to face them, hand still on his holstered weapon. The men in the car jerked spasmodically, their eyes wide and glassy. Kinney motioned for them to lower the side window. The operator fumbled for the switch, then the window slid down.

Marta couldn't quite hear the conversation taking place. But she did see the obviously rattled men both produce what appeared to be high-end cameras with telephoto lenses and hold them up with shaky hands for Kinney to see. Marta chuckled. Paparazzi. Nothing more than a couple of pathetic, opportunistic photo mongers. Kinney still hadn't relaxed but she doubted he would shoot them. They might be degenerates, but they were unarmed degenerates nevertheless.

Just then, one of the tag-playing boys seemed to notice Kinney. From his mischievous expression, Marta could easily discern that a plan was beginning to form in his impish little head. He took off at top speed, stopping ten meters behind Kinney who was still interrogating the photographers.

The next thing Marta witnessed chilled her blood and filled her with an overwhelming sense of imminent disaster. The boy reached beneath his t-shirt and pulled a menacing looking black pistol from the waistband of his cargo shorts. The tip of the barrel ended in jagged plastic and Marta realized in an instant that it was nothing more than a toy with the red safety tip broken off. A big grin spread across the boy's face. He closed one eye, squinting with the other, and held the toy gun out, pointed directly at Kinney's back.

At that instant, the man standing next to the RV, who Marta presumed to be the boy's father, took notice of the scene unfolding. He cupped his hands around his mouth and shouted, "Hey!"

Kinney's reaction was instinctive and instant. His sidearm popped free of the holster and he pivoted on his heel, while simultaneously dropping into a defensive crouch. His weapon was leveled directly at the child.

Marta cringed, waiting for the report to ring out. But it never did. It took only a moment for Kinney to size up the situation and lower his weapon to a ready position in front of him. He stood and crossed the distance to where the child was cowering, still frozen with fear.

"Ten'll get you twenty that kid just soiled them trousers," Chaz blurted out.

The boy's father rushed over and snatched up his son, glaring at Kinney. "You people are insane!" he screamed and trotted back toward their RV. Kinney just stood there and watched them hurry away.

A chime sounded from the pump beside her. Chaz flipped a lever on the nozzle causing a hiss as the gas trapped in the hose was vented and the pressure released. He disconnected the hose and flipped the port shut.

By then, Kinney had seemingly recovered his composure and reholstered his sidearm. He was walking toward them while they waited next to the hatch. As he approached, Chaz sucked in a deep breath as if preparing to speak.

Kinney sensed the impending taunt and pointed a finger threateningly at him. "Don't!" was all he said as he passed them and climbed up into the cruiser.

Marta glanced at Chaz, eyebrows raised. He just shook his head and shrugged his shoulders. Marta reluctantly ducked into the hatch and Chaz followed.

The next fifty kilometers passed in relative silence. Marta didn't really mind. She just stared out across the rolling countryside and allowed her mind to wander.

She watched solemnly as the shell of an old farmhouse drifted past. Remnants of a simpler time, a more idyllic era. Patches of white paint still clung to the ragged siding. A tattered sun-bleached curtain fluttered in one window, long devoid of glass. The front door stood open, a gaping hole into a world that didn't exist anymore, driven to extinction by the maddened climate and the rise of the corporate farms.

Behind the farmhouse, a splintered pile of rubble marked where a barn had once stood. A gravel drive, overgrown with weeds, had become the final resting place for the skeletal remains of a pickup truck that looked like it dated to well before the turn of the century.

Marta surmised the people who once lived here might be long dead.

Or they might now reside in one of the many shanty towns that were overflowing with displaced farmers and their families; migrant communities that had sprung up to meet the labor demands of the corporate farms. Those corporations, themselves owned by giant conglomerates, had the resources to weather the inevitable crop losses that had broken the backs of the family farms.

Twenty years ago, the vast majority of farms across the country had been privately owned family affairs, reverently passed down from one generation to the next. Then, as the teetering climate tipped over into full-scale upheaval, came the Great Heat, the storms and the decimated crops. As the family farms faltered and lapsed into foreclosure, the farmers had no choice but to sell their land and abandon their legacy just to feed their families and salvage a pittance of their life savings.

Such sacrificial offerings were greedily snatched up by the corporations. Homes were demolished, outdated equipment liquidated, and their lands assimilated into ponderous tracts that many times exceeded a million acres. The farmers who had once answered to no one found themselves laboring for faceless, merciless entities that could thrive in the face of the new adversities through their sheer size, questionable labor practices and near unlimited monetary resources.

Then there were the generous government subsidies granted the farming corporations by politicians with hefty personal investments in those very same corporations. All told, it was easy to see how the corrupt consortiums had so quickly and deeply entrenched themselves. For the public, it had simply meant escalating food prices. But for the bankrupt and destitute farmers, what had once been a desperate bid for survival had now become a way of life.

Marta heard the squeal of the brakes a moment before she was thrown sideways, her head rebounding off the thick armored glass. She caught a glimpse of something tan and white streaking across the highway just ahead of them. Her fingers dug into the armrests of her chair. Then the cruiser was skidding across the road into the oncoming lane. Somewhere a horn blared. The hood of a car flashed past the windshield. Two more abrupt lurches to the right and left and it was over. Chaz had them back on the road, safely in their own lane.

"What the hell was that!" Kinney bellowed from the floor where he had landed in a heap.

"Whitetail. Damn near walloped the little bugger," Chaz answered.

Kinney sat up, scowling venomously. "A deer? You swerved, in a twenty ton vehicle doing 100 kilometers per hour on a highway packed with other vehicles driven by civilians we are sworn to protect, for a deer?!?"

Chaz seemed to consider that for a moment. Then he nodded vigorously. "Yeah, that just about sums it up."

"Have you lost it?" Kinney shrieked.

"Well, I sure as hell wasn't going to splatter one of God's creatures all over the tarmac if I could help it," Chaz shot back.

"You damn near killed the three of God's creatures that are sitting right here!" Kinney screamed, slapping the floor in rage.

"Aww, it wasn't that close." Chaz glanced behind him and did a double take when he saw Kinney sprawled out on the floor. He frowned. "Whatch'all doin' down there?"

"Stop the vehicle," Kinney demanded, pulling himself up to his knees.

Chaz looked at Marta questioningly. "You'd better humor him," she said.

Chaz complied, pulling over onto the shoulder. Kinney slapped the hatch release and clambered out.

Chaz sat in his chair, waiting for Marta. She swung her arm toward the exit. "After you, St. Francis."

Chaz frowned at her.

"You know. Patron saint of animals?" Marta explained.

Chaz shook his head and started for the hatch. "I might have a soft spot for animals but I sure as hell ain't no saint."

"Maybe not," Marta said as she followed him. "But I think you're about to be martyred," she muttered under her breath.

Kinney was pacing on the gravel shoulder of the road as they emerged from the cruiser. Chaz leaned casually against the fender, stuffing his hands into the pockets of his coveralls. "Well?" Chaz prompted. "Go on, pardner. Let me have it."

Kinney stood and glared at him as if considering his options. "Fine," he said, rushing Chaz and going nose to nose. "Do you have even the slightest inkling of what a stupid stunt that was? You endangered our lives and the lives of all of the other people on this road, not to mention that ten million dollar vehicle you could have destroyed."

Chaz seemed uncharacteristically at ease, despite having a raving hulk of a man shouting directly in his face. "Dude, I said I had it under control," he answered calmly.

"You're a menace," Kinney growled.

Chaz snorted derisively. "And you're not? They don't call you Killer Keller for nothing."

Marta shut her eyes, sensing that Chaz was about to open a wound that wouldn't be easily closed. She wanted to intervene but decided to let them vent their frustrations, hoping it would cool their blood for awhile. Taking sides wasn't an option either. She wasn't even sure whose side she would have chosen.

"Hell, you damn near plugged that kid back yonder," Chaz taunted.

Kinney's eyes were smoldering, his fists clenched. Chaz showed no sign of intimidation or fear as he continued. "What's the latest tally over in Korea. I hear tell they're still digging bodies out of the rubble."

Marta knew that nothing good would come of resurrecting unkind ghosts from Kinney's military past. He had never seen fit to discuss any details of his tour of duty and that was his prerogative. But Marta had read the e-news and heard the rumors as nearly every American citizen had. His name had figured prominently in the media with rampant accusations that he had singlehandedly laid waste to a sizable chunk of North Korea's capital just before the war had ended.

Officially, he'd been demoted for insubordination but no other charges had ever been filed, further rankling the ire of the peace activists but planting a seed of skepticism in Marta's mind concerning his guilt. She was one of the few who chose to give him the benefit of the doubt and not condemn him for acts she personally knew nothing about. Chaz, on the other hand, was all too eager to accept the media's accounts as gospel and concede to public opinion.

Kinney sneered. "You're just an ignorant civvie. You know nothing about that. It was war. Those were incidental losses."

Chaz crossed his arms over his chest. "Is that what they call it now? Military's always coming up with some fancy schmancy term for it. Casualties of war, collateral damage. Just another way to make light of the killing of those who ought not to have been killed. Now I'm just a simple southern boy, born and bred in the sweet Carolina hills and I've always been partial to the phrase my pappy taught me for those kinds of happenings. Stone-cold black-hearted murder."

She was waiting for Kinney to pounce in rage. But instead, he snickered and turned away. "Never thought I'd meet one of those mythical creatures."

"Do tell. What sort of creature am I now?" Chaz said, playing along.

Kinney looked Chaz over from head to foot. "A redneck with a bleeding heart," he said.

It was Chaz's turn to snicker. "Touché, touché. Maybe I do wear my heart on my sleeve. But at least I have one." He clicked his tongue and pointed a finger at Kinney.

Kinney's expression hardened once more. When he spoke, his voice was a menacing, guttural snarl. "Congratulations. You just earned yourself the rare opportunity to strike a commissioned officer in the United State Army without the risk of repercussions. Legal ones, at least."

Chaz grinned. "Damn straight? Well how can a pigeon-toed hillbilly pass up an offer like that?" he said, rolling up his sleeves. He walked up to Marta, removed his hat and gingerly held it out to her as if presenting her with a priceless artifact.

"Marta, if you would be so kind as to hold my hat for me. Sorry you have to be here to see this. I'll make it quick." He winked at her as she took the hat, then turned to face his adversary. He sauntered toward Kinney, his swagger growing bolder with each step he took.

"You fixin' to turn me into one of those incidental losses you been harping about?" Chaz taunted. He brought his fists up into a fighter's stance and started shifting his weight from foot to foot. Kinney just stood there, arms at his side.

"You best defend yourself, Keller. Cause I aim to teach you a lesson you won't soon forget. Now let's dance."

Chaz pranced closer and threw a jab at Kinney's face. Kinney dodged it effortlessly, then repaid the gesture with a lightning-quick jab of his own that caught Chaz square in the nose. His head snapped backward, eyes fluttering. He staggered for a moment but managed to stay on his feet.

Kinney's arms were back at his side in a relaxed posture. He watched disinterestedly as blood began to trickle from Chaz's nostrils. Chaz stood up straight, tilted his head back, and simply walked away.

Marta was waiting near the hatch. She held out Chaz's hat as he approached. He still had his head tipped back and was breathing heavily through his open mouth.

"That *was* quick," Marta said, trying hard not to smile.

Chaz snatched his hat back. In a nasal tone, he said, "Thanks," and disappeared into the cruiser.

Kinney hadn't moved. Marta glowered at him. "Proud of yourself?" she scolded before following Chaz up the ramp.

CHAPTER 5

Marta was just finishing up applying her lipstick when her car parked itself in a crowded, paved limestone lot. To her left, she could see the rock studded shore of Lake Hefner. A line of vehicles with boats in tow stretched back from the pair of boat ramps that extended out into the placid waters.

Marta climbed out and felt the noonday heat and humidity wrap itself around her. She was dressed in a tight bikini that showed off her still considerable curves. She was thankful that middle age hadn't quite caught up with her yet. She did have a more conservative one-piece for those times when she felt like being more modest. But today wasn't one of those days. Today she felt like being daring.

She grabbed a blue waterproof tote from the backseat and started walking toward the water. She spotted Chaz bent over on a nearby pier inspecting a strange looking watercraft tied to one of the rusty stanchions. He was wearing just a pair of board shorts, giving her the opportunity to make a quick preliminary assessment of his physique. He was a bit on the scrawny side for Marta's taste but the sinewy bands of muscle that wrapped around his midsection more than made up for it. He did a double take when he spotted her approaching. It was only then that she saw the purple bruising around his eyes. She decided to pretend she hadn't noticed.

Chaz whistled appreciatively, looking her up and down. "Well, you sure clean up nice."

Marta smiled. "Thanks...I think."

Chaz held up a hand submissively. "Not to imply that you ain't perty otherwise. Just that those baggy coveralls don't do much to show off your...assets." He drew out the last word long enough she wasn't sure that the last syllable would ever come out.

Marta nodded, feeling a bit of red seeping into her face.

Chaz continued to study her and rubbed his chin thoughtfully. "You do look a might peaked though."

Marta glanced down at her pallid ivory complexion, noticing the sharp contrast from Chaz's golden brown skin. "Any suggestions?" she asked.

He reached down into a duffel bag sitting on the pier, pulled out a copper aerosol can and tossed it to her. She scrutinized the label for a moment, then began spraying a thin layer of clear liquid onto her skin, starting at her feet. It dried almost instantly. Within seconds, the treated skin turned a deep and even bronze hue. She applied it indiscriminately, not worrying about getting it on her suit or in her hair, knowing that the active tanning agent would only react with exposed skin.

When the tanner had completed her transformation, she held her arms out and spun around. "Better?"

Chaz bent low. "I bow down before the sun goddess of Oklahoma City."

Marta ignored him. She turned toward the odd looking craft tied to the pier. "So this is your boat?" she asked. The narrow two-tone fuselage, its belly painted glossy white and the top a bright yellow, resembled a cross between a jet ski and a porpoise. Two cylindrical channels bored through its length housed a pair of ducted fans. The tail section curved upward, ending in a horizontal stabilizer, not unlike the tail of a plane. Then there were the stubby swept-back wings that extended out to either side, their tips angled steeply upward. A vinyl seat sat atop the fuselage just behind a pair of chromed handlebars.

Chaz propped his foot up on the pier's stanchion. "This here's the Yellow Rose."

Marta squinted at him. "A skimmer, isn't she?"

Chaz nodded proudly. "That she is."

Marta came closer and knelt down next to it, running her hand over the smooth hull. "I've never seen one up close."

"Not many people have. Rare as hen's teeth these days."

Marta looked up at Chaz and raised an eyebrow. "If I recall, their safety record isn't so impressive."

Chaz waved dismissively. "Aw, that's bullshit. They can roll on ya, 'specially if ya put a wingtip in the drink, but all I ever had happen was a couple of belly flops when I stalled her out. She's like a fine woman, you just gotta know how to handle her."

"How high can she go?"

"Meter and a half, give or take. Then the lift peters out as the ground effect tapers off. O'course I can tease her up a might higher but she just doesn't want to stay there."

Marta smiled. She knew she should have been feeling a bit of reluctance. Perhaps even a twinge of fear. But she was beyond that now. It was easy to throw caution to the wind when you were feeling invulnerable, filled with a euphoria that set her nerve ends tingling. She hopped onto the wing of the craft and flung her leg over the seat. "Well? What are we waiting for?"

"Amen to that," Chaz said and tossed his duffel bag into a storage compartment near the base of the wing. He gave the rope a tug, releasing the knot that held it to the stanchion and allowing it to retract into a small hole in the fuselage.

Mounting the seat just ahead of Marta, he grabbed the handlebar's molded grips. The small display panel recessed into the fuselage lit up and told him his identity was recognized. A bar graph started climbing. The turbine spooled up with a keening whine.

Feeling the power surging beneath her, Marta's body shuddered. She wrapped her arms tightly around Chaz. As the bar graph topped out, Chaz thumbed the throttle. The ducted fans spun up, lifting a whirling mist from the surface of the water directly behind them.

A moment later and they were skimming the water, gaining speed, lurching and bouncing as they followed each peak and trough of the windblown waves. As they accelerated, the belly of the craft began slapping at the water's surface intermittently. Then the Yellow Rose made the elegant transition from watercraft to aircraft and they were soaring, frictionless, above the waves. Marta felt a sudden burst of exhilaration and held her arms out to her sides. "Wooo!" she screamed, pure elation flowing through her veins, feeling like nothing could ever bring her down.

They followed a narrow channel, passing a cavalcade of fishing boats making their languid way toward the main body of the lake. Several bobbing sign posts swept past, warning that they were in a no wake zone. Marta assumed it must not apply to them since they were sailing over the water instead of through it.

The channel opened up and Chaz banked the skimmer, sending it into a graceful arcing turn that pointed them away from the crowded shoreline and out toward the middle of the lake. Marta relished every moment as they floated along above the surf. A pair of sailing boats drifted by. Marta waved to the stunned passengers who, judging from their gaping mouths, had apparently never seen such a craft before.

A few minutes later and they had crossed the majority of the lake. They were coming up on a marina nestled along the eastern shore.

"My turn," she shouted into Chaz's ear.

"You sure?" he asked warily.

She nodded enthusiastically. He eased off on the throttle, bringing them gently down to the surface. They coasted to a stop. Chaz tapped the touch screen a few times, keeping his left hand on the grip.

"Give me your right hand," he instructed. She slipped her hand into his and he guided it to the hand grip. The display lit up as it mapped her handprint.

"Good. Now your other hand," Chaz said. She leaned into him further, sliding her left arm along Chaz's, her hand slipping over his. Then he slackened his fingers and allowed hers to slide between his on the hand grip. Her cheek nuzzled against the side of his face. Chaz swallowed hard, then reluctantly pulled his arm away, leaving her holding both handgrips.

"She knows you now," he said, ducking his head underneath her arms and slipping around behind her.

"All yours," he said, wiping the beads of sweat that had formed on his forehead.

Marta wasted no time gunning the throttle and nearly sending Chaz flying off the back of the skimmer. He pulled himself back into position and bearhugged Marta.

Despite never having operated a skimmer before, she was feeling fairly confident of her abilities. She had the craft up above the water and edged it toward shore. Banking too hard, she felt the craft shudder as a wingtip grazed the surface.

Chaz brought his mouth close to her ear and issued instructions. "Mind your turns, not too steep. And steer clear of the congested areas."

Marta nodded her understanding, then disregarded his advice entirely and swung toward the busy marina. She was feeling rebellious and more than a little bold and she wanted to be seen.

She hit an icon on the touch panel shaped like a musical note. In response, speakers tucked into the fuselage began barking out a rhythm that defied all manner of symmetry or tempo. A jumbled wreck of clashing notes peppered with guttural croaks that Marta could only imagine must be lyrics. What she found even more bizarre was that she liked it. Or at the very least didn't abhor it like she usually did. She even started bobbing her head to the ungodly beat.

"Thought you didn't like my tunes?" Chaz shouted.

Marta shrugged her shoulders. "I changed my mind. Woman's prerogative you know."

With the discordant melody pounding in her head, her first move was to buzz a yacht that was anchored in the bay. From their vantage point a meter and a half above the water, she could see clearly onto the deck of the massive luxury ship. Three women and two men sunning themselves on loungers somersaulted to their feet as they swept past.

Marta burst into laughter. She laughed so hard that she barely saw the wind ski in time. She banked hard to starboard, again slicing the water with the tip of a wing but she lessened her lean and once more averted disaster.

Chaz pointed urgently straight ahead. Marta's mouth dropped open. There were swimmers in the water just ahead and sailboats to either side. She cringed, knowing they should be a good meter higher than any swimmer's head could possibly protrude from the water. She tightened her grip on the handlebars and shot straight over their bobbing heads.

She glanced over her shoulder at the shocked expressions etched on the swimmer's faces. "My bad," she yelled. "I am so going to hell for that one."

Chaz didn't seem too concerned, grinning from ear to ear. "I'll see ya there. We'll do shots."

Marta felt it wise not to push her luck too far. She swung the nose away from shore and headed out toward calmer waters, leaving her hapless victims to fume in her wake.

The skimmer bobbed serenely in the water along a peaceful slice of shoreline where thick forest crept up to the water's edge. Marta was sprawled out on one wing, her feet resting on the upturned wingtip. Chaz was lying down on the opposite wing, his hat covering his face. His head rolled from side to side, neck muscles twitching nervously.

Suddenly he sat up, eyes wide. "Pa!" he screamed. Coming to his senses, he fumbled to catch his hat before it tumbled into the water. He sat there for a moment, breathing hard while the lingering memories from the nightmare slowly retreated back into his subconscious.

"Bad dream?" Marta asked.

Chaz didn't answer. He ran his hand back through his hair and rubbed the base of his neck.

Marta lifted a nearly empty bottle of vodka cooler in front of her face and stared at it, trying to focus on seeing just one bottle. It wasn't happening so she finished it off and reached for another from the icebox in the side of the fuselage.

"I'd take it a tad easy on those coolers, Marta. They pack a mean punch."

"Don't worry. I know my limit," she said, slurring her words slightly.

Chaz rolled over and looked down at her, a clear expression of disappointment on his face. He glanced out to where the sun's glow was rippling on the face of the waters.

"Be getting dark soon," he said, scratching his head thoughtfully. "The Rose doesn't have much in the way of navigational lighting. I reckon we ought to get back."

Marta frowned. "Already?" She slapped the wing in mock frustration, then her face lit up. "I'll drive!"

Chaz shook his head. "I'm afraid y'all are hereby restricted to passenger status on account of you are majorly pissed up."

Marta grinned stupidly. "I'll drink to that," she said and drained a third of the newly opened bottle.

Chaz glanced to his right and saw the silhouette of a boat motoring closer. He squinted, holding his hand up to shield his eyes. Then his face tightened. "Uh oh," he droned.

"What uh oh?" Marta asked, spinning her head around too quickly and inducing a brief wave of nausea.

"I reckon we got company," Chaz said.

Marta instinctively panicked and flung the bottle she was holding into the lake. "Marine patrol?"

"Worse," Chaz said.

Marta turned and saw a large speedboat pull up alongside. It had a sleek, streamlined hull, immaculately polished, and painted turquoise and lavender blue with white trim. A tall, solitary man stood at the helm. His features kept going in and out of focus but finally Marta's eyes brightened in recognition. "Kinney?" she called out.

"Commander," Kinney grumbled in a low monotone.

Marta couldn't remember ever seeing him dressed so casually. Gray swim trunks hugged his tree trunk sized thighs. Above his trim waist, a plaid short sleeve shirt hung open at the front, exposing his well developed chest.

"Fancy meeting you out here," Chaz said cheerlessly.

"Contrary to popular opinion, we GI's do have lives outside of the military."

Chaz stared down at Kinney's boat. "Wow. That thing looks prehistoric. Bet that's older than you are."

A familiar sneer creased Kinney's features. "It's an '85 Wellcraft Scarab. It's a classic," he said, clearly emphasizing the last word.

Marta stood up and pointed at the craft. "Hey. You can't have that out here. It's illegal. It's in violation of the emission...thingie."

Kinney ignored her obvious drunkenness and just answered the question. "Originally, it was equipped with twin 454 big blocks. Running those would probably cost me a year's salary in fines. However, I retrofitted it with twelve liquid-cooled superconducting synchronous electric motors."

"I stand corrected," Marta said, only a moment before she slipped on the wing and went down hard, still somehow managing not to spill her drink.

Again Kinney seemed to completely ignore her stupor, staring affectionately at his boat instead. "Pumps out nearly 3 megawatts. Top end...around 110 knots."

Chaz whistled. "Not bad."

Kinney turned his attention to the skimmer, frowning in distaste. "Better than that fluttering deathtrap you call a watercraft. Where'd you find that? Was it the toy surprise in a crackerjack box?"

Chaz seemed taken aback. "Surely you jest! There ain't another waterfaring craft in the whole of Oklahoma that could match the speed and prowess of the Yellow Rose."

Kinney's mouth turned up slightly. "Would you care to make a gentleman's wager on that point?"

Chaz sniffed disdainfully. "I don't dance unless the band is playing my song."

"Let's keep it simple," Kinney said and pointed across the water toward the far southwest shore. "We follow the southern shoreline west to the Overholser canal. Whoever passes under the Lakeshore Drive bridge first wins. Five hundred bucks says the Widowmaker will blow the petals right off your pretty little Rose."

"Ya'll got yourself a bet," Chaz said, grinning widely.

"Conditionally," Kinney said.

"I'm listening," Chaz said, helping Marta to her feet.

"Marta rides with me," Kinney said. "She'll be safer that way. This boat's a fortress compared to your skimmer. That thing looks like it would fold up in a stiff breeze."

"I believe that should be the lady's decision," Chaz said and looked at Marta.

Marta threw up her arms defeatedly. "Fine. Toss me around like a sack of dirty laundry. What do I care?"

Chaz guided Marta out toward the wingtip where the gentle swells were exaggerated, making her feel like she was riding a roller coaster standing up. The undulating motion nearly dislodged her from the slick surface and challenged whatever equilibrium she had left. Kinney held out his arms. She reached for him, her foot slipping at the last moment. But before she could fall he had snatched her up and effortlessly lifted her into the Scarab.

"Wow! You're strong!" Marta exclaimed. Without thinking, she reached out and squeezed his bulging bicep, garnering no reaction from Kinney whatsoever. Marta thought it rude that he paid no attention to her complement but simply guided her to the passenger seat and gently eased her down into it.

She didn't complain. The chair was a lot more comfortable than the seat on the skimmer. She was feeling like a nap anyway. But she also sensed that this race was going to be a spectacle that she wouldn't want to miss. So she sat up straight and concentrated on staying conscious.

On her right, Kinney was throwing switches on the console. She looked to her left and saw Chaz perched on the skimmer right beside the Scarab. He smiled up at her and she smiled back. Then she swung her head back toward Kinney.

"We go on Marta's mark," Kinney said.

Marta frowned, trying to discern his meaning. They both seemed to be watching her closely. Then it dawned on her. "Oh, right," she said and raised her right arm above her head.

"Ready.....go!" she yelled and dropped her arm.

Kinney slammed a pair of levers forward. She felt her head snap back as the Scarab lurched ahead under full acceleration. Behind the boat, roiling water exploded from the surface as the twin props dug in. She could barely hear the steady hum of the pumps and electric motors over the roar of water being churned and displaced behind them. She likened it to standing at the base of Niagara Falls.

A sudden surge of adrenaline flooded into Marta's bloodstream and helped to sober her. She was surprised to realize that she was still acutely aware of her surroundings despite her obvious impairment.

Marta noticed the Scarab was pulling ahead of Chaz but she could now hear the shrieking whine of the skimmer's turbine spooling up to full power. She watched as the Yellow Rose planed, then lifted clear of the surface. Its speed quickly matched that of the Scarab and it clung tenaciously to its position slightly to port and only a few meters behind them.

The shore on their left rushed by in a dizzying blur. Up ahead, a sloop, sails unfurled, was just emerging from the city docks. Their heading, parallel with the shore, put them on a near collision course. Chaz was still hanging off their port side so Kinney banked hard right to veer around the sailboat. Chaz broke left.

They each swung around the sailboat, Kinney at their bow and Chaz at their stern. A sustained gust of wind inflated the sails of the sloop, pushing it faster. To compensate, Kinney had to steer further around to maintain a safe distance. When the Scarab and the skimmer swung back in to rejoin their parallel path Chaz had gained the advantage and had a lead of at least twenty meters on them.

The channel leading to the bridge that marked the finish line was coming up fast. Marta could tell Kinney wasn't about to give up. He was busy flipping old-fashioned toggle switches, turning dials and nudging levers. His efforts paid off and the gap began to close.

By the time they entered the narrow channel, they were dead even. To Marta, the channel had looked barely wide enough for the two craft to navigate side by side and she'd been right. Neither Kinney nor Chaz seemed dissuaded by the tight quarters. They kept their throttles pegged. Kinney steered the Scarab closer to the middle of the channel where the water was deepest to avoid grounding the boat. Chaz stayed alongside, skimming over the shallow water at the edge of the channel.

Marta glanced behind them to see massive tidal waves of water break on the levee to either side, courtesy of the wake from the Scarab's powerful motors. She also saw several onlookers standing atop the levee, pointing and watching in awe.

When she turned back forward, she could already see the bridge that marked the finish line in the distance. She couldn't make out many details but the open arch beneath it looked unnervingly miniscule. They covered the distance rapidly. As it loomed ever nearer, the bridge grew larger but the arch still seemed much too narrow for more than one craft to fit through. She looked up at Kinney. His face was a hardened mask of concentration and determination. He seemed to be steering them ever so slightly to port, lining up the Scarab with the middle of the canal and crowding Chaz toward the steep banks of the levee. Tall aquatic weeds and cattails growing near the water's edge were neatly chopped off by the skimmer's wings, leaving a trail of green flotsam on the water behind them.

Marta saw Chaz mouthing words and imagined they were some of the more colorful southern expletives she'd heard him occasionally resort to during particularly harrowing missions . She expected to see him start backing off. The bridge was just ahead and his skimmer was heading directly for the stonework. She couldn't reason what type of suicidal venture he was on.

Just seconds remained. She imagined seeing the skimmer shatter into splinters as they passed through the narrow arch, Chaz nothing more than a damp crimson stain on the stone. But at the last moment, Chaz tilted the skimmer's nose up. It resisted his efforts. But finally it began to climb, slowly at first. Then it shot upward, just as things went momentarily dark and they blasted through the archway.

Marta hadn't felt an impact or heard an explosion which she took as encouraging signs. They were past the bridge in an instant. Marta glanced behind but failed to see the skimmer. Something struck her as odd. There appeared to be a shadow being cast down upon the Scarab. And it was suddenly raining. She looked up, her still fuzzy mind not quite comprehending what she was seeing. All of a sudden they had a glistening white roof over their heads but one that was shedding streaming rivulets of water. Then she noticed the edges of the odd roof ended in stubby wings. Wings that were shuddering violently.

"Get your head down now!" Kinney yelled. A burly hand grabbed the back of her head and forced it down beneath the console. She felt a sudden deceleration push her forward. Her head slammed into the console. Then came an ear-shattering crash from just behind them. The boat rocked and swayed.

Marta lifted her head. The first thing she saw was Kinney, still standing at the helm but facing rearward. His arms were raised as if in supplication. His expression was one of disbelief. Then Marta turned and saw what Kinney was gaping at.

The skimmer had crashed down into the Scarab just behind their seats, shattering the overhead radar arch and crushing the engine compartment access panels. The bulk of the skimmer's fuselage rested on the deck but one wing hung over the edge. Wisps of black smoke curled up from the Scarab's engine compartment.

Chaz was slumped over the handlebars. Slowly, he sat up and shook his head. As his weight shifted, the skimmer teetered precariously.

"What the hell have you done?!?" Kinney screamed.

"The Rose was stallin'. I had to park it somewhere fast. It was either back here or right on your noggin'."

"You're going to wish you'd set it down on my head," Kinney growled.

"That's the thanks I get for saving your life?" Chaz asked.

"Saving our lives?!?" Kinney said, chuckling maniacally.

"Damn straight!" Chaz called out just as Kinney viciously kicked the skimmer and upset the delicate equilibrium that had been keeping it stable. It keeled over sideways. Chaz scrambled off the fuselage and landed on the deck of the boat just as the skimmer toppled overboard, its hull screeching as it slid over the side. It landed with a splash in the water below.

Chaz crawled across the deck and peered over the edge. He seemed relieved to see the skimmer had landed upright and appeared buoyant. He climbed to his feet. "Ya'll are lucky the Rose is still floating."

Kinney was beyond distraught. "I'm lucky? I'm lucky?" he said and took two steps toward Chaz. Marta knew what was coming and pulled herself to her feet. She stumbled between the two men.

"No!" she shouted, extending her arms to keep the two potential combatants at bay. To her relief Kinney halted his advance.

"Not again! I'm your commander and I'm ordering you both to...". Marta stopped midsentence. Daylight seemed to be bleeding from her field of vision. "To," she said, trying to continue. The light continued to dim until she saw nothing but shadows and ghostly silhouettes. "To," she said once more. The strength suddenly drained from her legs. They crumpled beneath her. The last sensation she felt were hands tightening underneath each arm as Kinney and Chaz arrested her fall. Then darkness took her.

ard R. HENKE

CHAPTER 6

Marta's eyelids fluttered, then eased open. Bright, stabbing light flooded in and she squeezed them back shut. Her next attempt met with marginal success. She managed to keep them open long enough to see a dark complected man in a white lab coat staring her in the face. Her head recoiled back into what felt like a soft pillow.

"Welcome back to you, Marta," said the man in a familiar, pleasant voice with a heavy Indian accent.

Marta knew she was lying on her back. She practiced moving her limbs and found them all functional, albeit a bit sluggish to respond. "Where am I?" she managed to croak out.

"Ah, you are in good hands at the psychiatric evaluation ward of Glendale hospital," he said.

That got her attention and her eyes widened. She'd been there before of her own volition. That had been nearly three years ago when she'd first sought help for her condition. Her vision was returning. She could make out round wire-framed glasses perched halfway down the man's nose and thick black hair streaked with gray. "Dr. Raajeev?"

The man gave a quick nod. "The very same," he said, offering a tight-lipped smile. "At your service."

Marta rubbed her forehead and hoped that she hadn't somehow been involuntarily committed. She struggled to recall recent events but couldn't remember doing anything particularly illegal. At the very least, nothing that would get her committed. "So I'm back in the looney bin," she said dejectedly.

The doctor cringed, his face contorting in apparent agony as if he'd been physically stabbed by Marta's sharp choice of words.

She smiled sheepishly. "Sorry."

The doctor's pained expression slowly faded and he returned her smile. "I am accepting your apology. To be exact, since you are my current patient, you are here by my order so we could observe you upon waking."

Marta pulled herself up in bed and glanced around the room. "How did I get here?"

"Two very nice gentlemen brought you here. They said you just collapsed," the doctor said, picking up a data pad and scribbling some notes on it with a stylus.

Marta frowned, studying the doctor closely for a reaction. "Did they also tell you I'd been drinking?"

The doctor looked up at her over the top of his eyeglasses, still scribbling. "It did occur to me to ask them."

"Because you know me so well?" Marta asked, smiling uneasily.

"Yes that. And the fact that you smelled like a moldy beer keg full of rotten fruit." He finished his notes with a dramatic flick of his wrist and set the data pad down. His eyes stayed glued to Marta.

"Vodka coolers," Marta offered meekly.

The doctor smacked his lips. "Ah. Very nice," he said and then pointed an accusatory finger in her direction. "When consumed responsibly by adults who, preferably, do not suffer from serious psychiatric disorders."

Marta smiled uncomfortably. "That would be me."

"That would be you," he agreed. "Tell me. Have you been taking your medication?"

Marta sighed heavily, knowing there was no use lying. "I don't like how it makes me feel, doctor."

"I will regard that as a definitive no," he said, his eyes narrowing.

Marta threw her hands up in frustration. "You don't understand. When I take it my hands shake, I have to pee every ten minutes and it makes my mouth feel like I swallowed a bowl of cotton balls."

"Yes, yes. I realize those are common and very unpleasant side effects. But I really think they are the lesser of two evils."

Marta glared at him. "So I can either not take my medication and be miserable or I can take my medication and be just as miserable. What's my motivation here?"

The doctor leaned forward and spoke in a calm, controlled voice. "You are a rapid cycling manic depressive. You need to moderate your mood swings or they will only become more frequent and more severe. And the only way you can do that is by taking your prescribed medication every and each day without exception."

"Yes but why can't I just take it when I feel an episode coming on?" Marta reasoned.

"Being manic depressive is not like having a headache. And taking lithium is not like taking an aspirin. The medication needs to be maintained at a level that is therapeutic in order to effectively moderate your moods. All the time. Not just when you feel like it."

"Maybe I don't need as much as you prescribed," she suggested.

The doctor stared at her in silence for several seconds before replying. "Take your lithium, Marta. As prescribed."

"Yes, doctor," Marta said, hanging her head in defeat.

The doctor started for the door, then turned back. "And for the sake of goodness, stay away from the booze. It does not mix well with the medication and it does not mix well with your disease."

Marta chuckled. "Ain't it just grand being bipolar."

"You should count your fortunate stars that it is a treatable disorder," the doctor answered, swinging the door open. He waved without looking back. "Bye bye," he said and disappeared down the hallway.

"Yep. I'm lucky alright," Marta mumbled to herself.

RANDY R. HENKE

CHAPTER 7

It was well known that Storm Strike paid their employees reasonably well, always handsomely compensated the families of any crew member killed in the line of duty, and consistently made certain any equipment that would see active duty was well maintained and meticulously tested. But where they had failed miserably, in Marta's opinion, was in purchasing their fleet of company vehicles. They had chosen an economy model sedan from Jianghuai Motors.

The cars were used mainly for short distance errands or sometimes as a courtesy vehicle for visiting executives or dignitaries. They were also pressed into service for ferrying field officers out to the shanty towns when their storm shelters came due for inspection. That was the duty that Marta was in the midst of fulfilling and it was one of those sedans that was currently proving to be the bane of her existence.

She'd decided to take the car out of autodrive as soon as it had started acting up. The event that had qualified for 'acting up' status had occurred nearly fifty kilometers back when the car had drifted off the highway and followed an exit ramp. It would have been a nonissue had the car not been travelling at highway speed while attempting to negotiate a thirty kilometer per hour curving offramp. The ensuing incident, replete with squealing tires, blaring warning sirens, and a side window smeared with lipstick, had left an indelible impression on Marta's psyche as well as upon the cracked plastic floorboard where she had solidly planted her feet.

It had been awhile since Marta had taken manual control of a car but it proved to be a pleasant distraction and helped to pass the time. Lately, it had seemed as if time was passing by much quicker than usual anyway. It had already been three weeks since she'd woken up in the hospital and two weeks since she'd returned to work. She'd taken a week of administrative leave upon discharge to clear the medication-induced cobwebs from her mind.

She was well aware that she owed her continued employment to the nearly inviolable medical non-disclosure laws. Her superiors at Storm Strike were still none the wiser concerning her psychological malady. Of course, she'd taken the psychiatric screening that was mandatory for all field crews. Having been wavering between extremes at the time, she'd passed without eliciting so much as a raised eyebrow from the resident shrink.

Kinney and Chaz, of course, were acutely aware that she had some rather disquieting mood swings but she'd played the gender card and led them to believe it was just one of those inscrutable womanly things that men couldn't possibly comprehend. Still, it was obvious they had their suspicions that something more sinister was afoot.

It was easy for her to rationalize her deception. The impeccable performance record of her team spoke for itself. They'd never missed an intercept. Her emotional state had never interfered with her work and that was all that really mattered. The bottom line was that she'd proven herself competent and she was damn good at her job.

These days, it seemed like half the population was being diagnosed and treated for some type of emotional disturbance anyway. Just a sign of the times and certainly not a valid reason to discriminate against someone just because they had a few off days once in a while.

Marta glanced down at the climate control display as it flickered and rolled for the third time in the past hour. She slapped it with her palm. The glowing icons and digital readouts snapped back into alignment and the AC started purring again. She wiped at the sweat pouring down her neck and wondered how many more times she could tolerate these glitches before she finally lost her resolve and used the heel of her foot rather than her hand to goad it back into operation.

But resolve appeared to be something she had in abundance. She hadn't gotten angry in the past week. She hadn't really felt much of anything. A sure sign that the lithium was doing its job, keeping her emotions on an even keel. So even, in fact, that sometimes she felt disconnected from her own life. Not that it was currently much of a life anyway. One day seemed to blur into the next. Even when she was out in the stormcruiser hunting shredders, the euphoric high she'd come to expect, even embrace, just wasn't there anymore.

The car momentarily lurched and shimmied, then settled back into a steady cadence. U.S. 281 was mind numbingly flat and straight just south of Lawton as it cut through a shallow valley, bisecting an endless rolling sea of green. As far as the eye could see, soybean plants rippled in the morning breeze.

Every few kilometers a cluster of stubby towers topped by sprawling white saucers rose up from the fields like giant glossy mushrooms. They were called GGRUs, short for greenhouse gas reclamation units. She'd even played a small part in their design as an undergraduate in the Atmospheric Sciences and Meteorology program at NYU. That had been nearly twenty years ago and now the machines were as ubiquitous as trees.

Atop each saucer sat an array of solar panels that powered the units, pulling air up through a wire mesh at the bottom of the saucer and passing it over polymer gills that greedily snatched up the carbon dioxide. When the polymer sheets became saturated, heating elements coaxed them to release their plunder of CO_2. Then a spindly network of pipes at the base of each tower carried the gas to a central pumping station and, from there, a deep shaft deposited it into any convenient geological formation. In Oklahoma, those were typically abandoned coal mines or oil fields. Theoretically, the gas would remain sequestered there indefinitely.

There were nearly 5,000 of the units operating in Oklahoma alone and over 5 million worldwide. They'd proven themselves an effective supplement in the global effort at reducing greenhouse gas concentrations in the atmosphere. But, in the end, it was still too little, too late.

Marta turned off the highway onto a paved drive that passed one of South Central Conservation and Cultivation's largest farming operations in the state. A row of seven immense equipment sheds fronted the road. Behind them twelve silos reached up toward the sky and an enormous galvanized metal orb hung from struts like a Chinese lantern near a canopied natural gas fueling station.

Just as she passed by, a group of farmers clambered out of a rusting hulk of a school bus. Marta grimaced, wondering what it would be like to lead such a nomadic, impoverished existence. For the youngest who'd been born into such servitude, it was all knew. But most of them were old enough to remember better days.

Two miles from the highway, the Comanche County wind farm complex drifted past on her right. She gazed out at row upon row of concrete platforms, a towering mast anchored to the center of each one. Atop each mast, a gigantic triple-bladed propeller spun, their glossy white surfaces glinting in the sun. There had to have been at least a hundred of them, whirling silently in the gentle breeze.

A half mile further off the highway, Marta turned onto a one lane gravel road, still muddy from the rains the night before. She tried avoiding the worst of the potholes in an effort to prevent further trauma to her car. There was still hope that it would get her back to Storm Strike Alpha before breaking down completely.

Large black letters scrawled onto a piece of plywood and nailed haphazardly to a post told her she'd taken the right road. Grayson Flats, or at least the current incarnation of it, was just ahead, strung out along the gravel access road in a hodgepodge arrangement of shacks and sheds. Their weather-beaten corrugated tin exteriors reflected the sun's rays dully like corroded nickels.

Marta pulled up in front of the only brick structure in sight, it's chipped and faded front wall shaded by a covered wooden porch. She sat there for a moment, watching as a group of children frolicked near a puddle at the other end of the makeshift town; a poignant snapshot of a new kind of life. All that it needed was a modern day Norman Rockwell to capture its essence, breathe life into it and romanticize it for posterity. Someday, people might even look back upon it fondly. History had a way of glorifying even the most trying eras, imparting a sense of nostalgia to the most mundane existences and trivializing the hardships. But like it or not, shanty towns were becoming as deeply entrenched in Americana as baseball and apple pie.

She rummaged in her purse and pulled out a pill bottle. A silent curse passed her lips as she repeatedly attempted to open the child proof container. The persistent tremor that had developed in her hands over the last couple of weeks didn't help matters either. Finally she managed to pop the lid off and shook a single tablet of lithium out into her palm. She made a mental note to herself that only five tablets were left in the bottle. She'd have to get it refilled tomorrow morning before her next shift started. Three doses a day; morning, noon and night. That's what it took to conform to this society's brand of normalcy.

But there was a price for that compliance and Marta was already paying it. The tremors were just one of the manifestations. Her mouth was parched constantly. Her tongue felt like a dried up dishrag. Then there was the nausea that crept up on her without warning at any time of the day or night. Sleep had become elusive, coming in fits and starts when it came at all, and leaving her perpetually drowsy and lethargic. All of that on top of the vague, inexpressible feeling that she just wasn't herself anymore.

She swallowed the pill with a swig from a bottle of water and swung her feet out of the car. After an hour of sitting, her legs had stiffened considerably. She winced as she stretched them out, feeling much older than her thirty eight years. Then, slowly, she stood up, willing her tired muscles to contract.

Marta paused a moment to gain her balance. She tugged at her standard issue coveralls to work out some of the creases. Then she swung the car door shut, just as a three-legged German Shepherd bounded around the front fender, its scruffy tail wagging furiously. Marta smiled tentatively.

"Hi, boy," she said, holding her hand out but ready to pull it back if the apparent good-natured greeting turned out to be a ruse.

"The name's Chance," came a coarse, gravelly voice from the nearby doorway. Marta glanced that way. A tall, grizzled shank of a man stood leaning against the doorframe, watching Marta and rubbing at the gray stubble on his deeply weathered face.

While she was distracted the dog sensed an opportunity and closed in. Marta jumped back, startled, as Chance started licking her palm. Then she relaxed a bit and gave him a scratch behind the ear with her free hand.

"Short for second chance. Found him in an irrigation ditch after the twister that leveled Tishomingo two years past." He stepped off the covered porch and approached, an open hand snapping out toward her.

"Now that you've met one old dog, allow me to introduce you to another. I'm Brock Massey. I'm the mayor here at Grayson Flats. "

Marta gave the dog one last pat, stood, and shook his hand. "Marta Astin. Pleased to meet you, Mayor Massey."

"Pleasure's all mine but, please, call me Brock. Mayor is more or less of an honorary title really since we don't have need for much local authority here. But then again we don't have much town." He swept his hand in an arc that encompassed the sparse extent of Grayson Flats.

"How many people?" Marta asked.

Brock squinted off into the distance. "Last count was fifty-eight. That was before we took in some itinerants from Nebraska. Closer to seventy now."

Marta produced a data pad from her pocket and keyed in the numbers. "Children?"

"Twenty-two under fourteen years." A roguish grin creased his face. "Don't waste much time on pleasantries, do you, Marta?"

Marta's fingers froze, her hand still hovering over the data pad's display. She smiled timidly. "Just thought I'd get some preliminaries taken care of."

The grin stayed on Brock's face but some of the kindness in it withered. "Contrary to what the board members of South Central C&C would have you believe, we are more than just a set of numbers here."

"I am acutely aware of that, Mr. Massey." Marta caught her error and smiled apologetically. "Brock," she corrected.

"Good to know," Brock said, a hint of doubt evident in his voice. "Walk with me?" he asked, motioning down the street.

Marta nodded and kept pace beside him as they started down the street, sidestepping the larger rain-filled ruts as they went. Surveying her surroundings, she would have rated Grayson Flats a couple of notches higher than most shanty towns she had visited. Here, some of the residences had at least a couple of glass-paned windows. And solar panels graced the roofs of nearly every structure. Even the few tents that were pitched here and there seemed well patched and securely battened down.

It quickly became apparent that most of the men had already left for the day with the exception of two elderly gentlemen in lawn chairs who disinterestedly watched them stroll by from their perch on a rickety front porch. One of them was half-heartedly attempting to coax a yo-yo back to his fluttering hand as it bounced at the end of its string. The other was meticulously rolling a cigarette, his eyes never wavering from Marta. She did a double take when the old man stuck his tongue out at her.

The women of the town seemed every bit as aloof as the two seniors. They scurried about, carrying groceries or crates. But while they didn't stop and stare, she felt their unkind eyes graze her in passing. The children seemed more curious than anything, peering at her from the corners of windows or from behind the protective legs of their mothers who quickly ushered them away.

One portly young woman stood in a clump of tall grass between two of the shacks. A perpetual sneer was seared onto her face. She was hanging laundry on a frayed rope strung taut between a sapling oak and an aluminum pole with a red warning siren mounted at its peak.

Marta pointed up at the siren. "Does it work?"

Brock snickered. "Of course it works. But you have to realize that, out here, the best we can hope for is maybe two minutes warning from the nearest radar station. We tend to rely more on our own eyes and ears."

"And when your eyes and ears tell you it's time to haul ass for cover, where do you go?"

Brock's grin widened at her choice of words. He tilted his head toward the far end of town. "Storm shelters are a bit further."

Marta smiled. "Lead the way."

Brock started walking and Marta again fell in stride beside him. Chance lagged a few steps behind, sniffing at the damp ground as he trotted along. "How are the sanitary facilities?" she asked.

Brock teased a cigarette from his shirt pocket and lit it. "We do alright. Water is graciously provided by mother nature. We store the rainwater in cisterns and each point of use has its own purifier. Latrines drain to a common holding tank that gets pumped regularly."

Marta keyed in some more notes on her pad. Then she veered closer to the line of buildings along one side of the street. She tapped a tin wall, listened to the reverberating echo and stepped closer to examine a window opening.

A sudden surge of water burst from the window. Marta leaped back, her quick reflexes narrowly saving her from a drenching. A kerchiefed head peeked out from the opening. Marta backed up a few steps further, her widened view revealing a sixtyish woman holding a bucket in her hands. She had a disappointed look on her wrinkled face.

"Sorry. Didn't see you there," she grumbled.

Marta turned and rejoined Brock who was making no attempt to hide his amused expression. They continued down the street.

Marta did a quick three sixty, taking in the whole of Grayson Flats in one sweep. "I don't see much for insulation in these structures. How are the winters?"

Brock took a long pull on his cigarette before answering. "Quite manageable. We spend our winters near Killeen, Texas. A might more temperate and the government was kind enough to set aside a few hundred acres for those communities willing to make the journey. They have cabins, wood for the cutting, and the Red Cross, with their farmer relief program, keeps us in good stead when it comes to medical care and provisions. They make damn sure no one starves to death. Don't know what we'd do without them."

Marta smiled, feeling a twinge of motherly pride. "My son and daughter are both volunteers in that program."

Brock stared at her a moment. "Well, God bless 'em," he finally said.

A door flew open on a house just ahead, its walls and roof nothing more than a hodgepodge of overlapping corrugated sheets of metal. Two children ran out. They spotted Marta and froze. The boy couldn't have been more than five and he wasted no time darting back into the doorway. But the girl, a couple of years older than her brother, stood there, regarding Marta curiously.

"Hello there," Marta called out. The girl didn't respond but she didn't run either.

"What's your name?" Marta asked, slowly approaching the porch where the girl stood.

"Trina," the girl said softly, her eyes never leaving Marta.

Marta reached into a pocket and pulled out a small pin. "Well, Trina, how would you like to be an honorary member of Storm Strike?"

"Why?" the girl asked.

Marta chuckled. "Because we need good brave people like you to help us keep all of the other people safe."

"How?" Trina asked, continuing her line of questioning.

Marta knelt before the girl. "By making sure that everyone in your family makes it to the shelter when you hear the siren. Can you do that?"

Trina's brow furrowed, as if considering the scope of her responsibilities before answering. "Okay," she finally said, nodding vigorously.

Marta fastened the pin to the girl's shirt collar. "Then consider yourself a member of Storm Strike, Trina."

The girl waited for Marta to finish attaching the pin. Then she glanced down at it, tugging and stretching her collar to get a better look. The corners of her mouth crept upward into a wide smile.

A woman appeared in the doorway. "Trina!" she yelled and the girl jumped. "Inside now," she commanded. The girl quickly obeyed. As she walked past her mother and through the door, she glanced back toward Marta, her tiny hand lifted to her forehead in a timid salute. Marta returned the salute, ignoring the woman's glare as she followed the girl inside and slammed the door behind her.

Marta lowered her head and sighed.

"Don't take it personal," Brock said. "You've just got to understand how they see things. Storm Strike's primary agenda is to protect the interests of the farming consortiums. And those are the bastards that took their farms from them. To these people, any friend of an enemy is an enemy all the same."

Marta shook her head. "I don't know why things have to be so complicated."

Brock took a long puff on his cigarette. "They don't have to be, but they are."

Marta nodded solemnly and continued on. They walked in silence until they reached the far end of the town. Brock motioned toward a row of three rectangular cement foundations jutting several centimeters out of the ground, each capped by a steeply angled aluminum door.

Marta leaned down and swung one of the doors up on its hinges, its hydraulic supports hissing. A set of concrete steps disappeared down into darkness. Marta unclipped a flashlight from her belt and shined it down into the opening. The cellar extended back not more than five meters. Crates of food hugged the walls and bulging burlap bags cluttered the dirt floor.

Marta went to the next door, opened it and repeated her inspection. The second cellar proved to be even more congested than the first. She advanced to the third cellar and peered in at the jumble of boxes and plastic storage containers strewn throughout its interior. She shook her head.

"I know what you're gonna say," Brock uttered preemptively.

Marta planted her hands on her hips and turned to face Brock. "Then I'll just say it. Unacceptable. These aren't storm shelters. You couldn't even fit a handful of people in them, let alone over seventy."

Brock returned Marta's blistering gaze. "They're all we have. At the very least, the children would fit."

Marta didn't miss a beat. "Irrelevant. Those doors would last about two seconds against the vacuum that an F7 can generate."

"We'll manage," Brock shot back defiantly.

"I don't think you understand, Mr. Massey. I've seen what they can do. I'm not just blindly spouting regulations."

Brock flicked his cigarette and ground it into the dirt with his heel.

"With all due respect, Marta, you're preaching to the choir here. I've seen plenty with my own eyes to know what can happen. I seen a farmhand get caught out in an open field with a twister bearing down on him like the devil himself. The man wrapped a length of rope around his wrists and bound himself up tight to a well fitting, thinking he could ride it out."

Brock winced and Marta could tell he was reliving the entire spectacle in his mind's eye.

"Well, when that twister passed over him, his body went taut, boots to the sky. The next instant, his arms were wrenched from their sockets. All I saw was a swirl of red leading up into the heart of that beast. And all that we had left to bury were those two wretched arms, still knotted to that pipe."

Marta nodded and looked away. She knew the pain that Brock felt from witnessing such a horrid event. But she had her own story that she felt compelled to share.

"Do you recall the Mud Creek massacre?" she asked softly.

"I reckon I do," Brock said, giving her his full attention.

Marta glanced down at the cellar doors as she started to lose herself in the memory. "I was there. Less than an hour after it hit. My crew and I were some of the first responders to step foot into their shelters."

She turned back to Brock. "Inadequate shelters. Nothing more than root cellars, like yours. They'd seen fit to put the children in the deepest sections as an extra measure of safety. They thought the shredder would have to go through them first."

Her lips curled up in a humorless grin. "They were partly right. Those closest to the doors never had a chance. The hinges and latches sheared away like paper. We found men's and women's bodies, or what was left of them, scattered across the entire southwestern quadrant of Oklahoma."

Marta's face tightened. Her breaths came in quick swells, just short of sobs. "But the children were still there, huddled against the far wall. We heard their cries. And when our flashlights played across their trembling forms, we saw the blood trickling from their mouths, from their noses, their ears and their eyes."

Marta paused, trying to push back the hot emotions that came flooding back. "They were all deaf and blind. The tornado had passed directly overhead and had produced a vacuum so intense that it had ruptured their eardrums. Their eyeballs had burst from their sockets. And their tiny lungs were shredded from the pressure because they had held their breath in terror. Half of them died. Some would say the lucky half."

Marta's eyes had welled up with tears. She blinked and swiped at them with her hand.

Brock shook his head. "Makes you question everything, don't it? Even your own sanity."

Marta glanced up at him, caught off guard by his choice of words. She wondered for a moment if he had some insight into her own mental disorder. She quickly shrugged off the feeling as nothing more than paranoia.

"Bearing witness to such ungodly atrocities, it takes a piece of your soul," Brock said.

Marta sniffled and nodded. "I don't want to see it happen again here," she said.

"Nor I. But the simple fact of the matter is, we haven't got the resources to purchase shelters."

Marta brushed her hair back from her face and collected herself as best she could. "There is aid that you can apply for."

Brock smiled knowingly. "Yeah. And paperwork that could choke a longhorn steer. It's all been filed. And yet here we are."

Marta knew he was being honest. She'd heard it before a dozen times.

Chance strolled over and sat down at Brock's feet. Brock bent down to give him a scratch behind the ear. Then he angled his head up toward Marta. "Southwest C&C has been promising to bring in some prefabs and plant 'em for us. O'course by the time they get around to it, we'll be moving on. Next month we'll be over by Coalgate dismantling an irrigation system on 5,000 acres."

"Sounds like you move around alot," Marta said.

Brock groaned and pulled himself back up to his full height. "We go where the work takes us. Some of the other migrant communities are trying to sprout roots and settle down again. They want to recapture a sense of stability and belonging. More power to 'em. But most of us here feel it's to our advantage to not get too comfortable in any one place. We tried that once and look where it got us."

Marta smiled. She looked back toward her car. "Well, I guess my job here is done. I'll forward my findings and recommendations to C&C as well as to the Red Cross and I'll make sure you get a copy as well."

Brock nodded. "I got some business to attend to on this side of town so I trust you can see yourself back to your car. But for what it's worth, thank you kindly. I can tell that your heart is in the right place."

A frustrated bark sounded from a patch of sandy ground near the shelters. They both turned to see Chance, butt in the air, his head and shoulders submerged in a large hole. He barked once more, then tried to wriggle himself in even deeper.

"Chance! Knock it off!" Brock yelled.

The dog reluctantly complied, popping his front end up out of the hole and sauntering over beside his master.

"Damn badgers. They dig up the whole area. He'll learn his lesson if he ever manages to actually crawl into one of those dens. Mean sons of bitches."

Marta backed away a couple of steps. "It was nice meeting you, Brock."

"Likewise, Marta."

"Take care," Marta said and started walking back down the street.

"Tell you what," Brock called out after her. Marta turned around.

Brock took a moment to study Marta before continuing. "You seem like a nice gal. What say you come by on the 4th and we'll show you how a bunch of dirt pushin' farmers celebrate Independence Day."

Brock's eyes roamed down to her uniform. "Storm Strike attire strongly discouraged," he added.

"Sounds inviting," Marta replied only half seriously.

Brock swung his hand in an arc, indicating the nearby residences. "These here are good people. But let 'em see you for who you are before they see you for who you work for. Give 'em a chance and they'll warm up to you."

Marta glanced around, surprised that she found herself actually considering his offer. "I'll check my calendar," she offered genuinely.

"You do that," Brock said, sounding pleased. He laughed and swung his hands up in the air. "Hell, bring a friend."

Marta smiled and started back for the car. She was grateful that she didn't see much activity along the street as she walked, not wanting to deal with any unpleasant confrontations. A strong breeze had sprung up. Out of habit, Marta looked to the sky to see a bank of threatening thunderheads rolling in from the west.

A growing sense of malaise gnawed at her insides and urged her to hasten her pace. By the time she reached the car, she'd broken out in a cold sweat. She collapsed into the operator's seat and swung the door closed. A sip of water only served to nauseate her further.

Upon power up, the car's display panel flickered. A sharp rap from her fist set it to glowing bright and steady. She jabbed the "Take me home" icon and sat back while the car performed a slow, clumsy y-turn and haltingly started back down the narrow, dirt trail.

In the few minutes it took to get to the road, her stomach churned incessantly. Marta slapped her palm down on the red emergency stop button on the console. The car dutifully edged to the side of the road and braked to a stop. Marta swung her door wide, leaned out, and evacuated the frothing contents of her stomach onto the blacktop. She stayed in that position for several minutes, leaning her head against the open door, too weak to move. Waves of heat from the blacktop radiated up at her downturned face as she reflected on her situation.

In just a few short weeks she had went from a high functioning manic depressive to a barely functioning heavily medicated manic depressive. Marta wondered how anyone could possibly consider that an improvement.

Finally she found the strength to pull herself back inside and swing the door closed. She reengaged autodrive, not really caring whether it got her back to Storm Strike Alpha in one piece or not. As the car accelerated, she heard the rise and fall of sirens. They were quickly growing closer. Before she could react, three stormcruisers, their warning lights blazing, barreled past in the opposite direction. They were heading west toward the approaching storm front.

On most days, she would have been cursing her luck for not being in one of those cruisers, eager to hear the roar of the turbine and smell the acrid fumes of spent explosives. But today she had no such ambitions. She was quite content just lying back in her seat, closing her eyes, and letting the blessed numbness of sleep carry her away. It was as close to nonexistence as she could get, short of dying.

CHAPTER 8

The car delivered Marta back to Storm Strike Alpha without any major incidents. Or, at least, none that she was aware of, having been comatose for most of the journey. A pair of fresh dents in the front fender left her wondering but not quite curious enough to check the car's nav logs for any sudden jolts or erratic maneuvers that she might have slept through.

The parking bay on sublevel three was deserted. Marta was thankful that she didn't have to interact with anyone in her current state. She simply uploaded the files from her data pad at a terminal in the corridor just outside the parking bay, then exited the building and headed for her own car. She passed two people whose faces registered a semblance of alarm, no doubt from her haggard appearance. But, mercifully, they said nothing and left her alone.

Marta slumped into the operator's seat of her own car and got it moving toward home. Glancing up into the rear view mirror, she was horrified to see just how bedraggled she really did look. She spent most of the ride home coaxing her hair into a state of semi-presentability and applying just enough cosmetics to her pallid face so she wouldn't scare her own children.

As she walked up to the door of her apartment, she could hear two lively young voices laughing and shouting. She wondered what could possibly have them so wound up. Then she heard another voice. A deep, familiar voice. One that nearly made her turn on her heel and run.

Steeling herself, she slipped the key in the lock, turned it and swung open the door. It creaked on its hinges. Three heads turned toward her. Two of them were Bonnie's and Quinn's, bright smiles lighting up their faces. The third was a man who regarded her with cold, malevolent eyes and a rapidly fading smile. His contemptuous expression chilled her blood and sent a shiver racing down her spine. But what pained her far worse was her awareness that she deserved his hatred. She'd earned it with her own stupidity.

Marta swallowed hard and tried to appear calm. "Hi kids," she said, forcing a quick smile.

"Hi Mom!" Quinn called out. Bonnie just stood there uneasily. Being older and more intuitive, she could sense the sudden tension and was acutely aware of the history behind it.

Marta turned to face the man. She had to admit to herself that Brad Pinchot still cut a sharp figure with his custom tailored three-piece suit and neatly styled blonde hair. She supposed that was part of the reason she had agreed to marry him all those years ago.

"Dad decided to drop by," Bonnie blurted out in a futile effort to defuse the situation.

"I can see that," Marta said, trying to keep her voice steady and impassive.

Brad resurrected his smile and directed it toward the children. "Why don't you kids go down and start the car. Get the AC going. It'll recognize your handprint, Quinn."

"Awesome!" Quinn yelled. Then he noticed his mother's displeased look and hesitated. "Can we, mom?"

Marta took a deep breath. "Where are you taking the children, Brad?"

"To the zoo," he answered, his voice betraying a latent animosity, subtle enough for the kids not to notice but aimed directly at Marta.

"And the mall!" Quinn added.

Marta narrowed her eyes and snickered. "Of course." She looked toward her children. "Go ahead, kids. Just make sure you're back before dark."

She glared at Brad, awaiting a confirmation.

"They will be," he said.

Marta waited for the children to shut the door behind them. She stared at the closed door for a moment in an effort to prepare herself for the inevitable confrontation, knowing that any pretense of civility was about to be utterly abandoned.

Slowly, she swung around to face him. "So what really brings you to Oklahoma City, Brad? Other than to bribe your children into loving you?"

"I don't need to bribe my children to love me, Marta. And the only reason they are here with you this summer is because I thought it might be good for them to spend some time with their mother."

Marta's eyes widened in mock surprise. "Am I supposed to somehow show my gratitude for being allowed to see my own children for two months out of the year?"

Brad held up a hand in supplication. "Look, Marta. I didn't come here to fight."

Marta felt a sudden bout of dizziness and placed a hand on the wall to steady herself. "Then what exactly did you come here for? You still haven't answered that question."

"I came here to check on the welfare of our children which is my right as I am the parent assigned sole custody to them."

Marta's eyes smoldered. "And what did you think you were going to find?"

Brad shrugged his shoulders. "To be honest, I had no idea what I would find. But you do have a history of making questionable choices."

"It all comes down to that, doesn't it?" Marta asked.

"Yes. In fact, it does," Brad half yelled. His eyes burned with a rage that he was finally allowing to boil to the surface. "You had it all, Marta. Tenure as a professor of meteorology at a prestigious university, two wonderful children, and a husband who loved you very much. You threw it all away on a fling with a punk grad student."

Marta winced as the impact from his tirade settled in. "Thank you. Thank you for once more reminding me of the biggest mistake of my life."

Brad's visage softened, almost as if he regretted his caustic outburst. "At least you're finally willing to admit that it was your mistake and not just lay all the blame on your so-called mental illness."

Marta was having difficulty maintaining her train of thought. "My so-called mental illness. No, Brad. It was me. It was all my fault. And now I'm paying for it. Is that you want to hear?"

Brad took a few steps toward her and held his palms up submissively. "All I'm saying is that you need to stop making excuses and start taking responsibility for your actions."

A wave of nausea washed over Marta. She clutched her stomach and swallowed the bile that rose up into her throat. Feeling completely tapped, she just wanted this over. "Message received. Now if you don't mind…"

"You look like shit, Marta." He leaned closer and studied her face with apparent concern. "Your eyes are bloodshot, pupils dilated. And you're shaking like a leaf."

"I'll be fine," Marta assured him.

"Are you on something?" Brad asked.

Marta kicked herself for believing it was genuine concern she'd seen in his eyes. Instead, it was just another slap in the face. "Now you're accusing me of being on dope?"

"Well, look at you. You're a wreck. And the apartment is in complete disarray." He swept the apartment with an open hand. "It looks like it hasn't been cleaned in months."

Marta exhaled forcefully. "I've been living with two teenagers for the past month."

"I live with them all of the time and my home is spotless," Brad countered.

Marta forced herself to stand straight and meet his accusatory gaze. "Well, in case it hasn't occurred to you, I can't afford to hire a maid like you. I have child support. I have a twelve year old car that I still make payments on. Hell, I haven't even paid off my student loans yet. And on top of all that, every day at work I get to see human suffering on a scale that your pampered little ass can't even imagine. So, at this point, as much as my life sucks it's actually a fucking miracle that I'm not mainlining heroin."

Brad's eyes flicked down to her arms. "Is that what you're doing?"

Lunging toward her, he grabbed her by the wrist, yanked her arm out straight and pulled the sleeve of her coveralls up. Marta tried twisting away from him but he tightened his grip. He squinted, looking closely for any sign of needle punctures.

"Let me go!" she screamed.

He ignored her and continued his examination. Marta kept resisting but found she didn't have the strength to pull away. So she exercised her only remaining option, balled up her free hand into a tight fist and swung. The punch caught Brad across the jaw. He reeled backward.

"Don't ever touch me again!" she growled.

Brad stumbled back into the couch and toppled over it. Arms and legs flailed as he tried to regain his footing. His head caught the edge of the coffee table as he went over. When he came up, he kept his eyes locked warily on Marta and maintained a safe distance as he sidestepped toward the door. He pulled a handkerchief from his pocket and dabbed at the blood dribbling down his chin from his split lip. With his other hand, he fumbled for the doorknob.

"Bonnie and Quinn will be coming back home to New York next month. Be thankful that I'm not taking them home with me right now. The only reason that I'm not is because I know how much their work for the Red Cross out here means to them so I won't take them away from that. But if you ever want to see them again, I suggest you get your life in order."

Marta watched him slam the door as he left. Then she burst into tears. Sobs racked her body. Just when she didn't think it possible for her life to get any worse, she was proven wrong yet again. She felt miserable and weak and cursed herself for not defending herself more vehemently.

But she simply couldn't rally the passion or the energy. And she knew why. It was the damn lithium sapping her strength and dulling her wits.

Grabbing her purse, she stumbled into the kitchen and dumped the contents onto the counter. She rummaged recklessly through the detritus that had collected over several years. A pack of gum tumbled to the floor. Her cellphone slid across the counter and slammed into the toaster. Then she saw what she was after. Her trembling hand closed around the pill bottle.

With one violent twist, she wrenched the top off the bottle. After flipping the faucet on, she hit the garbage disposal button. A gravelly whine filled her ears as it spun up to speed. Then she unceremoniously dumped the remaining pills down the drain and listened to the raucous clatter as they were pulverized and washed away.

CHAPTER 9

A balmy dusk was settling over Oklahoma. Long, faint peels of thunder rolled across the land, like the low, threatening growl of a rabid dog; a harbinger that another imminent clash with mother nature was about to take place. Just southwest of Hugo, a trio of stormcruisers held the high ground. They were perched side by side on a knoll overlooking a wide expanse of grassy savannah, facing west toward an approaching wall of hostile, writhing clouds. With their anchors firmly entrenched and their missile carriages deployed, they were waiting for the storm to come to them.

In the front of the median cruiser, Marta sat alone. The driver's seat had been vacated by Chaz several minutes before when he wandered off to relieve himself, a direct result of the insane quantities of soda he constantly drank. Kinney was at his station behind her but his attention was focused on his console, giving her the opportunity to quietly watch the spectacle unfold outside.

Brilliant vertical slashes of lightning etched the darkening sky. A pattering of rain drops lashed the windshield every few seconds as a subtle prelude to the coming onslaught. Even now, the winds were picking up, slapping at the tall prairie grass and sending fleeing birds into haphazard spins and dives. It was a front row seat to the raw savagery of nature.

Only an hour ago a similar front had rumbled through the area, leaving ample destruction in its wake. A pair of twisters had carved sinuous paths across the countryside. They'd mangled several vehicles on State Route 3 and effectively removed an entire agricultural research station from the face of the earth. There was no reason to believe the next front would be any less violent. She only hoped that she was ready to confront it.

It had been five days since she'd swallowed her last lithium pill, but instead of her emotions ramping up as she'd expected, they had plummeted further. Still, the thick mental fog had receded and her ability to think and act was returning. Even battling the depths of depression was far preferable to a constant drug-induced state of infirmity and the numb desolate ache of feeling nothing at all.

She twisted in her seat, taking in a quick visual sweep through the side windows. To the north and east endless fields of soybeans stretched out to the gray horizon. They were here to defend those fields. But more importantly, at least to Marta, they were here to defend those who labored in the fields as well as any other unfortunate souls who strayed into the killing path of a wind-driven monster.

But the storms brought more than the twisters. There were other destructive weather-related phenomenon that couldn't be effectively defended against. Hail shredded entire crops in seconds. Straight-line winds leveled fields and devastated manmade structures. Flash floods swept away anything in their path. Even lightning claimed its share of victims. But Marta knew it was folly to dwell on things that could not be prevented. It was far better to concentrate on those that could.

Chaz broke the spell of silence as he clambered up the steps and shut the hatch behind him. Before he had even taken his seat, Marta's nose wrinkled in revulsion as a pungent, foul odor assaulted her senses.

"What the hell did you do?" Kinney yelled out, taking the words right out of Marta's mouth.

Chaz shrugged and sank into the driver's seat. "I know, I know. I smell riper than a polecat in heat."

Marta was trying her best not to gag as the smell permeated the cabin.

Chaz shook his head. "These suits might be flame proof, shockproof, and waterproof but they damn sure ain't skunk proof."

Marta pointed toward a locker at the back of the cruiser. "There's a spare suit in there. Use it. Please."

"Happy to oblige," Chaz said. He slipped past a choking Kinney, rummaged through the locker and pulled out a crisp, fresh pair of coveralls. As he started to undress, he glanced up warily at Marta.

"Now don't y'all be peeking at my bare essentials," he warned.

Kinney fixed his gaze straight ahead, his lip curled up in disgust. "Two hellish tours in a warzone never prepared me for this," he grumbled.

The radio crackled to life just as Chaz finished dressing and sealed his befouled suit inside the locker.

"Whiskey Romeo One, this is Storm Strike Alpha. Do you copy?" uttered a steady matronly voice in Marta's headset.

Marta smiled and tapped the icon on her console that put her on air.

"Roger, Storm Strike Alpha. We copy loud and clear, mom," she replied, applying the call sign that everyone affectionately used when conversing with Jane Cormorant in dispatch. She was a pleasant woman in her early fifties who'd done a short stint in a stormcruiser until an F4 had sent a rod of iron rebar through the side panel of her cruiser, impaling her thigh, shattering her femur and costing her the use of her right leg. It was that mishap that had prompted the retrofitting of reactive armor panels on all stormcruisers.

"Could I get a sitrep from you?" Jane asked.

"Affirmative," Marta said. She sighed as she mentally summed up their current status before responding. "We are deployed two miles southwest of Hugo. Two units in support. We have visual and radar acquisition of intense storm front approaching from the west with strong indications that tornadic activity will be prevalent."

There was a long pause as Marta waited for dispatch to reply. She could envision Jane conferring with her supervisor back at base. Then a quick burst of static preceded Jane's voice. "So you have three cruisers on the ground. Could you make do with just two?"

Marta raised an eyebrow, her curiosity piqued. "That shouldn't be a problem. Two missile batteries should be more than sufficient. What's up?"

This time the reply was almost instant. "We have a situation, Marta. One of our cruisers has gone dark."

Marta could feel Kinney's and Chaz's eyes on her. "For how long?"

"We lost contact about fifty minutes ago. And, Marta?" She tensed, staring down at the console, waiting for Jane's next words. "It's Alpha Alpha Five."

Marta winced. "Pete?" she asked.

"I'm afraid so," came the reply.

Pete Griffeth's smiling bearded face intruded into Marta's thoughts. He had been a good friend to her since her first mission. Already an experienced commander at the time, he'd mentored her through the vagaries of command, instilling in her a sense of honor and duty that she still carried.

"Last location?" Marta asked.

"Five miles north of Moyers, heading south."

Marta already had a virtual map floating in front of her. Moyers was a straight shot by highway twenty-five miles north of them.

The radio crackled again. "It's at your discretion which of your support units you send," Jane added.

Marta glanced at Chaz, then back at Kinney. She got nods from each of them. "I'll do you one better than that. We're going ourselves."

Chaz was already spooling up the turbine and retracting the anchors when the reply came back. "I'll need to clear that with command first."

"No time," Marta snapped back as she fastened her restraints. "Ingram in Delta Sierra Six has been commander almost as long as I have. I'll leave him in charge here."

"I'll relay your intent to command," came the response.

"Roger that, mom. Whiskey Romeo One, out."

Marta flipped the switch to kill her transmission just before Jane's voice came back to issue a final plea. "Go get them, Marta. And bring 'em back home."

Marta looked at Chaz. "You heard the lady."

That was all the encouragement Chaz needed. Tires tore into the ground, sending up a spray of dirt and grass. The cruiser swung around and followed their own tracks back down the hill toward the highway.

By the time they reached downtown Moyers they had seen no sign of the lost cruiser. Marta was poring over the virtual map, hoping intuition might give her some insight into Alpha Alpha Five's whereabouts. She'd already tried to raise them on the radio several times, hoping beyond hope that it had just been long range interference that had been responsible for the lost radio contact. But that hope was quickly vanishing as nothing but static greeted them.

Marta had also taken the liberty to access and read the order log for Alpha Alpha Five. They'd been instructed to continue south through Moyers which would have taken them on the exact route that they themselves were traversing, only in the opposite direction.

Marta's first impulse was to continue north, backtracking Alpha Alpha Five's intended route. Then it occurred to her that it might be prudent to inquire from some of the locals if they'd seen a stormcruiser pass through, knowing that it would be hard for anyone to miss such an imposing vehicle racing past with its lightbars flashing and siren blaring. That would at least tell them if they'd gotten that far. If they had passed through, the best course of action would be to turn around, head back south, and search any side roads that adjoined the highway. If not, they would continue north.

Her plan quickly hit a snag once they turned onto main street and found the entire downtown district deserted and submerged under half a meter of water. The cruiser, with its high ground clearance, had no problem navigating the flooded streets. Chaz had slowed their speed to a crawl but the cruiser's ponderous mass still sent rolling swells crashing into the cars parked along the curbs.

Chaz shook his head as he surveyed the disaster. "If the water gets much higher we best start paddling," he quipped.

Kinney snickered. "These cruisers go twenty tons. They're about as buoyant as a lead cork. Feel free to paddle your little ass off. You'll still be sucking bottom."

Marta let her crew's harmless banter pass without reprisal, staring out at the surreal desolation encompassing them. They passed by a grocery store, its sliding glass doors frozen open like a gaping maw. Stagnant, murky water pooled within its darkened annex. Just beyond it, a small brick building stood, a vacant flagpole and rusting blue mail receptacle out front; remnants of the long defunct postal service.

Marta finally spotted a small aluminum fishing boat with what looked to be a family of three cruising down one of the side streets. She was just about to inform Chaz when she felt a tap on her shoulder. She glanced back and saw Kinney pointing up ahead toward a closed wrought iron gate, behind which sat a Mercedes with its headlights on. A short, pudgy man in a soggy business suit stood just inside the gate and appeared to be trying to force it open.

Marta pointed him out to Chaz who nodded his understanding and slowed the cruiser even further. As they drew near, Marta noticed the residence that sat in the background. Twin columns of marble framed the entrance to a three-story plantation style mansion. The sprawling monstrosity looked totally out of place in this quaint small town community. Then she noticed the sign above the gate. It read: *Buford Dreyfus, CEO. Shantilly Soybean Producers.* That explained the incongruous nature of such an extravagant estate.

"You sure you want to ask this dude?" Chaz inquired.

"Why not?" Kinney asked, leaning forward.

Chaz sighed in exasperation, as if the answer should have been self-evident. "Well, being the CEO of one the largest farming consortiums, ergo one of Storm Strike's biggest investors, he's sorta kinda like our boss."

Marta raised her eyebrows. "Your point?"

"I just reckon it's a might ill-advised to be prattling to one of your superiors that you done lost one of his very expensive vehicles."

Kinney put a hand on Chaz's shoulder. "Just drive. Don't try to analyze everything. You might hurt yourself."

Chaz shrugged and pulled the cruiser up next to the gate and braked to a stop. Marta and Kinney were already standing next to the hatch when it swung up.

The man gave the gate one last rattle, then ceased his futile struggle, cocked his head to the side and stared up at them derisively.

"Lightning fried the damn electronics," he yelled as if he realized how ridiculous he looked standing in half a meter of water and attempting to manhandle a locked iron gate.

"Mr. Dreyfus, is it?" Marta began.

With an open palm, the man wiped the rain from his face and slung it away. "Yeah, that's right. What do you want?"

"We were wondering if you'd seen or heard a stormcruiser pass through town within the last hour or so."

Dreyfus sneered at her. "What kind of a question is that?"

Marta was already regretting their decision to stop but it was too late to cut and run so she sucked in a deep breath and prepared herself for the inevitable verbal skirmish before she answered him. "We lost contact with one of our units and we're trying to locate them."

Dreyfus let loose with a demented chuckle. "That's rich! We count on you to protect our interests and you can't even take care of your own." He shook his head and waded over to a pole with a touch panel mounted on it. A wave of his hand caused the panel to glow blue and project a jittery, flickering virtual keypad on its surface.

Dreyfus stabbed his finger repeatedly into the keypad while continuing his tirade. "With as much money as we throw at you people, you'd think you'd be able to keep track of your own damn vehicles."

Marta exchanged a frustrated glance with Kinney.

"We'll take that as a no," Marta said and started to turn away, hoping to disengage from this uncomfortable exchange as expeditiously as possible.

"FYI, yes, I did see a stormcruiser barrel through here about an hour ago," Dreyfus shot back. He pointed in the direction of the estate behind him. "Came in from the north on route two, sirens screaming, lights blazing. Making enough damn racket to wake the devil himself. Then it turned right around and went back north the way it came in."

"You said it headed back north," Marta reiterated haltingly.

"That's what I said. Doesn't make a hell of a lot of sense to me either," Dreyfus yelled, slamming his fist down on the touch panel.

"Thank you," Marta said and eagerly headed back to her seat. Kinney disappeared back into the stormcruiser momentarily, then reappeared holding his rifle at the ready. Dreyfus took one look and stumbled backward, nearly toppling into the water. He watched, wide-eyed and grim-faced, as Kinney took aim and fired. The sharp whipcrack of the report echoed through the town. A shower of sparks and small fragments of metal exploded from the gate's latch mechanism. Then the two halves of the gate drifted apart a few centimeters.

Kinney lowered the rifle and slapped the button to close the hatch. Dreyfus continued to stare in stunned silence.

"You're welcome," Kinney growled as the hatch swung shut.

In the front of cruiser Chaz watched amusedly as startled residents of the inundated town suddenly peered out from doorways and windows, the sound of the gunshot still echoing through the streets and alleys. Several attempted to flee, splashing frantically through the floodwaters until they made it to cover. He shook his head. "And we wonder why people don't like us."

Kinney finished securing his rifle and dropped into his seat just as the cruiser did a u-turn and headed back toward the highway. The clouds to the west formed a nebulous black veil that fouled the sun's last rays and cast a sickly yellow pallor across the landscape. Their brief time in town had cost them several minutes and allowed the leading edge of the approaching storm front to reach them. Gale force winds were already hurling sheets of rain past the cruiser.

They were just turning onto the main road when a fiery orb shot skyward to the north. Marta's head snapped around to follow its ascent. She jabbed her finger at the glaring streak of crimson.

"There!" she shouted.

Chaz and Kinney had already seen it. "Emergency flare," Kinney said.

They all watched as the glowing sphere reached the apex of its arc and plummeted back to earth.

"It must be them," Marta said. She judged it had been launched less than two kilometers away. Suddenly Chaz braked hard, violently throwing all three of them forward against their restraints.

"What now?" Kinney shouted.

"Road's washed out," Chaz said.

Chaz pointed ahead at the road or what was left of it. A torrent of water coursed across the highway from right to left, bringing with it a mass of mangled tree limbs and uprooted saplings. It flowed with enough force that it had eroded the asphalt and left a deep ragged crater that blocked their path. Even as they watched, enormous chunks of pavement broke off and were quickly swept away.

Marta brought up a map on her console. She spied the cause of the inundation just to the east of them. "Kiamichi River must be flooding its banks," she said. Her fingers danced over the glass console, scrolling and zooming the map, until she found a road that paralleled the highway before rejoining it a short distance ahead.

"Alternate route, Chaz," she said. Her hand swept across the console, flinging the virtual map across to Chaz where it reintegrated itself into a plotted 3-D navigational route. "Backtrack through town and take Old Moyers Road. I'm going to pop a bot and follow this highway north."

Chaz waited for Marta to darken her visor, bring up her virtual display and launch the drone. Then he got the cruiser turned around and headed back toward town.

The winds tugged at the drone, threatening to overturn it. But the automated stabilization system did an admirable job keeping the craft upright. Marta guided it past the imposing crater carved into the asphalt by the raging waters and onward down the flooded highway. She held its altitude at five meters; high enough to clear most obstacles but low enough for the surrounding tree cover to provide shelter from the worst of the wind.

She activated the infrared camera, overlaying the thermal imagery over her visual of the drone's surroundings. As she turned her head, the drone's camera pod rotated in unison with her movements, providing a panoramic view of the area. No heat signatures stood out to her yet. Marta felt the cruiser swing right and accelerate. She knew they were again heading through town but kept her full attention centered on piloting the drone.

Chaz spared a moment from his driving to glance over at Marta. He watched as her upraised hand dipped and tilted, mimicking the maneuvers that the drone was performing.

"Watch out!" Kinney shouted.

Chaz saw the oncoming car at the last instant and jerked the wheel to the right. His eyes widened when he realized it was the same vehicle that had been parked behind the gate just a few minutes before. He felt a mild shudder as the Mercedes met the unyielding mass of the cruiser and glanced off the angled steel brush guard that wrapped around the cruiser's hood. Chaz watched behind them in his mirror as the car hopped the curb, plowed into a thick hedge and skidded to a stop.

"What was that?" Marta asked, blindly turning her helmet toward the noise but seeing only the drone's point of view.

"Pot hole," Chaz lied. He turned to see Kinney shaking his head. Chaz didn't bother stopping to render assistance and risk the further ire of the antagonistic CEO. He just shrugged his shoulders, gritted his teeth and pressed on through town, turning north at the next intersection.

Marta's hand quivered in midair in an attempt to battle the winds that buffeted the drone. The stabilizing systems alone were no longer able to fully compensate for the turbulence. Marta found herself feeling queasy from the erratic, choppy view being relayed to her from the drone's camera. She noticed an urgent red light flashing in her right peripheral vision and swung her head in that direction. It was a collision warning and it only took her a moment to determine the danger.

The trunk of a towering oak tree had split at a high crotch. Its canopy had already broken from the treeline and was in freefall, plummeting directly toward the drone. Marta angled her hand forward sharply and tightened it into a fist, signaling the drone to accelerate forward at full power. As its speed ramped up, it began to lose its equilibrium. Marta did her best to keep it level.

"Oh shit," she mumbled under her breath, eliciting glances from Chaz and Kinney. But they knew better than to ask about her situation and risk distracting her.

Marta craned her neck, looking back, and saw that her effort at evasion wasn't going to be enough. Branches were crashing into the water just behind the drone. The remainder of the canopy was still descending. She had hope for a moment as it looked as if the drone might just burst clear. Then a limb clipped the top of it, swatting it down like a fly, and driving it under the water.

Marta didn't give up. She knew the tiny craft was waterproof but it was never designed to be a submersible. It wouldn't take long for the water to find an opening and short out the electronics. Her hand jerked spasmodically as she attempted to break the drone free from the obstruction. First down, then up. Then side to side. To her crew, it looked like she was having a seizure. But every movement was deliberate and calculated. The spinning fans churned the water into a spiraling froth. Twigs snapped. Leaves were shredded. The drone slipped through narrow gaps between the branches on its path toward freedom.

Finally, only one thick branch was all that held the craft down. But the drone was wedged tightly underneath it. She revved the ducted fans up to redline and held them there. The drone shuddered violently. Then she noticed a slight movement upward as the branch began to bend. When it suddenly snapped, the drone shot upward, bursting from the surface and into the air, shedding water from its plastic skin.

Marta jumped in her seat but quickly regained her composure and guided the craft onward, oblivious to the happenings in the cruiser around her.

Old Moyers Road had several centimeters of water washing across it but Chaz had deemed it navigable and kept the cruiser at an alarmingly brisk pace. Any risk of hydroplaning was averted by the sheer weight of the vehicle. The deep treads on the massive tires sent up geysers of water arcing out to either side of them.

It still wasn't completely dark but Chaz had already activated the illuminators, throwing their surroundings into sharp relief. The enhanced visibility served him well as he spotted the obstructions lying in the road in plenty of time to bring the cruiser to a stop. Several sprawling oak trees had fallen across the road in a tangled mess.

Chaz tapped his hand on the steering wheel, deliberating. The trunks extended from the treeline on one side of the road, all the way across to the opposite treeline. There would be no going around, only over.

Chaz set his jaw and gripped the steering wheel tightly. "Hold on. We're fixin' to do some tree creeping."

"I had a feeling you were going to say that," Kinney said as he braced himself.

Chaz activated an icon on the console. A series of clunks and a new whine from the transmission told him that all-wheel-drive was engaged. He eased the cruiser forward. The brush guard nudged aside a couple of saplings. Then the front tires came up against the first solid trunk. The twin sets of rear tires held their traction and pushed the front end up and onto the deadfall. Branches scraped against the armored undercarriage.

Two large trunks shifted beneath them, opening up a gap between the web of branches and allowing the left front wheel to slip through. The cruiser leaned precariously. Pneumatics hissed, pumping air in and out of the suspension to counterbalance the sudden shift in stability. Chaz tugged at the steering wheel, expertly shifting their trajectory and weight distribution and bringing them back onto semi-solid footing.

Twenty seconds later, their front wheels dipped down and struck pavement, quickly followed by the rest of the vehicle. Chaz shifted the transmission and got them moving back down the road.

Meanwhile, Marta had managed to keep her hand remarkably steady during the violent jostling. The drone made a few lurches and wobbles but held true to its course. She noticed a driveway on her right that disappeared back into the trees. A rustic wooden sign identified it as the Great K Campground. Dangling between the sign post and another post on the opposite side of the driveway, a heavy rusted chain effectively blocked access to the grounds. Another smaller sign hung from the chain but Marta couldn't make out the wording.

Marta urged the drone past the driveway, then caught sight of another flare racing skyward. It was on her right, still a significant distance from the road, but appeared to have been launched from the direction of the campground.

"Do you boys see that?" Marta asked, her head twisted up and to the right as she watched the flare in her visor. To Kinney and Chaz it appeared as if she were looking the wrong way. They both had their eyes on the distant flare to the northeast through the windshield as it slipped back below the treeline.

"We certainly do," Kinney replied.

"Looks like it's coming from a campground. I'm taking the drone in. When you get back to the highway, turn right, head for the Great K Campground and follow my breadcrumb trail on your nav screen."

"Roger that. I'll be on your ass in no time," Chaz said. Kinney shot him a reproving look for his ambiguous choice of words but held his tongue.

Marta maneuvered the drone over the hanging security chain and headed down the tree-lined gravel path. It continued several hundred meters before opening up on a wide expanse of waterlogged lawn. The path branched off with one leg heading toward several log structures that could be seen to the north but Marta ignored them, knowing the flare had come from further east. She continued to follow the trail that way as it once again entered the trees and descended steeply.

She toggled the thermal overlay several times. Then she spotted a stationary heat signature up ahead glowing a greenish-yellow through the heavy foliage. It was definitely large enough to be a stormcruiser. As she drew closer, she could see a vehicle's running lights peeking through the trees. They flickered almost imperceptibly and blazed brighter than the lighting on most civilian vehicles. Her heartbeat ratcheted up a notch as her hopes rose.

She piloted the drone down a steep ravine, almost colliding with a tall stone monolith and an imposing bronze statue that overlooked the flooded banks of the Kiamichi River. The waters currently looked less like a gentle-moving stream suitable for recreational activities and more like a hardcore class-four rapids that only the most ardent of death defying thrill seekers would dare to venture into. The rushing flow was being churned into a seething white froth as it tumbled past boulders and tangled jumbles of freshly uprooted trees. She could hear its roar in her headset through the drone's external microphone.

And there it was, just fifty meters upriver from the drone's location: a stormcruiser caught halfway across the river, its right side pinned against an enormous boulder by the sheer strength of the current.

Marta quickly sized up the situation. The crew of the stranded cruiser was making no immediate efforts to extricate themselves from their predicament. Marta knew that meant one of three things. It was possible the occupants were incapacitated. It was also possible that their vehicle was disabled. Or they may have already attempted to free themselves, found it futile, and had settled in to ride out the storm or wait until help arrived, whichever came first. Marta preferred the latter possibility.

The punishing force of the water would make any attempt at rescue perilous at best. But with another storm front quickly moving in, things were going to go from bad to worst case scenario in short order. A stormcruiser was designed to take one hell of a beating but it did have its structural limitations. If the force of the water surging against it became great enough, and from the look of things that was a foregone conclusion, then its hull would be crushed just as easily as a booted foot on a tin can.

With her mental risk assessment complete, she just needed to know the status of the cruiser and its occupants before she could hope to devise any strategy for rescue. With that thought in mind, she aimed the drone for the cruiser and started across the rampaging waters, keeping the drone's altitude high enough to avoid the majority of the whirling spray.

The drone approached the cruiser from the front. She adjusted the illuminators to high intensity and watched as their beam played across the battered hull of the cruiser. From the gouges, dents, and scorched reactive armor panels, she could tell it had already taken a pummeling. Even the three centimeter thick windshield had a diagonal crack running its entire width.

She thought she saw movement in the interior but the glare from the drone's reflected light made it difficult to know for certain. She flashed the illuminators off and on several times to signal the crew to the drone's presence. Banking the drone left, she brought it around to the side of the cruiser. The hatch appeared to be intact which she took as a good sign. Then she spotted the mangled wreck of an aluminum canoe wrapped around the jagged edge of one of the smaller boulders nearby.

Before she could pivot the drone around to inspect the smashed canoe, the cruiser's hatch swung open. A pair of hands reached out, snatched the drone in midair and pulled it inside the cruiser. Marta's view went crazy, tilting and bobbing. She closed her eyes to prevent the spinning blur from making her any dizzier than she already was.

When she opened them again she found herself staring into the haggard face of a man. Dark, bedraggled hair hung down over his forehead, partially cloaking his eyes but doing nothing to conceal the deep, heavy circles beneath them. For a moment she wasn't sure who it was. Then she noticed the neatly trimmed salt and pepper beard and the stub of an unlit cigar caught between opposing incisors and all doubt vanished. He was holding the drone up in front of him, careful to avoid the ducted fans with his fingers. Marta instantly killed the power to the drive motors and allowed the fans to spin down.

"To whom am I speaking?" Pete Griffeth, the commander of Alpha Alpha Five, asked, eyeing the drone warily.

Marta tapped an icon that activated the public address system onboard the drone. "Pete, this is…", she began but cut herself off as she noticed Pete grimacing in obvious discomfort. She dialed down the volume and tried again. "Pete, this is Marta."

Pete pinned his cigar to the corner of his mouth and smiled. "Well, well, well. Am I glad to hear your sweet voice."

Marta grinned back. "And I'm glad you're still alive. What happened?"

Pete shrugged his shoulders. "We caught some radio chatter that there were some campers stranded in the river so we came looking for 'em. Got blindsided by a wall of mean water. I'm guessing a dam collapsed somewhere upstream."

Marta frowned. "Why didn't you radio in for assistance?"

A fresh peal of thunder forced Pete to shout to be heard. "Lightning countermeasures misfired. We took a strike that fried our radio, our transponder, and our fire control."

Marta nodded. "You just hold tight, Pete. The cavalry is on its way. And hang onto that drone for me. I don't need to get my ass chewed for losing another one."

Pete snickered. "Will do, Marta. Oh, and one other thing. Not to burden you with any more responsibility but we have some guests."

Pete swiveled the drone to point its camera at five shivering forms wrapped in blankets. At least two of them were children.

"They were canoeing the river when the flash flood caught up with them. We found them clinging to some rocks and managed to pull them out before we got ourselves into this fix."

Marta didn't miss a beat. "It's not a burden at all, Pete. It doesn't matter how many of you are in there. You're all coming home with us. Alive."

Marta recognized the grim tension behind Pete's smile. It told her that he knew how dire the situation actually was. "Glad to hear it. I'll leave you to do your thing. Call me if we can assist in any way."

"Roger that, Pete. Talk to you soon."

Marta killed the connection to the drone, her visor once more becoming transparent. She checked the map on her console and saw that they were already on the highway and coming up fast on the campground's entrance.

"They're all alive and well for the moment," Marta said.

"Let's hope we can keep it that way," Kinney said.

Marta opened a channel on her radio. "This is Whiskey Romeo One. We have located the missing cruiser. Situation critical. Moving in to assist. All available units please converge on our coordinates."

After signing off, she quickly filled her crew in on what they were going to be facing. Then the driveway loomed ahead on their left. With the visibility that the cruiser's illuminators provided, Marta could make out the sign hanging from the chain across the entrance. It read: *Campground closed due to inclement weather.*

Chaz saw the chain but didn't slow. It snapped taut against the center angle of the grille guard and sheared away like a brittle strand of taffy. Through his visor, he kept his eyes on the trail and the dashed line being projected on top of it that indicated the path that the drone had taken only minutes before.

Just as the cruiser exited the trees, the alarms started sounding.

"Tracking an F2!" Kinney shouted as he frantically scanned his displays. "Shit! Coming down right on top of us!"

"Good time to try out those new warheads! Arm missiles!" Marta screamed.

"No good!" Kinney shot back. "We're too close. Can't target it and we'd be crushed by the shockwave. There could also be people taking shelter anywhere in these woods."

Chaz saw it first. An ethereal gray spiral that touched down just ahead of them. He yanked the wheel hard over to the left. They found themselves heading north, running parallel with the newborn shredder.

Chaz veered left again just as the twister lurched ahead and tore into a small log cabin. The structure came apart like a set of Lincoln logs. Marta watched in horror as one of those logs came hurtling straight for the cruiser. She could see that it was going to hit on her side. There was no time to do anything.

The log smashed into the side panel adjacent to where she sat. Marta waited for it to penetrate through the hull; to feel the pain as her legs were wrecked. Instead, an explosion reverberated throughout the interior of the cruiser. Through her window she saw a brief spout of flame erupting from the panels on her door as the reactive armor did its job. Shaped charges detonated on impact, expending their energy outward and repelling the incoming debris. In an instant, the log had become nothing more than a swarm of flickering embers dancing on the winds.

"I'll never get used to that," she uttered, still badly shaken. She watched the shredder slink off, carving a path through the forest as it went.

"Nothing like fighting fire with fire," Chaz said. He swung the cruiser around, lined it up on the trail and headed east toward the river. As they rolled down the hill, Chaz slowed to a crawl. The ominous stone monolith slipped past. Next came the statue. Then they were at the shore.

Despite the deluge of rain, the cruiser's active illuminators eerily turned the falling darkness into daylight and gave them a startlingly clear view of their surroundings. To Marta, the raging river looked even more menacing in person than it had through the drone's compact optics. The cruiser was still out there, looking still and lifeless, with the water pounding against its hull. But, now, Marta knew that there was life inside. And she was determined to keep it that way.

"Suggestions, gentlemen?" Marta asked. Her mind was already devising a plan but she'd learned long ago to entertain all options and she had come to value her crew's opinions.

Kinney leaned forward into the cockpit, his eyes narrowed as he took in the situation. "Nothing we can do from here." He pointed to the cluster of jagged rocks that surrounded the disabled cruiser. "And if we get close enough to attempt a direct evac, we're going to end up just as FUBARed as they are."

"Agreed," Marta said. "Options?"

Chaz scratched his head, his eyes roaming up the rocky, foam-shrouded shoreline. "Ain't nothing stopping us from heading up yonder. If we can get upstream, maybe we can snag their ass end with a cable and haul 'em out."

His plan paralleled the one she'd mentally formulated, albeit worded somewhat less eloquently. She glanced at Kinney who nodded his approval.

"Move out at your discretion, Chaz."

Chaz nodded and got them moving north up the shoreline, crawling over rocks and past the remnants of washed out firepits. A derelict fiberglass kayak shattered under the weight of the cruiser. The occasional screech of metal filled the cabin as their steel-plated belly scraped against offending outcroppings of rock.

They passed by the imperiled cruiser and continued another fifty meters. Then Chaz angled their cruiser back to face them.

Marta reestablished the radio link with the drone but instead of viewing the video feed in her helmet she routed it to her console so she could keep her sense of presence within her own cruiser. Within a few moments, Pete's face appeared.

"Pete, we're going to try to get a line to you," Marta informed him.

Kinney had already donned a black rain slicker and exited the vehicle. They watched through the windshield as he made his way to the front of the cruiser and unwound a length of cable from their forward winch, coiling it on the ground next to him. He turned to face the river, a length of cable in his hand and the hook dangling near the ground.

The hatch on the stranded cruiser opened and Pete stood in the doorway, waiting. Kinney twirled the length of cable vertically, aiming several meters upstream from his target. He let the hook fly. It sailed through the air and landed in the water but far short of the cruiser. After two more tries, it was clear that, even with the lightweight nano-steel cable, the hook was still being dragged down by wind and gravity before it could reach its mark.

Kinney reappeared at the hatch, rain streaming down his face. "It's no use! It'll never reach them. Reel it back in, Chaz."

Marta lowered her head, trying desperately to come up with another option. Then she saw Kinney reach under his slicker and unholster his sidearm. He held it out to her, grip first.

"Here," he said.

Marta stood and took the weapon, frowning. "What are you doing?"

"Hold onto it for me. I don't want it getting wet," Kinney said.

"What do you mean?" Marta asked, still confused by his sudden action.

"I'm going to take the cable out to them," he said matter-of-factly.

"You're going to what!?" Marta exclaimed.

Kinney calmly went about snugging the zipper on his slicker and cinching up his collar. "I'll be fine. I just have to avoid the rocks, watch out for underwater obstructions, steer clear of any floating debris, and keep a firm grip on that tow line."

"And not drown," Chaz added.

"Yeah, that too," Kinney agreed, rolling his eyes.

"Be careful, Kinney," she said, her gaze taking in every nuance of his face, wondering if she would ever see him alive again.

"No worries," he said and gave her a fearless smile.

As Kinney ducked back out into the tempest, Marta slumped in her seat and closed her eyes. When she opened them, he was already waist deep in the water. She could see that he had looped the cable around his midsection and secured it with the clamp. The strength of the current forced him to lean at a forty-five degree angle just to maintain his footing. He swayed unsteadily as he shuffled out another couple of steps. Then, before his legs could be swept out from under him, he launched himself into the torrent. Muscular legs and arms tore at the water. Slowly he made progress. Behind him, the cable remained taut as it free-spooled out from the winch. He dangled from its end like a hooked trout struggling for its freedom.

Twice he disappeared beneath the roiling maelstrom and twice his head bobbed back above the surface. It was obvious that he was far past the threshold where most men would have succumbed to exhaustion. His movements were becoming more uncoordinated and sluggish. But he soldiered on. Marta knew he was swimming not just for his own life but for the lives of those they were trying desperately to rescue. To a man like Kinney that made all the difference in the world.

Finally he was within a meter of the rear of the cruiser. The current slackened somewhat as a large boulder just upstream parted the waters and diverted much of the energy to either side of him. He reached out with a shaking hand, his arm stretched to its limit. His boots touched rock and he used that solid footing to uncoil his legs against it in one final lunge toward his objective. As he surged forward, his fingers tightened around the thick steel plate that formed the bumper.

Marta tensed as Kinney unfastened the cable from around his waist, knowing that if he were to lose his grip now, he'd be swept away to a certain death. But he managed to latch the clamp to the rear hitch, giving the cable a tug for good measure. He rested a moment, his back against the bumper, letting the force of the water hold him there. Then he worked his way around to the side of the cruiser to the open hatch where Pete was waiting for him.

Once he was safely inside, Marta breathed a sigh of relief. She glanced at the video feed and saw Kinney, looking more like a drowned rat than a soldier, peering into the drone's camera.

"Alright, Marta. Get us the hell out of here," he said.

Marta smiled. "Make it happen, Chaz."

Chaz dropped the anchors. Once the spinning blades pushed aside the surface rocks they quickly augured into the ground. Then he activated the winch. They waited while the arc of the cable slowly became a straight line as the slack was taken up.

"Come to papa," Chaz said, keeping his finger on the slider control for the winch so he could regulate its speed. The cable snapped taut and they heard the groan of metal as the cruiser's frame took on the load. Then the stranded cruiser shifted. Its rear end swung around to face them and its hull slowly eased away from the boulder that had immobilized it.

"Thataway," Chaz said as the stranded cruiser was slowly but steadily dragged closer.

Marta had to remind herself to breathe. The fact that the anchors had sunk into the soft sand so effortlessly had worried her. A moment later and her concern proved all too warranted. Their own cruiser began inching toward the river. Marta glanced out her side window, angling her eyes toward the ground. The anchors were still in place but they were carving deep trenches in the sand as the cruiser was inexorably dragged along.

Chaz instantly had the cruiser in reverse and was applying just enough power to get the treads to dig in deeper. Still they were pulled forward. Their front end dipped. Foam and water washed up over the windshield. Marta could see the tires on the other cruiser spinning as well as they tried to find purchase on the riverbed.

"Looks like we're goin' swimmin'," Chaz said.

They felt the last of their traction give way. Then they were caught in the current and began drifting downstream, still tethered to the other cruiser.

Marta swung her head around, surveying their predicament, trying desperately to think. This had been a hastily implemented rescue attempt and she'd devised no contingency plan for it. She wanted nothing more than to bury her head in her hands and cry. They'd tried their best and failed but ultimately that failure would be her sole responsibility as commander. Now people were going to die because of her ineptitude. A crushing weight descended on her and she couldn't shrug it off. She didn't even try.

Chaz was still revving the turbine, churning up water as he tried to get the tires to dig in. But it was futile. There was nothing more that any of them could do. The current was far too strong. Without a solid mooring to cling to, they would be mercilessly swept away. Perhaps to be crushed by a boulder. Or pulled into deeper water where they would sink and drown in an armor-plated tomb.

She glanced forlornly at the beach and the trail that led up from it. So close, but it might just as well have been a hundred kilometers away. She saw the statue that stood there clearly for the first time. It was a tall, smiling man in a business suit bearing a strong likeness to their recent acquaintance, Buford Dreyfus. One bronze arm wrapped around the shoulders of a shorter man dressed as a common laborer and holding a platter with what appeared to be a variety of prepared vegetables. The wording on the plaque at its base was large enough to read. It said: "*Support your local farming consortium. We put food on your table.*"

Marta's eyes traveled up the trail to the monolith, probably some type of geographical marker. Perhaps they would erect a new monument nearby to honor the bravery of those who lost their lives here today. But she doubted it.

She glanced at the drone's video feed. The drone had been unceremoniously dropped on the bare diamond-plated flooring behind the cockpit, its camera facing toward the front of the doomed cruiser. It was chaos there. Pete was in his command chair She could see more than one set of arms reaching out for controls and could hear the unintelligible chatter of the crew there as they struggled on valiantly. Occasionally the back of Kinney's head swept past the camera as he leaned into the cockpit.

If the drone were an order of magnitude larger she could have used it to ferry all of them across to the shore, one by one. Its motors were powerful but not even close to being able to lift a small child. Marta frowned, the seed of a thought forming. The drone couldn't lift a person but what could it lift? She stared out through the windshield, her eyes going to the cable stretching between the cruisers. It could easily carry a cable. But she wouldn't have released their grip on the other cruiser even if that had been possible.

Her eyes opened wide as a sudden epiphany dawned on her . She fumbled for her helmet's microphone and held it close to her mouth. "Pete! Kinney!" she shouted. It was obvious their attention was elsewhere. She tapped the volume slider and flicked it up to full volume.

"Hey!" she yelled. Her headset squealed as her own voice was fed back to her. The response was instant. The men in the cockpit jumped, instinctively cupping their hands to their ears. Marta brought the volume back down just as Kinney picked up the drone and held it up in front of his face, pain still evident in his features.

"Sorry about that," she said.

Kinney shrugged. "Losing our hearing is the least of our worries right now."

"How do you feel about risking your life one more time?" she asked.

Without hesitation, he said "Talk to me." Then he listened intently as Marta quickly summarized her idea.

Kinney wasted no time in executing her plan. He reappeared in the hatch of the cruiser and clambered up onto the roof. Lying on his belly to prevent the wind and waves from dislodging him, he slid down the windshield and onto the cruiser's hood. Then he lowered himself over the front edge of the hood, one hand clinging to the grill guard. He reached down with his other hand and retrieved the hook for the winch. Then he climbed back up onto the hood.

As he scrambled back up toward the windshield, his foot slipped on the slick, wet surface of the grill guard and he slid backward, nearly plummeting into the churning river, his legs dangling precariously over the front of the cruiser. But he managed to grab one of the thick wiper blades that were designed not just to wipe away rain but also to clear debris from the front of the cruiser. The wiper blade's steel support arm easily sustained his weight. Exhausted, he hung there for a few moments, rallying his strength.

Rain sluiced down the windshield past Kinney. Still too weak to pull himself up, he lifted his head and found himself staring into the cruiser's interior through the windshield. He saw Pete tap an icon on his console. The next thing he knew, the wiper blade began to climb up across the windshield, dragging him with it, his rain slicker acting like a giant squeegee as it slid across the glass. It abruptly stopped when it reached the top of the windshield. He saw Pete inside give him a thumbs up. Taking advantage of the boost he'd just received, he transferred his hands to a grab bar that ran across the rim of the windshield and managed to swing his legs up and onto the roof.

Pete was waiting for him at the hatch as he swung himself back over the edge and into the cruiser where he collapsed from exhaustion on the floor. Pete completed their part in the plan by popping the pin that fastened the hook to the winch cable. Then he attached the cable directly to a loop of metal that protruded from the rear of the drone.

"Ready," Pete said directly into the microphone so Marta would hear him over the roaring current.

Marta transferred the video feed back to her darkened visor and engaged the drone's lift fans. Pete extended his arms out through the hatch and released the craft as gently as if it were a dove. It hovered there a moment and then swung toward shore, dragging the cable behind it. That cable was their lifeline and Marta took every precaution to ensure that it made it to shore. Several times a powerful gust of wind rocked the craft and she slowed to a hover, allowing the drone to regain its equilibrium before continuing on.

Even before the drone reached shore, Marta was scanning the terrain ahead, looking for a suitable anchor point. There were several large oaks in the vicinity but the combined weight of the two cruisers would be well over forty tons. It would be a formidable load for even the stoutest of trees.

She considered the statue but its base was already submerged beneath the rising waters. Then she caught a glimpse of the monolith. Perched on the side of the hill, its base obviously extended down into the ground to a significant depth. In addition to its solid anchor point, the monument itself had to weigh several hundred tons. Under the circumstances, it was their best shot.

Piloting the drone past the statue, she steered for the monolith. Behind it, the cable draped itself across the shoulder of the tall granite figure that represented the farming consortiums. The drone continued up the hill a good distance past the monolith. Then Marta swung the craft back around, wrapping the cable around the base of the massive stone pillar. She performed this maneuver three more times. Then she spiraled the drone around the cable and brought it back through the loop that had formed, thus securing the line with a rudimentary knot. The drone came to rest dangling from the end of the cable. Marta cut power to it and looked over at Chaz.

"Now or never, Pete," Marta spoke into her microphone.

Marta and Chaz watched intently as the other cruiser's winch cable stretched tight into very nearly a straight line between the cruiser and the monolith, the only deviation being a slight curve where the cable bent around the neck of the statue's most prominent figure. But that had been unavoidable, the statue having been located in the direct path between the cruiser and the anchor point.

"I sure hope that puny cable is as strong as it's bragged up to be," Chaz said.

"It has to be," Marta replied.

"Give me a good old-fashioned braided steel cable for my money," Chaz mumbled, staring out at the cruiser as its winch gathered in the cable and the front end of the vehicle slowly rotated toward the shore. "These days it's all nano this and nano that."

Marta didn't bother replying to Chaz's rant but a slight grin creased her face when she noticed that the other cruiser's movement downstream had been arrested. It hung there in the current for a moment and then began creeping steadily toward the shore twenty meters away.

Their own cruiser drifted up behind them and continued downstream until its cable snapped taut. Marta's finger hovered over the cable release icon glowing an ominous red on her console. This was the moment she feared the most. The moment when the full weight of both vehicles would be brought to bear on the single cable that stretched to shore.

She knew that if that cable failed, it would probably do so in a single sudden snap. But if she had any warning that something was amiss or if their own mass began to overload the winch, she was ready to sacrifice herself and Chaz in the hope that the others would still make it to shore.

Chaz was still young, vigorous and had most of his life before him. It was likely that countless opportunities lay ahead of him on a bright, clear path that was untarnished by past deeds. But for her, it would simply be an end to her torment. Her children would go back to New York with their father and be well cared for. And she would finally be rid of her demons. The misfiring synapses deep within her brain would be stilled. She would finally find the peace that she longed for.

She glanced down at the console and saw that her hand was trembling violently, her finger coming alarmingly close to tapping the icon that would seal their fate. She blinked repeatedly as if emerging from a trance. Then she withdrew her finger and squeezed her hand into a tight fist. She couldn't allow herself to do it. She had to wait a few moments. Wait for the first hint that something wasn't right.

Their cruiser quickly fell into line behind the first and they found themselves creeping slowly but steadily toward salvation. Marta wiped the sweat from her brow. A cold shiver rippled through her body as she realized how close she had been to forfeiting their lives.

A klaxon blared from Kinney's unmanned console behind her. A radar screen materialized in midair above it. Chaz and Marta stared at it through their ER visors. It showed a massive blip converging on their location from the south. They looked at each other.

"This is not our damn day," Chaz said.

"We can't arm our missiles without Kinney," Marta said. She looked out toward the other cruiser, hoping to see their missiles rotating into position. Then she remembered. "Shit! Pete told me their fire control was damaged."

"I reckon we're nothing but ducks in a shooting gallery," Chaz quipped.

They both saw it at the same time; a massive funnel looming large in the dimly lit sky to the south. Its girth spanned the river and engulfed the wooded banks on either side. Saplings and full grown trees quickly lost their battle with the monster as they were wrenched from the earth and tossed like kindling.

"And this ole boy's got good aim," Chaz added.

They were out of options. There was no way to fight it and no way to dig in. By Marta's reckoning, they had perhaps thirty seconds to live. Then it would be over for all of them. All that would be left would be mangled steel and broken bodies.

Then four plumes of fire erupted from the shore and raged skyward. Marta squinted against the sudden glare and saw two stormcruisers stationed near the crest of the hill. Each had launched a pair of missiles and all four of them were relentlessly homing in on their target, leaving whorls of smoke and steam in their combined wake. She grinned. The cavalry had arrived.

The warheads exploded near enough that they lit up the entire sky like a million flashbulbs going off at once. Shockwaves from the almost simultaneous detonations rocked the cruiser but Marta barely noticed. Her attention was focused solely on the shredder. It shuddered as flames belched from four ragged wounds in its wind wrapped silhouette. Water vapor and debris drifted down from the sky as the funnel's strength ebbed. No longer capable of gripping its prey, the monster was shedding its hoard of airborne wreckage. Then the dark, swirling winds faded to a hazy gray, finally dissolving into a harmless mist and was gone.

Marta barely acknowledged the hooting and hollering that Chaz was engaged in next to her. She just leaned back in her seat, let her pulse drop below redline and started breathing again.

Several minutes later they were all safely on shore. Marta was standing just outside the hatch of her cruiser watching the other crews disembark from their vehicles. Pete emerged and headed straight for her. He latched onto her and swung her around in a bear hug.

"Damn glad we had you along for that ride," he said after releasing her from his iron grip. He smiled broadly and squeezed her shoulder.

She noticed Chaz rummaging around in the weedy undergrowth next to the trail. He came out of the thicket holding a severed bronze head that he was playfully tossing back and forth between his hands. She glanced up at the statue to where the businessman's head had been cleanly lopped off by the thin strand of winch cable.

"I reckon lots of folks been hankering to do this," he said, smirking.

Kinney finally appeared in the hatch of Alpha Alpha Five's cruiser, carrying a small girl in his arms. She clung to his neck. His eyes locked with Marta's. A weary smile crept up his face.

Marta tried returning the smile but her lips just quivered. Out of nowhere, a rush of overwhelming despair hit her like a rogue wave. Hot tears flooded her eyes and she began to sob. She turned away, embarrassed and unable to control the sudden outburst of emotion. Kinney's smile faded as he stood there regarding her with a mixture of confusion and pity.

CHAPTER 10

Marta felt anxious and uncomfortable as she sat alone in the small office, hands resting in her lap, her fingers interlaced tightly. Her superiors had decided to have the members of each crew debriefed individually so that their responses could be scrutinized for discrepancies. It was her turn.

She stared at a small translucent cube that sat on the corner of the glass-topped desk. She'd seen similar ones before. They changed color in accordance with the local weather. When she'd entered the office twenty minutes ago it had been glowing a serene blue. Now it was pulsing a muted pink. But she had no idea what each color represented.

A portly stump of a man with dark crescents under his eyes and a ruddy complexion lumbered into the room, carrying a cup of coffee in one hand and a data pad in the other. He nodded to Marta and unbuttoned his suit jacket, allowing his belly to burst forth from its confinement. As he took his seat behind his desk, the ridiculously undersized chair squealed in protest.

He placed the data pad down on the desk. As he did so, a glowing red outline formed around it on the clear surface of the desk. Then a pulsing red line shot across the desk and expanded into a rectangle of scrolling text positioned directly in front of him.

"Pardon my disheveled appearance. I'm not used to these early morning debacles. But the powers that be wanted these interviews carried out post haste." He leaned back and shrugged his shoulders. "So here I am."

Marta, still reeling from her recent ordeal and not in the mood for bureaucratic drivel or banal small talk, just stared blankly at him.

"And here you are...," he said, balancing a narrow pair of glasses on the tip of his nose and leaning forward to read her name off the desk's surface display. "Marta Astin. And I'm sure you're just as pleased to be here as I am."

He grimaced and tapped his forehead. "Forgive me. The name is

Jude Montgomery, humble inquisitor and revealer of truths." He pointed to a business card holder. "I even have a card that says that. Not really. But I do have my own parking space. And now that I've made a glorious first impression let's get down to the nitty gritty, shall we?"

Marta could tell the man was trying to add a bit of levity to the situation but he was failing miserably and she was growing impatient. All she wanted was to go home and calm her ragged nerves with a couple of medicinal shots of Kentucky's finest.

"Would you care to relate to me without undue embellishment precisely what," he paused, his fingers wagging out quotations in midair, "went down last evening, dated 2 July 2038. And I can tell that you are a talkative lass so please make this as concise as possible."

"I'll do my best," she said.

He nodded appreciatively and tapped an icon on his desktop. Another red line streamed out from the icon to a camera that faced toward Marta mounted a few centimeters above the desk's surface. A red light on it began flashing.

Marta didn't relish having her testimony recorded but she didn't have anything to hide so she launched into her account of what had transpired the night before. She managed to summarize the event in just a few minutes, while her interviewer sat quietly, picking lint from his suit and taking an occasional sip of coffee. When she was finished, Jude Montgomery leaned forward once more and started reading disinterestedly from an apparent script on his desktop.

"I thank you for your presumed candor. You are to be commended for preventing the loss of a stormcruiser by sheer ingenuity and uncommon courage and devotion while under extreme duress." He glanced up at her, one eyebrow raised, then continued reading. "I am now to inform you that no disciplinary actions are warranted. Blah blah blah. You have not been implicated in the pending insubordination claims."

Marta snapped to attention. "The what?"

Montgomery seemed taken aback by her sudden interest in what he obviously considered formalized drivel. "Insubordination claims. That's where someone naughty doesn't do what they're told."

Marta sneered at him. "I know what insubordination is."

"Well, apparently, Peter Griffeth doesn't. He's been charged with just that and relieved of duty. Likewise his loyal crew. Guilt by proxy, I believe is the proper term." Montgomery regarded her with a smug look on his chubby face.

"What kind of horseshit is that?" Marta yelled.

Montgomery rolled his eyes. "Allow me to enlighten you with the unabridged version." He flicked his finger across the desktop and scrolled to the appropriate section of the report. "Here we are. The disciplinary action being brought against Alpha Alpha Five's commander and crew is based upon indisputable evidence that aforementioned crew did willfully venture into an area not mandated by the Storm Strike charter whereupon they engaged in rescue operations without authorization and against direct orders. By these actions, the aforementioned crew unduly endangered Storm Strike property and imperiled the personnel and property of nearby farming consortiums."

Montgomery looked up at Marta expectantly. She felt the urge to lash out physically but managed to contain her rage and channel it into her emphatic response. "And in what godforsaken barbarous corruption-ridden hellhole of a society is it deemed justified to let innocent people die while we prance off to protect some wretched fields of fucking plants?"

Montgomery placed his hands on the desk and leaned toward her. "To my understanding, it all comes down to one intrinsic necessity. To gratify the needs of those who provide the not insubstantial financial support that allows Storm Strike to exist."

"If that's the case, then Storm Strike shouldn't exist and this world is even more fucked up than I thought."

Montgomery held up his hands in resignation. "I believe the old adage 'Don't shoot the messenger' would seem to apply here."

Marta's lip curled up in disgust. "The very fact that I am sitting here listening to you spout this bullshit makes you part of the problem."

Montgomery patted his chest. "I am merely a vessel sent to dispense the profound wisdom of those high above my pay grade."

Marta's eyes narrowed to burning slits. "Fine. Then dispense this wisdom back to your powers that be. You can tell them that if they suspend Pete Griffeth then they should fucking suspend me, too. Because if I had been in his position, I would have done the same damn thing he did. And they can take their fucking commendations and shove them up their asses."

Montgomery snatched up a stylus and began scribbling across his active desktop. "Your comments are duly noted in the event report. Every...last...expletive."

Marta stood up. "Good. Are we through?"

Montgomery eyed her warily, looking reluctant to continue. He rubbed his thick jowls nervously. "There is the small matter of defacing the likeness of the Shantilly consortium's CEO."

Marta frowned, not immediately comprehending what he was

referring to.

"Statue? Beheaded?" He slid a finger across his throat. "Of course, you won't be held accountable for that most regrettable casualty despite some rather nasty intimations from said CEO that heads should roll. Pun intended."

He grinned for a moment, proud of his quip. Then he quickly retracted the smile when he saw Marta's face flush even redder.

"And!?" she snarled.

He swallowed hard, withering under her heated gaze. He cleared his throat. "They simply wish to emphasize that you should be more careful in the future with such revered community icons."

As Montgomery finished that statement, he tensed, appearing ready to dive underneath his desk for cover.

"Un-fucking-believable," Marta mumbled to herself. She turned and stormed out of the room.

"I do believe that concludes our interview," Montgomery called out after her. "Go home and get some rest, Ms. Astin. Maybe have a drink." He breathed out a heavy sigh. "I know I intend to."

CHAPTER 11

Marta leaned back on the verdant bed of moss that carpeted the rooftop of her brownstone and watched as blades of lightning tore jagged rifts across the night sky. Tucked protectively under her left arm was a nearly depleted bottle of bourbon. It had been blessedly full when she'd arrived home that morning and had her obligatory two shots to quell her anxiety. Then she'd slept for several hours before awakening with an unquenchable thirst for more of the potent tonic.

So she'd indulged herself, her mind being unable to detach itself from thoughts of Pete's suspension as well as her own uncertain future with Storm Strike. In retrospect, her ultimatum may not have been the wisest of moves but she didn't regret it. At least not yet. Someone had to show those arrogant bastards that they couldn't trample over decent, caring people without repercussions.

The more she drank, the more she found herself able to slowly disengage from her troubles. The thoughts were still there, flitting about hazily. But they didn't matter as much. And when she'd drank enough, she finally found herself in that highly coveted, blissful, nirvanic state of not caring.

Such a state of not caring eclipsed even time itself. She didn't care about the past and how she had made a dreadful mess of her life. She didn't care about the present where injustices went unpunished and corruption flourished like a virus. She didn't even care about the future where her children might very well grow up to forsake her, prompted by their father's incessant brainwashing and their own misconceptions.

No one really understood what her life was like. If they did, they wouldn't dare judge her for seeking solace with a few drinks occasionally. And it was better than that damn lithium. At least when she sobered up, she could think clearly and function physically which was far preferable to ambling about like a perpetual zombie. In that state, she wouldn't have even been able to attend the Red Cross luncheon that her kids had invited her to.

She frowned and swiped her hand over the smooth rectangular object lying in the moss next to her that looked like a thin slice of pink slate. It registered her motion and its surface lit up, displaying a keypad and calendar. The 3rd of July. It had been today. Damn. She blinked slowly and shrugged, her level of intoxication sufficient to allow her to trivialize even that unconscionable negligence. She'd make it up to them, she thought.

Perhaps she'd buy them lunch tomorrow at one of the trendy new biome cafes that served rich, decadent foods with customized blends of bacteria to ensure that no calories would be absorbed. They were all the rage with the younger generation. Then she realized she'd maxed out her debit card when she'd bought the two bottles of bourbon yesterday. It would have to wait but she wouldn't let herself forget this time.

She took another pull of bourbon, feeling the warmth bloom in her belly, and set the bottle down between her legs. She stretched her arms behind her, resting her palms on the velvety moss blanket. Now that night had fallen, it was cool to the touch. During the day, the Oklahoma sun baked it relentlessly but somehow it managed to retain its moisture reserves. It had been bioengineered to do so, flourishing where its indigenous shade-loving cousins would wither and crumble to dust.

Some of the designer strains even glowed a soft emerald hue. She could see a handful of buildings that utilized them in the surrounding districts from her current vantage point. The eerie rectangles glimmered here and there, looking like alien landing platforms or perhaps windows looking down into the poisonous cores of nuclear reactors. But there was nothing radioactive about the effect.

The glow resulted from the insertion of a bioluminescent gene borrowed from the genetic code of fireflies. The strains were expensive and were mainly reserved for the posh buildings where the higher classes lived. Frequently the roofs were converted into outdoor havens where the well-to-do tenants could treat themselves to moss-lit cookouts and games of croquet.

A decade ago there had been healthy government incentives to develop such hardy CO_2-hungry designer strains and employ them in new construction. It was seen as an opportune means to help fight the runaway greenhouse effect. Owners of older buildings, wanting to cash in on the incentives, had retrofitted their roofs to accommodate the new green standard. Tar that had provided waterproofing was stripped away down to the bare wood planking. Then a thin rubber membrane was laid down, followed by a few centimeters of soil-like growing medium into which the moss was planted.

More times than not, the owners never bothered to consult with a structural engineer about the added weight. The overloaded roof would frequently fail, perhaps after a heavy snowstorm or one of the summer deluges that had become so prevalent. Innocent people had paid for such ignorance with their lives. In the aftermath of such disasters, the incentives had dried up and the practice had fallen out of favor. But its legacy remained as few would cough up the funds needed to revert their roofs to a more conventional design or at least reinforce those deemed most vulnerable to collapse.

Marta had her suspicions about the very building beneath her and was relieved that the top floor had been relegated to storage which would limit any damage to possessions rather than people if a section of the roof did give way. She glanced to a spot on her left where the moss had sunk several centimeters. Small fissures radiated out from a central depression. She'd nearly stepped into the crater the first time she'd come up. From the moment her foot had touched down, she'd heard the crack of splintering wood and felt an unnerving sponginess before she'd retreated.

Just to get to the corner of the building where she was now sitting and avoid the potential pitfall, she had to climb up on a narrow ridge of cement skirting the base of a derelict air conditioning unit that they'd never bothered to remove. She would sidestep along the ledge and hop down into a secluded little corner where she could watch the world go by.

No one ever came up here. The access door was chained and padlocked from the stairwell side but she had pushed it open just wide enough that her slim frame could slip through. So she'd claimed this spot as hers. Behind her, a sizable wooden crate held the remnants from her last few visits. And once she'd drained the last few swallows of bourbon, she'd be adding one more bottle to her growing collection.

The flashes of lightning out on the horizon formed a constant barrage now and she could hear the distant rumble of thunder. She could tell from experience that this front would be passing Oklahoma City by. But she knew that there were stormcruisers out there right now. Twice that she could recall, on previous nights, she had even seen the flare of an explosion blossoming in the distance and knew that a battle had been joined.

There were seeder planes out there as well. She could see three of them; the faint red and green flicker and intense white strobe of their navigational lights. They circled the raging storm, flying where the winds were still manageable. Gradually they would drop their payload of calcium chloride crystals to coax the storm to shed its moisture and deplete its energy reserves. It was a proven tactic to mitigate the intensity of wind and hail and to help prevent the spawning of twisters. But oftentimes the storm just didn't cooperate, preferring to vent its fury in a more destructive manner.

Her phone chirped. She glanced down to see a thumbnail image of Kinney glowing on its surface. She briefly debated if she should answer it. It was quite obvious to her that she was rather significantly impaired. But as long as she concentrated on carefully enunciating her words she reasoned that he would be none the wiser. Why it was even important that she sound sober to him she didn't know. It was her day off after all.

She picked up the phone, fumbled it, then brought it to her ear. "Hello, stranger," she said with only a mild slur.

"Marta, I'm glad you answered," Kinney began, as if he'd sensed her uncertainty.

"What's up?"

A moment of silence, then "Pete sends his compliments."

Marta frowned. "What?"

"Your little show of defiance apparently worked. He and his team are back on active status."

Marta's mouth dropped open. "I'll be damned."

"You very well could have been. But for what it's worth, Marta, if I'd known what was happening, I would have backed your play one hundred percent."

Marta smiled. "I know that, Kinney. Sometimes you just have to stand alone." She gritted her teeth when she realized just how corny that line had actually sounded.

"I just thought you should know," Kinney said.

"Thank you for that," Marta replied.

An awkward silence ensued. There was something Marta wanted to ask Kinney but even with the copious quantity of liquid courage that was surging through her bloodstream she was still having difficulty bringing herself to ask.

"Have a good night, Marta."

With her opportunity quickly evaporating, she summoned the requisite courage and yelled "Wait!" into the phone.

No reply. She hadn't heard a click to indicate he'd terminated the connection but she knew that he must have done so before hearing her plea. He wasn't the type to hesitate. So she decided to just blurt it out and let her words float across the airwaves even though no one was listening.

"I thought maybe we could get to know each other a little better and I was wondering if you would you like to go with me to a little Independence Day celebration at Grayson Flats tomorrow night?"

There, she'd said it. More silence. But it had felt good and no harm done.

"When?" she finally heard Kinney ask. Expecting only silence, the sound of his voice startled her. But, at the same time, never had a single word sent such an electric thrill through her entire body.

She quickly realized she hadn't actually thought far enough in advance to plan out a set time. "Ah, seven?"

"I'll be there."

This time she heard the click. She dropped the phone next to her, tilted her head back and stared up into the vast sky where she suddenly saw limitless possibilities. Sometimes she had to marvel at how quickly her emotions could flip-flop with all the subtlety of a planetary pole shift. What was down suddenly became up.

Usually the process was much slower. But there were certain triggers that could flip her mood like a light switch. To feel such a sudden surge of elation almost made it worth being bipolar. But what went up also came back down. And it was those inevitable descents that truly terrified her.

But if things ever became too much for her to contend with, there were always other options. She leaned to her right and peered over the building's edge. It wouldn't be the first time she'd entertained such notions. And she doubted it would be the last.

RANDY R. HENKE

CHAPTER 12

On most summer evenings, Grayson Flats gently settled into a sleepy cadence, its bone weary residents eager to dismiss another day of endless toil. But not on this evening. It was Independence Day and, despite their hardships, they were gearing up for a celebration.

Marta's car rolled to a stop next to a small grove of cherry and persimmon trees at the far north end of the makeshift town. She got out, smoothed her red silk blouse and adjusted her blue stretch jeans. On her feet, white leather cowgirl boots completed her patriotic color scheme. She realized she might draw a bit of attention, not just from the vibrant, contrasting colors but from the tight cut of her jeans and the three buttons that she left open at the top of her blouse. But that was fine with her. She was feeling more brazen than she had in weeks.

She walked to the front of her car and leaned against the hood. A freshly mown glade, alive with activity, spread out just beyond a thick veil of branches. Here and there, flickering kerosene lanterns hung from iron rods bent into the shape of shepherd's hooks. Their glow cast an orange hue that was supplemented by the pale blue light of a crescent moon hanging low in the sky.

Families were spread out across the meadow. Some huddled around picnic tables, some sprawled out on blankets and some stood in small clusters, laughing and talking boisterously. Giggling children darted about, tumbling and roughhousing.

She could see two fires blazing, a whole pig roasting over each of them. Every so often, a favorable breeze offered her a tantalizing hint of the rich, smoky aroma. That same breeze brought rousing notes of the Star Spangled Banner from a trio of fiddlers.

The sullen, defeated looks she'd observed on her first visit were gone, replaced with a vibrancy that defied their meager status as farm laborers. She found herself envying them. These were people who were trapped in an existence where they lived by the sweat of their brow, barely making ends meet. A good day for them was any day with food on the table. But it was obvious that they had one thing in abundance that

Marta found fleeting. Hope.

"Whatcha doin', lady?" she heard a small voice ask.

She turned to see a young boy with dirty blonde hair clad in sun bleached bib overalls. Beside him stood a raven-haired girl in a tank top and work trousers with her pant legs rolled up to her knees. In their hands, sparklers twirled through the damp evening air.

Marta smiled down at them. "Waiting for a friend."

The two children just stood there, peering up at her, their sparklers fizzing and spitting.

"Is Brock around?" Marta finally asked.

"Sure he is," the boy said.

"Could you tell him that Marta Astin took him up on his invitation?"

"Okay," he replied and they both took off skipping through the grove in the direction of the festivities.

Behind her, she heard the whine of an approaching vehicle's turbine. She turned to see a black Jeep Rhino coast to a stop beside her car. The door swung open and a pair of military style boots emerged. Next, came a set of sturdy legs in faded jeans. Then Kinney's head leaned out and he stood. A denim jacket draped loosely over a black t-shirt completed his civilian attire.

Kinney walked up beside her, hands on his hips, and eyed the gathering. The pop and crackle of small scale fireworks drifted on the air.

"Sounds like the party has already started," Kinney commented dryly.

Marta looked at him and grinned. "Then what are we waiting for?"

They had just slipped through the trees and entered the glade when Chance bolted up to them much faster than Marta would have thought possible for a three-legged dog. He greeted Marta first who gave him a quick pat on the head. Then Chance walked over and pressed his lanky frame up against Kinney's legs.

Kinney kneeled down, rubbed the dog's scruffy back and leaned in a bit too close. Chance took the opportunity, reared up and struck with an unrelenting flurry of licks across his chin and nose.

"I don't know you," a low, gravelly voice shouted at them.

Marta looked up to see Brock Massey appear out of the shadows, heading straight for Kinney. Kinney quickly stood, slipping instinctively into a fighting stance.

"But they say dogs are exceptional judges of character. That and the fact that you're accompanying this fine, young woman leads me to believe that you must be a good man." Brock held out his hand. "Brock Massey," he said.

Kinney's muscles relaxed as his defensive instincts throttled back to their default level. He shook Brock's hand. "Kinney Keller."

"Military?" Brock asked.

"How'd you know?" Kinney replied.

"The imposing 'don't mess with me' way that you carry yourself for one thing. Your solid handshake for another. But the dead giveaway was how you were sizing me up and fixin' to break me in half if I kept on coming."

"Old habits," Kinney said, shrugging his broad shoulders.

"Good habits. Can't be too careful these days."

Brock turned to Marta and held out his hand. She swept past it and gave him a warm hug.

"Good to see you again, Marta."

"You too, Brock."

As they relaxed their embrace, Brock gripped her lightly by the shoulders and held her at arm's length, his eyes roaming her up and down. "You sure do know how to make a bold patriotic statement."

"Too much?" she asked abashedly.

"Not a bit. It suits you. And it's Independence Day. A day for celebrating our God-given freedoms. To be whoever we want, say what we want and dress however we want."

His words didn't offer her much reassurance and neither did the amused expression that Kinney gave her when she glanced his way.

Brock widened an eye, his face suddenly stern. "Now, no disrespect intended, but I would strongly suggest that you not mention your association with Storm Strike for obvious reasons."

Kinney straightened to his full height. "I'm not ashamed of who I am or what I do. We save lives," he said defiantly.

"And you do it by risking your own," Brock offered in appeasement. "There's no reason for you to feel ashamed of that. But I think it's safe to say that your motives are perhaps a bit more benevolent than those of your superiors."

Kinney appeared ready to argue the point further when Marta shot him a warning glare. Then she smiled kindly at Brock and nodded. "We understand."

Brock motioned them on. "Shall we? I hope you brought your appetites."

They followed him into the clearing where the music grew louder, the smells more fragrant, and the atmosphere more jubilant. Brock led them through the crowd, his movements surprisingly spry for his apparent age. Revelers paid them passing glances that quickly turned to cordial smiles and friendly greetings once they realized who was leading the strangers through their midst.

An old woman in a plain gray dress waylaid Brock. She turned a suspicious eye on Marta and Kinney. Marta's heart skipped a beat when she recognized her as the same woman who had nearly doused her with a pail of water on her first official visit to Grayson Flats. She waited for the outburst that she knew would be coming.

"Who are the new faces, Brock?" she asked warily.

"A couple of old, dear friends. Neighbors of mine from when I lived near Broken Arrow. A lifetime ago," he said convincingly in what could only have been a premeditated response.

The old woman's eyes brightened and a smile rerouted the roadmap of wrinkles on her face. She grabbed Marta's hand and gave it a gentle squeeze.

"Any friend of Brock's is a friend of mine. Welcome…?" she said, her head tilting and her voice trailing off questioningly.

"Marta. And this is Kinney," Marta replied with a lingering sense of unease, even though it was clear that the woman had not recognized her. Apparently, she'd never bothered to look further than Marta's Storm Strike badge and what it symbolized to her during their first unpleasant encounter.

"I'm Betsy. Be sure to try the cobbler. Made it myself," she stated proudly.

Marta nodded and smiled back, making a mental note to avoid the cobbler, and eagerly played catch up with Brock who was on the move again. They passed by a young mother sitting in a rocking chair, tenderly holding her infant's hands and tapping them together to the spirited notes of the Battle Hymn of the Republic.

A small boy and girl passed in front of them, trailing behind their parents. The girl's head slowly turned toward them. It was Trina. This time she wore a dress in place of the tattered rags and her blonde hair and face shined with not a hint of grime or smudges. Marta was quite sure it was her but all doubt was erased when the girl lifted her hand and snapped off a resolute salute that Marta quickly returned.

Near a row of benches carved from rough hewn logs Brock turned to face them. "You two make yourselves to home. I've got some things to attend to. I'll be around a bit later," Brock said as he turned to go.

Kinney and Marta watched Brock depart, heading toward one of the cooking fires. They made their way over to one of the benches and sat down. Marta's attention was quickly drawn to a table with a pair of tapped wooden kegs that people were serving themselves from.

"Be right back," she said and took off in that direction. Kinney sat there, surveying his surroundings, committing to memory as many details as possible just as his military training had taught him to do in any given situation, even one as seemingly innocuous as this one.

When Marta came back she was carrying a pair of drinks in tin cups. She held one out to him.

"Margarita?"

Kinney held up his palm. "Not for me."

Marta stared at him disappointedly. "If it makes you feel any better, it's a virgin."

Kinney thought it over and finally accepted the drink. "Never had a virgin before," he said unwittingly.

Marta smiled slyly. "Don't get your hopes up, soldier."

Kinney gave her a tight, strained smile and she realized how inappropriate her comment had been. She took a long quaff from her cup, feeling a rush of heat in both her stomach and her face.

Kinney sniffed his drink, his nose wrinkling. He took a taste, looked surprised and smacked his lips. "Not bad."

Marta sat down beside him, making sure their hips touched as a subtle teasing gesture. Kinney shifted uncomfortably and opened a tiny gap between them.

Marta sighed. In her experience there were probably only a handful of guys in the entire world who didn't respond to the direct approach. But it was just her luck that Kinney was going to prove to be one of them.

Over the next hour, they made small talk, then had a drink. They listened to the fiddlers who'd been joined by a teenage boy strumming a banjo and had a drink. They indulged in a plate of the most succulent roast pork they'd ever had and had another drink.

When Marta glanced up into the night sky and the stars were wheeling across the heavens of their own accord she knew that she should be tapering off her consumption. She glanced at Kinney who was tapping his foot to the beat of a lively rendition of *This Land is Your Land*. He had definitely loosened up a little but not nearly enough.

The song drew to a close and the musicians paused a moment to confer amongst themselves. They started playing an upbeat *When Johnny Comes Marching Home*. In response, several couples jumped to their feet and started swinging each other in circles around the center of the clearing. Legs pumped and dresses flared to the lively rhythm.

"Do you dance?" Marta asked.

"Not if I can help it," Kinney quipped.

As if he'd heard the exchange, a young man with long, wavy auburn hair and a farmer's stout build sidled up to the bench and bowed low to Marta.

"Care to dance, little lady?" he asked.

Marta gave Kinney a sideways smirk and allowed herself to be led into the fray. Despite her dizziness and slightly impaired balance she managed to keep up with her partner and draw a few looks for her exaggerated gyrations. For the entire time she was dancing she could feel Kinney's eyes on her. Once, she glanced his way and saw him raise his drink and down it in one fierce gulp.

When the song ended, she nodded to the young man and rejoined Kinney, slipping up beside him and pressing herself into his sturdy side. This time, at least, he didn't pull away. But he still seemed distracted and wary. She knew exactly what he was doing. His eyes constantly scanned the area. Any quick movements drew his attention. He was scrutinizing potential aggressors, looking for threatening gestures, searching for weaknesses that could be exploited if violence ensued.

It was the military mindset at work, ingrained to the point of becoming second nature. Vigilance bordering on paranoia. Intense distrust of unfamiliar people and places. It gave soldiers the edge in hostile territory. And it crippled them emotionally when they returned home. Kinney was a good man. She believed that. But she also knew he would never make a good husband, not that she was in that market anyway. Perhaps not even a good lover. People who couldn't let their guard down tended to be dispassionate and awkward when it came to intimacy.

In the midst of her reflections, Marta's cup slipped from her grasp and tumbled to the ground. She started reaching for it but Kinney quickly bent and retrieved it for her. As he did so, his jacket fell open and she spied the massive pistol that was strapped to his side. Kinney quickly realized what had happened and pulled his jacket back into position as he handed Marta the cup.

"Thank you," Marta said. She stared at him a moment longer. He was doing another quick sweep of his surroundings as if concerned that someone else might have noticed his momentary disclosure that he was armed.

Marta frowned at him. "Can I ask you why you're so on edge? And why you're carrying that artillery piece?"

Kinney looked down at his jacket, making sure his firearm was still concealed. Then he stared at her but said nothing.

"Well?" Marta said, impatience and aggravation simmering, fueled by both the alcohol and her borderline manic frame of mind.

"Need to know," Kinney replied in a cool monotone, an arrogant smirk on his face that Marta had to fight not to remove with a well-deserved slap.

Marta's eyes flashed with enough intensity that Kinney visibly recoiled. "Really? Really? Well there's something you *need to know*, too, then. I thought you were different from all the other square-jawed dim-witted Neanderthal lackeys roaming the halls at headquarters. But you're just like them. All you know how to do is follow orders and be an asshole."

Marta stood, glaring down at him. Her tirade had already drawn considerable attention. "Well, fuck your orders. And you can take your need to know bullshit and...."

Kinney stood up next to her and gently squeezed her arm. He glanced around furtively. "Let's take a walk," he said and released her.

She continued to stare at him, attempting to hold her raging emotions in check.

"Please," he added. Then he turned north and began following a well worn rock-strewn path up a long, rolling hill. Marta hesitated, still unsure if she should comply. Finally, her curiosity overrode her anger and she rushed to catch up.

"So are you going to answer me or did you just want to come up here so I can continue my outburst without causing a scene?"

Kinney cleared his throat but kept his eyes on the trail. "Let's just say that intelligence has recently come to light that there are certain factions looking to acquire thermobaric warheads."

Marta made a concerted effort to hide her shock at how effortlessly Kinney had blurted that statement out. Perhaps he was a bit more sloshed than he appeared. "From us? From Storm Strike?" Marta asked, falling behind a few more steps.

Kinney scaled a particularly steep section of the trail without even slowing, his voice never wavering as he continued. "Potentially. Stormcruisers are far from being soft targets but they do operate in areas where backup is not readily available thus making them vulnerable. All munitions officers have been made aware of the situation and security has been appropriately heightened around Storm Strike Alpha."

Marta struggled in vain to keep up with Kinney's unrelenting pace up the hillside. The moon had vanished behind a dark cloud, abolishing most of the ambient light. Despite the fact that she could barely see her own feet, Kinney seemed as surefooted as a mountain goat while she tripped over nearly every obstacle in their path. "I think we're out of earshot now.

Feel free to stop at any time."

Kinney reached the craggy summit and turned back toward Marta. When she caught up, she was perturbed to see that Kinney wasn't even breathing hard while she was literally panting for air. "So when were the crews going to be informed of this?" she managed to say between gasps.

"They weren't. We were told to withhold that information on the grounds that it would only serve to distract them from their duties. That could endanger lives and..."

Marta finished his sentence. "And endanger their precious equipment. Right?"

Kinney nodded.

Marta's breathing was beginning to settle into a manageable rhythm. "And just who are these factions?"

"Terrorists. Eco-terrorists to be exact," Kinney said.

Marta snickered. "What are they going to do? Go blow up a beaver dam?"

Kinney crossed his arms and puffed out his chest defiantly but continued to answer her queries. "The accords."

Marta looked at him quizzically.

Kinney tilted his head, one eyebrow raised. "The environmental accords? Being held in New York next month?"

Marta thought for a moment, unable to find any logic to that. "Why would terrorists concerned about the environment want to bomb the best hope we have of trying to save it?"

Kinney glanced down at the clearing, making sure no one had followed them. "It's more complicated than that. There are certain nations that still refuse to acknowledge the damage that their own industries are doing to the climate, China being at the top of that list. They only care about their own economic growth despite the fact that over twenty million of their own people have already been displaced from coastal communities by the rising sea level. The terrorists are going to target the delegates from those countries."

Marta frowned. "But didn't I read somewhere that all of the nations had agreed to sign some sort of treaty?"

Kinney snorted derisively. "The agreement that's on the table is a farce and the terrorists know it. It proposes a gradual reduction in CO_2 emissions over the next twenty years. Nothing more than a token gesture. No real teeth to it. No provisions for international monitoring. No increases in carbon sequestering. Not even any significant monetary penalties for failing to meet the requirements of the agreement."

Marta shook her head. "So their answer is to kill a few hundred people and make the world a better place."

Kinney stared out into the darkness beyond the hill. "Yep. Whether the bloodshed be in the name of God or nature, it's all the same in the end."

As they both stood there, silently contemplating the warped logic of such rampant fanatics, the curtain of clouds drifted past the moon and the landscape was once more bathed in a soft pale glow. Kinney saw it first, to the north. He stared at it, a look of awe etched on his face. Marta noticed Kinney's reaction and followed his gaze, her eyes widening.

"My God," she murmured.

Just beyond the hill that they stood on, tucked into a shallow valley, the sprawling wreckage of a town stretched out before them. They'd seen such wide-scale destruction a hundred times but always in the immediate aftermath of a disaster with first responders swarming the area, searching for survivors and clearing debris. This was something different.

It was a ghost town, resting still and silent. Stumps of wood-frame buildings, left to rot, lined the paved streets. A jumble of crumbling ivy-choked brick walls conspired to form fragmentary mazes. In a small open space that could have been the town square, a toppled water tower sat rusting, weeping red tears onto a pale cobblestone terrace. And everywhere, the ground was cluttered with odds and ends. Dented and battered appliances, broken furniture, tattered bits of clothing; the ravaged and weathered remnants of shattered lives.

For Marta, the most surreal aspect of the scene was the disquieting state of abandonment. It was as if the residents had simply walked away. She reckoned they were bearing witness to at least several years' worth of decay. Saplings had already sprouted up through gaps in the sidewalks. Cracks thick with weeds spiderwebbed the crumbling pavement. Nature was slowly reclaiming her territory. With one glaring exception.

Just west of the rubble sat a plot of well-tended lawn hedged by a short stone wall and sown with tidy rows of crosses and tombstones. Vibrant patches of wildflowers adorned the graves and fresh bouquets graced many a headstone.

Marta glanced southward toward Grayson Flats, then back to the north. Two towns. One transient and haphazard, one built for the ages yet destined for calamity. One alive, one dead; separated by nothing more imposing than a mound of dirt.

Something warm and furry brushed up against Marta's hand. She looked down to find Chance standing beside her. Surmising that Brock must be nearby, she turned and saw him trudging up the hill behind them. When he finally reached the summit, he took a moment to catch his breath, staring reverently down at the cemetery.

"This hill never used to be at the north end of town. Eight years ago, it stood at the south end." He pointed to the ruin. "And that, over there, was Grayson Flats. A great many of the folks who lived there..." His finger shifted to point toward the cemetery. "Are now buried there."

Brock smiled a humorless smile. "Damnable thing was, it wasn't even a twister. Just a mean bitch of a storm with a straight-line wind that basically disassembled the entire town. I believe you folks call it a microburst. We just called it fate."

"You were there?" Kinney asked.

Brock nodded slowly. "I was there that day. Buried my wife and son the day after."

"I'm sorry," Marta said.

Brock shook his head. "Nothing to be sorry for. Except maybe for being damn fool enough to conjure building that burg in the first place."

Marta and Kinney stared silently at Brock, their attention piqued. Brock lowered his head for a moment. When he finally looked up, his eyes had taken on a dreamy quality as his awareness shifted to that shadowy plane where deep memories reside.

"I was one of the few farmers who saw the crash coming and got out in time. Sold my land and my whole operation before the prices bottomed out. When they did, me and a few others decided to build a town, a haven where all of the farmers who'd lost everything could call home. We had it all planned out. A self-sufficient community. Off the grid. We'd eat what we grew. We had storm shelters, too. Most of us never made it to 'em."

Brock shifted his feet and blinked as if coming out of a trance.

"After the storm, we talked about rebuilding. But we didn't have the resources or the ambition. We left our shattered utopia to the elements. Kind of an offering to nature, you might say. Then we took up the nomadic existence that had sprung up all around us. Carried with us little more than the clothes on our backs. Bought just the essentials. Moved where the work was."

He cast one last weary look down upon the cemetery and then his gaze returned to his guests. "We make it back this way from time to time. Whenever C&C needs the help. Still call it Grayson Flats. The hill here provides just enough distance to dull the pain and dim the memories. But we do remember. And we pay our respects."

Marta realized that anything she might say would be just a feeble attempt at consolation so she said nothing and just nodded solemnly. In the next instant, the pain on Brock's face evaporated and he conjured a shallow smile. "Enough talk," he said.

Brock threw his arms around Marta and Kinney and swung them around to face the celebration below. "We're not here to dwell on the past tonight. Fireworks are about to start. C&C usually puts on a pretty good show for their annual shindig up at the farm. They can afford to. We just happen to have front row seats." He started leading them down the hillside.

Chance lingered behind, sniffing the air. His head turned toward a dilapidated old farm shed at the base of the hill. The fur on his back stiffened and a low threatening growl seeped from his throat.

Brock glanced back. "Come on, Chance. Nothing down there but ghosts and memories."

With one last glance at the shed, Chance turned and followed his master down the hill.

Seated on their bench once more, Marta's head rested on Kinney's shoulder. They watched intently as shell after shell of pyrotechnic wonder was launched from the C&C farm complex, just visible in the distance. The rockets burst and bloomed above them, painting the heavens in psychedelic splendor and casting shifting patterns of tinted light across their faces.

A dark-skinned man holding a pewter pitcher walked up beside them. "Last call for margaritas."

Marta eagerly held out her cup and he refilled it.

Kinney pointed to his cup. "Any virgins left?"

The man stared at him in obvious confusion.

"The drink? I've been drinking virgins," Kinney clarified with just the hint of a slur in his voice.

The man shook his head, looking bewildered. "Don't know where you got your drink, man, but we ain't got no virgin margaritas. This here is homebrewed tequila and lime juice. Smooth as molasses and kicks like a mule."

"Then no thanks," Kinney said, giving Marta a nasty look.

"Suit yourself," the man said and stepped away.

"Trying to get me drunk?" Kinney asked, still glaring at Marta.

Marta shrugged innocently.

Just then, the finale started. They both tilted their heads back as several volleys shot upward at once, splashing the open sky with a kaleidoscope of shimmering colors accompanied by the crackle and sizzle of exploding pyrotechnics. It was a dazzling spectacle worthy of a major theme park.

As soon as the show had ended, the celebration broke up quickly. Kinney walked Marta back to her vehicle. Once there, Marta spun toward him, looking up into his face expectantly. Kinney froze, as if unsure what his next move should be.

"So was this a date? Or just two friends getting together?" Kinney asked.

Marta furrowed her brow. "And this matters because...?"

Kinney rubbed his neck, looking flustered. "If it's a date, then I'm obligated to kiss you."

Marta's eyes went wide. "Obligated?"

Kinney winced. "Poor choice of words. What I meant was that on a date it's customary to kiss before saying good night."

An amused grin crept over Marta's face. "Better. Try one more time."

Kinney pulled in a deep breath and exhaled forcefully. "May I kiss you?"

Their eyes locked for a tense moment that Marta drew out as long as she dared. "You may," she finally said.

Kinney moved in tentatively and bent down toward her. The moment their lips touched, Marta wrapped her arms around Kinney's neck and pulled him into her. Kinney tensed momentarily, then let himself be drawn in. They both lost themselves in the sudden passion. When Kinney finally eased away, they were both breathing hard and fast.

He ran his hand through his hair and shook his head as if to clear it. Then he took a single step back. "I think we've both had too much to drink tonight to make rational decisions."

Marta countered his move by stepping toward him. She ran a finger down his arm. "What's wrong with making a few irrational ones from time to time?"

Marta knew that Kinney was a strong willed man but his resolve was weakening. She was sure of it. Then, just as she thought he was about to take her into his arms again, he suddenly turned away.

"Goodnight, Marta," he called out without looking back. He climbed into his truck, set it for autodrive and allowed it to usher him away. Marta stood there a moment, stunned that her attempted seduction had failed.

"That's the last time I throw myself at you, Kinney Keller. Who needs you anyway?!?" she screamed into the sudden stillness of the night. Then she sunk into her own car. She was about to set the autodrive to take her home but decided she wasn't quite ready to call it a night yet. From the row of favorite destinations flashing on her dash she tapped the one labeled "Mandi B's"'. The car started moving and took her back down the gravel road toward her next stop.

Her taillights were still visible when a sleek black Toyota Lancer Z sports coupe, illegally rigged for silent running, rolled quietly out of the nearby farm shed just beyond the grove of trees. With its headlights dark, it accelerated rapidly and followed in Marta's wake.

CHAPTER 13

Perched on a bar stool, Marta stared down at a row of three square buttons that she saw recessed into the intricately etched patina of the copper countertop before her. She narrowed her eyes into a tight squint and for a moment the three buttons coalesced into a single one. But her concentration quickly foundered and they diverged into a blurry trio once more. Relying on past experience, she pressed the middle one. A chime sounded.

Marta looked up, her focus improving significantly as she shifted her vision to more distant objects. The first object she saw was the buxom form of Mandi B gliding toward her from behind the bar, responding to her summons.

The bartender was sliding along a single tubular rail suspended at waist height, low enough that most seated patrons wouldn't see it. But it was the perfect height to provide the illusion that Mandi B was standing.

The bartender lurched to a stop before Marta, her long blonde hair swaying and her ample bosom bouncing from the sudden stop. A smile that appeared almost genuinely human crept across her smooth unblemished complexion.

"What can I get you?" Mandi B. asked in a sultry feminine voice.

Marta didn't see the playful wink that Mandi B gave her, having averted her eyes from the bartender's strikingly beautiful but uncanny face. Her gaze dropped to the bartender's skin-tight beige t-shirt and the words printed across her hilly chest, its bold capital letters highlighting the acronym for Mandi B. It read: *Mechanized ANDroid Interactive Bartender*.

Marta was careful not to lower her gaze any further, always feeling an awkward and lewd sense of shame whenever she caught a glimpse of Mandi B's nether regions which protruded beneath the t-shirt and consisted of a pair of belt-driven rollers which the bartender used to propel herself along the steel rail.

"Gin and tonic, please," Marta uttered in a low tone.

The bartender's head tilted slightly to the side. Marta could feel

Mandi B studying her and knew instantly that she had not spoken loudly enough. Having not heard Marta's request through her microphoned ears, she was running algorithms through her processors, trying to derive the intended order by analyzing the movement of Marta's lips that the cameras behind the vivid blue eyes had recorded.

"I'm sorry. I didn't understand you," Mandi B finally said.

Marta smiled, her mind fabricating a deeper meaning to the words. "That's okay. No one does."

"I'm sorry. I didn't understand you," Mandi B repeated.

Marta forced herself to look the bartender in the face. "Gin and tonic," she said loudly, enunciating her words as carefully as her current state of inebriation allowed.

Mandi B instantly went to work. Her torso swiveled at its base and a pair of impeccably manicured hands retrieved a tumbler from a shelf and squeezed a lime wedge into it. Then Mandi B expertly poured in the gin and tonic and added two spheres of ice, dropping each in with a flamboyant flick of her mechanized wrist.

Marta glanced down at her phone resting on the bar as its surface lit up, showing a summary of recent purchases, an inordinate number of which came from Mandi B's. Her bank account balance was displayed in large bold numerals at the bottom of the screen. As she watched, the number decreased by twenty.

"Twenty dollars have been deducted from your account," Mandi B informed Marta as she set the drink down in front of her. "Enjoy," she added affably before gliding off to serve another customer.

Marta took a sip, her eyes traveling around the oval bar. There were only a handful of customers and the noise level was remarkably low. That was how Marta liked it. Mandi B's attracted its share of curious spectators and techno geeks who marveled at the latest in robotic technology but they seldom returned once the novelty wore off. Apparently, most people preferred a bartender with whom they could enjoy a more lively repartee.

Marta came here when it was too late to buy liquor at the vending machines or when her emotions were soaring in one of her manic phases. Tonight, it was both of the above. She happened to enjoy the impersonal nature of the bartender and the lack of the usual obligatory small talk. Her only interactions here were typically with the guys who occasionally hit on her. Most of the time, she took great pleasure in shooting them down. She'd never had any time for desperate horny drunken slobs looking for a quick score. But she had made her share of rash and regrettable decisions from time to time.

She'd already been hit on twice since she'd arrived half an hour ago. One troll had been old enough to be her father. The other had been handsome enough but even more drunk than Marta and an obvious lecher who couldn't stop staring at the bartender's fake boobs that jiggled realistically with every precision movement of her mechanized torso. His polished Rolex watch and the well-tailored cut of his suit told her that there was probably money there. Lesser women would have seen him as an exploitable resource. It wasn't her style.

Marta knew she was an attractive woman but she'd never stooped to using her comeliness as a crutch to get what she wanted. That type of behavior was reserved for bimbos and hookers. But she saw nothing wrong with being flirtatious around men she was genuinely interested in, even when the outcome didn't immediately pan out.

She hadn't given up hope on Kinney yet. She knew he had feelings for her. But his pride, stoicism and sordid elements from his own past kept getting in the way. Despite that, he had always been there for her. When she was feeling vulnerable, he offered security. When she was distraught, he consoled her. She'd come to associate his presence with stability and comfort. In many respects, she thought of him more as an older brother than a prospective lover and anything more than friendship seemed to remain just out of her reach.

As her raging emotions aroused raging desires, she found her thoughts wandering to Chaz with his carefree spirit and the boyish charm that would make any woman swoon. She wasn't exactly sure how deeply his feelings for her ran. She reasoned they were more akin to a school boy crush than anything serious. But what she found most tantalizing was thinking of herself as the proverbial schoolgirl. She felt young and alive when she was with Chaz.

Marta stared down at her phone. Then she snatched it up, selected Chaz from her list of contacts and typed two words into the text window: "You there?" Her finger hesitated over the send button. Then she tapped it and set the phone back down.

Marta took another sip of her drink. As she had the glass raised to her lips, someone bumped into her from behind. Gin and tonic spilled down the front of her blouse. Marta rolled her eyes and waited for the lame excuse that would surely follow.

"My bad," she heard an oddly tinny but distinctly womanly voice say as she dabbed at her blouse with a napkin. "Excuse my clumsy nature." Then the woman's face appeared next to hers. Her features were angular and she wore glasses with thick, black frames. But what Marta found most disconcerting was the fact that she towered over the other patrons and had the frame of a linebacker bulging out from beneath her black cocktail dress. The woman frowned, then her eyes widened in recognition.

"Oh my gosh!" the woman gushed, holding a hand to her chest.

"Marta? Marta Astin?" the woman continued.

Marta turned and studied the mountain of womanhood standing before her but said nothing.

"You don't remember me, do you? Toni Mitchells?"

Marta shook her head. "Yeah, no."

"Toni Mitchells from NYU? Only now it's Toni with an I. It used to be with a y."

Marta blinked repeatedly, suddenly recalling a Tony Mitchells from her meteorology classes in college. A socially inept fellow student who had played football but, unlike most jocks, had proven himself to be a prodigy in his studies.

"Toni, yeah. I do remember you. I'm so sorry I didn't..." Marta hesitated, swallowing hard, "recognize you."

Toni plopped down on the stool next to Marta and waved her hand in the air dismissively. "Perish the thought, honey. Happens all the time."

Marta continued to stare, still a bit flustered by this intrusion into her own little world. "Wow. So what brings you to Oklahoma City?"

Toni looked around cautiously. In a hushed tone she said, "My vocal chords didn't respond well to the hormone injections. I didn't want to look like a Victoria and sound like a Vic. So I had a voice chip implanted. Now it's on the fritz. Keeps switching octaves on me. And at the most inopportune times. Bad for my love life."

Marta realized her mouth was gaping and shut it, then took a long pull from her drink.

"My surgeon hails from here in Oklahoma City. Best in the business. So I'm back in town for a tune-up, so to speak," Toni said. Then she grinned. "Pun intended," she added and broke into a fit of laughter, its pitch rising and falling in short bursts that sent shivers down Marta's spine.

"There it goes again, damnable thing," Toni said, rubbing her throat before continuing. "Anyhow, his name is Dr. Pelletier. Best in the business. I swear, he could make tits grow on an oak tree."

Marta glanced down at Toni's formidable chest. The thought crossed her mind that that was exactly what the doctor had made happen.

Toni caught Marta's glance and proudly thrust her breasts out, plumping them with her huge hands. "You don't think they're a bit much, do you? Hard to make them proportional to your stature when you go nearly two meters."

Marta, speechless, just nodded her head.

Much to Marta's chagrin, Toni made herself even comfortable. She wriggled her large butt, imprinting it deeply into the cushioned stool, and slapped both palms down on the countertop as if claiming her spot. Then her head twisted toward the door as two new patrons walked in. "Now there's something you don't see every day," Toni said, frowning.

Marta followed her gaze toward the door. The new arrivals were young men with bony, chiseled features and light brown skin. Both had long, flowing black hair, a single feather dangling from a lock at the side of their head. Each had a necklace of white and black beads around their sinewy necks. And both wore matching tan leather jackets adorned with tassels front and back and along the sleeves.

Their gazes seemed immediately drawn to Marta but they quickly looked away and took up seats at the far end of the bar. It was almost like seeing a pair of American Indian warriors step out of the distant past. Marta assumed they were more than likely part of some Native American convention or possibly even extras in a film being shot locally. But she did find it strange they would be wearing leather jackets when it was still nearly ninety degrees outside.

Toni leaned close. "Have you noticed how this bar attracts some of the oddest characters?" she whispered to Marta.

Marta turned to stare at her, completely taken aback by her comment. She shook her head slowly. "No, I hadn't."

Marta took a long, much-needed drink while Toni again repositioned herself. This time, she leaned forward, her elbow resting on the bar and her chin resting on her hand. She gazed intently at Marta. "Enough about me. What's new with Marta? Last I heard you were teaching back at NYU?"

Marta finished off her drink and eagerly stabbed the call button. "I was. Now I work at Storm Strike."

Toni's eyes narrowed. "A worthy cause, to be sure. But, and far be it from me to judge, it just seems like a waste of a good meteorologist's talents."

Marta ordered another gin and tonic from Mandi B, then turned to glare at Toni. "Meaning?" she said defensively.

Toni sighed. "It's just that Storm Strike is fighting the symptoms and not the disease." She made a thick fist and shook it. "That's where we need to rally our forces."

Marta gave her newly delivered drink a stir. "I agree. But that's easier said than done."

"No argument there. But it can be done and my company is on the vanguard of that effort."

Marta started to take a drink and set it back down. She found herself suddenly intrigued. "Your company?" she asked.

"Mitchell Engineering. I've been a busy girl, Marta. Well, initially, a busy boy. As I am sure you are aware, the business sector will always be biased against the superior sex. So I decided to live a lie until I entrenched myself in the insular corporate hierarchy and could do what I damn well pleased."

Marta's initial opinion of Toni as eccentric and annoying still applied, but she also found a seed of respect beginning to grow.

"So what exactly does Mitchell Engineering do?"

"We're a geoengineering firm. We design CO_2 scrubbers and bioreactors but our primary impetus is as a think tank for innovative solutions to our current climatological predicament."

Marta nodded. "What proposals are on the drawing board?"

"We have several promising candidates. The one that really shines has been around for awhile but recent advances in materials fabrication has made it both economically and technologically feasible."

Toni stopped and bit her lip as if pausing for dramatic effect.

"And that is?" Marta prompted.

"We use the oceans as a storage depot for all of that excess CO_2 floating around in the atmosphere," Toni said and pressed her own call button despite the fact that her glass was still three quarters full of what looked like orange juice that Marta surmised must be a screwdriver.

Toni pointed to her glass. "Imagine this drink represents the oceans."

Mandi B slid to a stop before Toni. "Shot of black vodka, please."

A moment later a shot glass filled with a dusky liquid was sitting on the bar before Toni. She picked it up and, very slowly and carefully, poured half of the shot into her screwdriver where it pooled at the top, forming a thin black layer.

Toni pointed to the top layer of liquid in her glass. "This black is the surface layer chock full of biomass in the form of fish and phytoplankton along with plenty of dissolved carbon. Below that layer are the vast depths. Nutrient rich water but with very little trapped CO_2. So we give it a stir."

Toni swirled a green stir stick through the drink, dissolving the top layer.

"Now all of that biomass and trapped CO_2 is on its way down to the abyss and we have cold, nutrient rich water at the surface capable of supporting a fresh crop of biomass."

Toni poured the rest of her shot into the glass, forming another obsidian layer. "The new biomass pulls carbon from the atmosphere, removing more CO2. We stir again."

She stirred the drink again. "The cycle repeats until we've reversed the greenhouse effect and used only a fraction of the ocean's massive untapped potential to sequester CO2."

"How many pumps?" Marta asked.

"Simulations favor ten thousand," Toni said without missing a beat.

"Now that's a big construction project," Marta said.

"It is. But we could use the new juggernaut-class multi-material printers that they're using to construct the latest skyscrapers. One printer could crank out ten floating platforms a day, complete with a functioning pump assembly powered by wind or waves and a hundred and fifty meter intake/outtake pipe. Half of the pumps would pull water up. The other half would force it down."

"Sounds like you have it all figured out," Marta intoned.

Toni shook her head. "Au contraire. Much work to be done yet. More simulations, more research, more limited scale trials and a hell of a lot more proselytizing of those stubborn asses who hold the purse strings in the government."

Toni downed half of her drink in one swig, then turned back to Marta. "One thing I'm sure we can both agree on is that mother nature is a vindictive bitch and we don't stand a chance against her in a knockdown dragout fight. We need to appease her. Correct our mistakes."

Marta smiled, wondering if Toni realized just how true her statement actually was.

"Maybe it's just time for the dominant species on this planet to go away," Marta blurted out, struck by a sudden moment of defeatism.

"Honey, we're not going anywhere. We just need to take responsibility and set things right," Toni insisted. Then she touched Marta's hand.

"We could use you," Toni said, studying Marta carefully.

Marta froze, her drink suspended halfway to her mouth. She turned to look at Toni.

"You'd have to move to California but I know your qualifications and I remember your passion," Toni continued.

Marta quickly averted her gaze, focusing on her drink once more.

Toni produced a thin green phone from her pocket. "No need to make any decisions now. Think of it as a standing offer." She tapped her phone to Marta's, still resting on the copper bar. The surface of Marta's phone lit up, displaying a small thumbnail image of Toni along with a few lines of contact information. Marta stared down at it.

"If you don't mind working for a woman, that is. God knows we can be fickle," Toni said and threw back the rest of her drink. She swallowed wrong and broke out in a violent fit of coughing. Her voice chip went berserk, issuing an intermittent stream of wavering trills and whistles, coinciding with each cough.

Two men standing nearby backed up cautiously. Toni waved at them. "Don't mind me," she said in a hollow, metallic chipmunk-like voice. She stood and turned back to Marta. "Gotta run," she said, patting Marta on the shoulder and started backing toward the door. As she uttered her next sentence, her voice dropped to a growling baritone. "Don't you forget about me, you hear?"

Toni swung around and collided with a small nervous-looking man just walking in. Toni towered over him. In an apologetic gesture, she patted his chest. "Excuse me," she said but her voice came out in a guttural, demonic roar. She slapped a hand to her mouth in utter shock at the menacing sound of her own electronically distorted voice. But the damage had already been done. The terrified man let out a shrill, effeminate yelp. He launched himself toward the door, narrowly missing his target. His shoulder glanced off the doorframe and he landed in a heap on the floor.

Toni bent to help him up. The man's eyes bulged when he saw her burly outstretched arms reaching for him. He let loose with an ear-piercing scream, scrambled to his feet and bolted out the door, nearly sending two women to the pavement in the process.

Toni stood there, aghast at the spectacle she had just caused. She glanced meekly at Marta, shrugged her broad shoulders and then slinked out the door.

Marta turned back to her drink as the other patrons began talking amongst themselves in hushed tones. She smiled. "Don't worry, Toni," she said to herself. "I never black out. Which means I'm going to remember every last excruciating minute of this whole pathetic evening."

Marta was still trying to decide whether her implacable memory was a blessing or a curse when her phone chirped and vibrated and Chaz's picture appeared on its surface. Marta tapped a finger on the bar, deliberating. Then she picked it up and answered it.

A faint buzzing roused Marta from her slumber. Her entire body felt like it was floating. She forced open her heavy eyelids and blinked at the blinding light emanating from a tunnel just beyond her feet. Then the silhouette of a figure emerged from the light, drifting toward her. She wondered for a moment if she might be dead and this was an angel. The buzzing in her ears grew louder.

She blinked again and the illusion dissolved. She found herself lying in her own lumpy disheveled bed, covers askew. The light was spilling from the open doorway to her cramped little bathroom. And the figure resolved into the naked form of Chaz, grinning down at her and holding a buzzing electric razor to his stubbly face.

"Top of the mornin' to ya, princess," he said.

Marta sat up quickly and felt a stabbing jolt pierce her skull. She winced at the pain and then winced again as all of the vivid memories from the night before came rushing back to her in all of their inglorious lucidity. Reaching up, she swept her tangled hair back from her face, deciding then and there that a gaping void in her memory would have been far preferable.

RANDY R. HENKE

CHAPTER 14

A shimmering virtual keyboard glowed within the surface of Marta's console just beneath her fingertips and a virtual monitor, displaying blocks of text, plotted graphs, and radar snapshots, hovered half a meter in front of her heavy-lidded eyes. Deciding she needed a break from the partially completed shift report, she lifted her visor and stared out the cruiser's windows as a typical weekday morning unfolded around her in the town of Ada, nestled snugly in the rolling hills of southeastern Oklahoma.

Marta could tell the neighborhood they were passing through was upscale. Smartly dressed business people carrying briefcases and steaming travel mugs were vacating their tidy brick townhouses, walking across their well-manicured lawns and climbing into their late-model luxury Chinese imports, ready for their morning commute. A few hardy souls, clad in vibrantly colored running suits, jogged along the sidewalks. Their skin glistened with sweat prompted by equal measures of exertion and brutal humidity. They made Marta weary just watching them. But their day was just beginning. And, thankfully, hers was about to end. The cruiser was heading northwest toward Oklahoma City and they were little more than an hour away from their home base of Storm Strike Alpha.

Marta was surprised she'd made it through the entire night without nodding off. The twelve hour shift had proven to be an uneventful one and she hadn't slept since waking up next to Chaz early yesterday morning. After she'd convinced him to leave, she'd spent a few uncomfortable minutes explaining the casual nature of her relationship with him to her children. Then she'd spent the remainder of the day attempting to clean her apartment but accomplishing very little because of the thick melancholia that had hung over her.

It was quite apparent that the powerful wave of euphoria she'd been riding was collapsing beneath her as it inevitably always did. The tide of her emotions was ebbing as was her ability to concentrate. Both extremes of her manic-depressive swings were debilitating, each in their own unique way.

When caught in the throes of a manic phase, her mind raced at light speed. Random, sometimes aberrant, thoughts assailed her in a mad, chaotic rush that left her reeling and unable to sort through the disarray. Rational thinking eluded her. Over the years she had found ways to cope; to force herself to focus, to exercise discretion in her decisions and to examine each option from all possible angles before committing to a particular course of action.

Conversely, when she found herself slipping into the depths of depression, it felt as if her brain were mired in a viscous, suffocating sludge. Her entire thought process slowed to a crawl. The very act of making decisions seemed futile. Where was the incentive when cruel fate dictated all outcomes anyway? That was where she found herself now; her withered spirit locked in a small grey cell where just the effort of continuing to breathe seemed overwhelming. Yet she clung to a tattered shred of her awareness that told her that even this impenetrable fog of despair would eventually dissolve, if only she could hold on that long.

Marta continued staring numbly out through the armored glass as the town of Ada awakened around them. She marveled at how the residents were routinely going about their daily lives, totally oblivious to the foreboding storm clouds lurking in the western sky. But it was human nature to become desensitized to danger when confronted with it continually. Kinney had explained it to her once. It was what kept a soldier's stress levels from redlining in hostile environments. But there was a double edge to such innate survival mechanisms.

Desensitization dulled a soldier's senses, lulling them into lowering their guard. On the battleground, that cost lives. To counter it, the military trained its soldiers to maintain a high alert level during prolonged periods of stress. But civilians, untrained in such psychological tactics, allowed their defenses to wane. And on this battleground, in the midst of a war being fought on friendly soil in the heartland of America itself, such carelessness could prove just as deadly.

Chaz slowed the cruiser as they entered a school zone. A line of school buses crowded into a curved drive fronting the arched entrance to Ada Elementary. Hordes of pre-adolescent children converged on the glass double doors. One boy glanced over his shoulder, then turned and pointed in the direction of the cruiser, shouting something to his classmates. A few others turned to point and stare. Within seconds, the entire assembly was watching their passing with wide-eyed wonder.

Chaz gave the air horn two short blasts that heightened the children's excitement. Marta waved to them. In unison, a hundred tiny arms waved back. It was clear from their obvious delight at seeing the cruiser that the ire that most of their parents undeniably felt for Storm Strike had not yet been instilled in their offspring, whose fascination with powerful vehicles and the adventurous souls who crewed them still held sway over their beliefs. In their untainted minds, heroes still existed, monsters could be vanquished, and good always eclipsed evil. In time their convictions would change as harsh reality set in. But Marta's determination to protect them would not.

Marta felt a tear slide down her cheek and wiped it away, wishing she could do the same with the thought that had prompted it. Perhaps not so much a thought as a question. Why did people still feel obliged to bring such innocent little beings into such a cruel and ugly world. Was it just for the parent's own selfish gratification? Couldn't they see that they were simply perpetuating another generation to suffer the consequences of the mistakes that they and their ancestors had made? And their children would go on to make new, and potentially even more devastating mistakes of their own, the repercussions of which they would pass on to their own unwitting progeny.

She had asked herself the same question regarding her own children. But she'd felt differently when she was young, naive and in love. She had seen hope for the world and hope for a future for her children. Now there wasn't a day that went by that she didn't wonder what horrors awaited them in the years to come.

A sudden barrage of fat raindrops pelted the cruiser, then dissipated just as quickly. Marta suspected that the approaching front was moving in faster than the predictions had forecast. She contemplated checking the radar to confirm her suspicion but decided it wasn't her problem anymore. There were others who could deal with any impending outbreaks of mayhem. She leaned back in her chair and closed her eyes.

"Whiskey Romeo One, this is Storm Strike Alpha, do you copy?" the radio belched loudly. Marta opened an eye and saw Chaz glance over at her expectantly. She pointed a finger lethargically toward the console.

"Be my guest," Marta uttered lowly.

Chaz toggled his radio link on. "Whiskey Romeo One here. Nice of you to call, mom."

"I'm afraid it's not a social call, Chaz. I realize your shift is over but we're going to have to put you back on the clock. We have a situation developing," Jane replied grimly from the dispatch office at Storm Strike Alpha.

Marta rolled her eyes, rubbed a hand over her face and sat up straight. She flipped her visor back down and activated her comm link.

"This is Marta, mom. What's happening?"

"Do you have your situational map up?" Jane asked.

Marta flicked a small placeholder icon on the center console, sending it flying up a narrow glowing track and exploding into a large map on the dash where Chaz and Kinney could also view it through their own visors. The map showed a topographical view of their surroundings. A moving green dot indicated their own cruiser's position as it moved northwest out of Ada on Hwy 3W. The entire western edge of the map was engulfed by swirling hostile masses of red, green and yellow.

"We do now," Marta replied.

"Good. As you can see, we have drones at the leading edge of the storm front."

Marta noticed several small white dots near the storm's periphery.

Jane continued, "They're already reporting tornado genesis and intense electrical activity."

Marta squinted down at the map, seeing a larger dot flashing red to their southwest with a transponder id attached to it. She read the crew's call sign.

"Mom, it looks like you already have a unit in position. Tango Sierra Two. That's Beckett's crew, isn't it?"

"Affirmative, Marta," Jane confirmed.

Marta continued to stare at the blinking dot. She frowned and said, "Their transponder signature is flashing red. Are they in distress?"

A burst of static preceded Jane's voice. "Not in distress but definitely out of commission. Turbine seized up. They've dug themselves in but without power they can't move and they can't launch. They'll be sitting this one out. That's why we need..."

A ribbon of lightning unraveled across the morning sky, so bright that it lit up the interior of the cruiser. Marta shielded her eyes. Another burst of static issued from the radio. Then the audio cut out completely.

Marta shot Chaz and Kinney a worried look. "Say again, mom. Lightning is wreaking havoc with our comm reception."

A few tense seconds passed before Jane responded. "Your orders are to defend the western border of Ada. Engage any funnels that pose an immediate threat to the town."

Marta's expression hardened as she felt a small measure of resolve begin to grow inside her, nudging the oppressive gloom to the periphery of her awareness. "You can count on us, mom."

"I know we can, Marta. Take care."

"Whiskey Romeo One, out," Marta said and switched off her comm. She took a deep breath and let the air simmer in her lungs before forcing it out. She was still dispirited and bone weary but there were people who were counting on her and she wouldn't let them down. She turned to her crew. "Questions or concerns?"

Kinney shook his head. "Nothing to say. We've got a job to do."

Chaz touched his Stetson, making sure it was still tucked neatly next to his seat. Then he adjusted his helmet. "I'm good to go. I can use the O.T." He gave Kinney a cold look. "I still have some repairs to make on the Yellow Rose."

Kinney glared back. "I didn't know duct tape and super glue were that expensive."

Chaz raised a finger and opened his mouth to reply but Marta cut him off. "Not now!"

Chaz retracted his finger, shut his mouth and placed both hands firmly on the wheel. Marta was already studying the map, searching for a location that would give them the best tactical advantage. They were two kilometers outside of town and the storm was already upon them. Rain flung itself into the side of the cruiser, driven nearly horizontal by the roaring winds. Streamers of lightning rippled across the charcoal sky ceaselessly.

"We haven't got time to double back toward town. Chaz, take 19 West at the next intersection," Marta instructed.

"Electric field sensors are going crazy," Kinney interjected, his attention never wavering from his console.

Marta wasn't surprised. She glanced out the windows and saw the entire sky awash in blazing tendrils of lightning.

"Strike imminent!" Kinney shouted. One index finger hovered over a red square on his console. His other index finger deftly manipulated a virtual joystick. The visor of his helmet glowed from a video feed generated from a camera at the rear of the cruiser. The view was panning in response to the joystick's movements.

On the roof, at the rear of the cruiser, a small but menacing looking Gatling gun mounted on a turret had popped up from a recessed bay. The turret rotated in unison with Kinney's targeting, sweeping across the highway until all eight barrels pointed down toward the shoulder of the road.

"Launching countermeasures!" Kinney shouted and tapped the red square on his console.

Flames belched from the top barrel of the gun. A titanium rod shot out, embedding itself into the asphalt at the side of the road at a nearly vertical angle. Then a projectile was launched explosively skyward from the rod's hollow core, like a fourth of July bottle rocket, only this one trailed a thin copper filament in its wake, still attached to the rod.

The tiny rocket had sailed upward several hundred feet when a jagged finger of blue current reached out and obliterated it. The bolt of destructive energy sizzled down the filament in a blinding flare, vaporizing the copper strand instantly. But it had already done its job, distracting the lightning away from its intended target and leading it to ground where it dissipated harmlessly. A moment later the accompanying thunderclap shook the ground.

"Close," was all Kinney said.

Marta suppressed a shudder, knowing just how close they had come to having their own cruiser disabled. A direct hit could easily fry every electrical system they had. The same fate had befallen Alpha Alpha Five and very nearly ended in disaster and death. That harrowing episode would live in her nightmares for the rest of her life.

Chaz had slowed the cruiser and steered it onto the ramp leading to Hwy 19. Cars that weren't faring as well against the wind and rain cluttered both sides of the road, their emergency flashers blinking. Marta noticed Chaz was preoccupied with the rear view monitor on his console. She leaned over and glanced down at it, seeing a pair of headlights coming up fast behind them.

Then she turned just in time to see a streamlined Sinotruk Longhauler barrel past them in the oncoming lane and swerve over right in front of them, its trailer swaying in the gale force winds.

"Someone's in a hurry" Kinney said.

Chaz just shook his head and fell in behind the reckless semi. "That ole boy is fixin' to get somebody killed," he muttered.

Marta sneered ahead at the rear of the trailer. "What do they care?" she scoffed. "Sitting up there in their reinforced cab. They know that if there's an accident they'll be just fine. Never mind the people in the other vehicles that they grind into the asphalt. Just as long as they make good time, deliver their cargo and collect their payment."

She tried to shake off the loathing she felt for such despicable lowlife and went back to studying the map, looking for a good side road to take that would afford them a defensible vantage point. But her thoughts were quickly interrupted when a vicious crosswind caught them and shoved even the massive cruiser toward the shoulder. Chaz quickly corrected and brought them back under control.

The Longhauler in front of them wasn't so lucky. Its trailer fishtailed violently as the driver fought for control. Then its tires lost all traction on the rain slick road. The big rig slid sideways and jackknifed, its velocity barely even slowing as it hydroplaned down the road. The cab was now facing back toward them and in the oncoming lane of traffic. The derelict driver, visible through the domed windshield, was frantically working to straighten out his course but it was too late and he soon realized he was just along for the ride.

Marta could still see the road ahead through the gap between the rig's inverted cab and the trailer. What she saw made her gasp. A half kilometer ahead, a pile-up had occurred. Cars were facing every direction. She could see silhouettes of people walking in the stagnant beams of headlights. And she knew without any doubt that what would happen next would be a nightmare rivaling anything she'd seen before. With the semi hydroplaning sideways down the road toward the throng of people, the outcome was inevitable.

"Oh Lord!" Chaz shouted.

Marta could already picture the aftermath. Torn metal and dismembered bodies littering the roadway. Blood mingling with the rain. More lives decimated. And the cycle continued.

Suddenly she felt the tug of g-forces slamming her back in her seat. Her head turned toward Chaz and a chill went through her when she saw the crazed look of determination in his eyes as he redlined the cruiser's turbine and steered across the centerline.

"This can't be good," Kinney grumbled and braced himself for what he rightly surmised was coming.

Marta looked up to see the semi driver's eyes go wide when he saw the cruiser closing in. He vaulted over the front seats and disappeared into the sleeper portion of his cab. Not just a fool but a coward as well, Marta thought.

"Sorry ole boy but ya'll should'a known better," Chaz hissed without a hint of remorse at what he was attempting to do.

Chaz manipulated a lever mounted on the steering wheel's hub. A loud hiss sounded as air was bled from the suspension, lowering the vehicle and significantly enhancing its stability. The deeply treaded tires were shedding forceful streams of water at all four corners. At their current speed, it was the only protection they had against hydroplaning and losing control themselves.

Marta grimaced just before the impact. Chaz's aim was true and their armored bumper connected with the rig's angled front end. Then, somehow, he coaxed even more power from the turbine. It whined in protest but kept the cruiser accelerating even against the added resistance.

The enormous weight and momentum of the big rig proved no match for the tightly concentrated mass and brute power of the cruiser. The cruiser's armored hull gave not a centimeter but crumpled the front end of the rig as it applied more and more force. Then the acute angle between the cab and its trailer lessened. The trailer straightened until it was running true down the right lane, the cruiser alongside it with the cab pressing against its bumper, still at a right angle to its trailer. But the cruiser kept powering ahead, nudging the cab until it, too, slipped into alignment.

Now the crux of the problem shifted. The semi was hurtling, driverless, down the right side of the road and the cruiser was hurtling down the left side. Only a hundred meters separated them from a bloody massacre of stranded motorists. Marta held her breath.

Chaz didn't hesitate in his course of action. He veered the cruiser into the side of the rig. The impact detonated several of the reactive armor panels on the cruiser's right side. They exploded outward, opening up gaping holes in the wall of the trailer. Shrapnel blew several of the trailer's tires, sending it fishtailing once more. But the cruiser's forceful nudge had already sealed the rig's fate. It hit the soft shoulder of the road, skidded and rolled down the ten meter embankment, enveloped in mist and gravel.

Before the wreck had even come to rest, Chaz had braked and swerved the cruiser off the right side of the road and onto the shoulder. The tires skidded perilously on the loose gravel but found purchase at the last moment. Clinging to the edge of the road, they shot past the pileup and the dumbfounded motorists standing amidst their vehicles, spraying them with gravel and mud but otherwise leaving them unharmed.

Marta watched Chaz wipe at the sweat rolling down his forehead through his helmet's opening. Then she waited for the tirade she knew would be coming from Kinney, chastising Chaz for his recklessness and blatant disregard for Storm Strike regulations.

She saw Kinney lean forward and place a firm hand on Chaz's shoulder. She saw Chaz tense as he prepared himself for the inevitable rebuke.

"Well done," Kinney said.

Chaz looked stunned at the completely unexpected compliment. Words eluded him and he just nodded modestly.

Marta smiled for a moment before turning back to the vibrant swirling colors on her display. "Well, boys, that was more than enough excitement for one day but I'm afraid we aren't done yet. Take the next left, Chaz. Let's find a place to dig in."

Rain continued to lash the cruiser as it turned off the highway and proceeded south down a narrow tree-lined drive that skirted a cemetery. Rows of granite tombstones swept by in a blur. Twice more, Kinney was forced to deploy countermeasures and twice more a searing shaft of lightning followed the dangling copper wire to ground.

Consulting the map, Marta guided them to a strategic spot that offered a clear field of fire. The cruiser rolled up to the sandy edge of a large oval pond over which they could launch their missiles without obstructions. Judging by the network of rusting pipes emerging from its murky waters, Marta assumed it had once served as an irrigation pond but had been abandoned for some time.

At each corner of the cruiser, heavy augurs emerged from their recesses and buried themselves in the loose soil, anchoring them to the spot. Atop the roof, three missiles slowly rotated into launch positions along the angled rails. Then they waited.

Marta's eyes were glued to the radar screen, looking for the telltale tornadic signatures; white dots surrounded by spinning clusters of red pixels. Kinney's screen showed the same data but allowed him the added functionality of tracking any potential targets from the moment they demonstrated the proper characteristics to be considered a threat. As he watched, a yellow reticle popped up near the storm front's leading edge, framing a swirling red mass.

"We have a bogey," Kinney warned.

"I see it," Marta said, her eyes homing in on the same disturbance.

"Forming fast," Kinney shouted. Marta nodded, watching the swirl grow larger. She still had her fingers crossed that it was only a transient anomaly that would fail to descend. Then all doubt was erased when she saw the white core form at its center as the newborn touched down and started lifting dirt and wreckage.

"I'm picking up debris clutter. Looks like she's already on the ground," Kinney said.

"Confirmed," Marta replied.

Watching the newly formed funnel creep across the radar screen, she could discern that it was still ramping up in size and power as it traveled east toward the town of Ada. But what she found more disturbing yet was the fact that the disabled cruiser was just south of its projected path.

"We have a target. I recommend going hot," Kinney offered.

"I concur," Marta said. She pressed her hand down on the transparent surface of the center console. A sliver of white light rotated beneath her hand, reading every whorl and ridge of her palm and fingertips. Her right hand hovered over a virtual keypad projected in her visor, her fingers tapping out a ten digit code. Kinney followed the same procedure from his own station.

When they had finished, a row of status lights turned green on

Kinney's panel. "Authorization confirmed. Warheads armed," Kinney said. As if in response to Kinney's announcement, another burst of lightning fractured the sky, followed by a long, rolling rumble of thunder that Marta could feel in her bones.

"Do you have a lock on our target?" Marta asked.

Kinney frowned down at his tactical display, his fingers flexing and unflexing. "Affirmative. But we have other issues to contend with."

"I know. Tango Sierra Two," Marta said. On the map, her index finger touched the shape of the twister while her middle finger came to rest on the symbol for Tango Sierra Two. A new menu popped up and she selected a launch simulation option. Vector lines streaked out from both their own marked location and just ahead of the twister, plotting its suspected path. Where they coincided, a circle indicating a blast radius expanded. Its circumference stopped expanding just short of Tango Sierra Two's location.

Marta bit her lip. "The safety margin is narrow but I think the risk to them is minimal."

Kinney checked his console again and shook his head. "I disagree, commander. We're now carrying missiles tipped with SCORCH-5 warheads. The new ordnance has a much greater explosive yield than what these simulations are showing. And there's also the possibility the shredder might swing south toward the disabled cruiser. If that happens, the missiles will blindly follow it and Beckett and his crew will be in a world of hurt."

Marta tensed, knowing their options were limited. She said, "But if we wait until the shredder is past the cruiser, we risk casualties in the outlying areas of the city from the detonations."

Kinney looked up from his console. "It's a tough call but policy dictates we stand down when our actions could endanger anyone, including our own crews."

Marta twisted in her seat, her eyes meeting Kinney's. "What about the remote destruct codes? If the tornado shifts course away from the town and toward the cruiser we could detonate the warheads."

"On a good day, yes. But with all this electrical interference we can't rely on those codes getting received intact. And if we can't intercede, then those missiles will home in on their designated target, regardless of what path it takes or what collateral damage is caused."

Marta felt her frustration growing. "Let me talk to them," she said and opened her external comm link. The hiss and crackle of electromagnetic interference filled her ears. She dialed back the volume to a manageable level.

"Whiskey Romeo One to Tango Sierra Two. Do you copy?"

To her surprise, the response was prompt but the reception was badly garbled. "This...Tan...ierra two. We copy."

"Commander Beckett, are you mobile yet?" Marta asked.

"Nega...still...dead in...water."

"Shit," Marta said and pounded her fist on the console.

Kinney said, "I have to recommend standing down, commander."

Marta winced, not wanting to give up so easily but knowing that any action they took could endanger more lives. Her thoughts went back to the community they had just passed through only minutes before. "But that town," she whispered, more to herself than anyone else.

"The sirens have already sounded there," Kinney said reassuringly. He leaned toward Marta. "The residents have had ample opportunity to seek shelter."

Marta knew he was right but she couldn't clear her mind of the images of those children standing outside their school, waving at her. "You saw those children this morning. They're looking to us to protect them."

Kinney sighed. "The chances are that those children are all five meters underground by now with thick slabs of concrete between them and anything that shredder could throw at them."

She tried to believe Kinney but the images wouldn't fade. She kept seeing the faces of those children, no longer smiling but wracked with terror as the shredder closed in. She made her final decision then. "Yes, chances are they're safe. But chances aren't certainties. I can't risk the lives of those people on a loser's gamble. Stand by for launch."

Marta saw a worried glance pass between Chaz and Kinney.

"Are you sure you've thought this through, Marta?" Kinney asked softly.

Marta glared back at him. "Are you questioning my competence or my command authority, major?"

Kinney's face hardened at the accusation. "No, sir."

Chaz opened his mouth to speak.

"You got something to say?" Marta growled.

"No, ma'am. Just stretching my jaw," Chaz retorted.

"Good. Then prepare to launch," Marta said, still scowling.

Kinney went back to work at his console. "Target is currently classified as an F4. The new warheads are still untested so protocol dictates we use a double tap to ensure termination."

Marta nodded. "Two missiles, it is, then. Fire."

Kinney waited for the steady tone that indicated a positive target lock. Then he tapped the launch button. The cruiser shook as two rocket engines ignited just above their heads. Flames flared against the windshield, clouding it with a thin layer of soot which quickly melted into the rain. Then they watched the missiles pull away above them, gliding low over the pond. Their exhausts parted the water behind them, cutting v-shaped trenches in the rain-dappled surface.

"Missiles away," Kinney said.

Still rapidly accelerating, the missiles quickly became nothing more than specks in the gray sky. Marta's attention turned to the radar where she watched the twin blips close in on their prey. Thirty seconds passed and the shredder's course remained eastward. Then, just as Marta began to unclench her jaw, the shredder's direction became erratic. It shifted a few degrees north. Then it sharply curved to the southeast, away from the town but on a nearly direct path toward Tango Sierra Two.

"No!" Marta cried out, feeling the color drain from her face.

"We got us a sidewinder," Chaz intoned.

"Orders?" Kinney asked, his fingers already hovering over two orange icons.

"No choice. Destruct the missiles!" Marta shouted.

Kinney tapped the twin icons. "Codes sent," Kinney said. A moment later, he shook his head. "As I feared, the signals aren't getting through."

"Keep sending," Marta uttered breathlessly, her eyes glued to the display as the twin blips followed in the wake of the shredder, quickly closing the gap.

Then, some eight kilometers distant, the lead missile's control module successfully decrypted its destruct code. Its warhead detonated in mid-flight, sending out a massive blast wave that rippled through the sky, hurling black clouds ahead of it.

The second missile vanished into the cloud of smoke and flames. But a moment later, it shot back out of the maelstrom, corrected its skewed course, and continued on toward its target, unscathed.

On Marta's screen, one of the twin blips winked out. She felt a momentary upwelling of hope that was quickly crushed when she realized the second missile was still there.

"One missile down but one still airborne. Twenty seconds to impact," Kinney said.

Had Marta been a religious woman, she would have been spending the remaining few seconds pleading with a higher power. Begging for divine intervention. Praying for deliverance for the three souls she had just condemned to death. Instead she just vainly willed the last missile to explode. But she knew she was just waiting for the inevitable.

"Ten seconds," Kinney said.

The shredder was nearly on top of the disabled cruiser.

"Five."

Marta closed her eyes.

"Impact."

She opened her eyes and saw an expanding circle sweep out from the missile's last position. Looking out the windshield, a small glimmer of white light near the horizon confirmed the detonation. On the screen, the funnel icon disappeared as it was engulfed by the circle which continued to swell. Its border swept across the icon for Tango Sierra Two and the cruiser's transponder instantly went dark.

"Funnel has been terminated," Kinney said.

"Oh my God," Marta muttered, her voice wavering. Tears rolled down her cheeks.

Next to her, Chaz lowered his head in reverence.

Despite the sounds of the storm raging around them, Marta's world fell silent as she reflected on the sudden finality of it all. She could feel the guilt welling up inside of her. If only she'd waited a few more seconds to launch. If only she'd listened to Kinney's warning. If only.

The radio crackled loudly, prodding Marta back to semi-awareness. She thought she heard a distinctly familiar voice concealed in the burst of static. It must have been her imagination. But then she saw Chaz and Kinney cock their heads and sit up ramrod straight in their chairs. They'd heard it, too. She leaned forward, her entire body going rigid with anticipation, and listened intently.

"Whiskey Romeo One, do you copy?" a male voice asked over the comm link.

"Who is this?" Marta said, breaking radio protocol with her vernacular reply but not caring.

"This is Beckett," the voice replied.

Chaz whooped. "Well, kiss my rosy ass!" he blurted out.

Marta was struck speechless. She held a trembling hand to her mouth, unable to believe what she was hearing.

"What's your status, Commander Beckett?" Kinney asked, opening his own comm.

"Well, we took a pounding but we're still breathing. Mayer is spitting teeth and Johnson thinks his arm is bending in one too many places but, all in all, not too bad for being a stone's throw from ground zero. Word of warning though. From the look of things you might need a can opener to get us out. Over."

"Thank God you guys are alive," Marta gushed, feeling a fresh burst of tears welling up in her eyes.

"No hard feelings, commander. But next time it's your turn to put the apple on your head, over."

For a brief moment she smiled at the joke, issued by a man who should have been a ghost. Then a cold chill swept through her as she acknowledged the guilt and the shame she felt for almost ending the lives of the three men sitting in that cruiser. She could feel Kinney's and Chaz's eyes on her but she didn't turn. She didn't acknowledge their presence. She just doubled over in her seat and cried.

CHAPTER 15

It felt like deja vu. Marta found herself in the same small office facing the same small desk. Behind it, the contrastingly large Jude Montgomery slumped back in his seat, hands resting on his bulging belly, twiddling his fat fingers. Marta wasn't sure if his leering gaze was meant to portray bitter disappointment or utter contempt. But she did her best to ignore it and just focused on reciting every regrettable detail of that morning's mission, her voice droning on low and steady.

"When the storm had subsided, we assisted in the extrication of Tango Sierra Two's crew and the treatment of their injuries. Then we returned to base," Marta said, finishing her narrative. She sat calmly and waited.

Montgomery leaned forward and switched off the camera that was recording Marta's account. He smiled a Cheshire cat smile.

"Your version of events appears to be well corroborated by the mission logs and data recorders that have already been preliminarily reviewed. So. We have that out of the way. Now, unfortunately, we have some rather unpleasant business to attend to," he said with a predatory grin.

Marta said nothing. She just lifted her eyes to meet his cold gaze as he continued.

"At 8:42 a.m. this morning, some ten kilometers west of Ada, Oklahoma, missiles were launched in violation of, and with blatant disregard to, proper operating protocol. Do you wish to refute that statement?"

"No," Marta said bluntly.

"So you acknowledge your negligence in this matter?" he asked, raising an eyebrow.

"I acknowledge that I took a chance trying to save a town full of innocent people and it didn't work out like I'd hoped."

Montgomery snorted. "I would say it didn't work out. A ten million dollar vehicle has been rendered unsalvageable by your unmitigated naughtiness."

Marta stared down at her hands. "I did what I thought was right," she said resolutely.

Montgomery wagged an index finger in her direction. "And that, my dear, is why we have procedure. So you don't have to fret over what's right or what's not. You just follow procedure. It's a very simple concept. Really. Here, let me show you."

Montgomery produced a tiny pair of square-lensed spectacles and perched them on the tip of his nose. Reaching out near the edge of his desk he plunked a finger down on the binding of a virtual book laid out in a row of similar books displayed in high resolution on the glass desktop. He dragged it over in front of him. Then he flicked open the cover and flipped through several pages, each page flip accompanied by a simulated electronic rustle of paper, before finding what he was looking for.

"I refer you to the operations protocol section of our field manual. Section 12B. And I quote. 'If a proposed intervention endangers Storm Strike property or personnel, said intervention will not be executed. Crew will stand down and allow nature to take its predestined course.' There. That wasn't so hard, now was it?"

Marta lifted her gaze to Montgomery as he sat back and gloated.

"Am I being reprimanded or not?" she asked.

Montgomery again leaned forward . He flipped closed the virtual book, slid it back into place and dragged another one over in front of him.

"Let's find out what the official procedures have to say on the subject, shall we?"

He flipped through several pages.

"This time we'll refer to the administrative procedures manual under disciplinary actions. Section five dash twenty-one. Any crewmember accused of dereliction of duties leading to damage or destruction of company property, either directly or indirectly, shall be suspended from field duties pending an investigation and until an official arraignment is held."

Montgomery peered smugly at her over his glasses.

"You're suspending me?" she asked.

"Procedure demands it. Effective immediately, you will be relegated to certain supervised non-critical functions here at Storm Strike Alpha."

Marta felt a hot flash of anger. "Would this be happening if that tornado had been threatening one of your precious corporate farms?"

Montgomery delicately removed his glasses and placed them back in his pocket. "Irrelevant and if you wish to dispute this issue further, I have been given the authority to upgrade your suspension into a full termination. Just say the word."

They stared at each other for several long seconds before Montgomery took her continued silence as answer enough.

"Very well. Report to meteorology on Monday at 7:00 am."

Marta got up and turned to leave.

Montgomery leaned back in his seat and rested his hands behind his head, making his belly protrude even further. "It's all for the best, Ms. Astin. Who knows? Perhaps a more regimented and docile work environment might suit you. I actually prefer it. You might say it grows on you."

Marta turned back, her eyes meeting his. Then her gaze dropped to his voluminous midsection, her lip curling up in disgust. "I can tell," she said and took her leave of the office, leaving Montgomery to stare shamefully down at his own inflated gut.

Marta ambled down the row of administrative offices wondering how she would possibly be able to tolerate being confined to a single location for an entire shift when Lydie Wright burst out of one of the offices and shut the door behind her. She leaned back against it with a dreamy, delighted look on her face.

Marta cringed, knowing it was too late to turn around and walk the other way. Lydie's face lit up even more when she spied Marta. She bounded over.

"Marta! You're the first person I'm going to get to tell! I just got assigned to a crew!" she said, her voice brimming with enthusiasm.

Marta forced a smile and quickened her pace toward the elevator lobby. "That's great, Lydie."

"I know! A position just opened up!" Lydie raved, her short legs struggling to keep up with Marta's longer gait. She glanced down at the assignment sheet in her hand. "Whiskey Romeo One! Do you know who that is?"

Marta felt her stomach plunge and a cold sweat begin to form beneath her uniform. She reached the bank of elevators and anxiously hit the call button. "Yeah. I've heard of them."

"Are they a good crew?" Lydie asked.

"The best," Marta choked out, swallowing back the emotions trying to break free.

"Well, I guess I'll be seeing you around, commander," Lydie said.

She stood at attention and issued a rigid salute.

Marta returned the salute weakly just as the elevator door slid shut. As soon as it had sealed her off from the rest of the world, her hand tightened into a fist which she used to give herself a couple of sharp raps to the forehead. She slapped the stop button while the elevator was transitioning between floors. Then she clamped both palms firmly over her throbbing temples, squeezed her eyes shut and slid to the floor in the corner of the elevator car, hugging her knees to her chest. Knowing she couldn't lapse into a complete breakdown here she allowed herself just thirty seconds to compose herself. Then she pulled herself up, took a deep breath, and set the elevator back in motion.

Half an hour later, Marta inserted her pitted key into her apartment door, twisted it and shoved the door open. She assumed her children would be out on one of their Red Cross assignments, giving her a chance to decompress before having to face anyone else.

But when the door swung wide, she saw both of them leap from their perches on the sofa and quickly stand at attention, side by side. They were dressed casually in jeans and t-shirts which probably meant she would have to contend with their presence all day in spite of her current distraught state and her desire to be left alone to wallow in more or less equal measures of self-pity and hard liquor.

She smiled at them and they smiled back but their smiles seemed contrived and stiff making her immediately sense that something was wrong.

"Hi," she said tentatively.

"Hi, mom," they both said nearly simultaneously.

"What's up?" she asked. Bonnie and Quinn shared a knowing glance between them that made Marta even more suspicious.

Bonnie bit her lip before replying. "Mom, we just want you to know that we love you. And we support you."

"And we want you to get better," Quinn added.

"What is this?" Marta asked, completely stupefied by her children's uncharacteristic actions. "What...what are you doing?"

"It's called an intervention," Bonnie said meekly.

Marta frowned. "Intervention?"

"You need help, mom," Bonnie replied, shifting back and forth on her feet nervously.

"You need to take your medication," Quinn added.

"And stop drinking," Bonnie finished.

Marta's eyes went wide. She glanced into the kitchen and saw two empty bottles of vodka sitting on the counter next to the sink.

"Oh, God. You didn't! Not now!" Marta yelled, bolting for the kitchen. She dropped to her knees and flung open the cabinet beneath the sink. She rifled through the contents, flinging dish towels and scrubbies through the air and sending a bottle of dishwashing detergent skittering across the linoleum.

"It's all gone," Bonnie said matter-of-factly.

Marta closed her eyes and collected herself, letting her raging blood cool, before she said something she would later regret.

"Okay, fine," she said, curling her lips up into a semblance of a smile. "You've made your point."

She rose to her feet, straightened her shirt, and walked back into the living room. Grabbing her purse, she turned back to her children who were still watching her.

"I think we need to talk, mom," Quinn said, his look of utter seriousness coming off as slightly comical on the face of a thirteen year old.

"About your problem," Bonnie added.

"We can talk about it later. I need to...I need to run some errands," Marta said and turned to the door. Then she hesitated and turned back. "And I think it would be best if you were to call your father and tell him to come and get you. As soon as possible."

The shock and hurt that flooded into her children's faces hit her like a bullet between the eyes.

"I didn't mean that," Marta said. "I just need to be alone right now."

Quinn cautiously approached her and held out his hand. A business card was clutched tightly between thumb and forefinger. "What's this?" Marta took the card. It was an old-fashioned paper business card for a Dr. Heath Merriwether, a psychiatrist, and from the subtitle he apparently specialized in bipolar disorder.

"Dad told us what's wrong with you," Quinn blurted out.

Marta looked at them, her mouth agape.

"He's supposed to be the best," Bonnie said.

Marta didn't know what to say, shocked and horrified that her own children thought that she was not just a drunk but a crazy drunk, no less. She hastily left the apartment, slamming the door hard behind her. She half-expected them to follow her out into the hall but no one appeared. Taking one more look at the card, she stuffed it into her purse and started down the hall.

CHAPTER 16

Mandi B's seemed unusually deserted until Marta realized it was only mid-afternoon and most of the socializers and casual drinkers wouldn't show up for another two or three hours. She ordered her sixth gin and tonic from the buxom robotic bartender. Glancing around at the few patrons present, she cringed when she spotted her gender-bending friend, Toni, sitting at a small table in a front corner of the bar. She hadn't even noticed her come in. Toni smiled and gave her a brief effeminate finger-wiggling wave but made no move to come over. Then Marta saw the slightly built, weasel-faced man sitting across from her, swaying gently on his stool. His lustful, bloodshot eyes were drinking in Toni's every curve and bulge.

"To each his own," Marta mumbled to herself and took a swig. Her thoughts quickly returned to her current plight or, more accurately, series of plights. Foremost on her mind was her demotion and what it would mean for her. A serious pay cut was inevitable. She had barely been scraping by on her former salary. After the monthly outlays for her still formidable student loans, child support, car payment, and rent she'd had just enough left for the basic necessities of life. The food she subsisted on was already cheap, prepackaged and barely palatable so there were no corners to cut there.

She looked down at her phone as its surface sprung to life, displaying her bank account summary. Another line item was added and the already diminutive balance decreased by twenty dollars as her latest drink was deducted. She stared down at the list of expenditures. The vast majority were for Mandi B's or Acadia Ale & Spirits, the name advertised on the front of the beverage vending machine at the corner of 3rd and Dale. She scrolled the listing upward, skimming over the debits for the past several days. More of the same.

She looked at the gin and tonic in front of her. Picking it up, she raised it halfway to her lips, then set it back down again. Her phone chirped. Its faux slate surface brightened, displaying the profile image for Bonnie's cellphone. An incoming text message appeared beneath it: "Staying at Jackie's. Sorry for upsetting you. We love you."

Marta thumbed a return message: "Love you too. Sorry." She sent it.

Leaning forward, she tapped her finger on the profile image, bringing it to full screen size. She stared at it. The beaming faces of Bonnie and Quinn stared back. They had on their Red Cross uniforms and were standing proudly in front of the open hatch of a stormcruiser parked just outside the hangar doors at Storm Strike Alpha. Marta stood between them dressed in her Storm Strike uniform, her arms around their shoulders.

She recalled that the photo had been taken toward the beginning of the summer on one of her good days. A day when her emotions had idled in neutral and her urge to drink to contain them had never surfaced. Those days were rare in the endless cycle of euphoric peaks and desolate valleys that defined her existence. There was always the lithium. But she'd been down that road before. A road nearly as treacherous and every bit as debilitating as the one that her own impaired rhythms coaxed her to follow.

Her life was a shambles. She'd destroyed her marriage, alienated her children and now she'd gotten herself discharged from the only worthy endeavor that had ever given her a sense of purpose and a fleeting taste of redemption. Fate was a cruel dictator and she was growing weary of living under its iron rule. As she sat there, staring down at her half finished drink, it occurred to her that, perhaps, it was time to call an end to it.

There were no good ways to die but Marta already knew how she would consummate her final deliberate act. She'd dwelled on it many times. Her end would come with a single brave step from a familiar precipice followed by a triumphant five-story plunge onto hard, unyielding cement. Quick and painless. She lowered her head and closed her eyes.

It gave her a perverse pleasure to think that the misfiring cells in her brain that had conspired against her for most of her adult years could soon be spilled on an unforgiving patch of concrete where they would bake, sizzle and die in the potent afternoon sun. Their time for relentlessly tormenting her would blessedly end. She wondered if they might have some primitive sentience of their own and realize that, even now, the sane and rational part of her brain had finally had enough of their treachery and was plotting their demise.

"This seat taken?" she heard a woman say next to her. Snapping out of her psychotic daze, her first thought was that Toni had exhausted her romantic options and chosen to join her but the voice was far too feminine. She turned to see a tall, slim woman dressed in faded jeans and a white blouse with the sleeves rolled up gracefully slip onto the stool next to her without waiting for Marta to give permission.

Mandi B glided over in front of the woman. "What can I get you?" she asked in her sultry voice.

"Water," the woman replied, keeping her gaze fixed ahead of her.

Marta took the opportunity to study her new companion. Sharp but delicate facial features defined her profile. Her smooth auburn skin glowed with a natural radiance despite a complete lack of any discernible cosmetics. Straight, raven-black hair cascaded down to the small of her back. Marta's immediate impression was that this was a strikingly beautiful Native American woman.

Then the woman turned to regard her. Instinctively, Marta recoiled. A deep jagged scar carved a trench down the left side of her face from just below her eye down to her jaw line. Another grisly fissure crisscrossed the first, climbing nearly to the tip of her nose across a misshapen crater that used to be her nostril. Marta quickly composed herself but felt the heat of shame seep into her face.

The woman seemed amused rather than offended by Marta's startled reaction. A hint of a smile crept across her marred features. "Do not be ashamed. I know my scars can be alarming. But I carry them with honor."

Marta wanted to ask what she had meant by that cryptic statement but was still a bit flustered. "I'm sorry. I'm Marta. Marta Astin. And you are?"

"I am Yanaba," the woman said, bowing her head slightly.

"Yanaba," Marta repeated slowly. "That's a beautiful name."

The woman took a sip of water. "Thank you. It is my Navajo name. I grew up on a reservation not far from here."

Marta nodded, giving her gin and tonic a stir.

"Where are you from?" Yanaba asked.

Marta shrugged. "New York originally."

"You are a long way from home, Marta," Yanaba said, studying Marta closely.

Marta shook her head and in a somber tone said, "It's not home. Not anymore."

Yanaba raised an eyebrow and tilted her head. "And Oklahoma is?"

"It's where I live," Marta stated flatly.

Yanaba nodded slowly as if pondering Marta's implied meaning. Her eyes remained fixed on Marta but, for a moment, her gaze seemed to turn inward. "The Navajo say that home is where our hearts feel rested and a warm hearth fire burns."

Marta chuckled. "For me, it's more along the lines of where I can afford the rent."

Yanaba smiled at the wry humor and took another sip of water. Marta suddenly noticed the maze of tangled tattoos running up and down both of her arms. Most of them depicted bold, geometrical patterns or colorful figures that she took to be idols from her Navajo heritage. But the one that stood out to her was a vivid representation of a tornado that extended nearly from elbow to wrist on her right inner forearm. The swirling winds formed a face with two glaring red eyes peering out.

Yanaba noticed Marta studying her tattoo and held up her arm. "You like it? It is my wind demon."

Marta smiled. "I've heard them called many things but never that."

Yanaba ran a finger down the edges of her facial scars. "It is what gave me these."

Marta looked baffled. She furrowed her brow and stared down at her drink.

"What is it?" Yanaba asked, sensing Marta's dismay.

"Nothing," Marta said. Then, not wanting to offend her companion, she decided to share her impulsive appraisal. "It's just that most people who get bit by a rabid dog don't choose to brand themselves with a likeness of it."

Yanaba chuckled. "Wind demons do not attack out of malice but in defense of their earth mother," she stated matter-of-factly.

Marta eyed her new companion a bit more warily, wondering what other outlandish beliefs this woman subscribed to.

"Believe me, I've seen plenty of them up close. I know they don't really think or reason but when one of them is coming straight at you, they look pretty fucking malicious," Marta said. She gestured toward Yanaba's scars and added condescendingly, "You should know that."

Yanaba ignored the subtle snub and watched Mandi B drift past on her rail. She turned back to Marta, her eyes narrowed. "How is it that you have had such intimate encounters with them?"

"I work for Storm Strike."

Yanaba's eyes widened. "Ah. I am not surprised. You look like a woman of courage."

Marta snickered softly at the attempted flattery but said nothing.

Yanaba licked her lips and stared off into the far corner of the bar, her eyes glazing as if in deep recollection. A full but distant smile crossed her face, tugging at the scars until her cheek formed a sunken pit. "My people say that there was a time when the wind demons obeyed their wishes. They would shout "go that way" and the wind demon would turn away. They do not listen anymore. Their ears have grown deaf to our words. Their hearts are hardened by rage at the injustices that humans have heaped upon their earth mother. I do not blame them."

Marta couldn't be sure if this woman seriously believed such nonsense or was just recounting tribal lore. She chose to believe the latter. "I bet that makes a nice bedtime story," Marta joked.

Yanaba's head snapped around toward her. Her dark eyes flashed and Marta quickly realized that her mysterious companion did actually believe what she was saying and that she had just inadvertently insulted her by making light of her bizarre convictions.

"Do not mock what you do not understand," Yanaba hissed.

"Okay," Marta said, suddenly feeling very uncomfortable. She started to stand and reached down to pick up her phone.

Yanaba's hand shot out like a cobra's strike and clamped down on her wrist. Marta stared at her incredulously. A moment later the iron grip loosened and Yanaba patted Marta's hand lightly. A rigid smile creased Yanaba's lips but never reached her deep, black eyes. "Marta, please. Stay a moment."

Not wanting to make a scene, Marta cautiously sat back down but kept her phone in her hand in the event that she found a convenient occasion to slip quietly away. It was quite obvious to her that she was dealing with an unstable and potentially dangerous personality.

Yanaba sighed deeply. When she looked up at Marta, the fiery belligerence had faded from her eyes, replaced with a shallow facade of humility and kindness. "You see, Marta, it's all about accountability. We were chosen ages ago to be the caretakers of mother earth. But the human race collectively made the decision to pollute the atmosphere, to poison the waters, to defile the land that they call home."

Her voice wavered slightly while she fought to reign in her obviously mounting emotions as she continued. "Now, instead of facing the retribution that humanity deserves, they devise unnatural means to fend off the judgment and the wrath that they themselves have perpetrated. Mother earth has every right to lash out in defense against us. People need to be punished for their traitorous actions. Penance must be served before balance can be restored. That is why Storm Strike itself is a blasphemy against nature!"

Marta had just watched, awestruck, as the woman's serene gaze had transformed once more into a fiendish sneer. Her hands were clenched into tight fists. Then, just as quickly as before, she seemed to quench her rage and smiled. "I hope that does not offend you. You are an intelligent woman, Marta. And, I sense, a woman of vision who has seen her share of strife and misfortune."

"Where are you going with this?" Marta asked.

Yanaba clasped her hands together and rested them on the bar. "Many nations, including the U.S., have made great strides to redeem themselves in the eyes of nature. Renewable fuels. Cleansing the air and water of toxins. I commend them for their efforts. But other countries, too consumed by their own greed, do not share such noble ambitions. Their efforts are nothing more than empty gestures meant to appease their neighbors. If we are to achieve a lasting peace with mother earth, the world must be unified. We simply wish to send a message to those arrogant countries that remain in opposition and we need warriors who are not afraid of sacrifice for a worthy cause."

Marta's mind was reeling from this woman's senseless propagandistic ranting. "Who the hell are you?" she asked.

Yanaba sat tall and prideful on her stool. "I speak for the Order of the Shining Winds."

Marta couldn't recall ever having heard of such an organization and she doubted there ever had been one. She had her suspicions she was talking to a lone nutjob who'd skipped a few doses of her medication. That thought brought an old but remarkably applicable adage to mind. 'It takes one to know one', she mused to herself before putting herself back in the moment. "What do you want from me?" she asked candidly.

Yanaba glanced around warily as if ensuring that no one else was within earshot of their conversation. Then, in a hushed tone, she said, "You have access to the tools we need to convince the heretics of their offenses against mother earth."

"You mean weapons?" Marta corrected bluntly.

Yanaba's eyes burned. "Violence can be a useful tool. A tool that is seldom ignored."

Marta felt her face flush red, a sudden burst of anger beginning to flare over this woman's arrogance and disregard for human life, nutjob or not.

"Listen, Yanaba, or whatever your name really is. I'm not saying you don't have a valid point but I don't believe in terrorism and that is exactly what you are proposing. And I don't believe in killing people in the name of God, nature, mother earth or anything else."

Yanaba's hand snatched Marta's wrist once more and squeezed until her fingers turned white. But, this time, Marta's reaction wasn't shock but unmitigated rage. She glared down at her restrained hand and then back up into Yanaba's face, her indignant expression issuing its own warning before she even spoke. When she did, her voice came out as a menacing growl. "And if you don't remove your hand from my person, I will take great pleasure in removing it from yours."

To Marta's surprise, Yanaba's grip relaxed. The woman smiled and held up her open palm in a gesture of submission. Still cautious, Marta stepped back, turned and started for the door.

"Ituha!" she heard Yanaba call out behind her. She turned back to see the woman looking past her toward the door and making a slicing motion with her finger across her throat. Marta's blood ran cold as she contemplated who the gesture was meant for and the possibility that she might have seriously underestimated this woman.

Marta quickened her pace but a dark, giant oak of a man stepped from the shadows beside the door and blocked her path. She stood there, frozen, as he reached under his black leather trench coat and grasped something. As he slowly withdrew his beefy hand, Marta saw the glint of the long steel blade and knew her end would come quicker than she'd imagined.

Suddenly the floor trembled. Marta heard a rumbling that brought to mind a stampeding bull. A blurred flash of something massive moving fast to her left caught her eye. It caught the eye of her assailant as well who turned his head just in time to see Toni bearing down on him, and apparently quite anxious to put her linebacker physique to good use. As she closed in, she let loose with a blood curdling howl of rage.

At the moment of impact, Toni's roar hopped up an octave as her voice chip took the jolt. Despite suddenly sounding like a rampaging chipmunk, Toni still had the brute strength of a rhino. Her momentum lifted the man off his feet, snapping his head brutally to the side. The blade clattered to the floor. Not even slowing, she continued her charge and drove his limp body into the far wall. Then Toni stood there, breathing heavily, and watched the man slowly topple over, leaving a body-shaped imprint in the crumbling plaster. She reached up and rubbed her neck tenderly, then probed her Adam's apple with her finger. Her voice chip trilled like a deranged sparrow.

"Aw, hell," she uttered in a high-pitched squeak.

As much as Marta wanted to thank Toni for her courageous and selfless act, she deemed it wise to take her leave of the bar while she still had the chance. She made it out onto the sidewalk and staggered, partly from the effects of the alcohol and partly from the sudden blinding brightness of the Oklahoma sun. Yet, despite her limited vision, she still recognized the two bronze skinned men who emerged from the backseat of the black Toyota Lancer Z parked at the curb.

As they turned toward her, their long black hair whirled behind them. They both wore tan leather jackets, just as on the night she'd met Toni when they'd entered the bar and done their best to look inconspicuous. Now, it was clear that all pretenses had been dropped. They stared directly at her, like two panthers taunting their prey, waiting patiently for her to make the first move.

They didn't have to wait long. Marta turned and sprinted down the sidewalk, doing a reasonably good job of adhering to a straight line. She glanced briefly behind her to see the two men taking up pursuit and, behind them, Yanaba standing and calmly watching it all unfold.

Marta wasn't sure which direction to go or what course of action to take. She was running on instinct, adrenaline and an unfortunate amount of gin that only served to cloud her good judgment which was probably why she found herself running toward her apartment building two blocks and one bustling street away.

She suddenly realized that her phone was still grasped tightly in her hand. She brought it up in front of her and flicked through the contacts. With the presence of law enforcement being scant at best in this crime-ridden tract of Oklahoma City, the notion to call the police did not even enter her frantic mind. Instead, she searched for the one face that had always instilled a sense of security in her. Finally, she found it and tapped the thumbnail image of Kinney looking heroic and dapper in his crisp army uniform, a photo she'd scavenged from an online database of military personnel returning home from Korea after the last war.

She brought the phone up to her ear and clumsily dodged a startled patron exiting a coffee shop. Her raised arm caught the man's steaming cup, sending its contents splattering to the sidewalk. She ignored the string of expletives hurled after her and listened as the phone rang four times, anxiously waiting for Kinney to pick up. "Come on, answer, damn you!"

She heard a promising click from the phone. "Kinney!" she shouted.

"You've reached Major Kinney Keller. Please leave a message," Kinney's flat recorded voice announced before a solitary beep sounded.

"Shit!" Marta yelled. She glanced down at her phone. Almost as an afterthought, she swiped at a button that had appeared on the screen.

"Your location has been shared with this contact," an automated voice announced.

Then she stuffed the phone back into her pocket and urged her legs to carry her faster. She still didn't have a plan but it did occur to her that she might be able to lose her attackers when she crossed the next intersection.

It was rush hour now and Potosi Avenue would be a torrent of speeding traffic. It also occurred to her that, if she bounded out into the swarm of cars at her current pace without waiting for a walk signal, she might not make it across alive herself.

She was ten meters away from the street when the walk signal for crossing pedestrians faded out and traffic began to pick up speed. Marta cursed her timing. By the time she vaulted the curb, all four lanes, two east and two west, were zipping past perilously fast. A fortuitous gap in the traffic in the first lane allowed her unobstructed passage. Seeing two cars approaching fast in the second lane she skidded to a stop and waited for them to race past. Then she bolted forward again.

Nearing the narrow median that divided eastbound from westbound traffic, she clumsily tripped over her own feet. Stumbling forward, she fell to her knees in the middle of the third lane. When she glanced up, a city bus was already bearing down on her. Its air horn sounded. Tires screeched as the bus's sensors instantly detected her presence and applied full brakes to its own lumbering mass.

Marta squeezed her eyes shut, waiting for the crushing blow but it never came. When she opened her eyes, the grill of the bus was only a few centimeters from her face. She didn't have time to celebrate but instead pulled herself up and dashed past the bus and right into the path of an oncoming Jaguar. The car's collision avoidance system dutifully calculated that impact was imminent. With not enough space to stop in time, it chose the only alternative to colliding with a human being. It swerved, hopping the curb and plowing into a light pole. Marta saw the white flash in the passenger compartment as the airbags deployed. She quickly gained the sidewalk and ran past the totaled vehicle and its single occupant, still struggling to free himself from the jumbled mass of deflated fabric.

By now, all four lanes of traffic were in gridlock, vehicles piled up bumper to bumper; a direct result of Marta's breakneck dash. Gasping for breath, she slowed and turned to look back. Her pursuers had just made it to the crossing and they weren't slowing. They effortlessly pounced onto the hood of a Mercedes in the first lane, then leaped across to the hood of another smaller car. One of them dropped to the pavement and rolled beneath the bus while the other expertly clambered over it with the uncanny agility of a monkey. They met up again in the fourth lane. By then, the man in the Jag had extricated himself from the deflated airbags and tangled belt restraints and swung open his door.

"What the hell is going on!" he bellowed just as one of the men kicked the door shut on him, sending him tumbling back into the Jag's seat. Marta had already lost precious seconds watching her pursuers navigate the maze of stalled vehicles. She picked up speed down the sidewalk again but found herself tiring quickly, her energy reserves nearly depleted.

There were few people on the sidewalk that she could seek assistance from and none that would stand a chance against two assailants, especially if they were armed which it was safe to assume that they were. She was less than a block away from her apartment building when the thought crossed her mind that she should just go home and barricade herself inside her apartment. The building itself was run-down and decrepit but the doors were solid. She also knew her children were staying with a friend so she didn't have to worry about trapping them with her in the apartment with two murderous lunatics determined to break in.

With no other options presenting themselves and feeling more and more drained with every step she decided it was the only course of action that made any sense. It would buy her some time at the very least. While she didn't keep a gun in her apartment she would have another opportunity to call for assistance. If the door held for just a few minutes, they might even arrive in time.

She saw the familiar front door coming up on her left and quickly ducked into it. The lobby was deserted as she tore through it and down a short hallway. Knowing she didn't have time to wait for the sluggish elevator she ran straight past and threw open the door to the seldom used stairway. She bounded up the first flight, tripped on the top step and slammed into the far wall of the landing, her shoulder absorbing the majority of the impact. Taking a moment to recover, she heard the clatter of footsteps approaching the stairwell door below and knew she had to keep moving.

She made it to the second floor and then the landing leading to the third. It was on the next flight that a small chunk of concrete crumbled from one of the steps as her foot touched down. She managed to keep her balance and continue on but a sketchy idea popped into her head, made all the more promising by the liquid courage still circulating in her veins.

When she reached the third floor where her apartment was located, she continued upward two more floors. Then she climbed further still, toward the roof. The last two flights proved the most challenging. She stumbled twice on the uneven steps, utterly exhausted and panting for air. Frantically, she wriggled through the narrow opening between the doorframe and the chained door leading to the roof.

She backed slowly and stealthily away from the door, hoping that

STORM STRIKE

seeing the intact chain might convince her pursuers that she'd slipped out quietly on one of the floors below. Those hopes were dashed when the chain was sheared cleanly in two by some type of heavy-bladed weapon. The rusting door creaked open and the two men who resembled each other enough to be twins stepped through the doorway and took up positions on either side of it.

Marta glanced down and saw the gleaming hatchets that they both carried. She froze, watching the men for what seemed like minutes. Their eyes never wavered from hers but they made no move to approach her. They just stood there, brandishing their evil-looking weapons, twirling the blades with subtle flicks of their wrists, taunting her. They were obviously waiting for something. She thought about slipping the phone from her pocket and feigning a call to the police to goad them into action.

But such efforts proved unnecessary when Yanaba walked through the door, a conceited smirk on her face. She strolled forward with the ease of someone who knew they were in absolute control of the situation. Behind her, her two cohorts gently shut the door to the stairwell and stood guard on either side of it, arms crossed over their chests.

Yanaba gestured back toward the two men with a grim smile. "You haven't met my associates." She pointed to each in turn. "Atsidi and Ahiga. They are brothers by blood and cause. I had hoped you would become a sister to that cause."

Yanaba shook her head and sighed. "Marta, I am so very sorry that I approached you today. I misjudged your sense of honor and your courage to do what needs to be done. I can see that now."

Marta started backing up toward her familiar corner of the rooftop. Yanaba matched her pace, slinking like a cat of prey. She shrugged her shoulders. "But what's done is done and now we have a dilemma."

As Marta continued to back up, she felt a disconcerting sponginess under her feet as she approached the weak spot in the roof. The derelict air conditioning unit was just to her left. She debated slipping up onto the narrow ledge that supported the unit as she usually did to reach her secluded corner but realized that Yanaba's suspicions would be instantly aroused. Instead, she skirted as close to the unit as she could where the framing would be strongest and concentrated on setting each foot down as gingerly as possible.

Yanaba continued to advance toward her. "We cannot allow our cause to be jeopardized by anything or anyone. Now that you know of our existence you have a become a liability for us."

Marta felt the roof sagging under her feet but she continued moving backward. Finally the heel of her foot bumped into the lip at the edge of the rooftop, nearly sending her off balance. A wave of panic washed over her as it dawned on her that she had willingly trapped herself here with a raving, demented woman in front of her and a five-story drop behind her.

For a brief moment she savored the irony of it. The very place where she had conspired to end it all was now where she had chosen to make her stand to live. But she knew it would be a short-lived stand. Even if her ill-conceived plan worked, there were still the woman's two associates to contend with.

Yanaba stopped just two meters away. She feigned a pout and placed one palm on her chest. "I am deeply saddened that it has come to this." Slipping quickly into a fighting stance, her hand disappeared up her sleeve and came back out holding a short-bladed knife.

"If you do not struggle, this will be quick and painless," Yanaba said as she crouched low and began to move in for the kill, holding her knife at eye level beside her head but pointed straight at Marta.

Marta just nodded and lowered her head in apparent submission. But she quickly snapped to attention when she heard the first dull snap as a rotted beam splintered. Yanaba immediately sensed the danger. A series of cracks appeared through the moss and spiderwebbed out beneath her feet. Her eyes widened and she stared at Marta in disbelief. Then the roof gave way and Yanaba began her plunge through the opening to the floor below. Just before she disappeared from sight, Marta saw the knife she was still holding rebound off a protruding section of beam and carve a cruel gully down the previously unmarred side of her face. Then she was gone.

Marta took a tentative step forward and peered down to see Yanaba lying motionless on the fifth floor's polished concrete flooring several meters below, surrounded by rubble and stacked storage crates. Marta looked back up at the two men still flanking the door. The initial shock on their faces at seeing Yanaba fall had been quickly replaced with murderous rage as vengeance fueled their thoughts. And Marta's bag of tricks was empty.

She jumped when her phone unexpectedly chimed. Not even knowing why she bothered, she pulled it from her pocket and glanced down at it. An animated smiley face grinned up at her and a notification from her social networking app popped up in a bubble just above it. It read: *You have a friend near your current location.*

Marta frowned in confusion. Then she looked up just in time to see Kinney kick open the door to the roof, his service pistol held out at the ready. The steel door delivered a bone-rattling full-frontal body slam to the man Yanaba had earlier identified as Atsidi. He'd been standing on the hinged side of the door and took the full force of the kick that Kinney had delivered to it. The impact sent him sprawling backward into the brick wall, his head rebounding off the solid surface with enough force to render him senseless. He slid to the ground, unmoving.

It was obvious to Marta from Kinney's abrupt and noisy entrance that he was relying more on the element of surprise than on stealth. But Ahiga's position next to the door frame kept him out of Kinney's peripheral vision, allowing him to evade detection just long enough for him to recognize the new threat and execute a single swift downward chop with his hatchet toward the arm protruding from the stairwell.

Marta didn't have time to warn Kinney before Ahiga's hatchet came crashing down into the gun's barrel, knocking the weapon from Kinney's hand. Then the hatchet reversed direction and swung upward toward his face. Kinney's finely honed fighting instinct kicked in. He leaned back, dodging the blow. The hatchet clattered against the doorframe in a shower of sparks. Then it was time for Kinney to take the offensive.

He advanced on Ahiga, raining down a series of punishing blows with his fists and the backs of his hands that staggered his opponent. It was clear that Kinney had at least fifty pounds on either one of the two men and he knew how to use it to his advantage. Just as Ahiga dropped to his knees from the brutal punishment he'd just absorbed, Atsidi shook off his daze and lunged at Kinney from behind. Kinney heard him coming and swung around to meet the new threat. He leaped back just in time as a hatchet whistled past his midsection.

Kinney glanced over his shoulder and saw that he was nearly out of room to maneuver. The edge of the building was less than a meter behind him. Beyond it was a seven meter gap separating the brownstone from a neighboring rooftop where Kinney caught a glimpse of an array of solar panels under construction. Looking up, he saw a steel gantry that spanned the gap between the two buildings. Snaking along the skeletal frame of the gantry were several electrical cables that would eventually allow the partially constructed solar array mounted on the adjoining rooftop to share its renewable power with the apartment building.

While Kinney was taking this in, looking for something he could use to gain an edge, Atsidi made his move. He leaped up, latching onto the gantry with both hands. His legs coiled and then struck out at Kinney, both feet catching him solidly in the chest. The blow knocked Kinney back a couple of steps but failed to send him over the edge as his solidly muscled body absorbed the impact. Atsidi lashed out with one more kick but this time Kinney was ready for him. He caught Atsidi's legs and twisted, breaking Atsidi's grip on the gantry but losing his own hold on the man's legs at the same time.

Using the spin imparted by Kinney, Atsidi executed a somersault, coming up on his feet. Before he could recover his balance and counterattack, Kinney had closed the gap and latched onto his jacket. He swung him around, wrapped his arm around Atsidi's neck and attempted to put him in a sleeper hold. But the proud Navajo brave refused to give up the fight. He lashed out, scratching and kicking at Kinney like a wild animal as he struggled to free himself. Then Kinney noticed Ahiga stirring.

Knowing his chances would be considerably diminished facing two opponents at once, Kinney reached out and snagged a dangling power cable. Wrapping it tightly around Atsidi's neck several times, he spun around and hurled the flailing man from the rooftop.

The cable went taut and Atsidi was left hanging by his neck halfway between the two buildings. His hands reached up and grasped the cable to prevent it from strangling him. His legs thrashed, seeking a purchase, but finding nothing but empty space.

Kinney turned his full attention to Ahiga who had reclaimed his own hatchet and was now glancing forlornly at his struggling brother suspended helplessly between the two buildings. Then Ahiga's focus shifted back to Kinney and he began to cautiously advance on his unarmed adversary.

Kinney saw a glint of steel near his feet. He reached down and picked up the other hatchet, testing its heft and taking a test swing through the air. With the trace of a smirk, he faced off with Ahiga and made a cocky come hither gesture with his hand that caused his attacker's advance to falter.

Kinney saw the sudden uncertainty in his opponent's eyes and knew there was fear there as well which could only work to his advantage. Then, without warning, the young Navajo brave whooped a loud war cry. With one final glance up at his brother, Ahiga raised his hatchet and rushed at Kinney.

Kinney had been hoping for just such a desperate attack. As Ahiga came within striking distance and swung his hatchet, Kinney brought his own up to parry the blow. The blades clashed together, handles entwined. Kinney followed through, rotating his arm in a wide arc and sending Ahiga's weapon flying through the air while maintaining a firm grip on his own.

Before Kinney could counterattack Ahiga bolted past him, sprinting for the ledge. Then he leaped from the building and caught hold of his brother's dangling feet. Kinney heard a pop as the added weight proved too much for Atsidi's precarious grip on the cable. His spine snapped like a twig.

Ahiga used his brother's limp and lifeless body like a pendulum, allowing the momentum from his jump to carry him close to the neighboring rooftop. He timed his release perfectly and landed hard, dropping into an acrobatic roll to absorb the brunt of the impact. He came back up on his feet and, with a pained glance back at his brother and a fierce glare at Kinney, he raced across the rooftop and vanished from sight.

Marta had been watching the entire battle play out from her corner of the roof. Her heart was pounding nearly as hard as it had been racing up the stairway. When it was over, she breathed a deep sigh of relief and felt her muscles relax. She smiled at her hero, Kinney, who was returning her stare.

"Oh, thank…" Marta started to say just as she took a short step back. Her heel caught the crate of empty liquor bottles and her balance faltered. "Shit!!!" she shouted. Her arms flailed as she tried to shift her weight further forward, away from the ledge and the five story drop that loomed just behind her. Eyes wide, she saw Kinney break into a mad dash across the roof toward her.

One of her feet came off the ground at the same moment that Kinney hurdled over the air conditioning unit. Then, just as she was about to lose her battle with gravity and her own compromised equilibrium and tumble into the void, Kinney was there beside her. His arms snatched her back from the brink.

For a long moment they just stared into each other's eyes. Marta thought she sensed a reluctance as Kinney slowly released her. He gestured toward the crate of empty bottles that had very nearly led to her demise.

"That stuff can kill you," he said with one eyebrow raised.

Marta caught the double meaning right away and felt a hot flush spread across her face. She nodded weakly. "I know."

Kinney studied her face a moment longer. Then he turned and cautiously shuffled his feet toward the collapsed section of the roof and stared down through the ragged hole. Marta peered down as well, clinging to Kinney's arm for support.

Yanaba was gone. Only a small pool of blood in the midst of the fallen debris remained. Marta gasped. She glanced at Kinney. Then her eyes traveled up to the body still swinging from the gantry. She pulled out her phone and was about to hit the emergency services button.

"What are you doing?" Kinney asked.

"We have to report this whole thing to the authorities," Marta said.

Kinney placed a hand over her phone and gently pushed her arm down. "Leave that to me. This is more of a military matter."

Marta frowned. "Military matter?"

"Where are your children?" Kinney asked, completely disregarding her question.

"Staying with a friend," Marta answered. She was now thoroughly confused and suspected there was much more that Kinney was failing to tell her.

Kinney nodded. "Good enough for right now but I'll need that address so I can assign a security detail to them."

Marta placed her hands on her hips in a half-hearted show of defiance. "Just what the hell is going on, Kinney?"

Kinney reached down and took her hand, squeezing it tightly. "Right now, I need to get you out of here. We can talk then. Deal?" Kinney said.

Marta wasn't sure what to do. But she did realize that Kinney had just risked his own life to save hers and that was enough reason to offer him the benefit of the doubt. She nodded apprehensively and followed Kinney as he led her past the gaping hole and toward the stairwell.

CHAPTER 17

Marta leaned forward on the black leather sofa and took another gulp of steaming coffee. Kinney had brewed it strong and the bitter taste made her cringe. She only hoped the hefty jolt of caffeine would wash away the last of the mental cobwebs still floating through her head, courtesy of her latest binge which had almost turned out to be her last as well.

From her current perch on the edge of the sofa she could turn her head and see the majority of Kinney's small apartment. It was just as she'd imagined it would be. Spartan but spotless with a few military artifacts on display including a civil war era dress sword hanging from one wall and a bronze likeness of a minuteman from the American Revolution that graced a small side table next to the sofa. The only thing that differed from her fantasies was the reason for her being there.

She could see Kinney in the kitchen, talking intently with someone on the phone and pacing on the shiny linoleum. She could only hear bits and pieces of the conversation but it was clear from his sharp tone that there were some points of contention surfacing.

Every few minutes for the past half hour Marta had been glancing down at a day old newspaper lying on the coffee table, using the headlines as an improvised visual acuity test. The text had finally stopped drifting across the page, a positive indication that her head was beginning to clear. As her senses returned so did a vague uneasiness about everything that had happened. She had a suspicion that Kinney knew more than he had told her and she was just waiting for him to finish his conversation before confronting him about it.

Finally, Kinney set the phone down on the counter. He stood there for a moment as if deliberating his next move. Then he left the kitchen and sat down next to Marta on the sofa. He cleared his throat and exhaled forcefully before beginning. "There's a field team at your apartment building right now cleaning up the mess that we left there."

"When will I be able to go back?" Marta asked.

"That's a good question", Kinney said, running a hand back through his hair. "My superiors feel that protective custody for you and your kids is unwarranted. They believe the chance of them coming after you again is remote since they've already tried to recruit you and failed. Also you've already had a chance to tell us everything that you know so there's no reason for them to feel obligated to eliminate you."

"Other than personal ones," Marta pointed out.

Kinney held up an index finger. "There is that. But our dossier on these people suggests that they don't take unnecessary risks for any reason. Their only actions are those that further their cause."

Marta set her mug down hard on the coffee table and cast a wary glance at Kinney. "You have dossiers on these people?" she asked accusingly.

"We've known about them for some time," Kinney admitted, looking uneasy. "They call themselves the..."

"The Order of the Shining Winds," Marta said, finishing his sentence for him.

Kinney nodded. "An extremist group. Complete whackjobs but they do have a clear agenda and apparently the balls to try and pull it off."

A sudden realization hit Marta. She pointed her finger at Kinney. "This is the group you were referring to back at Grayson Flats. The eco-terrorists."

"One and the same," Kinney replied bluntly.

Marta stared down at the drab tan carpeting, trying to absorb everything she'd been told. Then a cold chill swept over her. "Are my children in danger?" she asked.

"Not very likely but I'm not taking any chances. I have a couple of friends who are keeping an eye on your kids. I served with them in Korea so I can vouch for their skills and their loyalty is beyond reproach."

Marta breathed a sigh of relief and smiled. "Thank you for that."

Kinney seemed ready to say something, then hesitated. Finally he said, "You're welcome to stay here as long as you like."

Marta stared at him questioningly, somewhat taken aback and more than a little flattered. She felt her breaths coming a little quicker as she deliberated over whether there might have been a subtle innuendo hidden in that offer.

Kinney quickly broke eye contact and fidgeted on the couch. "I mean I'd be plenty comfortable out here on the sofa. You, of course, can have the bed."

Marta's hopes collapsed and she silently cursed herself for even entertaining such thoughts, especially given the circumstances. "I'm quite capable of taking care of myself," she said with a sudden edge to her voice.

Kinney winced at the slight and rubbed his palms across his pants. "At least stay the night," he offered.

Marta sighed, knowing she didn't have anywhere else to go and feeling a bit sorry for snapping at Kinney over his benevolent offer just because it hadn't included a gratuitous romp in his bedroom. She nodded. "Okay. But I'll take the couch."

Kinney smiled. "Deal," he said.

Marta glanced down and noticed the nasty bruises lining Kinney's forearms and the backs of his hands. "Oh my God!" she exclaimed, reaching out to examine them.

"I've had worse," Kinney said.

Tears formed in Marta's eyes as she gently caressed his hands. "This is my fault, too. I got you involved and almost got you killed. Just like Beckett's crew this morning," she said, her lip quivering.

Kinney grasped Marta's hands tightly and looked into her eyes. "I'm still alive and so are they. And if you hadn't called me you wouldn't be around to be feeling sorry for yourself," Kinney reasoned.

Marta shook her head vigorously, feeling her emotions swelling. "I screwed up today, Kinney. I almost got those three men killed. I was responsible for what happened."

"No," Kinney protested. "You were doing your job to the best of your ability and trying to save as many lives as you could. It's not a matter of responsibility. It's about calculated risks and making the best decisions you can make given the circumstances."

Mara looked away, unable to hold his stern gaze any longer. She pulled her hands out of Kinney's grasp and twisted away from him, hoping he would leave and let her wallow in her own self-pity. But he didn't.

"August 14, 2036," Kinney said in a low, deliberate tone.

Marta slowly turned back to face him. "What?"

The distant glaze that settled over Kinney's eyes told Marta that he was already someplace else. He grunted. "Hard to believe it was almost two years ago," he mused, more to himself than Marta.

Marta suddenly recalled the significance of that day. "The day the Korean conflict ended," she offered.

Kinney nodded grimly. "Everyone knows I'm the one who pushed the button. And they know I did it without command authorization. That was enough for the press to brand me 'Killer Keller' and turn me into a pariah. But what they don't know...what's still classified...is why I did it."

Marta decided to put her own troubles on hold and give Kinney her undivided attention, eager and honored to learn something about this man that no one else knew. She could see the strain on his face as he began.

"I was the launch coordinator for a battery of Dragonfire cruise missiles near Munsan, less than eight kilometers from what had once been the DMZ. The war had turned it into a killing field. Shelled bunkers. Hulled tanks. Bodies so thick you couldn't see the ground. Over a million dead."

Kinney let out a quick breath as if to steel himself from the painful memories he was stirring up. Then he continued his story.

"It was chaos on an unimaginable scale, made even more so by the unexpectedly advanced nature of the weaponry being supplied to the north by the Chinese. Both sides were using the latest jammers, effectively wiping out all communications short of couriers. The brass had anticipated such a contingency and our orders reflected that. In the event of communication disruption each forward unit was given the authority to act autonomously as long as such actions served to expedite our objectives and didn't endanger our troops. That's a hell of a lot of latitude to extend to a brigadier general with 256 missiles at his beck and call. Don't you think?"

He let the question hang for a moment, not really expecting an answer, before continuing.

"We were already on high alert because of two ballistic nukes that the north had lobbed toward Seoul. Berserkers, we called them because of how effectively the missiles had attempted to evade our interceptors using countermeasures and erratic course changes. We brought them both down before they reached their target but it was close. It gave us a damn good idea of just what that war mongering bastard, Kim Jong-un was capable of. Satellite surveillance showed several dozen mobile missile batteries moving south. If we allowed them time to set up and launch, the odds were good that several of those berserkers would make it through our defenses. Even one of their fifty kiloton warheads would level a city."

Kinney's shoulders sagged and his frame seemed to melt into the couch as if the very act of recollection was sapping his strength. His gaze remained fixed on Marta but it was what he was seeing in his mind's eye that consumed his thoughts at the moment.

"Then my communications officer managed to decrypt an enemy communiqué that pegged Jong-un's location at a command post in Pyongyang. It was the first solid lead we'd had on his whereabouts in months. I decided to act on it and put an end to the conflict by lopping off the head of the dragon. I already had authorization to use tactical nukes to prevent any incursions across the DMZ. I took the liberty of extending that directive. We armed two Dragonfires with three kiloton warheads, downloaded the coordinates for the command post into their guidance systems and then I gave the order to launch."

Kinney studied Marta as if he expected to see a discernible reaction upon such a bold admittance of his culpability. He took another deep breath and continued.

"Five minutes later, the war was over. Jong-un was dead. Downtown Pyongyang was a wasteland. The brass expressed their gratitude to me in private for ending a war they weren't sure they could win. Then they explained how they had no choice but to publicly reprimand me. Partly to appease the Chinese and partly to conceal our knowledge of just how advanced our enemy's weapons technology had become."

His gaze dropped to his tightly intertwined hands resting in his lap. A muscle in his cheek twitched momentarily.

"I could understand their need for a scapegoat so I went along with it. It had been my decision to launch. I killed over a thousand innocent civilians. Men, women, children. But I got that son of a bitch. It ended the war and it undoubtedly saved countless lives."

Marta reached out and touched Kinney's shoulder. His piercing steel-blue eyes flicked upward toward her.

"They demoted me to colonel and assigned me to Storm Strike where I would be out of the public eye and less of an embarrassment to them. I've never felt the need to explain myself to anyone. I prefer to let people think what they want. And when someone recognizes me, and they're not too busy spitting or slinging expletives at me, they sometimes ask if I have a clear conscience."

His intense stare bore into her as if he were waiting for her to ask the same question.

"The answer is yes. My conscience is clear. I regret the deaths of those people but I don't regret the decision that I made. I think about the people that I saved, not those that I killed. When you're in a war, whether it be against another country or against nature itself, there will always be sacrifices that have to be made. You do what you have to do to save the most people that you possibly can."

Kinney didn't wait for Marta to say anything. He got to his feet, walked to a linen closet and pulled out a neatly folded blanket. He strolled back to the couch and handed it to Marta.

"You should get some rest," he said and bent down and kissed her tenderly on the forehead. "Goodnight, Marta," he said softly. Then he disappeared into the bedroom.

There weren't many occasions when Marta was dumbfounded but this was one of them. She dimmed the lamp, laid back and pulled the blanket over her, resting her head on a throw pillow. Kinney was proving to be an impossible man to comprehend. His stoicism, even when recalling clearly painful memories, was virtually impregnable. Then there were the subtle shows of affection that he bestowed upon her but the blatant shunning of any advances that hinted at anything more than friendship.

It was an exercise in frustration to try to unravel such a conundrum. But she also knew the same could be said for herself. Her mood could shift radically and instantly. She could be laughing one moment and burst into tears the next. Kinney was a perceptive man. Perhaps he sensed her emotional instability and knew the pitfalls that awaited anyone naive enough to get involved with her. Of course, it was also possible that he recognized how emotionally damaged that he, himself, was and that pursuing a relationship with anyone would be predisposed to failure.

Suddenly, it occurred to her that she was rambling within the confines of her own head. An endless train of thoughts were assailing her despite her best efforts to quiet her rampant mind. She tried to mentally follow the breadcrumb trail back to when her thoughts had veered away from her own guilt and settled on her infatuation with Kinney. Unable to do so, she quickly concluded that she must once again be swinging toward a manic phase.

She found herself craving another drink and the calming effect that she always derived from it. As she wriggled beneath the blanket in an effort to get comfortable her hand brushed against something protruding from her pant pocket. She pulled it free and brought it out into the dim light. It was the business card that Quinn had given her just that morning.

She studied it, turning it over in her hand. Then she made a promise to herself that she would call the number embossed on it in the morning. Her decision imparted a sense of peace that allowed her to drift off into a tranquil sleep.

She awoke at 2:30 in the morning. Feeling restless, she sat up and glanced around at the dark shadows that lurked in the nooks and crannies of the unfamiliar apartment. Her gaze fell upon a small rectangular object sitting on the coffee table. As the fog of sleep cleared she realized it was Kinney's G-phone, the same one that Kinney had used to link with the mysterious colonel's data pad in the parking lot of Storm Strike headquarters.

Curiosity got the better of her. She picked it up and touched the screen. It lit up, displaying a prompt asking for a thumb print. She deliberated for a moment. Then, moving quietly, she carried it to the open bedroom door and peered in.

While Kinney was definitely asleep, his slumber was anything but sound. Sweat beaded on his forehead. Muscles twitched and jumped in his face, his head rocking from side to side. He was mouthing words that came out in short, brisk huffs. Marta listened closely, trying to discern what he was saying.

"Too many, too many. All dead. No, no, no," was all she could make out. Then he seemed to slip deeper into a more restful sleep. The twitches and jerks subsided. As he relaxed, his left hand slipped free of the covers and hung limply over the side of the bed. Marta saw her chance and quickly knelt down. Activating the phone's security screen, she gently brought it up to the pad of his dangling thumb.

Then she backed out of the room while the phone checked the acquired print against the one stored in its security profile. It chimed as identity was confirmed. A home screen appeared with a brief weather summary and a notification that two unread messages were waiting for retrieval.

Marta slipped quietly into the bathroom and shut the door behind her. Deciding that she would draw the line at reading someone else's personal messages, she left those alone and instead called up a screen listing recent activity. Sorting it by date, she scrolled back to the day she'd seen Kinney and the colonel conversing. It showed several phone calls and a single entry for an app download. The time coincided perfectly with when she had witnessed the conversation taking place. She tapped the listing.

In response, an app opened with the seal of the U.S. Army prominently displayed at the top of the screen. Amongst a jumble of military designations and lingo were several dropdown selection boxes. When she tapped one it presented her with a listing of the team call signs at Storm Strike. She selected her own former call sign, Whiskey Romeo One. Another box allowed her to select between several different spans of time that ranged from several minutes down to zero seconds. She set it to thirty seconds. A large red button at the bottom of the screen was labeled 'Commit.'

Her thumb hovered over the button, wondering if this was some sort of direct comm link with the fleet of stormcruisers and how such a system might benefit the military. Her curiosity finally got the better of her and she tapped the button.

A message in bold red letters flashed onto the screen: *Retina scan required. Initiating...*

Before she could react, a blinding red light shot out of a small aperture concealed in the bezel of the phone. It swept across her face, homing in on her eye. She tilted the phone away but the tracking software compensated faster than her reflexes. The next thing she knew her left eyeball was being bombarded with a blaze of red laser light.

She let out a short yelp and dropped the phone. It clattered against the tile floor. Taking a step back, she stumbled over the toilet bowl, lost her balance and fell backward. She ended up sitting down hard on the toilet. Thanks to Kinney's bachelor status, the seat had been left up, allowing her rump to plunge momentarily into the tepid water, soaking the back of her jeans and sending water sloshing from the bowl. She mouthed a silent curse. Regaining her feet and worried that the noise might have startled Kinney, she cracked open the door but heard nothing to indicate he'd been roused from his slumber.

Cautiously she picked up the phone, examining it for damage and thankfully finding none. Then she saw the message glowing on the screen: *Destruct sequence cancelled.* She frowned, unable or unwilling to fathom what that message might portend, what the military might be planning and what Kinney's involvement might be.

After hastily cleaning up the spilled water and patting her jeans dry with a towel, she snuck back out to the sofa, replaced the phone on the coffee table and spent the next hour lying awake, her imagination awash with conspiracy theories and terrorist plots. Finally she drifted off and her dreams took over where her waking imaginings had left off. When she awoke at six the next morning, her mind had blurred the line between dreams and reality. She couldn't easily distinguish between what she'd dreamt and what she'd actually experienced in those early morning hours.

She left the apartment before Kinney was up, preferring not to face him as the dark foreboding images from her nightmares gnawed at the back of her mind. She summoned a cab on her phone from the street outside the apartment building. The sun was just peaking above the skyline but she could already feel the heat from its glaring rays. While she waited for the cab, she found herself doubting her mental stability even more than usual. As she factored in the distinct possibility that she'd suddenly become delusional and paranoid, she wondered if she'd somehow developed schizophrenia to go along with her bipolarity.

The cab arrived and Marta climbed in. She thought about returning to her own apartment but couldn't quite bring herself to face that eventuality yet so she decided to grab a bite to eat at her favorite cafe. The morning commuter traffic slowed the cab's progress to a crawl. That was fine with Marta. She glanced down at her cellphone held tightly in her hand. It gave her the time that she needed to make a very important phone call.

CHAPTER 18

Seated on a concrete park bench, Marta gawked up at Frontier City's latest coaster through the shimmering heat waves of the afternoon sun. A train of five cars, packed with screaming riders, was just reaching the apex of the first five hundred foot drop. A moment later the Dancing Cobra claimed twenty more victims as they plummeted at a near ninety degree angle toward the ground along a perilously thin steel rail. Their cries of demented glee echoed throughout the park.

Marta hadn't come here to join in the exhilaration and excitement but, instead, to meet someone. She had thought it somewhat odd that a doctor of psychiatry would agree to a client consultation in such a public place brimming with distractions. When she'd spoken to him on the phone just that morning he'd queried her on her choice of locations for their initial "getting acquainted" meeting as he had aptly put it. He'd asked her to think of a place that she had an affinity for or a latent fascination with. A place she felt comfortable. Without hesitating, she'd chosen Frontier City.

The trainload of thrill seekers crested another hill and they let loose with roars of delight. Marta smiled and finished off her corn dog just as a dapper gentleman dressed in a smart tweed suit broke from the surging crowds. He approached with a subdued limp and settled onto the bench next to Marta. She quickly appraised him out of the corner of her eye. If he was who she thought he was, he was younger than she'd imagined; perhaps thirty with a perfectly coifed mane of blond hair and a neatly trimmed van dyke. In his hand, he held a cane with an ornate golden eagle head.

Marta had the uncanny feeling that this man was surreptitiously studying her just as closely as she was studying him. He extended a well-manicured hand in her direction and smiled warmly.

"Marta Astin I assume?" he asked in a delicate English accent.

She turned toward him and shook his hand. "Yes," she said politely.

"Dr. Heath Merriwether. At your service," he said, bowing his head slightly. Then he tilted his head to the side, watching Marta closely.

Furrowing his brow, he said, "You seem a bit perplexed. Does my appearance not match your expectations?"

"No, it's not… I just thought you'd be…older," Marta stammered.

"I would not presume to be as experienced as some of my senior and more esteemed colleagues. But there is something to be said for the impartiality of youth. New perspectives sometimes yield revelations disregarded by those of a more inveterate nature. Old dogs and new tricks, as it were."

He smiled again, his intense brown eyes twinkling.

Marta immediately found herself liking this young man who was eagerly taking in his unfamiliar surroundings, his face filled with a fresh, almost childlike quality.

"Tell me, Marta. What prompted you to select such a novel venue?"

Marta thought for a moment. "Well, I've always liked roller coasters. Back in New York as a child my parents took me to Coney Island three or four times every summer."

"Ah. Hearkens back to your youth," he said, nodding his understanding. "Many fond memories, I'm sure."

Marta smiled, feeling more and more at ease with her new acquaintance.

"Do you ride much?" he asked, gesturing toward the roller coaster.

Marta pursed her lips, thinking. "Sometimes. But mostly I just like to watch."

Heath's attention was drawn back to the coaster overhead. His eyes narrowed and Marta could tell his mind was pursuing some newly conceived angle.

"I'd wager your appreciation goes much deeper than that," he finally said.

"What do you mean?" Marta asked, intrigued that Dr. Merriwether already felt he had insights into her psyche.

"Have you ever likened your condition or perhaps life in general to a roller coaster ride?" Dr. Merriwether asked.

Marta's eyes widened. It was, in fact, an analogy that she had thought about many times as she watched the trains make their circuitous loop.

"Well, yes. Actually I have," she admitted.

"In your own words, would you describe for me how it is you feel that your bipolarity is similar to that roller coaster?" he asked, crossing his legs, resting an elbow on his raised thigh and stroking his van dyke thoughtfully. His eyes never left Marta's.

Marta felt a touch of nervousness being put on the spot like this. "I guess if you think of a normal person's life as a roller coaster, there are the curves that life is always throwing at them. There are times when they're up at the peaks feeling great. And then there are times when they are down at the bottom, in a pit of sadness and depression and feeling like they'll never rise back up out of it again. Then there are the straight-aways where everything just kind of goes."

"And how would your life compare to that of an average Joe's?", Merriwether asked, his eyes narrowing as he studied her.

A sudden spark glimmered in Marta's eyes. She felt a flood of emotion as she imagined what such an amusement ride would be like. Then she let her excitement spill out with her words which came in a fluid torrent.

"It would be a roller coaster five miles high. That's my life. When I'm up there," she said, pointing up toward the tallest peak. "I'm on top of the fucking world. You couldn't bring me down if you tried. Hell, if someone pointed a gun in my face, I'd still be convinced that I was going to live forever."

Noticing that her pulse had accelerated and her breaths were coming faster than normal, she tried to calm herself as best she could. Then her eyes fell until she was looking at where the track nearly touched the ground. The glow faded from her eyes.

"But when I come down...and I always come down...I crash, hard. It's all I can do not to blow my brains out. So that's the kind of wild, insane ride that I'm on."

"And what about the straight-aways. Where everything just kind of goes, as you put it?" Dr. Merriwether asked.

Marta shook her head. "There aren't any."

She felt tears well up in her eyes. But when she glanced over at Dr. Merriwether he was smiling widely.

"Splendid, Marta. Simply splendid. You just described to a tee the formidable trials and tribulations that every manic-depressive faces in their life. And you did so with quite a flare for words if I might say so."

Marta felt a crimson bloom wash over her face but the doctor didn't seem to notice. He took a deep breath.

"I have reviewed all of your records, Marta. I am acutely aware of your extreme distaste for lithium and your proclivity to use alcohol as a crutch which is unfortunate but understandable given your current dilemma. Is it safe to assume that you are not currently on any prescribed medication?"

"Yes," Marta answered sheepishly.

"And your alcohol intake? Would you say it is excessive?"

Marta shrugged her shoulders. "I like to have a few drinks once in a while but who doesn't?"

Dr. Merriwether smiled knowingly. "It simply does not do to lie to your therapist," he said in a disapproving tone.

Marta sighed. "Yeah, I drink a lot. Okay?" she shot back, then quickly regretted her gruffness.

The doctor raised an eyebrow at Marta's obvious annoyance. "No. It is not okay. But we are going to work on that together." He leaned forward, a stern look on his face. "Now, if I were to prescribe a new medication, would you be willing and able to take a respite from your indulgences?"

"If it works, I will," Mara answered candidly.

The doctor slapped his knee. "Well that's the kicker, isn't it?" He reached out and patted her hand. "What we need to do here is establish a threshold of trust, you and I. I need you to trust that, regardless of what therapy I choose to utilize or what medications I prescribe, I have your best interests at heart. And, conversely, I need to trust that you will not lapse into old habits and cause a potentially dangerous reaction with the medication that I prescribe."

"May I ask what the medication is?" Marta asked.

The doctor nodded amicably. "Yes you may. It is called Zepherin and it belongs to a new class of very promising mood moderators that just completed clinical trials. Of course, lithium is still considered the preferred first line of treatment for bipolar disease by most psychiatrists and for good reason considering its track record. But I, for one, believe that when a patient is suffering from debilitating side effects, perhaps it is time to seek more palatable solutions."

"Is it safe?" Marta asked warily.

Dr. Merriwether snickered. "As safe as any drug can be that alters the functioning of the most sophisticated and vital human organ of all," he said, tapping his head. Then he took his cane and drew an exaggerated sine wave in the churned up dirt at his feet.

"Think of this as representing your mood swings. Peaks and troughs. A drug like lithium works remarkably well to even out those rhythms but in some patients it works a little too well."

He drew a straight line cutting through the middle of the waves. "You end up having your emotions dulled to the point of feeling like a zombie."

Marta nodded, knowing exactly what he meant from past experience.

"Zepherin is a different animal altogether. It still allows your emotional highs and lows but it attenuates the extremes." He drew another sine wave overlapping the first but with less exaggerated curves. "Effectively tapering off your mood swings but not entirely eliminating them. After all, mood swings are an integral part of the human experience. To deny yourself those highs and lows is to deny yourself an essential part of being human."

"It sounds too good to be true," Marta said.

The doctor nodded gravely. "There are no magic pills that can cure your malady but there are many treatment options that can be explored on your path to achieving a sense of normalcy. If, for some reason, Zepherin doesn't work for you, we'll find something that does. Stop by my office tomorrow morning. I'll have a prescription waiting for you, you can set up an appointment for our next meeting in a more formal setting and we'll take it from there. How does that sound?"

Marta chuckled. "Don't take this the wrong way, but I've never met a doctor quite like you before."

"No offense taken. I have been accused by an astonishing number of my peers as being unconventional in my approach to therapy. My methods are a short jaunt off the beaten path, so to speak. But, then again, there's nothing wrong with being a bit different, now is there?"

Marta shook her head. Then Dr. Merriwether stood and began slowly walking away. He paused and turned back. "There is hope for you yet, Marta Astin," he said and winked. "Mark my words."

Marta sat there a few minutes longer, taking in the lively, frenetic atmosphere and daring herself to believe that the doctor was right. Perhaps, just perhaps, there was reason for hope.

CHAPTER 19

Marta shuffled swiftly away from the concessions stand balancing three cones of chocolate custard in her hands. She dodged and weaved her way through the throngs of families milling about on the maze of walkways. It was a sweltering summer afternoon at the Oklahoma City Zoo and she was in a race against time, the melting custard already beginning to flow down the sides of the cones.

Nearing her destination, she glanced ahead at a deeply moated enclosure, its spacious confines made to resemble an arctic tundra, alive with patchy stretches of grass and small shrubs. In one corner stood a large pond, its margins spattered with clumps of lush, green sedge. All along the guardrail that surrounded the steep moat, humbled spectators stood, staring in awe at the reinvention of a species.

The two creatures stood side by side, grazing on tussocks of thick grass; their long, curved tusks scraping across the ground with each dip of their massive heads. Reddish-brown fur hung like tufts of coarse silk threads from their towering frames, rippling in the ragged wind. They hadn't changed position during Marta's brief absence, preferring to loiter in the same spot until the spotty vegetation was stripped down to the bare ground. But when they did move, they carried themselves with a fluid grace that belied their incredible size and latent strength.

Marta spotted Bonnie and Quinn, taking in the spectacle that still drew record crowds after two years. She came up behind them.

"Get 'em while they're cold," she said, holding out the treats to her children. They turned, smiling, and eagerly relieved her of two-thirds of her burden.

"Thanks, mom," they said nearly in unison.

Marta stepped up between her children and watched the two mammoths eating. The smaller of the two animals, which Marta surmised was the female, lifted her head and held Marta's gaze for a long moment and she realized that they had the same gentle and knowing eyes of an elephant, their closest living relative.

Quinn looked up at his mother. "I can't believe they brought them back from the dead," he said.

Marta squinted and shook her head. "It's not really like they came back from the dead. It was humanity's fault that they went extinct in the first place. Now we're just giving them another shot at living."

A big grin spread across Quinn's face. "Kind of like your new doctor is doing for you," he said.

"Kind of like that," Marta agreed.

"We like the new you," Bonnie said with a smile.

"It's not the new me. It's the real me," Marta explained.

Just then, they heard a series of oohs and aahs from the crowd. They turned to see a baby mammoth not more than a meter tall peek out shyly from behind its mother's legs.

Marta glanced down at the interactive display screen mounted on a post in front of them. Information scrolled down the left side while, on the right, a video interview with the zoo's administrator played.

"It says that the baby is only the third full-blooded mammoth to be gestated naturally," Marta said, repeating one of the facts she had just read.

Her phone vibrated in her pocket and she pulled it out. A notification popped up on the screen informing her that Chaz had just sent her a text message. She tapped on it and read: "Any chance for dinner tonight? If not, how about tomorrow night? Or the next night? Please?"

Marta sighed. She couldn't keep ignoring him. She knew that. Perhaps later, once the children were back at home, she would go and talk to him. She owed him that much.

For the past month, her new position at Storm Strike Alpha and her preoccupation with getting reacquainted with her own children had taken priority over everything else in her life. She hadn't seen Chaz since their last patrol together. She hadn't even seen Kinney since she'd left his apartment that morning in July, the day after the traumatic episode that had nearly claimed her life

Only a week ago, she had climbed the stairs leading to the roof of her apartment building, wanting a glimpse into her troubled past and curious if any trace of the violent confrontation or her solitary drunken interludes remained. She'd found the door latched tightly shut, secured with a thick deadbolt controlled by an electronic keypad. She'd resigned herself to the fact that it was a part of her life that was now closed off and that wasn't exactly a bad thing.

She hadn't been back to Mandi B's either. No longer needing to dilute her runaway emotions or numb her pain, alcohol held no appeal for her anymore.

She owed a great deal of her recent transformation to her new doctor and the little purple pill that he had prescribed. For the first time that she could recall her emotions floated on an even keel in calm seas with not a storm in sight to the far horizon. For the first time that she could recall she felt good.

A few minutes later Marta and her children were headed for the exit gate. They took their time, strolling casually along the walkway, enjoying the time spent together as a family.

Suddenly, Bonnie's face lit up. "Guess what, mom? You know that shanty town you were telling us about?"

Marta nodded. "Grayson Flats," she replied.

"We're going to be there all next week as part of the farmer relief effort. We're bringing them supplies and helping set up a new sanitation system," Bonnie said, beaming.

Marta smiled. "They're good people. When you meet Brock, don't take him too seriously. Kind of a gruff old guy but he's got a heart of gold." She turned to Quinn. "And you are going to love his dog, Chance."

Marta spied one of the many photo opportunity booths located throughout the zoo and ushered Bonnie and Quinn over to it. Inside the cramped booth sat an unmoving chrome facsimile of a person holding what resembled an old point-and-shoot camera in its raised hands. The camera was pointed toward an alcove in an outcropping of rock just a few meters away. Just inside the stone recess a waterfall cascaded down over the rock face with small scooped-out ledges cradling colorful, blooming flowers.

Marta thought the scene provided the perfect backdrop for a family photo. She set her phone down on a small circular pad embedded in the booth's counter. The chrome man's eyes lit up. "Thank you for choosing Magical Moments Photo Opps," it said in a hollow, tinny voice. "Fifty dollars will be debited from your account. Please take your positions. Photo will be taken in twenty seconds."

They quickly slid into position in front of the waterfall, Marta in the center flanked by her two children. She bent down and pulled them tightly to her. A screen on the front of the booth gave them a preview of the photo as the timer counted down the remaining seconds. They were all smiling brightly when the photo was taken. Then they stepped back up to the booth and watched through a transparent panel as an eight by ten glossy was inserted into a resin frame of faux rock and then presented to them through a slot.

"A digital copy of your photo has been transferred to your phone. Have a good day," the metallic voice announced.

Marta stared down at the photo, her children huddled close, and realized that it really was a good day.

CHAPTER 20

Marta's car pulled to the curb in front of a spacious bi-level with an attached two-car garage. The house, with its recent coat of teal paint and freshly cut lawn, fit in perfectly with its neighbors in this decidedly middle-class suburban community.

As she climbed out of the vehicle, Marta couldn't help but chuckle to herself when it dawned on her that Chaz, as young and immature as he was, was actually living more comfortably than either her or Kinney. Walking up the sidewalk toward the front door, she tried to forge in her mind the proper words to say that would convey her feelings without damaging his.

As clichéd as it sounded, she did still treasure her friendship with him. But any interest in Chaz above and beyond that rapport had waned. She no longer found his juvenile antics as charming as she once had when her own rebellious emotions were flooding her system with potent endorphins.

She pressed the doorbell and waited half a minute, then pressed it again. Getting no response, she resorted to knocking loudly on the door. A minute later and still no answer. Marta frowned and stepped back. She glanced toward the front of the garage, confirming what she'd already seen. The overhead garage door was half open.

Cautiously, she walked over to the paved drive leading to the open garage. She raised a hand to shield her eyes, peering into the darkened interior but could see only shadows.

"Hello? Chaz? Anybody home?" she called out.

Ducking under the door, she stepped inside, her eyes quickly adjusting to the gloom. She was standing between two vehicles. The one on her left was covered with a black tarp. The one on her right was Chaz's pale blue 2025 Ford F150 LE, heavily modded for racing with thick treaded over-sized tires and a hood scoop feeding the massive turbine beneath its hood that, by Chaz's proud admission, barely met the stringent emission laws.

    Marta slowly moved forward toward a meticulously organized and spotless work bench that spanned the entire front wall of the garage. Shiny, chrome tools were laid out on the wall above it, mounted to a matte black pegboard. She noticed the door leading into the house was closed. Then her eyes were drawn to a row of four framed photographs on the wall next to the covered vehicle. Curious, she walked over and stood in front of them, examining each in turn.

    The first photo showed a young smiling couple sitting side by side in a swing on a small covered porch. On their laps, they were holding a small infant between them and holding its arm up in a mock wave. Chaz's blonde hair matched the woman's long tresses but his resemblance to the man was much more striking; from the aquiline nose to the thin lips to the tapering jaw. What's more, he had the same twinkle in his eye and the same mischievous grin.

    The second photo showed the same man dressed in a blue and white racing suit sitting on the hood of a vintage but race-worthy black Ford Charger. His arm was wrapped around a toddler who sat beside him, dressed in a tiny blue and white racing jersey with the number 22 boldly emblazoned on the chest.

    Moving on to the third photo, Marta saw a noticeably more weathered version of the man sitting in the driver's seat of a battle-ready cherry red Ford Mustang. A blond-haired boy of about eight years sat contentedly on his lap.

    The last photo showed the same boy, a few years older, seated in the driver's seat of the same Ford Mustang and giving an enthusiastic thumbs up. Though more pubescent, his visage was unmistakably that of a decade-younger Chaz. Kneeling next to the driver's window, the man was giving the same thumbs up, wearing a baseball cap with the number 22 on it. Marta squinted at the swooping lines of the car in the photo. Then she turned around and studied the contours of the car concealed under the cover. Judging from the shape, they were nearly identical.

    She lifted a corner of the cover and saw a polished fender painted bright cherry red. Wanting to see a bit more, she pulled the cover away from the front end of the car. It was definitely the same vehicle as the one in the last two photos. From her limited knowledge of sports cars, she guessed it to be a mid-teen model but heavily modified for race worthiness. On its hood was stenciled the same number 22 as in the photos.

    She circled around toward the front of the car. Her brow furrowed when she saw the entire left front side of the grill crumpled in. The leading edge of the fiberglass racing hood was shattered as well. Looking closer, she could see what appeared to be tiny flecks of dried blood spattering the damaged front end but with the red paint it was hard to be sure.

"Ain't you just a sight for sore eyes," a voice called out, startling her. She spun around to see Chaz standing in the doorway to the house, dressed in stylishly torn and faded designer jeans and a white t-shirt. He stepped down into the garage and shut the door behind him.

Marta composed herself and smiled nervously as he walked up beside her. His eyes shifted to the damaged fender and Marta thought she saw him wince. Then he looked back up at her and smiled weakly.

"What's a man gotta do to get your attention these days?" he asked.

"I've been kinda busy lately," she said.

Chaz scratched his head. "Too busy to take a good ole boy up on his offer to wine and dine you?"

"I've been trying to give my children a little more of my time lately and now that I'm no longer working twelve hour shifts chasing twisters with you and Kinney I've got a little more to give them."

Chaz nodded. "Well I can't argue with that logic."

A moment of awkward silence passed before Marta spoke again. "How are things with the new commander?"

Chaz rolled his eyes, looking a bit uncomfortable discussing Marta's successor. "Ah, you know. She's a bit rough around the edges but Kinney and I are grinding down the burrs. I guess you gotta appreciate how they wanted to put a newbie commander with an experienced, top notch, professional crew to break her in right."

"And I can't argue with that," Marta teased.

Chaz once more allowed his gaze to drop to the hood of the Mustang. He took a deep breath. "I see you've uncloaked the ole fireball as my daddy used to call her."

"She's beautiful," Marta said, glancing down admiringly.

Chaz nodded and breathed a long, solemn sigh . "My daddy's pride and joy. Took third in the Wintek Cup series with her two years running."

Marta grinned. "So that's where you got your love for driving."

"Yes ma'am. It's in the blood."

"Ever race yourself?" Marta asked.

"In my younger days, I dabbled," he joked. "Offroading was more my forte. Raced in the TORC Pro division in '35. Held my own, too. Until I hit a cement wall, that is. Snapped my spine clean in two."

Chaz turned around and pulled up his t-shirt. Marta gaped down at the grotesque s-shaped curve in his spine that bulged outward in his lower back. She was surprised she hadn't noticed it back at the lake.

He pulled his shirt back down and turned to face her. "Had to have stem cell injections to cinch it up. Took a year before I could walk right again."

"Wow," Marta said. She bent and slid her hand over the damaged grill.

"Did this happen in a race, too?"

Chaz stared down at the grill, his face turning ashen. "Haven't been able to bring myself to fix it just yet. It kind of serves as a reminder of just how dumb kids can be."

Marta frowned and waited for Chaz to explain. She'd never seen such a somber, pensive look on his characteristically buoyant face.

"I was twelve. Sitting right there in the front seat," Chaz said, pointing toward the driver's seat of the Mustang. "Near as I can recollect my daddy was tuning up the turbine. Had the hood up, bent over, fiddling with the injectors. I was an antsy little pecker, squirming around in my seat trying to get a better look at what my daddy was doing. My arm bumped the gearshift, popped the car into first. Next thing I know I hear a crunch and my daddy was pinned twixt the car and the wall. Deader than dead."

Marta held a hand to her gaping mouth. "Oh my God, Chaz. I'm so sorry."

Chaz nodded grimly. "So am I. Wasn't my finest hour but ya gotta roll with the punches." His eyes flicked up, roaming the ceiling. "I suspect he's up there somewhere, looking down, shaking his head, just waiting to see what kind of stupid ass stunt I pull next."

"It was an accident," Marta said, quickly realizing it was a rather feeble attempt to console someone who had been responsible for his own father's demise.

Chaz shut his eyes for a moment. "I know that. My daddy always said that no matter what kind of blame fool thing a fella goes and does, sooner or later, there'd always be a chance to redeem himself." He opened his eyes and they settled on Marta. "Guess I'm just waiting for my chance."

Marta, lost for words, just returned his stare. Then Chaz sniffled softly and flicked a single tear from his eye. "Hell, I do believe that's the first time I've ever told another living soul that story. Felt good."

Marta smiled. "You can talk to me anytime, Chaz."

Chaz turned his head to the side and Marta sensed he was still trying to shake off the memories that he'd just awakened. When he turned back to her his smile was wider but his eyes were still dim. "How 'bout you?

Got all your hens in a row now?" he asked.

Marta pursed her lips and peered outside through the half-open door. "I'm working on it. Just taking it one day at a time. But I think I'm doing much better. I feel much better than I have in a long time."

"Wasn't none of my business, but I kind of thought something would have to give sooner or later," Chaz admitted.

Marta's eyes widened, surprised by Chaz's candor. "It was that obvious?" she asked.

Chaz scuffed the cement floor with his boot nervously. "I've known you weren't right in the head for a while now. There were times I was just waiting for the pea soup to come spewing out your mouth and your head to start spinning 'round."

Marta couldn't help but laugh out loud. "Oh, really? How astute of you."

Chaz shrugged. "Doesn't take a rocket scientist."

"Well, that's good. Cause you're not one," Marta said, smirking.

"Shoot, I knowed that," Chaz said mockingly in his deepest southern drawl. His eyes flitted nervously about the room. Then he looked back at Marta, almost shyly. "So you want to go and grab a bite to eat?" he asked.

"I can't, Chaz," she said quietly.

"What do you want then?" he asked and Marta heard a sudden swelling of emotion in his voice. She took a deep breath before letting the words spill out.

"The truth is I don't know what I want yet. I need time to sort through what I'm feeling. Being able to follow a train of thought for more than a few minutes, to be able to get up in the morning two days from now and feel like the same person that I am today is new to me and I'm still getting used to it. I hope you can understand that."

Chaz flashed a genuine smile. "Don't sweat it, Marta. Hell, I'm as tickled for you as a hog dancing on a feather bed."

Marta reached out and squeezed his hand. "Are we still friends?"

Chaz chuckled. "Till the day I curl up my toes and get dirt up my nose."

"I'll take that as a yes," Marta said and gave Chaz a short, firm hug.

"You take care, Chaz. I'll see you around," she said and started for the door.

"Damn straight," he called after her. "I'll come look you up in your new office at Alpha. We'll do lunch," he said, throwing his arms up in the air for effect.

"I'd like that," she said and stepped out into the fading daylight.

CHAPTER 21

It was a hectic Tuesday morning in the crescent-shaped event room at Storm Strike Alpha. Outside, a ferocious cauldron of storms was brewing. Inside, the air crackled with tension and frenetic energy. A cacophony of voices shouted orders, issued weather updates and conversed with the crews who were out preparing for the next round in the never-ending battle against nature's fury.

Marta, relegated to a workstation in the far corner, took a sip of her morning coffee. Then she pushed her chair back from the console, removed her enhanced reality glasses and rubbed the blur from her eyes. When she opened them, she looked over her shoulder and took in the curving room with a quick sweep of her head. To the unaided eye, the seven other workers huddled at their stations and gesticulating madly at the clear slabs of glass before them, could have been a group of frenzied mimes prodding at imaginary walls or perhaps a den of meth addicts hallucinating on a bad trip, poking and swiping at things that didn't exist outside of their own warped reality.

Slipping the glasses back on, chaos gave way to order and madness to method as a virtual layer of reality was projected onto the lenses in front of Marta's eyes. The stark and lifeless transparent glass consoles instantly became awash with flashing icons, maps and radar displays. White glowing orbs representing raw data coursed from console to console as operators shuttled data between stations with a subtle flick of their wrist.

Her eyes settled on Jane Cormorant, one of the primary dispatchers for Storm Strike who had also become a close friend. Seated in her wheelchair behind the wraparound central workstation, she obviously had her hands full on this stormy weekday morning. Having served a stint as commander in a cruiser herself, she had more empathy for those men and women out in the field than most. Perhaps that was why they all adored her. Marta wondered if Jane would even take the time to have lunch with her as had become their custom over the past several weeks.

Marta turned back to her own console and tried to concentrate on the mundane task she'd been given. Her primary duty in her newly assigned position was to pore over international weather databases, sorting through terabytes of undigested data, looking for patterns that might lead to better event prediction. Of course, the Storm Strike mainframe did the hardcore number crunching. She just told it where to look.

To a trained meteorologist there was one glaring problem. The worldwide climate was in a constant state of flux. Temperatures were beginning to level off but were still climbing. The jet stream was undulating like a convulsing winged serpent. In such an unstable environment, data gathered this week was meaningless next week.

She set the mainframe loose on a table of wind current data she'd just imported from a Russian database and tried to tune out the background noise. But, as was usually the case, the harder she tried to tune it out, the more she found herself listening in and catching fragments of conversations.

"Massive supercell...vectoring in from southwest...32 meters per second...shaping up to be a monster...what do we have on the ground in sector 7B...currently no presence in 7B...warnings being issued for the City of Lawton...evacuation notice for Southwestern Conservation and Cultivation...settlements in immediate path...several transient farming communities...Grayson Flats."

It was that last phrase that chilled her blood and quickened her pulse as she quickly recalled where her children were going to be stationed that day as part of the Red Cross's farmer relief efforts. She quickly switched her own display over to a live Doppler view of Oklahoma. Patches of red and orange dotted the entire state. One particularly vibrant patch of crimson rested like a fresh bloodstain just to the southwest of the Lawton area or sector 7B as it was designated on the grid overlying the radar map. A series of arrows popped up showing the supercell's projected path which took it straight over Grayson Flats. The color instantly drained from her face.

Marta fumbled for her purse, dangling from its strap on the back of her chair. She pulled out her phone, frantically brought up Bonnie's profile and placed the call. It rang several times before the voicemail announcement played in Bonnie's chipper voice: "Uh, oh. Not here. Give me a reason to call you back. Bye."

As soon as the beep sounded, Marta said, "Bonnie, some really bad storms are heading your way. When you get this message, don't call back. Just get to a shelter. If you can, try to make it to Southwest C&C. They have secure shelters there. If not,....do what you can. When you're safe, then call. I love you."

She ended the call, slapped the phone down on her console and stared at it, willing it to ring.

"You okay, Marta?" Jane asked, ungluing her attention from her own console.

Marta looked up toward her friend. "My children," she said numbly.

"What about your children?" Jane prompted her.

"They're...well, they're at Grayson Flats with the...ah...with the Red Cross," Marta managed to stammer as images flashed through her mind of what happens when a shredder hits a shanty town. Sheets of corrugated tin flying through the air thicker than a flock of starlings, their edges razor sharp. She'd seen the aftermath and would never forget. It had looked like a scene straight out of the Texas Chainsaw Massacre.

"If it makes you feel any better, the warnings have already gone out," Jane offered.

"It doesn't. She didn't answer her phone," Marta said despondently.

Jane threw her hands up. "Well you can't be sitting around here while your children are out there," she said sternly.

Marta blinked, having trouble comprehending Jane's meaning. "I can't very well stow away on a cruiser," she said.

"You can if you're invited," Jane replied. Then she turned to the woman sitting on her opposite side. "Kate, put this young lady on the roster as a ride along on the next departing cruiser for sector 7B," she said assertively. The woman nodded and went to work on her own console.

Marta frowned. "Won't you get in trouble?"

Jane smiled. "Honey, the only rule for ride alongs states that they have to pass a background check. Yours is on file. I see no problem," she said, shrugging her shoulders.

"Thank you," Marta said, trying to regain control of her breathing which was coming in short gasps.

Jane turned back to her console and brought up a virtual page with an inordinate amount of fine print on it. "Before you can go, you'll need to sign this," she said, pointing to the page hovering on her display.

Marta walked over. "What is it?"

"A waiver. So you can't sue Storm Strike if you incur bodily injury or die. Rules are rules," Jane said with a smirk.

Marta brought her thumb up and touched the page in the small box where it indicated her print should go. Then the page condensed into a ball of light that shot down the glass panel and disappeared beneath a data pad that was sitting on the flat part of the console. The data pad's display lit up with a photo of Marta, a few lines of text and a barcode. Jane picked it up and held it out to Marta.

"Here's your ticket for one hell of a thrill ride," Jane said as Marta took the data pad from her.

The woman seated next to Jane looked up. "There's only one crew scheduled for imminent departure," she said to Jane.

"Put her down," Jane ordered.

Marta glanced at the woman in charge of the roster. "Which one?" she asked.

The woman looked down at her console. "Whiskey Romeo One," she answered.

Marta winced, suddenly not sure this was such a great idea.

"Beggars can't be choosers. You're all set. Now get on out of here," Jane said with a wink.

Marta nodded. Then she turned and bolted from the room.

For sentimental reasons, Marta had held on to her mission suit after cleaning out her crew locker, having transferred it to her new staff locker on the main floor. Not wanting to risk being seen using the ready room, she'd taken the suit with her into the women's restroom and was just zipping it up when she glanced into the mirror and saw her name badge still affixed to the lapel.

With a pained look, she grasped the tag and tore it loose, then deposited it in the trash receptacle. With one last look at her reflection, she slipped the helmet over her head, not even bothering to bundle her hair beneath it but letting the long brown locks spill out the back of the helmet to just below her shoulder blades.

Then she hurried back out into the corridor and headed for the elevators. The halls were teeming with Storm Strike staff as they rushed between departments. Marta felt it wise to lower her tinted visor to prevent anyone from recognizing her and asking unwanted questions. Just ahead, she spotted the pudgy form of Jude Montgomery, lumbering down the hall with a cup of steaming coffee in his outstretched hand.

As she overtook him, an urge she just couldn't resist came over her. Just as he was about to take a sip, Marta deliberately bumped into him as she hurried past. Coffee splashed up against his face and drenched the front of his immaculately clean and pressed white dress shirt. He yelped in pain and frustration and stumbled back against the wall.

"Clumsy lout!" he shouted after her.

Marta ignored his protest and increased her pace even more until she made it to the elevator bank and headed for the sublevel that housed the hangar bay.

Kinney, Chaz and Lydie were standing next to their stormcruiser, parked in one of the dank underground hangar bays, getting ready to embark on their imminent mission. Suddenly the thud of rapid footfalls echoed throughout the labyrinth. They turned to stare as a single form ran toward them from down the connecting passageway.

Kinney raised a hand cautiously and motioned for Chaz and Lydie to enter the cruiser. "Get inside," he said firmly and they quickly complied. Then he brought his hand up to his sidearm as the helmeted figure dressed in mission garb rapidly approached.

"Identify yourself!" Kinney shouted.

The figure slowed to a walk. "Kinney, it's me," pleaded a female voice.

Kinney's eyes widened in recognition. "Marta?"

Marta walked up to Kinney and pulled off her helmet. Then she held out the data pad. He accepted it and gave it a brief look.

"Are you sure this is a good idea?" he asked sharply.

Marta huffed disgustedly. "Good to see you, too."

Chaz and Lydie both reappeared in the hatch of the cruiser. Lydie held out her hand toward Kinney who handed her the data pad. She studied it a moment and then looked at Marta.

"I can verify that she is authorized as a ride along. Major Keller, you can let her pass," Lydie said and then broke into a broad smile.

Marta smiled back and the tension in the air seemed to evaporate.

Chaz motioned toward the interior of the cruiser. "Whatcha'll waitin' for, people? Don't let the snails nip ya in the ass. We got us a mission to complete." He disappeared back inside.

Marta climbed the steps and paused before Lydie who was holding out her hand. She grasped it firmly.

"Welcome aboard, Marta," Lydie said.

"Thank you, Lydie," Marta said and then quickly corrected herself. "Commander," she said, emphasizing the single word.

Lydie nodded proudly and followed Marta into the cruiser. Then Kinney mounted the stairs and disappeared inside. Behind him, the hatch swung shut and latched with a clunk.

CHAPTER 22

Barreling down Hwy 281 just south of Lawton, the lone stormcruiser, its lightbars blazing, had the two southbound lanes of the highway nearly to itself. The air was heavy and still but the brooding clouds to the southwest cast a grim yellowish tinge over the landscape, adding to the strong sense of foreboding that the entire crew instinctually felt.

Marta shifted uneasily in her cramped foldout guest seat, her back against the side of the cruiser behind Chaz. If she leaned slightly forward, tugging against her restraints, and looked left she had a clear view out the expansive windshield between Chaz and Lydie. But right now, her attention was focused on Kinney, seated just to her right behind his wraparound console. She had her helmet on and visor down so she was privy to the rapidly shifting virtual displays arrayed before him.

"Haven't seen you in awhile," Kinney said, not bothering to even look in her direction.

"I know. Lots of adjustments happening in my life lately," Marta said, trying to sound apologetic.

Kinney nodded, still refusing to meet her gaze and concentrating solely on his console. It was quite apparent that he was giving her the cold shoulder and she couldn't really blame him. But her trust in him had waned significantly since their last contact which had left more questions than answers regarding the people who'd attacked her and how far the military's involvement really went in that whole affair. One thing was certain. Her relationship with Kinney would never be the same now that a component of distrust had crept into the equation.

Just then, Marta felt the cruiser braking hard. She turned her head to peer out the windshield and saw brake lights ahead in the gloom. The way they zigzagged back and forth across the road told Marta instantly that something bad was happening.

"Looks like we got us a little game of bumper pool going on up yonder," Chaz commented dryly, just as the cruiser transitioned onto a bridge that crossed a deep wooded ravine. The careening brake lights had dimmed to just a single set of taillights and were now unmoving.

Chaz slowed the cruiser as they approached. When they were just twenty meters away, the wreck that they had watched play out from a distance in the eerie ballet of dancing brake lights materialized out of the gloom. Chaz eased the cruiser to a stop just twenty meters behind a two-vehicle accident. An enormous Mack dump truck faced sideways across the entire width of both southbound lanes of the bridge, wedged tightly between the cement guardrails. Pressed up against the side of the dump truck was an aging yellow Chevy Volt.

Lydie turned in her seat. "Major, see if we need to render any assistance. I'll call it in and get an emergency crew here."

Kinney unbuckled his restraints, got up and swung open the hatch. He turned to see Marta standing right behind him. He opened his mouth as if to protest and then thought better of it. Instead he turned and pointed at Chaz and Lydie. "You two stay put," he said sternly and slipped out through the hatch with Marta following on his heels. Kinney came to a sudden stop as he passed the right front corner of the cruiser. He held out his arm, blocking Marta. She glared at him but he didn't notice. His narrowed eyes were darting between the dump truck and the car.

Marta quickly surveyed the scene herself, wondering what he had seen that had him spooked. She immediately noticed the driver's door on the dump truck was wide open but the cab appeared empty. She also noticed that there was still a meter wide gap between the car's front bumper and the truck and no discernible damage to the car. Yet the driver of the car was slumped over in the seat, a hooded sweatshirt concealing his head and his face turned away.

Marta heard a pop and realized it was Kinney releasing the strap on his holstered sidearm. Her anger flared, knowing that he was wasting precious time with his constant paranoia when lives could be on the line.

"Kinney, we don't have time for this. People could be seriously injured here, for God's sake. Now go back and get the medkit from the cruiser," she admonished. Kinney didn't budge. "Please," she added, her features softening.

Kinney sighed and reluctantly took a few steps back toward the cruiser with Marta looking on. Then he froze in his tracks as a dark blue sedan rolled to a stop behind the cruiser. The passenger side door swung open and a tall, dark-haired man began to climb out. Kinney's finely honed battle instincts took over the instant he saw the muzzle of the submachine gun rise into view above the opened car door. Before the man could even level his own weapon, Kinney had drawn, aimed and put two rounds through the car door's window. The metal jacketed slugs shattered the safety glass and tore through the man's torso, dropping him to the pavement and ensuring that he would never get up again.

Then Kinney turned his attention to the driver who was standing behind his own open door and in the process of pulling the pin on a stubby cylindrical grenade. Kinney took careful aim and put a single bullet through his forehead. He watched as the man's eyes rolled up, his limbs went rigid and he toppled over backward like a felled tree. The grenade spilled from his hand, bounced once and rolled behind the car. Kinney ducked down, knowing what was coming. Three seconds later, the explosion sent a swarm of hot shrapnel whistling through the air but what the car didn't stop, the armored plating of the cruiser effectively blocked.

Marta had dropped to her knees near the front of the cruiser, stunned by the unforeseen violence that had just transpired. As the blast wave from the exploding grenade swept past, she noticed a black clad figure clamber over the guardrail and quickly close in on Kinney's crouched form from behind. She felt her throat tighten but before panic could claim her voice she screamed, "Kinney! Behind you!"

Kinney leaped to his feet and swung his pistol to cover whatever new threat he might be facing. The black figure ducked underneath his line of fire and pivoted on one heel, bringing his leg around in a blindingly fast arc that swept Kinney's legs from under him. He hit the pavement hard, air exploding from his lungs.

Dazed, Kinney had no chance to prepare for the swiftness of his attacker's next move. He leaped onto Kinney, his legs straddling Kinney's chest and trapping his left arm against his body. Kinney tried to raise the gun he still held in his free right hand but that arm was also quickly pinned to the ground. Then he saw the face glaring down at him. It was Ahiga, his long black hair hanging about his face, dark eyes wild with rage. With a blood-curdling war cry, he lifted a gleaming hatchet above his head and brought it down toward Kinney's skull.

In one single powerful motion, Kinney yanked his left arm free and caught the handle of the hatchet before the blade cleaved his head like a melon. Ahiga tried repeatedly to yank the hatchet free of Kinney's iron grasp but to no avail. He couldn't find the leverage and his other arm was busy restraining Kinney's dangerous right hand that still clutched the gun.

Marta had been watching Kinney's struggle, horrified. Witnessing the sheer savagery of the attack had left her in a near catatonic state of shock. She heard a car door creak open behind her. Still on her knees, she turned and watched a man climb out of the Chevy Volt and shrug off the hood of his sweatshirt to reveal a long, black ponytail. He turned toward her, a menacing long-barreled revolver tucked in his hand. The man smiled and started raising his weapon.

Kinney was still clinging for dear life to the hatchet's handle and watching with an almost amused expression as Ahiga desperately tried to free it with no more luck than if it had been embedded in solid rock. Then, out of the corner of his eye, Kinney saw the man emerge from the car in front of the cruiser, ten meters beyond where Marta knelt.

Knowing he had his hands full at the moment, Kinney sought help from the only source available to him. "Chaz! Run that bastard down!" he yelled into the open hatch of the cruiser.

Inside the cruiser, Chaz heard Kinney's appeal and threw the vehicle into gear. But as he watched the man raise his weapon toward Marta, Chaz's vision dimmed, his perception turning inward. In his mind's eye he saw his father standing there in front of the cruiser, a look of inconsolable grief on his face, his hand outstretched as if pleading with his son. Chaz's determination faltered. His foot refused to press down on the accelerator pedal. Beads of sweat broke on his forehead and his breaths came in shallow heaves. Eyes wide, he looked through the windshield at a ghostly recollection, powerless to act.

"I can't!" he yelled in defeat and exasperation.

Back outside, Kinney growled. "Damn bleeding heart redneck!" His face contorted into a mask of single-minded focus as he willed his pinned right arm to rise. Ahiga instantly threw as much weight as he could down on Kinney's arm to hold it in place. Veins in Kinney's forehead bulged. The sinewy bands of muscle in his thick neck swelled. Then he let out his own guttural warcry as his arm lifted above the pavement through sheer force of will and, somehow, he managed to line up a shaky shot with Marta's kneeling form nearly blocking his line of fire. He said a silent prayer to the gods of war and squeezed the trigger.

The single bullet left the barking muzzle of Kinney's gun and zipped along its straight-line trajectory, eager to inflict carnage on whatever happened to be in its path. Marta felt a searing sting as the bullet slashed her cheek on its way past her. It continued on, oblivious to the wound it had already inflicted, and closed in on its final mark. It hit the man directly center of mass, its hard casing stripped away by the impact as it shattered the man's breastbone to gain access to far more vital targets. The remaining lead expanded and bloomed, ripping a massive ragged channel through his chest cavity, severing vital arteries and obliterating half of his heart. Still holding the revolver out, the man's lifeless form crumpled.

Marta got to her feet, both hands clutching her wounded face. She stared at the still form lying next to the car in disbelief. Then she heard the whine of a turbine and a steady cadence of odd thumping that she could feel in her chest as well as hear. She turned around to see a sleek, black two-person mini-copter pop up above the bridge from the depths of the ravine below.

Before she could comprehend what was happening, she saw Yanaba lean out the right side of the chopper, holding a scoped assault rifle in her hands. Even from a distance, Marta could see the new gash that Yanaba's own knife had opened up on her face along with a black patch that covered her left eye. Yanaba grinned, distorting her features further as her scars stretched. For a brief moment their eyes met and Marta could feel the hatred and the overpowering urge for vengeance. Flames spit from the muzzle. The pavement at Marta's feet erupted as chunks of asphalt were blown out of the road's surface by the barrage of lead.

Marta ducked down and staggered toward the cruiser for cover, dodging behind the left side of the armored vehicle just as a line of bullets stitched across the armored hood, sending up sparks and metal fragments. She leaned back against the cruiser to catch her breath.

On the opposite side of the cruiser, Kinney was still engaged in his life or death struggle with a man hell-bent on avenging his own brother's death. Once Kinney had taken his shot at Marta's potential assassin, Ahiga leaped up and brought both of his knees down onto Kinney's gun arm, forcing it back to the pavement and jarring the gun loose from his grip. The weapon went skittering several meters across the asphalt.

Despite the loss of his weapon, Kinney took full advantage of his legs suddenly being freed. Maintaining his iron grip on the hatchet, he curled his torso, lifted his legs up and twisted sideways just enough to wrap his calves around Ahiga's head. Bringing both legs back down in one powerful thrust, he flipped Ahiga backward with enough force that he nearly broke his neck.

As Kinney scrambled up off the ground, he was amazed to see the smaller man correct his uncontrolled tumble, execute a reverse somersault and pop back to his feet, still brandishing his hatchet. They circled each other. Kinney, now weaponless, kept his eyes locked on his opponent but he used his peripheral vision to scan his immediate surroundings for anything he could use to gain an edge. Ahiga lunged, taking a swipe across Kinney's midsection with the hatchet that he barely dodged in time.

Kinney's cursory visual sweep paid off. A devilish gleam appeared in his eyes as he quickly devised a risky ploy. Slowly, he backed toward the armored hull of the cruiser. Ahiga played along, knowing he would soon have his prey backed into a deadly corner.

Kinney's back touched the side of the cruiser. He feigned surprise and dismay at being trapped with his back to an immovable object. He glanced nervously left and right as if seeking an escape route. Cautiously, Ahiga closed in on his quarry. He brought the hatchet up over his head, let loose another war cry, and swung. Kinney timed it perfectly. He dropped to the ground, just as a small voice in his head reminded him that he'd be completely defenseless if his plan didn't work.

Ahiga had thrown every ounce of his strength behind his furious swing. When his target suddenly ducked, there was no time to adjust the arc of his hatchet. The razor sharp blade pierced the outer layer of the cruiser's hull just deeply enough to trigger the reactive armor, priming it to repel any hostile force threatening the hull's integrity. In the blink of an eye, the shaped charge detonated, hurling Ahiga backward with the force of a cannon. His already mangled body hit the guardrail, glanced off and spun like a ragdoll before plummeting into the ravine.

Kinney stood and took several tentative steps away from the cruiser, shaking his head to clear the loud ringing in his ears. Before he even had time to gather his wits, the ground exploded around him as Yanaba opened up on him with her assault rifle from the hovering copter. With no cover for several meters in any direction, he was out of options and waited for the killing shot that would surely take him before he could even move.

"Heads up!" he heard Chaz cry out from the cruiser's hatch. He spun just in time to catch the rifle that Chaz tossed to him. In a single well-practiced movement he dropped to one knee, brought the rifle to bear on the copter and let loose a salvo. Tracers slashed through the sky like a line of angry glowing hornets. They closed in on the chopper as Kinney corrected his aim. The copter's bubble canopy popped and shattered where the bullets stung it. Then the pilot veered sharply away and the copter vanished beneath the bridge. Once out of imminent danger, his thoughts turned to Marta and he dashed around the back of the cruiser.

Marta had heard the last exchange of fire and was hoping it would be the last. She jumped when Kinney came flying around the rear corner of the cruiser. He grabbed her arm and spun her toward him, his eyes scanning her from head to toe. She knew that he was looking for any serious injuries that would require immediate attention.

"You okay?" he asked.

Marta nodded. "I think so," she said.

For a moment their eyes locked. Lightning flashed across the sky and a deafening peal of thunder shook the ground. But it was another sound that drew Kinney's attention as a motorcycle rolled to a stop on the nearby bridge for northbound traffic. The operator, his head concealed by a black helmet, slipped from the bike and took cover behind the cement railing.

"Down!" Kinney yelled and pushed Marta down behind their own bridge's railing. Bullets pinged off the cruiser's armor plating behind them as the motorcyclist opened up. A shower of sparks rained down on them. Kinney popped up above the railing and returned fire, his bullets sending up a cloud of concrete dust where they pitted the railing. Two more volleys were exchanged.

Marta cringed with every shot that hit the cruiser. She pointed at one of the dimpled armor panels. "Won't they explode?" she asked.

Kinney knew what she was insinuating and shook his head. "It takes more than small arms fire to set them off," he assured her. "A hatchet works real nice though," he mumbled to himself.

"What?" Marta asked, confused, having missed the entire incident. Kinney shrugged her off and sent back another volley toward their latest attacker.

Just as Kinney brought the rifle back down, the copter swung into view and Yanaba unleashed a burst of withering fire from her assault weapon that slammed into the cruiser. Several of the rounds ricocheted toward Kinney. One hit the rifle. Another caught Kinney in the left shoulder. He ducked down, howling in pain. Swinging the rifle barrel up to provide cover fire, he pulled the trigger. Nothing happened. Examining the gun, he saw a cratered hole where a bullet had burrowed into the receiver. Damaged beyond repair, he tossed the rifle to the ground.

Before Marta knew what was happening, Kinney had thrown her down flat on the ground and given her an urgent shove that rolled her underneath the cruiser. She took the hint and continued to roll. Then she noticed Kinney rolling along right next to her. They continued to roll until they popped out on the opposite side of the cruiser.

Kinney was on his feet before Marta and pulled her up beside him. Quickly, they clambered into the cruiser and Kinney shut the hatch behind them. He turned and pulled a medkit off the wall just as Marta plopped down in the guest seat.

"No. Take the console, Marta," he insisted. She didn't argue but slid behind the console and slipped her helmet on. Kinney sunk into the guest seat. Chaz and Lydie were staring back at them, still completely overwhelmed by what had just happened.

"How about getting us the hell out of here, Chaz!" Kinney yelled.

Chaz, snapping out of his daze, went to work. The cruiser lurched backward, accelerating straight for the car that had blocked them in from behind. On impact, the momentum of the cruiser spun the car sideways into the guardrail like it was nothing more than a toy. Chaz continued backing up until they were clear of the bridge.

"You've got to be shitting me!" Chaz exclaimed, just as a black Toyota Lancer Z and a compact silver pickup truck with two men standing in the bed cradling rifles screeched to a halt fifty meters further behind them. Chaz didn't wait for them to open fire. He gunned the turbine and steered the cruiser across the grassy median, throwing up chunks of sod, and into the northbound lanes of the highway.

The car and pickup made the same maneuver and took up the pursuit, with the cycle not far behind and the copter following along just above them. Bullets began pinging off the armor plating at the rear of the cruiser.

As if the situation wasn't already grim enough, the approaching storm's leading edge had reached them. Nature's assault ramped up quickly. Rain fell in heavy sheets. Winds buffeted the cruiser but, thankfully, had little influence against its enormous bulk. But it was only a matter of time before they would have more than just straight-line winds to contend with.

Inside the cruiser, Kinney had the medkit open on his lap and winced from the pain as he sprayed his shoulder wound with a coagulant to help control the bleeding. Looking up at Marta, he noticed the blood still oozing from the slash across her face and held out the spray to her.

Marta shook her head. "I'm okay," she said.

"Sorry about winging you," Kinney said, then he smiled. "Hell of a shot though, you've got to admit."

Marta tried to smile back but found it next to impossible as the pain flared to life in her cheek. She dabbed at her wound and glanced down at her trembling hand. "Speaking of shots, I could use one right about now. Maybe a double," she quipped, realizing there would always be occasions where a drink or two sounded more than a little inviting.

Marta listened in as Lydie tried calling for assistance on the radio but was met by a wall of static. She stared at Kinney who was just finishing up applying a gauze pad to his wound. "You recognized the man who attacked you, didn't you?" she asked.

Kinney nodded. "We knew they'd be back sooner or later," he said.

"You knew?" she asked, her eyes flashing.

"They want the new SCORCH-5 warheads," he said, setting the medkit on the floor. Another burst of gunfire ricocheted off the hull. "Very badly," he added.

"So you were using this cruiser as bait?" she asked.

"We were doing everything we could to track them down but they're very good at crawling under rocks and disappearing. We've also had two Saber gunships covertly escorting us just out of visual range ever since that little incident at your apartment building."

Marta peered out the windows, scanning the skies. "Where the hell are they?" she asked.

Kinney leaned back in his seat and closed his eyes. "They usually link up with us just after we leave Oklahoma City. Unfortunately they got caught in the damn storm."

Chaz turned in his seat. "Ain't no way we can outrun these guys!" he admitted.

Kinney's eyes popped open. He nodded solemnly. "I was afraid of that," he said. Marta watched suspiciously as he pulled his phone from his pocket, then glanced up at her. "I hope you understand. Those warheads we're carrying cannot be allowed to fall into their hands."

Marta recognized the app he opened on his phone. Her heart skipped a beat. "Too many lives at stake," Kinney said as he held his thumb to the phone's screen. Marta knew that any pleading with Kinney would fall on deaf ears. Her only chance was to make it clear just how many lives really were at stake.

"Lydie, how many cruisers are covering this sector?" Marta shouted up toward the cockpit.

"We're it," Lydie called back.

Kinney's phone projected a red beam that swept over his right eye. "Identification confirmed," a female voice stated.

"So if we don't get there to defend those towns...," Marta continued.

Lydie turned back with a grim look on her face. "They won't have a chance," she said.

Kinney's finger hovered over a glowing red icon on his phone. He looked up into Marta's pleading eyes and sighed. Then his finger shifted and he tapped a smaller green icon. "Cancelled," the voice intoned.

Marta took a deep breath and blew it out forcefully, knowing how close they'd just come to being vaporized by their own booby-trapped ordnance. When her heart slowed to a manageable pace, she turned her attention to the console and tried to make sense of the displays. The tactical radar was nearly identical to the one available to the commander but most of the controls were totally unfamiliar to her, having more to do with tracking and weapons delivery than the passive monitoring and communications systems that she was used to.

She felt the cruiser lurch sideways as Chaz steered them off the main highway and down a side road heading west. She didn't bother asking where they were going, trusting his navigational instincts to get them to where they needed to be.

The storm was hitting hard. Rain hammered at the cruiser's hull. Lightning streaked across the sky almost continually. The occasional ping of bullets deflecting off the hull served as a constant reminder that they were still under attack by man as well as nature.

Marta glanced through the windshield and did a double take. High-towered wind turbines rose like one-legged sentinels to the far horizon or at least to the limit of their weather restricted vision. Huge triple-bladed propellers spun rapidly all around them. She quickly deduced that Chaz had navigated them onto the maze of access roads that weaved through the sprawling Comanche County wind farm.

"Where the hell are you taking us, Chaz? We have to lose these assholes and get to the designated launch zone," Marta yelled over the constant din of rain and bullets.

"I'm working on it. Just thought our new friends might lose interest if we took the scenic route," Chaz shouted back.

"We don't have much time," Lydie reminded him, trying to raise her soft voice above the clamor, even as she dug her gloved fingers into her armrests for support.

"Well if them fellers hadn't plugged that bridge up on us I wouldn't have had to go all cattywampus."

"Cattywampus?" Marta asked, frowning.

Kinney shrugged. "Who knows? You'd have to grow an extra appendage and lose a few teeth to be able to understand half of what he says."

Somehow, over the racket of bullets, turbine, and weather, Chaz overheard the insult. "Hey now. I still got all my white and sparklies," he said, tapping his front teeth proudly.

Marta stared down at the radar display as it began tracking several new targets in the immediate vicinity. "We have funnels on the ground," she informed everyone.

"How many?" Lydie asked.

"Three F2's. Nothing big yet," Marta said.

"I've got a feeling the party is just getting started," Kinney chimed in.

Lydie was staring in abject terror at the huge rapidly spinning blades that surrounded them on every side. "My God! Why are they still turning? In a storm, aren't they supposed to lock them down or something?"

Kinney leaned forward and looked out. "The control station for the wind farm is only about half a klick from the bridge where we were just involved in a major firefight. I'd wager the operators got spooked by the sound of the gunfire and abandoned their post."

Chaz pointed off to their right. "There goes one," he said, just as flames erupted at the apex of one of the towers as the turbine overloaded. The propeller broke loose and hit the ground still spinning, sending it cartwheeling across the landscape until the blades splintered and the remnants collapsed in a heap.

While Marta and the crew were mesmerized by the destruction playing out around them, the motorcycle broke from the ranks of the pursuing vehicles and pulled up close on the right side of the cruiser. The rider lifted a short barreled shotgun and fired it at the commander's side window.

Inside the cruiser, Marta saw the spiderweb cracks form on the window next to Lydie. "Shit!" she shouted. Whatever kind of ammunition they were using, she was quite sure the armored glass in Lydie's window wouldn't take another hit from it without shattering. Suddenly, an alarm sounded from her console.

"Impending lightning strike," Kinney told her, glancing down at the panel. "Electrical potential building fast," he warned.

Marta knew what had to be done but her unfamiliarity with the tactical console was hindering her ability to act. Finally, she found the controls that activated the lightning countermeasures and brought them online. Her visor projected a view out the back of the cruiser with a targeting reticle in the center. She aimed toward the ground but then caught a glimpse of the motorcycle as it tagged along with the cruiser, the rider already angling for another shot. She swung the reticle up to point directly at the cycle. The Gatling-gun-like launcher mirrored her movements. "This is how you kill two birds with one stone," she snarled and fired.

The sleek tubular countermeasures package erupted from the barrel and hurtled toward the motorcycle. Its spiked tip caught the rider in the knee, punching cleanly through bone, flesh and cartilage. Then it embedded itself in the bike's frame just above the small turbine engine. Straight as an arrow, the conducting line shot skyward. In the next instant, a lightning bolt struck, sending a chaotic rush of energy hurtling down the line. The rider's knee vaporized in a puff of smoke and ash, leaving his booted foot and calf still perched on the pedal. Tiny streamers of current danced across the bike's frame and arced to the ground. One of the streamers found its way to the batteries. They exploded, tumbling bike and rider end for end. They vanished in an expanding wave of mud and flame.

Kinney looked impressed. "Wow. Remind me not to piss you off," he commented dryly.

Chaz continued on his erratic course through the wind farm, dodging debris and doing what he could to evade their dogged pursuers. Behind them, the copter was taking a beating from the storm. It shuddered and pitched as the winds tossed it about. The pilot brought it down close to the ground just behind the cruiser and Yanaba opened fire once more, raking the rear of the cruiser with bullets. Several rounds tore into the gimbal mount for the lightning countermeasures launcher, eliciting a quick flash of fire and puff of smoke. Then one of the reactive armor panels on the rear hull exploded outward.

Marta heard the explosion and knew what it was. She looked accusingly at Kinney. "What did you say about small arms fire not setting them off?"

Kinney gave her a lopsided sheepish grin. "Lucky shot," he said just as a second panel blew outward and he quickly looked away.

Another alarm went off on Kinney's console. "F2 on our right!" Marta yelled.

Kinney looked right and his eyes widened. "No shit!"

Just off their right flank, a spiraling column of wind and debris licked at the ground, paralleling their path. It veered closer. They all felt the left side of the cruiser lift into the air as the twister tugged at them. Chaz quickly veered away and the cruiser settled back to the ground with a jolt.

"Thought we were on our way to Oz there," Kinney commented.

Marta gestured behind them. "With that flying witch behind us, I thought we were already there."

Chaz chuckled. "Hell, I'd sure like to click my heels together and be home right about now."

Kinney snickered and said, "You'd have to trade in your shitkickers for a set of ruby slippers first."

Without missing a beat, Chaz tapped his Stetson and replied, "Nah. They'd clash with my hat."

Another armor panel blew out behind them as the copter shadowed their every move and Yanaba continued to direct salvo after salvo into the aft section of their cruiser. Chaz angled their course directly toward one of the spinning wind turbines, hoping that the pilot would veer off rather than risk following them underneath it. But the copter stayed right on their tail, just two meters off the ground. Gusts of wind pummeled the small craft, rocking it side to side. Despite the constant jostling, Yanaba continued to fire short bursts from her rifle, scoring hit after hit.

As the cruiser closed in on the wind turbine platform, Chaz watched the enormous blades slice through the air. He almost lost his nerve and veered off. Instead he just held his breath and prayed that his instincts would prove correct.

The cruiser passed beneath the propeller blades with just centimeters to spare. Behind them, the copter's pilot maneuvered even lower to stay clear of the spinning monstrosity. Just as they were about to pass safely underneath, a sudden updraft caught them and coaxed the ultralight aircraft to rise.

The pilot desperately fought against the controls to halt their sudden inadvertent climb. Just when he thought he'd succeeded, the winds shrieked like a banshee and drove the craft upward. They rose several meters. Yanaba saw the whirling blades as they hurtled toward them and fully understood what was about to happen. She lowered her rifle and waited quietly for the end.

One blade caught the copter across its midsection, shearing the fuselage neatly in two. The rear half continued on, crashed into the wind turbine's tower and exploded. The front section containing the doomed pilot and Yanaba tumbled and slammed into the ground, pulverizing their bodies to a bloody pulp on impact.

The crew of the cruiser had watched the whole thing play out on their monitors. Chaz grinned. "And that's why you don't fly in inclement weather, you dumb sons of bitches."

Marta snickered. "Scratch one witch. Maybe without their fearless leader her minions will decide to bug out."

Kinney just shook his head and Marta realized he knew better. Then she tensed up when Kinney grabbed his phone again. He held up a hand. "Relax," he said and began scrolling through his contact list. "I just need to make a call."

Marta watched as Kinney set his phone to speaker in another obvious attempt to ease her concerns over his intentions. She heard it ring twice. Then a female voice answered. "Oklahoma City Army Command. How may I direct your call?"

"General Ilea Coltrane," he stated plainly.

The woman's voice came back instantly and well rehearsed. "I'm sorry, the general is unavaila..."

"Codename Sleeping Giant, priority zulu one," Kinney broke in.

"Just a moment," came the stern response.

As they waited anxiously for someone to answer, lightning struck a wind turbine just ahead and to their right. The top of the tower disintegrated in a fireball. Chaz saw what was happening just as the hub of the propeller broke loose from its mount. He pegged the accelerator to the floor. The propeller assembly fell as if in slow motion. When the blades finally bit into the earth, they sent a hail of dirt and mud against the side of the cruiser and gouged a massive trench in the soggy ground. Then they pivoted ninety degrees and toppled over, narrowly missing the cruiser.

Chaz was just breathing a sigh of relief over the close call when he saw the Lancer Z come up alongside on their left. A long barreled weapon jutted out from the passenger window, pointed at the cruiser's double set of rear tires.

"Oh, hell no!" Chaz shouted and activated the left rear augur. The rotating shaft popped free of its recessed enclosure in the rear fender and swung down. A shower of sparks flew from the hood of the car as the giant drill bit tore a gaping hole and continued to dig deeper. The passenger in the car was so shaken he dropped his weapon. He and the driver watched helplessly as, less than a meter away, the augur penetrated the polished chrome turbine housing of their vehicle. With the screech of shearing metal, the Lancer Z's turbine expired in a quick burst of flame.

The driver spun the steering wheel left and right in a desperate attempt to break free but their impaled car was held tight. The downward pressure from the augur arm intensified, forcing the car to squat down, bottoming out its suspension. Then the tip of the augur pierced through into the wheel well. The tire popped loudly and the car, still secured to the cruiser by the augur's arm, started bucking violently from side to side.

The once sleek and sporty Lancer Z looked like a battered parasite clinging to its much larger host; a parasite that Chaz was preparing to rid themselves of. He tried repeatedly to retract the augur arm but it was lodged too securely in the scrambled innards of the car.

Chaz steered close to one of the towers, lining up the anchored car with the immovable structure and accelerated. The driver shoved open his door but, before he could jump, the car slammed into the tower, its front end folding in on itself like an accordion, crushing both men. The cruiser shuddered from the impact. Metal screeched as the augur arm was torn away, hydraulic fluid spewing from severed lines. The cruiser continued on, leaving a smoking pile of wreckage in its wake.

Behind them, the pickup, with two men hunkered down in its bed, was the last pursuing vehicle. After witnessing the destruction of their fellow terrorists in the Lancer Z, they slowed, allowing the cruiser to pull away.

"You reckon they're leaving?" Chaz asked.

Kinney glanced at the monitor showing the rapidly receding vehicle. "No. What I reckon is that they're opening up a kill zone," he said.

"Kill zone for what?" Lydia asked.

They heard a shrill whistle and saw a smoke trail streak past the windshield. Then flames erupted thirty meters away as a rocket propelled grenade cratered the ground. The shock wave from the explosion rocked the cruiser.

"Heavier weaponry," Kinney answered. Then a click sounded on Kinney's phone and General Coltrane's scowling face appeared on its screen.

"Major Keller, I trust this is not a social call?" said the general in her hard-edged voice.

"Far from it, general," Kinney shouted over the clamor of rain and the whine of the cruiser's turbine. "We are in active retreat from hostile forces. Taking heavy fire. Our options are limited. Request immediate support."

The general sneered. "Your support units, major, are still bogged down in OK City. You are aware of your responsibilities and your final failsafe option, are you not?"

Kinney shot Marta a knowing glance. "Yes, general, but I'm sure you recall that final determination to exercise that option was placed at my discretion and there are extenuating circumstances that preclude me from acting on it at the moment."

A glimmer of disappointment registered on the general's face. "Regardless, until our units can mobilize you are on your own, major."

Kinney took a deep breath before responding. "Request permission to wake the giant."

The general's face seemed to shrink and she took a step backward, obviously taken aback by the request, but she quickly recovered her stoic demeanor. "We can't afford any incidents that will reflect negatively on the army or suggest any intention to use Scorch Five in an offensive capacity, major. Do you foresee the potential for civilian casualties?"

"Other than the crew of this cruiser? No," was Kinney's deadpan answer.

The general nodded her head slowly. "Acceptable losses. Weapons free, Major. Terminate the threat with extreme prejudice."

"Thank you, general," Kinney said and ended the call.

"Going hot?" Marta asked.

"Fucking A," Kinney replied.

Chaz glanced back at them. "What was that part about acceptable losses?" he asked uneasily.

"I think that meant that we're expendable," Marta explained.

"Some more than others," Kinney grumbled just loudly enough to ensure that Chaz overhead it.

Lydie watched Kinney place his hand on the console for the requisite palm scan that would arm the missile system. She mirrored his movements on her own console.

"We might die today but it's not going to be at the hands of these assholes," Kinney assured everyone just as another rocket screeched past and plowed into the ground only meters away, showering the cruiser with shrapnel and debris.

"I hope," Kinney mumbled, this time low enough that only Marta picked up on it.

Kinney gingerly leaned over the tactical console and tapped a few icons. "Switching to ground target tracking mode. Bless those military engineers for not purging it from the system."

Without thinking, Kinney tried raising his left arm and winced. He leaned back in his seat and gripped his shoulder in pain. Marta looked at him worriedly. "I've got this one, Kinney," she said.

Kinney sank down into his seat and nodded, his face still contorted in a mask of agony. Marta shifted her attention back to the console and the radar display that had suddenly transformed itself. No longer did it show vibrantly colored spiraling winds and tracts of pastel-shaded rain. Instead, the screen glowed an ominous monochrome green, cluttered with well-defined stark white shapes that represented ground objects in their immediate vicinity. Several of them were demarcated by thin flashing trapezoids with a few lines of tiny text that indicated direction, speed, range and a few other parameters that Marta didn't recognize. One in particular drew Marta's attention as it shadowed their movements far behind them.

"I've got a target," Marta said.

The radar flashed a warning in red as a new smaller and faster moving blip appeared just above the object that held Marta's interest and rapidly homed in on their position at the center of the screen.

"Ah...incoming?" Marta shouted, not quite sure of what she was seeing but quite sure that a warning was definitely called for.

Chaz reacted, sending the cruiser into a skid as he changed direction and left the access road, hopping over to a parallel one. The road they had been travelling on blew apart, chunks of molten asphalt pelting the cruiser.

"Good call," Kinney said through gritted teeth.

Marta's eyes narrowed, focusing on the shape that she knew was the pursuing truck. Her finger tapped it. The trapezoid changed into a diamond and a solid tone sounded.

"I have a lock...I think," Marta said.

"Range?" Kinney asked.

Marta squinted at the text next to the designated target. "Six hundred meters," she read out loud, then looked up at Kinney whose expression of dismay and subtle shrug of his uninjured shoulder offered her no reassurance.

Then she glanced up at Lydie. "Commander?" she asked as a gesture of respect for the Storm Strike chain of command.

Lydie turned and looked Marta in the eyes. "Burn 'em," she said with an uncharacteristic amount of malevolence in her usual soft, squeaky voice.

"Roger that," Marta said and keyed in the launch sequence.

Above them, the missile carriage rose out of its armored crypt and rotated to face aft. A single rocket engine rumbled to life, its exhaust port glowing like an angry orange eye. Just as the missile began its upward slide along the launch rail, the cruiser momentarily vanished in a billowing cloud of smoke and steam.

Once airborne, the missile's guidance system quickly acquired its target and homed in, no longer programmed to seek a Doppler signature of spiraling winds and whirling debris. Dormant code in its processor awakened, transforming it from a life-saving tool into a cold-blooded killing machine.

The truck's driver saw the launch and watched in terror as the missile lay down a parabolic contrail and swiftly closed in on their position. He knew the end was near. In a futile, last ditch effort to avoid the incoming projectile, he swerved violently. The haphazard maneuver dislodged one of the men in the truck's bed whose limp body tumbled and skidded across the muddy ground.

Swooping down from the sky, the missile made a last second course correction, found its target and detonated. The truck and its occupants winked out of existence in a blinding flash. Flames, smoke, mud and debris coalesced into a rolling wave of destruction that swept outward in all directions. A dozen wind turbines toppled like dominoes as the expanding blast wave reached them, their blades sent hurtling through the sky like giant boomerangs.

The cruiser's occupants saw the shock wave coming and braced for the impact. It slammed into the rear of the cruiser like an iron fist, shaking the massive vehicle and sending bone-rattling vibrations throughout the interior. Marta clenched her jaw tightly shut to keep her teeth from chattering. Superheated air washed over the hull, blistering paint. Falling rain sizzled into clouds of dense vapor that enshrouded the cruiser.

Chaz kept the turbine wound out and the cruiser pointed away from the heart of the explosion. The turbine coughed as its supply of fresh air was momentarily interrupted but it kept dutifully churning out power. Gradually, the thunderous roar of the explosion died away, its energy dissipating, leaving only the howling winds and the steady whine of the turbine. Steam continued to pour off the cruiser's armored skin, still hot enough to instantly vaporize the rain that was pelting it.

"Scorched our ass hairs on that one," Chaz mused just as a splintered wind turbine blade came crashing down in the mud only meters away. With the immediate threat neutralized, he eased up on the throttle and loosened his grip on the steering wheel just enough to let blood flow back into his white knuckled fingers.

Marta knew the victory would be short-lived, as did her companions. By all indications, nature was about to unleash her own savage forces, pitting them against any creature that walked, crawled or flew. A single battered stormcruiser and her weary crew would be the only defense.

CHAPTER 23

Marta didn't allow herself even a moment to breathe a sigh of relief after the last of the terrorists were incinerated. Her finger tapped an icon on her console. "Switching back to weather tracking," she said and watched the radar display hovering before her light up with intensely colored splotches. She frowned, a sense of dread growing in the pit of her stomach as three tightly clustered swirling masses appeared at the edge of the screen.

"Stop here, Chaz," she said, hoping to tweak a bit more resolution from the image once their own motion was eliminated.

As they rolled to a stop, Kinney pointed out the windshield at a flashing white beacon moving slowly across the sky. "There, one of our seeder planes," he said. As they all looked closer, they saw that it was a plane silhouetted against the dark clouds. Its wings seesawed as it fought against the raging winds. One moment the nose tilted up, the next moment it pitched steeply downward. It was clear that the aircraft was rapidly losing altitude and already perilously close to the ground.

Marta thought she saw one wing dip just before the plane disappeared behind a hill. They all held their breath. A moment later, their worst fears were realized when they saw the plume of dense smoke begin to drift up from behind the hill.

"Damn," Chaz exclaimed.

Marta felt her stomach sink but knew she had to keep her focus. She stared down at the console. "If this radar track is correct, we've got our own problems right now," Marta said.

Kinney peered at the display. "A triad," he said, confirming Marta's suspicions. She'd never seen one before but knew the phenomenon existed. Three funnels orbiting about each other, drawing their energy from a common well of warm, moist air. Competing with each other in such close proximity, each tornadic element comprising the tight cluster never achieved a rating above F4 but they were notoriously difficult to bring down.

The lightning alarm squawked loudly. Marta could tell from the rapidly climbing bar graph of electrical potential that it was going to be a powerful strike. She quickly activated the countermeasures but she knew something was seriously wrong when her view through the launcher's camera spun out of control. Knowing they were out of time, she jabbed the fire button and hoped for the best.

The damaged launcher fired the countermeasures package at a nearly horizontal angle. The spike skidded along the ground with the tip barely penetrating the soil. Then the conducting line shot out but, rather than being launched skyward, it skimmed ineffectively over the ground before coming to rest.

A new alarm added an intermittent buzz to the higher pitched lightning warning. Marta searched her panel for an indication of what had happened but Kinney saw it first.

"Misfire!" he called out just before the bolt hit. Reaching down from the sky like the finger of an incensed god, the white hot streamer danced across the deployed missile pod and sent blazing tendrils of current streaking across the hull of the cruiser, searching for the path of least resistance that would take them to ground.

Inside the cruiser, the virtual control panels flickered from the sudden overload. Circuit breakers popped and all went dark. A faint haze of smoke hung in the air. Marta caught a pungent whiff of ozone that mingled with the acrid stench of scorched circuitry.

Kinney reached down to a panel near his feet, released an access panel and flipped several heavy switches. Power came back and the virtual displays winked on. Each system rebooted and quickly ran through its own series of diagnostics. Green lights flashed in quick succession across most of the panels as the systems miraculously checked out.

Chaz whistled. "Might have lucked out. I'm green across the board."

Marta watched the sequence of lights turning a cheerful green on her panel as well. The radar screen came back online without a hitch. Then a single red flashing light sent icy shivers down her spine.

"The fire control module in the turret isn't responding," Marta said.

"How serious is that?" Chaz asked.

Kinney looked grim. "Without it, we can't launch."

"I can fix it," Lydie stated resolutely and all eyes were suddenly on her. "Really. I worked in maintenance for eight years. I just need to swap out the controller board. I could do it hanging upside down and blindfolded."

Kinney looked doubtful. "But can you do it in gale force winds and driving rain with three shredders breathing down your neck?"

"I'll damn well try," Lydie shot back, releasing her restraints and climbing out of her chair without waiting for a reply. She rummaged through a storage locker behind her seat, pulled out a circuit board sealed inside a clear plastic container and slid it into a pocket on her coveralls. Then she pulled out a safety harness, slung it around her shoulders and latched the belt around her waist.

"I want everyone to stay inside the cruiser and that's an order. This won't take long," Lydie said, releasing the hatch.

"Make it quick, Lydie. There's vortex activity everywhere," Marta warned.

Lydie nodded, just as wind and rain started whipping into the cruiser. She braced herself against the frame of the hatch, took a deep breath and vanished into the maelstrom.

Lydie clung to the side of the cruiser and watched the hatch slam closed behind her. She worked her way around to the rear of the vehicle where an access ladder extended up. Taking a moment to steel herself, she began to climb. Twice, her feet slipped off the rain-slick rungs and she found herself clinging to the ladder with just her small hands as the wind attempted to fling her off.

Finally she pulled herself up onto the roof and lied there, prone, hugging the surface tightly with her body to prevent the howling wind from prying her loose. Slowly she crept forward until her helmeted head bumped into the base of the missile pod. Feeling blindly around, she found a grab bar and snapped the short safety line from her harness onto it.

Once she knew she was secured, she pulled herself up into a kneeling position and wiped the rain from the visor on her helmet. She popped open an access panel on the missile pod and tried to peer inside but her helmet banged into the pod's exterior and prevented her from getting close enough to see what she was doing. Without hesitation she pulled her helmet off and wedged it between her legs. Stinging rain lashed at her face but she ignored it and poked her head into the tight space.

She immediately identified the damaged circuit board by its burnt and blackened edges. With a gloved hand she popped it free of its slot and discarded it over the edge of the cruiser's roof. Then she reached into her coverall pocket for the replacement board. Grasping it firmly, she fumbled to remove the plastic container surrounding the board. Finally, it slid free of its protective sheath and she quickly went to work installing it.

Back inside the cruiser, Marta slammed her hand down on the console as yet another alarm blared to life. "Damn it!" she yelled. "We have an F3 right on top of us!"

Chaz activated the sequence to begin digging the cruiser in but, instead of hearing the comforting and familiar drone of the servo motors, more warning alarms shrieked. Glancing toward each corner of the cruiser, his visor traced a red flashing outline of the still-retracted augur arms in his field of view along with a haunting message: 'Critical hydraulic pressure loss. System failure.' When he turned to look back toward the rear left corner, his visor painted him a grim picture of the missing augur arm and the severed hydraulic lines.

"Augur arm hydraulics are dead. Digging in ain't gonna happen," he yelled over the furious winds.

Marta tapped the intercom on her helmet. "Lydie! Can you hear me? Get the hell out of there!" she screamed.

Outside the cruiser, Lydie barely heard Marta's warning as she finished snapping the circuit board in place. She had just enough time to glance up and see it coming. Then she was lifted from the roof, her safety line snapping taut. Her helmet sailed straight up and was lost in the heart of the twister. Lydie tucked her head between her arms and prayed that the safety line would hold. Her body swung to and fro a meter above the cruiser like a tethered kite.

Then she felt the cruiser tilt, barely perceptibly at first. But as the pervading winds found purchase beneath its bulk, the cruiser began leaning to the left until it was teetering on two tires. Lydie closed her eyes and prepared for the worst.

Inside the cruiser, Marta held onto her restraints as the cruiser pitched to the side. The angle grew steeper and steeper until finally the vehicle keeled over and landed on its left side with the sickening groan of stressed metal. The deafening roar of the winds subsided back to the keening gusts of a few moments before as the shredder moved away.

Releasing her restraints, Marta dropped to the wall of the cruiser which had now become the floor. Beside her, Kinney was still strapped into his now upward-facing seat, cradling his injured shoulder. Still a bit disoriented, she reached up over her head and hit the hatch release. Water, already pooling on the side of the upturned cruiser, poured in. Marta ignored the sudden deluge and pulled herself up and out of the hatch.

Using the steps as a handhold she eased herself over the side and dropped to the ground. Her boots sank into the mud. She sidestepped along the underside of the cruiser toward the rear and heard a loud splash. Looking back the way she'd come, she saw that Chaz had landed on the ground and quickly headed in the opposite direction toward the front of the cruiser. Then she made her way around the rear corner, dreading what she might find on the other side.

When she came around the edge of the roofline, she saw Lydie lying on her back, half submerged in the muck, with her legs pinned beneath the missile pod. To Marta's surprise, Lydie's eyes opened and she stared up into Marta's face.

"Lydie!" Marta screamed and knelt beside her, lifting her head clear of the muddy water. Lydie reached up and gripped Marta's arm firmly.

At the front of the cruiser, Chaz reached down, popped the winch hook free from its mount and flipped the free-spool lever on the winch's motor housing. Then he started back along the underside of the cruiser, pulling the winch cable with him. Looping the cable around one of the steel beams that ran from one side of the frame to the other, he started backing away from the cruiser, dragging the cable with him.

"Now to find me an anchor point," he said to himself and wandered off into the storm.

Thunder rolled and lightning crashed as Marta held Lydie's head above the water, trying not to apply too much force in case she had incurred any neck injuries.

"Are you hurt?" Marta asked.

Lydie's face twisted in pain as she struggled for a moment. "I can't get my legs out," she said in exasperation.

Marta squinted down at where Lydie's legs disappeared beneath the exhaust ports on the trio of deployed missiles. Her gaze followed the missiles up as water streamed off their glistening white surfaces. Her eyes finally settled on the red tips, pointed skyward like mute sentinels.

They heard another rumble but knew instantly it wasn't thunder. Their heads turned in unison as lightning seared the sky and illuminated their surroundings to the far horizon. They saw them in the distance; a group of three twisters revolving about each other, engaged in a sinister ballet.

Kinney popped his head out of the hatch and joined them in watching the ominous spectacle. He lifted his visor and peered down at Marta and Lydie. "Radar has them plotted on a direct course for Southwest C&C Farms. And just beyond that is Grayson Flats."

Lydie looked up at Marta, rain coursing down her face. "Fire control should be back online."

Kinney nodded in confirmation. "It is," he said.

Lydie blinked against the rain. "Marta, you have to launch."

Marta looked down at her, appalled. "No, I can't do that," she said.

"You have to. There are too many people's lives on the line," Lydie said, her eyes pleading.

Marta knew that Lydie was right. She tried convincing herself of what needed to be done. Even her children's lives were in peril. But when she confronted her own moral code, she suddenly realized that the undetermined potential for lives to be lost still wasn't enough for her to condemn a single person to certain death. She shook her head.

Lydie turned her head toward Kinney who was still watching. "Major Keller, you are to launch a full salvo immediately and that is a direct order from your commanding officer," Lydie barked in as steady a voice as she could manage.

"Stand clear, Marta," Kinney growled.

Marta glared up at him. "Don't you dare!" she shouted just as Kinney's head vanished back into the cruiser. Her heart began to pound. She had a strong suspicion that he was more than capable of carrying out what would become the last order that Lydie would ever give.

Chaz was struggling to pull the cable through the thick mud as he searched for a solid anchor point. Debris was strewn across the ground from the shredder's passing. Just ahead, he spotted the shattered remains of one of the wind generator's towers. Several twisted pieces of rebar and a single massive bolt protruded from the ground. Chaz's eyes lit up. "Hot damn!" he bellowed and redoubled his efforts.

Suddenly, the cable went taut, jolting him to a stop. He turned and gave the line a tug but it didn't budge. He dug his boots into the mud and tightened his grip on the cable. Then, putting all of his remaining strength and weight behind it, he heaved. Without warning, the cable broke free.

Chaz tumbled into the mire but, knowing that every second counted, he scrambled to his knees and quickly regained his footing.

He covered the last few meters and reached the steel bolt. Wrapping the cable around its girth twice, he latched the hook back to the cable to secure it. Then he removed a small remote from his belt just as he happened to glance up into the sky and see the three twisters gyrating in the distance. His jaw dropped. "The devil's own trident," he whispered.

Shaking off his momentary daze, he hit a button on the remote and the winch spool started turning.

Marta struggled in vain to pull Lydie free despite her cries of anguish that coincided with each forceful tug. Marta was aware that the suits they wore were fire proof but she also knew that there was no garment made that could withstand a superheated stream of rocket exhaust at point blank range. She heard an ominous fiery crackle from the base of the missiles. Sparks skittered across the ground and she knew the launch sequence had been initiated. She held back the sobs that were building in her chest and prepared for one final heave.

Before she could make her last desperate attempt to save her friend, the cruiser shifted slightly. Metal groaned in protest. Then the edge of the roof lifted by a fraction of a centimeter and Marta knew there was a chance. She rallied her strength, tightened her grip under Lydie's arms and pulled. Lydie's legs slid free just as flames sputtered from the three missiles' exhaust ports.

Marta had no time to get her clear. It would simply be a matter of whether their suits could survive the inferno that was about to be unleashed. Then, in horror, she realized that Lydie wasn't wearing her helmet. Instinct took over. Marta slammed the visor on her own helmet shut, sealing it. She hurled herself down and shielded Lydie's unprotected face with her own body.

Hellfire consumed them. Flames licked at their suits, probing, as if seeking out any gaps or seams that would provide a ready path to the vulnerable flesh beneath. The three missiles lifted off in quick succession, their exhaust gases washing over the cruiser's hull. Then the heat subsided and the smoke cleared.

Marta rolled off Lydie and lay beside her, their boots and uniforms still smoking. She lifted her visor and coughed. A moment later and Lydie joined her with a racking heave of her own. Marta sat up and studied

Lydie's face closely, looking for peeling skin or blisters but thankfully finding only a thin layer of soot.

"Are we dead?" Lydie asked, half seriously.

Marta didn't answer immediately. She reached behind her head and pulled free a clump of charred hair from beneath her helmet. She wrinkled her nose. "Not unless heaven smells like rocket fuel and singed hair," she quipped.

The cruiser was still lying on its side with the winch cable taut beneath it. Kinney reappeared in the upturned hatch. Marta glowered at him. "You almost killed both of us, you son of a bitch," Marta ranted.

Kinney seemed unfazed. "I told you to stand clear," he replied, then turned his head to watch the departing missiles streak toward their targets, like predators stalking their prey. Three white hot flashes erupted as they found their mark, casting brief stark shadows across the landscape.

Over a kiloton of rampant energy ripped through the triad, dislodging the tips of the funnels from the ground and sending them wildly thrashing through the faltering air currents. Then the three shredders dissipated into nothingness. But something troubled Marta. The debris should have been falling from the sky but instead it hung there, suspended by latent forces.

Marta held her breath a moment longer, unsure of what she was seeing. It seemed as if the spinning clouds that had just been violently disrupted and torn apart were once more coalescing into a unified cohesive force. Then, like a giant phoenix reborn from its own ashes, a single vortex spun up from the remnants, with the combined mass of all three of its predecessors.

Marta could hardly believe that she was witnessing the birth of an F8, nature's most bold and violent destructive force, with wind speeds upward of five hundred kilometers per hour. Only two had ever been documented before. They were a product of the last decade's climatic upheaval, before which the atmospheric conditions that allowed them to form had never even existed.

As she watched, it quickly overtook the Southwest C&C farm complex, shredding buildings, imploding silos, and tossing heavy farm machinery like it was made of styrofoam. It lifted so much dirt and debris that it actually carved a trench in the earth as it went.

It was clear that the newly spawned monster would miss the cruiser by a wide margin. But that was little cause for celebration. Turning her head ninety degrees, in the distance, she could make out a few of the buildings that marked the outskirts of Grayson Flats. As she swung her head back toward the F8, its path lined up perfectly with the shanty town. She closed her eyes as any hope of seeing her children alive again dwindled.

Chaz had been busy hastily trying to reposition the cable which had begun to slip from the ground-anchored bolt a few seconds after he had applied power to the winch. He had just managed to secure it for a second try at righting the cruiser when he heard a low growling rumble begin to build. He could even feel the vibrations seeping up through the soles of his boots. Looking up at the sky, he watched in awe as a monster was born and started its rampage across the countryside. Then he pressed the button on the remote again. The line snapped taut and held tight to the anchoring bolt.

He crossed his fingers. "Come on. Roll, baby, roll," he urged.

The cruiser jolted violently as the cable tightened and Kinney lost his grip on the frame of the hatch. His head vanished as he lost his balance and fell back into the cruiser. A moment later, the vehicle reached a brief point of equilibrium, teetering on two wheels. Then the cable gave it one last nudge that pushed it past the tipping point and brought the cruiser back down on all four tires.

When the two right tires hit the ground, the impact dislodged Kinney from the interior and he rolled backward out through the open hatch, down the steps and into the mud where he lay, stunned and in agony from the further insult to his injured shoulder.

Chaz stepped up beside him, looking down with a comical expression. "This ain't nappy time, soldier," he joked. Kinney ignored him, his gaze fixed on the dented and oddly canted missile pod atop the cruiser, still smoking from the previous launch. It was quite apparent from the visible damage alone that the launcher was permanently out of commission.

Chaz followed his gaze up to the wrecked pod. "That don't look so hot," he said.

Marta came around the rear of the vehicle supporting a badly limping Lydie. "It's coming," Marta said.

"And we've got fifteen missiles and no way to launch them," Kinney said, gesturing toward the cruiser and wiping the rain from his face.

Chaz seemed to deliberate for a moment. Then, with a determined look, he leaped over Kinney's prone form and hit the steps to the cruiser running. He disappeared inside. A moment later the hatch slammed shut, leaving the rest of the crew stranded in the deluge.

Kinney gingerly pulled himself up out of the mud. "What the hell does he think he's doing?" Kinney ranted as the turbine rapidly spooled up. Then the cruiser's tires spun and they were left standing there, watching it depart under heavy acceleration.

Marta tapped the comm button on her helmet. "Chaz! What in God's name are you doing?"

They heard a burst of static in their helmets and then Chaz's voice broke through. "You remember that chance at redemption I was harping about? I think I just might have found it."

It quickly dawned on Marta exactly what he intended to do. "Chaz, it won't work. You're just going to get yourself killed. Even if you somehow manage to get the cruiser inside that thing, the missiles won't detonate."

There was a short pause before Chaz responded. "I beg to differ. I watched Kinney and Lydie arm those suckers not five minutes ago."

"Tell him, Kinney," Marta said.

Kinney activated his own helmet's transmitter. "She's right, Chaz. The warheads won't detonate. There's a proximity sensor that prevents the detonator from energizing while they're inside the storage bay." He gave Marta a guilty look and sighed heavily before continuing. "But I can remotely destruct the cruiser and the missiles along with it," he added as Marta shot him a cold stare.

"The hell you say," Chaz exclaimed excitedly. "Well, boy, get ready to light me up then. Just try not to enjoy it too much. Guess I'll know what it's like to be a June bug on a bottle rocket when it's the fourth of July."

Kinney already had his phone in his hand as he and Marta continued to stare at each other without saying a word. Rain streamed down their sullen faces in rivulets. The ground trembled with the approach of the mega-twister. Already having amassed several hundred tons of debris spiraling upward toward oblivion, it appeared as a solid mass and dominated the sky behind them, visible with each flash of lightning.

"You're a fine woman, Marta," Chaz called out over the comm. "I'm mighty proud to have known ya."

All eyes went to Kinney's phone as he unlocked it with his thumbprint and allowed the pencil-thin beam of red light to scan his eye. The ominous glowing red button appeared on its display.

Marta, Kinney and Lydie all turned to watch the receding cruiser's lights shimmering and swaying in the distance as the cruiser bounced over rough terrain on a collision course with destiny. The F8 loomed over it, ravenously collecting debris from the collapsed wind turbine towers and the innumerable shards of propeller blades that littered the ground. In its wake, it left a massive gully where the earth itself had been ripped away.

"And as for you, Kinney Keller. I'll see ya in hell, yankee!" Chaz yelled through the comm before static overwhelmed it. Then they watched as the twenty ton cruiser was lifted clear of the ground. It rose higher and higher, orbiting about the six kilometer wide funnel, its illuminators still blazing and warning lights flashing.

Kinney didn't hesitate. He tapped the button and the sky exploded. A flash of searing white light froze a single moment in time, followed by a boom louder than a thousand thunderclaps. The fireball that erupted swallowed the monstrous funnel which became an enormous swirling wall of flames, biblical in proportion and utterly apocalyptic in appearance. Then the flames died out, the fueling winds dissipated and nature's most demonic creation faltered and perished. A thick cloud of debris rained down from the sky like a plague from an angry god.

The rolling, surging, superheated blast wave generated from the explosion continued to radiate outward, scooping up muck, rain and rubble and churning it into a thick, steaming porridge. By the time it swept past the crew, its strength had diminished and most of the debris had already settled to the ground but it still felt like a door to a blast furnace had been opened right in their faces.

Even with the sound of the lessening wind and rain, they were left with an overwhelming sense of stillness. Marta was the first to stir and break the spell. She threw her helmet down. Then she put her arm around Lydie. Kinney did likewise on her other side and, together, they walked in silence toward the barely discernible settlement of Grayson Flats.

Their path took them past the center of the blast zone. They stopped to stare at a torn, burnt out section of the cruiser's hull that had come to rest half-buried in the ground. A hundred meters away, they could see the kilometer-wide canyon-like rift in the earth that traced the twister's path back in the direction of the decimated farm.

They continued on a short distance and came to a spot where one of the enormous wind turbine blades had come to rest after slashing a deep trench in the soft ground. The bulk of the blade had actually fallen directly onto the excavated trench with only a small crevice near the tip of the blade descending down into its depths.

Marta's eyes welled up when she saw Chaz's prized Stetson lying nearby, drenched, muddy and charred. She walked over and delicately picked it up, feeling a hot flood of emotion sweep over her. She knew he'd gotten what he'd wanted. But redemption never came cheaply or easily. She closed her eyes and wished her friend a safe passage.

"I'm going to be wanting that back," a voice called out in an unmistakable Carolina drawl. Marta's heart leaped as she turned to see a battered and bloody Chaz struggling to climb out of the exposed section of trench. Kinney rushed over and pulled him out with his one good arm. Getting shakily to his feet, Chaz looked up into the smiling face of Kinney, staggered back a step and then let loose with a right cross that sent Kinney sprawling backward into the mud.

Chaz grinned down at him. "That there's for blowing my ass up," he said. Kinney rose to his feet, wiped the trickle of blood from his mouth and just shook his head, evidently deciding to let the incident slide in consideration of the lives Chaz had just singlehandedly saved.

"I don't believe it," Marta mumbled and hugged Chaz tightly.

"Well, once I had her lined up on the straight and narrow, I popped the hatch, tucked my tail and hoped for the best. Musta slid for 'bout two city blocks. Wound up right here next to this rabbit hole so I slithered on inside." He tapped the side of his head with his palm. "Don't know as I'll ever hear the same again."

"Not to break up this reunion, but it looks like they took some damage, too," Kinney said, pointing toward Grayson Flats where thin tendrils of smoke were rising and the wreckage of several structures could be seen.

Without waiting for her companions, Marta took off at a dead run. By the time she reached the edge of the settlement she was winded and wheezing from the exertion. The rain had diminished to a light drizzle and the wind was little more than a brisk breeze. Above her, the ominous grays and blacks had given way to lighter shades of milky blue, lending assurance to Marta that the bulk of the storm had passed. But it was what she saw on the ground that horrified her.

The town was a shambles. More than half of the cobbled together houses had taken considerable damage. Roofs were missing. Windows shattered. Walls fashioned from metal sheeting curled back like pencil shavings. The street and yards were cluttered with myriad personal items; papers, dishes, clothing, all pilfered and discarded by the rummaging winds.

People were emerging from the makeshift shelters that she'd inspected on her prior visit to the shanty town. They seemed dazed but Marta couldn't discern any major injuries. She even saw several young people dressed in the familiar Red Cross uniforms ambling about but she failed to see the two faces that she was desperately searching for. She saw Brock step from one of the shelters, disheveled but otherwise uninjured and raced over to him. Then Marta's eyes lit up as she saw Bonnie climb out just behind him.

"Oh, thank God!" Marta cried and hugged her daughter. She glanced at Brock who returned only a sullen stare. "Where's Quinn?" Marta asked, suddenly concerned as she'd expected him to be right behind his sister.

Brock shook his head. "Didn't make it to the shelters. Last I saw of him he was playing with Chance on the other side of town. No sign of him either." Brock angled his face away, trying to conceal his obvious emotion.

Marta took another look at the decimated town, not having the slightest idea where to start searching. "Quinn!!!" she screamed at the top of her lungs but there was no reply. She reasoned it could take hours to find him. And when they did, the chances were that it would be a small, cold and lifeless body that they would be pulling from the rubble.

A soft, muffled bark sounded but Marta couldn't place from where. A tiny ember of hope flickered in her heart as she scanned the area and waited.

"Chance?" Brock called. Then they listened intently. Another bark, this time louder and what sounded like claws scratching against metal. Brock, Marta and Bonnie walked over to a sheet of tin lying on the ground nearby. Brock reached down and lifted it to reveal the badger hole that he'd shown Marta. Chance instantly bounded up and out of the hole, shook himself off and greeted Brock with a furiously wagging tail. Then he spun around and barked inquisitively at the hole.

They waited an intense moment. There was movement from within. Mud shifted and a small hand emerged. Then Quinn crawled out of the badger hole on his hands and knees, a thick layer of mud coating his face. Marta lifted him to his feet and held him close.

Brock bent down on one knee, allowing Chance to lick his face. "Damn lucky for them that badger hole wasn't occupied."

"You okay?" Marta whispered to Quinn while brushing the hair out of his eyes.

"I'm fine, mom," he said calmly, smiling up at her. "How about you?"

She smiled back. "I'm just fine, too," she said.

CHAPTER 24

Standing before a sweeping tinted glass window in the main concourse of Will Rogers Airport, Marta watched a jet soar from the runway, bank eastward and start on the first leg of its journey to LaGuardia. It carried Bonnie and Quinn, on their way back to New York and their father. They'd left on better terms than she could ever remember. It had been a teary-eyed farewell with warm embraces and the glowing promise of another visit in the not so distant future.

Clearly a maternal bond was forming that had been woefully absent before she'd managed to wrest a semblance of control over her own emotional issues. She still had her good days and bad ones but the debilitating extremes of mood that had plagued her for so long had been effectively blunted by the new medication which allowed her to function on a level that she had not known since her mental illness had manifested over a decade ago.

Once the jet became nothing more than an indistinct speck in the hazy blue sky, she turned and reached for the handle of her rolling black carry-on. With plenty of time to spare before her own flight was scheduled to leave, she strolled down a long corridor that would take her to another set of arrival and departure gates, one of which would serve as a portal to her new home.

New home. It had a bitter sweet ring to it. She was leaving behind a job that she still believed in as well as several cherished friends. But she was also leaving behind fog shrouded memories of anarchic moments best forgotten and the sting of regret at having squandered so much time before seeking an effective treatment for her disorder.

She'd never visited the west coast before and knew very little about California; Pasadena in particular. That was her destination. She'd decided to take Toni up on her offer of employment, leave the remnants of her former life behind and start anew.

It was late afternoon and the airport was saturated with fellow travelers, their expressions stern, their movements frenzied, intent on making it to wherever their travels were about to take them. As Marta walked along the expansive passageway, her own thoughts dwelled on those she was leaving behind. She'd made her intentions known to them but hadn't been able to bring herself to face them until the last moment and now it was too late. She wasn't fond of goodbyes, especially lasting ones. It was another regret that would probably haunt her.

A long line of square columns spanned each side of the walkway, their flat chromed surfaces diffusing and multiplying the reflections of passersby. As Marta approached each one in turn, its mirrored coating dissolved and she found herself watching a high-definition 3D advertisement that popped intrusively out at her. Each one was different, tailored to her own individual tastes and penchants. Such an intimate level of personalization was achieved by a series of antennas embedded throughout the airport that read the RFID chip embedded in the airline ticket that every traveler carried on their person. Their position was then triangulated in real-time. Polarized light and directional sound ensured that each traveler saw only the specific commercial intended for them as they walked past.

The first advertisement offered discounts to hotels in the Pasadena area where she would be landing in just a couple of hours and provided tantalizing glimpses of Jacuzzis, beds adorned with stacks of plump pillows and waiters presenting trays of decadent steaming entrees. The second ad gave her the option to reserve a taxi that would be waiting upon her arrival. The third made her smile. A shirtless male model holding out a glass in a mock toast. In his other hand, he held a bottle of Glenmore London Dry, Marta's favorite gin.

Toni had set her up in an apartment near the Mitchell Engineering main office thus rendering the first ad pointless. She was also personally picking her up at the airport to give her a brief tour of the city before stopping by the office and introducing her to her new co-workers. Thus the second ad was irrelevant as well. As for the third, she hadn't had a drink in weeks and felt no compulsion to partake any time soon.

The corridor opened up into a terminal with gates lining both sides to the far end of the building. Each gate had its own designated seating area. Gate eight was still beyond her line of sight, just past a lounge and coffee shop. She glanced down at her phone and checked the time. Her flight wouldn't be leaving for another forty-five minutes. Then she checked for new messages but found none. Out of habit, she opened her Doppler radar app. Sure enough, a long line of unsettled weather was rolling across the western border of Oklahoma. It would be a busy day for the crews out on the front lines.

Glancing up, she was surprised by how much ground she'd just covered, her gate looming just ahead. But she was even more surprised to see three familiar figures dressed in Storm Strike coveralls loitering nearby and watching her approach. The short-statured Lydie held crutches, still recovering from the sprained knee she'd suffered when Marta had unceremoniously yanked her out from beneath the cruiser. Chaz, his Stetson perched low on his forehead, hovered over her like an overprotective brother while Kinney hung back a couple of steps. Marta quickened her pace.

"Didn't think we'd let y'all hightail it out of here without a proper sendoff, did you now?" Chaz drawled out, a wide grin chiseling lines in his shadowed face.

Marta parked her carry-on behind her and smiled wistfully. "I'm glad you didn't," she said softly.

Chaz planted his hands in his pockets and rocked his knees back and forth. "So. California. Try not to have too much fun in all that sun and surf."

Marta snickered. "I think I'll be staying plenty busy."

"Busy saving the planet, I hear tell," Chaz asserted, raising a single mischievous brow.

"I'm going to do my part," Marta replied sincerely. "Just like you guys do every day out there."

Chaz shrugged off the subtle tribute. "It's a living."

Marta's attention turned to Kinney. She found his uncharacteristic aloofness disturbing.

"You're looking good, Marta," he uttered in a low tone, devoid of any perceptible emotion.

"Thank you, Kinney. I feel good," she said, narrowing her eyes, trying to pierce his stoic armor with her gaze but his face betrayed nothing.

Realizing she was fighting a losing battle she turned to Lydie. "Are you keeping these two in line?"

Lydie chuckled. "I'm holding my own," she said. Then she flipped her head back toward Kinney. "You can't find a more competent officer than Kinney. He knows what to do before he's even told to do it." She flashed a quick glance up at Chaz. "And Chaz...well, what can I say? He's Chaz."

Chaz bent low and wrapped his arm around her. "You wouldn't have it any other way," he quipped. Marta cocked her head, studying them. Something about the way that Lydie leaned into Chaz hinted to Marta that there was more than friendship brewing between them.

"I may be wrong but I think I'm sensing a bit more than professional courtesy here," Marta suggested cagily. Chaz and Lydie exchanged an amorous look that erased all doubt from Marta's mind.

"You might say we kinda hit it off," Chaz admitted.

Lydie reached up and gave Chaz's hand a delicate squeeze. "He's quite the southern gentleman. Just a little rough around the edges."

Marta grinned slyly. "Well, you'll just have to grind down the burrs then," she offered and watched Chaz's face flush as his own saying was tossed back at him.

Kinney snorted. "Grind down the burrs and there might not be anything left," he said in his classic deadpan style.

Chaz tilted his head and leered back at Kinney. "Said the man who damn near incinerated his own commanding officer."

"In case you've forgotten, I was following a direct order that she, herself, gave me," Kinney retorted with a sharpening edge to his voice.

Chaz retracted his arm from around Lydie and turned to square off against Kinney. "So I suppose if she ordered you to shoot me in the head you'd just be all too happy to oblige," he snapped.

Kinney gave a low chuckle but his eyes burned, never leaving Chaz. "I'd do that without being ordered to," he growled.

Lydie quickly went into action, using her crutches to boost herself up to her full height. "Alright, break it up, you two," she snarled and delivered a withering glare to each of them They both looked meekly away, abandoned their aggressive posturing and assumed a more relaxed stance.

Marta smiled, impressed with Lydie's spontaneous show of authority. "I see you've found your place," she conceded.

Lydie gave a forceful nod. "I certainly have," she said proudly.

Chaz jumped to attention as if a sudden realization had just hit him. "Hell, we gotta haul it," he exclaimed.

Marta frowned until Lydie filled her in. "Stormcruisers' double parked," she said and rolled her eyes.

Chaz broke into a broad smile. "Let 'em try to find a tow truck that'll budge that beast," he joked, even as he rushed forward and swept Marta off her feet in a tight bear hug that threatened to purge the air from her lungs.

"You take care, Marta," he murmured in her ear.

"You, too, Chaz," she said. Then he released his grip and backed away.

Marta stepped up to Lydie and gave her a gentle hug, taking care not to unbalance her. "You be careful out there, Lydie."

Lydie sighed. "I just hope I have what it takes," she said, her voice thick with doubt.

Marta took a step back and gripped Lydie's shoulders firmly. "I know you do," she said reassuringly.

Lydie hobbled over to join Chaz who both turned to stare expectantly at Kinney. Kinney gestured in the direction of the main terminal. "You two go on ahead. I'll catch up," he offered.

They both took the cue and vanished into the depths of the crowd. Kinney took a tentative step forward. "Marta, I just want to say...," he began but Marta cut him off.

"I know why you did what you did. And I'm not angry with you...anymore," she said as Kinney's eyes timidly met hers.

Marta reached out and took his hand into hers. "Most of us don't have the ability to stay focused on the bigger picture. We only see what's in front of us. But you don't let anything or anyone distract you from the broader perspective. You don't hesitate to do what you think is right. And you very likely saved my children and a lot of other people by giving them the time to get to a shelter. For that, I'll be forever grateful. Thank you."

Marta stood on her tiptoes and gently kissed his cheek, eliciting a warm glow that quickly spread across his face. For a long moment, they held each other's gaze. There was a tenderness in his eyes that she hadn't detected there before.

Eager to break the awkward tension, she pointed down at his empty holster. "I see that airport security doesn't make exceptions for military officers. You must feel naked without your gun."

"To be honest, I was more nervous about seeing you," he admitted, his eyes never wavering from hers. "When it comes to most people, I don't give a damn what they think of me. But with you..." He paused, his voice nearly breaking. He quickly composed himself and continued, "With you, I do. I value your respect, Marta."

"You have it," she said without hesitation.

Kinney breathed a deep forceful sigh. "So you're off to the city of roses. Can't say I blame you. Air's a little damp here for my taste, too," he said with a note of levity.

Marta squinted up at him. "Maybe you should try California," she said with a keen genuineness in her tone.

Kinney swallowed hard, his body tensing as if fighting a sudden impulse. Then he recovered a semblance of his usual stoic demeanor. He scratched his head and grinned. "Someone's gotta stay here and fight the good fight until you scientists figure out how to fix the climate," he said.

Marta nodded, knowing better than to pursue that line of thought any further. "Take care of those two," she said.

Kinney heaved his torso higher as if shouldering a burden. "I'll do my best," he promised.

Marta smiled softly. "I know you will. See you around, soldier."

Kinney stood at attention and saluted. Then he spun on his heel and followed after his crew. Just before she lost him in the throng of travelers, she saw him glance back over his shoulder. Then he was a memory.

She stood there silently staring into the mass of people a moment longer while a sea of possibilities washed over her. Then she felt the gate beckoning to her. Grabbing the handle of her carry-on she took the final few steps that she could ever conceive of taking in Oklahoma.

Marta leaned her head forward, fighting the g-forces straining to push it back and watched out the airliner's window as her world fell away. A new world would soon be taking its place once she landed in Pasadena and assumed her new role as research meteorologist at Mitchell Engineering. It was her intention to make it a better world.

She heard the low rumble as the landing gear went up. The plane continued to climb at a steep angle for the next two minutes, her ears popping as they rapidly gained altitude. Then they leveled off and the roar of the engines died back to a faint whine. She sat back in her seat, closed her eyes and allowed herself to relax.

Her cheek itched and, without thinking, she reached up to scratch it. Her fingers grazed the gauze pad that still covered her wound. It had taken twelve stitches to close it and would, no doubt, leave a scar for the rest of her life. She was fine with that. Scars served as gentle reminders of our past and who we used to be. She had her share of scars, most of them not visible to the naked eye.

The seatbelt sign winked out and Marta eagerly flipped the latch open on her lap belt and stretched out in her seat. "Would you like a complimentary cocktail, ma'am?" asked a bright-eyed blonde stewardess.

"Just water, please," Marta replied.

She ran a hand through her close-cropped hair, its downy tufts ending abruptly at the nape of her neck. She still hadn't gotten used to it. But sometimes change was good. It was time to stop fighting against what was and think about what could be. She would do what she could to help usher in a new era where nature's delicate balance was restored and her violent outbursts tamed. Climate remediation held the promise of a better world and that was a change worth working toward.

She peered out the window once more. To the south, another storm was brewing, making its way toward Oklahoma City. She craned her neck to see ahead of the plane toward the azure western horizon where the fiery orb of the sun was just beginning to set. She smiled. Clear skies were ahead.

ABOUT THE AUTHOR

Randy Henke lives a quiet and modest life in Wisconsin with his lovely wife, Robyn, and several spoiled four-legged companions.

He invites you to keep apprised of his latest writing projects by following his blog at unlovedauthor.com.

He also asks that you take a few moments to post an honest review of this book on Amazon. Reader reviews are the lifeblood of self-published authors.

Made in the USA
Coppell, TX
25 February 2020